LOVE SCENE, TAKE TWO

LOVE SCENE, TAKE TWO

ALEX EVANSLEY

Swoon
READS

SWOON READS NEW YORK

A SWOON READS BOOK
An imprint of Feiwel and Friends and
Macmillan Publishing Group, LLC

Our books may be purchased in bulk for promotional,
educational, or business use. Please contact your local
bookseller or the Macmillan Corporate and Premium Sales
Department at (800) 221-7945 ext. 5442 or by e-mail at
MacmillanSpecialMarkets@macmillan.com.

Library of Congress Cataloging-in-Publication Data

Names: Evansley, Alex, author.
Title: Love scene, take two / Alex Evansley.
Description: New York : Swoon Reads, 2018. | Summary: While
    filming a movie based on a bestselling book series, teen
    heartthrob Teddy Sharpe, twenty, falls in love with the books'
    author, eighteen-year-old Bennett Caldwell.
Identifiers: LCCN 2017041899 | ISBN 978-1-250-13570-4 (hardcover) |
    ISBN 978-1-250-13571-1 (ebook)
Subjects: | CYAC: Love—Fiction. | Actors and actresses—Fiction. |
    Authors—Fiction. | Motion pictures—Production and
    direction—Fiction.
Classification: LCC PZ7.1.E935 Lov 2018 | DDC [Fic]—dc23
LC record available at https://lccn.loc.gov/2017041899

Book design by Danielle Mazzella di Bosco

Emoji © emojidex https://www.emojidex.com

First edition, 2018

1 3 5 7 9 10 8 6 4 2

swoonreads.com

For Sam
For Ana
For Ashley
For Zoe
And for everyone who read this story on a screen,
long before it was ever a book.

Teddy Sharpe (actor)

Theodore Maxwell Sharpe (born September 3, 1997), or **Teddy Sharpe**, is an American actor and producer. He is best known for his costarring role on the hit <u>MTV</u> comedy-drama series _Testing Wyatt_. Sharpe made his film debut in 2016 in the independent film _Corduroy_ and starred in the film _Bistro on 5th_, which debuted at <u>Sundance Film Festival</u> in early 2017 to mostly positive reviews.

Sharpe is known for his energetic improvisations and slapstick performances, and has recently been praised for his craft versatility for such a young actor. Although he is relatively new to acting by industry standards, he has been described as one of Young Hollywood's brightest (and most promising) rising stars.

Filmography:

Television:

Testing Wyatt (2015–present) _[Recurring role]_
Lies Your Ex-Girlfriend Tells You (2016) _[Guest role]_

Film:

Corduroy (2016)
Bistro on 5th (2017)
Remember This Moment (2018) _[Uncredited]_
Parachutes (2019) _[Rumored]_

CHAPTER ONE

There are few things in life of which Teddy Sharpe is absolutely certain, and he's absolutely certain this audition is going to be a train wreck.

At least, that's what's running through his head when he bursts through the front doors of one of LA's fanciest office buildings, scaring the receptionist and a security guard half to death along the way. Teddy's had to run into last-minute auditions before, yeah, but never one he learned about an hour ahead of time. Never one he's had to go into completely blind because he hasn't seen the script yet. And never one that could launch his acting career into the stratosphere. He's a little on edge.

"You said you're here for the *Parachutes* auditions?" the receptionist asks, pulling her hand away from the button that releases the lobby's turnstile to smooth her hair. She looks unnervingly like Jennifer Coolidge. "Call times for those auditions started at seven a.m. I'm sorry, I can't let you up if you missed—"

"I just got the call from the casting director an hour ago," Teddy rushes out, a little out of breath and holding up his phone. It doesn't help that he came straight here from an early morning shoot for his TV show. He's been awake since midnight and probably looks as cracked out on caffeine as he sounds. "She said if I got here by nine, I could have the last slot of the day."

The receptionist looks unconvinced. "That's not how things are run—"

"I *know*," Teddy cuts her off again, then tries to cushion it with a smile. He gives her both the casting director's and the director's names. "My booking agent's been trying to schedule an audition time for me all week. We just confirmed it this morning."

"Let me see if I have a note about it. Just a moment," the receptionist says, typing something into her computer. Teddy checks the time on his phone, sees 8:56 a.m., and starts to panic all over again. He rubs a hand over his jaw and makes eye contact with the security guard sitting at the desk on the other end of the turnstile.

"I'm not seeing anything," the receptionist says slowly.

"Is there any way you could call up there? Tell them that Teddy Sharpe is here? They know I'm coming," Teddy tries one last time, subtly reaching around to unstick his T-shirt from his back. At least the *Testing Wyatt* stylist dressed him in mostly black this morning. Teddy's been stress sweating since his manager, Rita, picked him up from set and rushed him across LA to make it here on time.

"I'm sorry, sir, but auditions are still going on. I can't call to interrupt. This is why we have the call times policy—"

But see, the thing is, Teddy knows about policy.

He also knows he's been waiting for a shot like this for two years. So instead of listening to whatever boilerplate technicality she's going to pitch next, Teddy backs up from the desk, gets a running start, and vaults over the lobby's turnstile, earning himself a startled shriek from the receptionist as he sails by.

"Sorry!" Teddy yells over his shoulder. The security guard scrambles after him, sending an office phone clattering to the ground behind him, and Teddy definitely doesn't have time to wait for the elevators now. His foot slips out from under him on the marble floor as he bolts right, barely catching himself before slamming into the concrete stairwell.

So here Teddy is, sleep deprived and soaked in sweat, taking the stairs two at a time to get to the most important audition of his career with the building's security guard chasing after him. This is not the way he anticipated his day going.

The security guard is wheezing behind him in the stairwell, but Teddy's got him by at least two floors now. His legs, however, might give out before he makes it to the eighth floor, and every time he grabs the railing to swing himself around on a landing, the palm of his hand keeps less and less traction to curb his momentum. Finally his hand slips and he almost goes face-first into a door with a large number six painted on it. Luckily his shoulder is there to break the impact.

The eighth-floor door comes into Teddy's line of vision and he makes it up the last flight of stairs in three strides. He spills out into a long, carpeted hallway with a dozen doors on each side. His audition is supposed to be in the eighth-floor conference room, and Teddy checks the plaque next to each door as he sprints by. He comes to another hallway running perpendicular and makes a snap decision to go left, sucking wind and silently praying he made the right call. This hallway leads to several sitting areas and a couple of rooms with floor-to-ceiling windows.

"Excuse me, sir?" someone calls out. Teddy whips around. *Christ, it's another receptionist.*

"Yes, hi, I'm, uh—" He takes a deep breath in. "I'm Teddy Sharpe. I'm the last scheduled *Parachutes* audition today?"

The woman smiles warmly at him from behind her desk. "Great, they're expecting you. The audition before yours just ended, so you can head straight in. The conference room is the last door at the end of that hallway," she says, pointing to Teddy's left.

"Awesome, thank you," he says, like his lungs aren't about to implode. Why the hell couldn't it have been that easy eight flights of stairs ago?

Teddy checks his phone again as he breaks into a speed walk back down the hallway. With how fast everything happened in the past hour, he didn't exactly have time to dwell on what this audition could mean for him, so of course now is when his brain chooses to fully register the gravity of the situation. Waves of nerves hit him hard the closer he gets to the conference room.

This is big.

No—this is *huge*. And Teddy is hyperaware of how unprepared he is when he knocks twice, then twists the doorknob after someone on the other side calls to come in.

There are three people sitting behind a table in the middle of the room, a camera operator set up next to them—which is standard. There's also a small group of people sitting in the back corner—which is not standard. When Teddy walks over to the table to introduce himself and get his script, he's unsure if he should introduce himself to the group in the back as well.

"There's a red dash next to the monologue on page seventeen we'd like you to read," the casting director tells him.

First rule of auditioning: Don't waste any time, under any circumstances.

Teddy walks to his blocking position in front of the camera.

"Awesome—thanks so much for scheduling me. I'm Teddy Sharpe, auditioning for the role of Jack O'Heinessey," he says, and *oh, dear God, please let that be the way the name is pronounced*. No one corrects him, so he puts on his most charming smile, pretends like he has the slightest idea about the character he's auditioning for, and . . . points a thumb back over his shoulder and says, "I'm sorry, but just as a heads-up—a security guard might bust through that door in a second."

* * *

"Seriously, this could be your *Hunger Games*, Ted," Rita says for the third time since picking him up from the audition. She's driving Teddy back to the *Testing Wyatt* set to pick up his car and has spent the majority of the trip giving him another run-down on how crucial this could be for his career. "How are you feeling about it? Do you think it went well?"

"Sure," Teddy lies. He sits up straighter in the passenger's seat of her fancy sports car and doesn't mention that the audition happened so fast, the only thing he remembers is *not* feeling good about it on his way out.

"Come on, Ted! You gotta give me more than that."

Teddy glances over. Rita's been his manager since before he landed his *Testing Wyatt* gig three years ago, back when her hair was dark brown instead of platinum blond and when Teddy never went into auditions unprepared. Rita's one of the main reasons Teddy is where he is right now, and even though he can't stand lying to her, he doesn't have the heart to tell her he blew the audition she and his booking agent worked so hard to get him.

"No, I mean—you know how it goes," Teddy skirts, rubbing his hands over his jeans. He still hasn't stopped sweating. "They had me read a two-minute monologue, then I read a scene with one of the PAs. . . . Then they had me do some improv."

"Oh, thank *God*—you always kill it with improv. Did they say anything before you left?"

"Not much."

"Not even about scheduling a second round?"

Teddy shakes his head (further evidence the audition didn't go well), then realizes what a shitty job he's doing of putting up a front here. "Well, they mentioned something about the audition process being a little unorthodox because of preproduction conflicts, and that if I get the role, we should hear from them soon—what's been going on with preproduction?"

"I haven't heard much. Just that the script initially got held up getting green-lit and that the director is eager to get the ball rolling to make up for time," she tells him, turning into the *Testing Wyatt* set parking lot and pulling into the spot next to Teddy's car. "I don't think it's anything to worry about, though. It happens a lot with book-to-film projects. Especially in YA."

Teddy nods again. "I appreciate the lift today."

"Of course." She smiles and holds up her hands. "By the way, that receptionist thought you were on something when I came in to fill out paperwork during your audition. Did you jump over the turnstile to get to the elevators?"

"I didn't have time to wait for the elevator," Teddy says. "Had to take the stairs."

Rita laughs. "That's the commitment a manager likes to see."

Teddy shoulders open the car door and steps out into the Los Angeles sun.

"Wait, wait, before I forget," Rita says, reaching into the back-seat and presenting him with a Barnes & Noble bag. "For your flight to Miami this afternoon. In case you're in the mood for some light vacation reading."

Teddy peeks inside and forces himself to smile at the hard-cover copy of *Parachutes* at the bottom.

CHAPTER TWO

The flight attendant is really starting to stress Teddy out.

He's not trying to be a dick here, but only so much can be expected of him given the circumstances. She already insisted on personally escorting him to his seat, and now she won't stop staring at the duffel bag resting across his legs. It hasn't left his lap since he sat down on this Boeing 747 death trap that's supposed to fly him from one end of the country to the other, and he's too busy trying to regulate his pulse to worry about moving it.

Flying. Teddy hates it.

"Are you sure you don't want me to stow your bag in the captain's closet, Mr. Sharpe?" the flight attendant asks, popping up in the aisle next to him.

"Oh, uh—" Teddy clamps both hands down on top of it. "I'll keep it with me, thanks."

"Is there anything I can get for you? A blanket? Or a pillow?" she rushes out, undeterred and borderline manic.

Teddy barely gets out a quick "No, thank you" before she finally detonates, and it takes active effort for him to not recoil out of the blast radius.

"My daughter thinks you're just the cutest thing!" she gushes.

"She's going to just *die* when she finds out you were on my flight tonight!"

Teddy tries to laugh it off, despite how uncomfortable he is. He knew it was only a matter of time before she said something— he saw the recognition flicker across her face when she scanned his boarding pass at the gate earlier.

"No way, that's so sweet," he says, sending her into another fit of adoration. He's already a terrible flyer, and again, not to be a dick here, but there's no way he can deal with this on top of everything else right now. Not when he's still sleep deprived and wallowing in self-pity over his botched audition this morning. "Actually, yeah," he interrupts, "could I get a pillow?"

This appears to be a thrilling development. "Of course! Back in a second." She winks at him and then she's gone, and Teddy stares stoically at the tray table in front of him and tries to roll some of the tension out of his shoulders.

It's not that he doesn't appreciate the occasional attention he gets from people who recognize him. He knows it comes with the job. And he knows he's going to have to get used to it if he lands this *Parachutes* role (big, massive, ginormous *if*). Still doesn't mean he's used to it now, though. Teddy loves talking to fans, but he's always liked his space. Particularly when it comes to his personal life.

Speaking of which.

Teddy's connecting flight to Miami is going to cut it close. Since he has no idea where his next gate is going to be, he pulls out his phone and uses it as an excuse to start a conversation with Chelsea. She filmed on location in North Carolina a few years ago. Maybe she remembers her way around the Charlotte airport. . . .

Yeah, Teddy knows it's a stretch, but, you know, desperate times, desperate measures.

Thu, Jul 20, 6:43 p.m.

> Hey Chels. I'm landing in terminal E and I have like 15 min to get to my connecting flight in terminal B. . . . Are they close?

> Your all the way across the airport. I'd run.

Teddy sighs and holds back an eye roll. He and Chelsea have a complicated relationship (if you can even call it that anymore). One more reason why he's glad he's not much of a tabloid target by industry standards. One second they're on, the next they're off—Teddy can't keep up with it, and he sure as hell doesn't need *US Weekly* speculating on when "Teddy Sharpe and Chelsea Bordeaux finally call it quits."

Still, Teddy's looking forward to spending a long weekend in Miami with Chelsea. She planned this trip as an apology for canceling the last two trips they were supposed to go on because of her filming schedule. It's been more than a month since they last saw each other, and lately Teddy's caught himself wondering if Chelsea's as tired of keeping track of their time apart as he is. Assuming she's keeping track at all.

> Thanks for the tip 😞 you'll be in Miami by <u>tomorrow afternoon</u> right?

> Yep.

One-word answers have become a recurring theme with her. Teddy doesn't respond out of respect for his dignity.

"I brought you an extra, just in case."

Teddy's head whips up from his phone.

The flight attendant is back. She winks at him again and hands him two pillows. "Is there anything else I can get you?"

"Any way I could get a bourbon on the rocks?" Teddy asks, because screw it. He could use a drink right now. It's a gamble, though. He still has a few weeks before he turns twenty-one, and the flight attendant knows who he is, obviously, but maybe it'll work in his favor. He surveys her reaction, and—nope, gets confirmation that's not the case as he watches the smile disappear from her face, the illusion of Teddy being the perfect boyfriend for her daughter shattering.

"You'll have to wait until takeoff. And I'll need to see some ID," she says, narrowing her eyes at him before walking away.

"Okay, thanks," he calls after her, satisfied to put her off a bit.

He's still alcohol-less, though. And conversation-less with his girlfriend. And—now that he's alone with his thoughts—helpless to the preflight anxiety creeping in.

He needs a distraction.

Teddy pushes his duffel bag into the empty window seat next to him and digs through it, looking for his copy of *Parachutes*. Since he has a five-hour flight ahead of him, maybe perusing it to compare and pick apart his performance will double as enough masochistic entertainment to get him to cruising altitude. Or he can at least use it as a shield if that flight attendant comes back. He finds it toward the bottom of his bag, shoved under his toiletry kit.

Only the title and the author's name, M. B. Caldwell, are on the cover, with a faint silhouette of a deployed parachute in the background. Nothing spectacular. But apparently whoever M. B. Caldwell is knew what they were doing when they wrote the series, because "spectacular" is the word everyone keeps using to describe the type of opportunity this is for Teddy's acting career.

This could be your Hunger Games, *Ted.*

Teddy turns the book over and tries not to pout at all the praise written on the back.

If he were in the mood to be honest with himself, he'd acknowledge the real reason why he didn't feel good about his audition today. Regardless of how overprepared or unprepared he could have been, Teddy stills finds the whole prospect of auditioning for "the next major YA film franchise" spectacularly terrifying, and it messed with his head this morning. It's intimidating as hell to take on that kind of role and all the expectations attached to it. . . .

So much so, that Teddy can't even psych himself up to crack the book open now. He just sits there with his copy of one of the most hyped books being adapted to film in 2019, running his fingers over the slightly raised letters spelling out "M. B. Caldwell" across the top, and telling himself that God, he really blew it today.

Eventually Teddy's pulled out of his downward self-deprecation spiral when movement to his left snags his attention. There's a pair of jean shorts in his peripheral vision, and when he turns his head he's confronted with a spectacular view of whoever's ass is in the aisle next to him. His eyes wander north, all the way up to a blond braid spilling out from underneath a baseball hat.

Teddy's kind of a sucker for chicks in ball caps.

His gaze drops to the girl's jean shorts again when she

moves to sit in the opposite window seat. He tries to steal a glance at her profile, being nowhere near discreet, but her head is down and covered by the bill of her hat. He's so busy trying to get a look at her face that he almost startles back into the window seat next him when that same flight attendant comes out of nowhere and blocks his view.

"Would you like me to stow your backpack in the captain's closet, ma'am?"

"No, thank you," Teddy hears the girl reply. "I'll keep this one with me."

Subtlety has never been one of Teddy's strong suits, so it should come as no surprise that he doesn't have a talent for eavesdropping, either. As soon as the flight attendant walks away, he finds himself staring directly across the aisle at the girl in the baseball hat—staring, and trying to rein in the initial shock that runs through him when their eyes meet, because it only takes a split second of accidental eye contact to realize that he's definitely seen this girl somewhere before.

Her eyes flicker away, and Teddy goes back to staring at his tray table.

One of the flight attendants comes on the intercom a few minutes later to do the usual preflight safety routine, but now Teddy's too distracted to listen. He meets new people pretty much every week thanks to his career choice, and he's never had a problem with putting a name to a face before. He's worried about coming across as rude, and he's not trying to get a reputation in Hollywood as an unfriendly asshole who ignores people on airplanes.

Teddy's still flipping through his mental Rolodex of people he might run into on a flight to North Carolina when the pilot announces to prepare for takeoff, effectively upstaging all thoughts of jean shorts and baseball hats. You'd think with how much he flies that he'd eventually get used to it, but nope. Usually his anxiety level is already in the lower stratosphere by the time the plane pushes back from the Jetway.

Teddy thumbs through the M. B. Caldwell book in his lap without seeing anything on the inside and tries to ignore the way his stomach drops when the plane begins to pivot.

"'Scuse me?"

Teddy barely registers it at first. Then she repeats it and he glances left.

The familiar chick in the baseball hat is looking at him again—pretty sure she just spoke to him, too, now that Teddy's brain has had a chance to kick-start.

"Yeah?" His voice cracks. The corner of her mouth quirks up as her eyes drop to his lap, and Teddy's brain has no idea what to do with that.

"Sorry to bother you"—she levels her gaze with his again—"but I was wondering if you like that book you're reading?"

There's a subtle drawl to her words—a slow curve of the vowels that rules out any chance Teddy might have met her before. He would've remembered that.

The girl blinks at him, and at last it occurs to him that she's talking about the book in his lap.

"Oh—" Teddy looks down to hide the embarrassed smile spreading across his face. "Haven't started it yet."

She gives a polite, noncommittal hum, and when Teddy looks over, she's digging through her backpack despite the plane creeping toward takeoff.

"Have you read it?" he asks, watching her pull out a thick manila folder.

She doesn't look up when she says, "I have, actually."

Teddy almost asks her how she liked it, stopping short when the plane starts taxiing up the runway. He closes his eyes and pushes his head back into his headrest instead.

God, takeoffs are the absolute *worst* thing about flying. Except the landing. And the turbulence. And the annoyingly small snack bags—

"Hey."

Teddy's eyes snap open and he looks across the aisle.

Baseball hat is staring at him and trying not to laugh.

"You all right over there?" she asks.

"I'm good," he says, then blows out a breath that completely undercuts his attempt to not seem like the biggest pansy in first class today.

"Really? Because you kinda look like you're about to throw up."

Teddy gives up and points a finger at the roof of the cabin. "Not the biggest fan of flying."

"I can tell."

"Is it that—" He lets out another shaky breath as the plane picks up speed. "Is it that obvious?"

"Little bit, not gonna lie," she says, crinkling her nose.

He extends a hand to her. "I'm Teddy."

"Aw, man." She has to lean all the way across the seat next to her to return the handshake. "So you're not actually Buzz Lightyear?"

Teddy freezes, because there's only one explanation for why in God's name a stranger would ask him that, and he doesn't want to turn around to check for confirmation.

"You can totally see inside my duffel bag right now, can't you," he says.

Grinning, she slips her hand from his and says, "Little bit, not gonna lie."

Sure enough, when Teddy forces himself to look, a pair of bright blue boxer briefs are hanging halfway out of his bag—the apparent aftermath of rummaging around for his M. B. Caldwell book. The folded-over waistband is announcing to the entire plane: UZZ LIGHTYEA in bold white lettering.

Teddy's at a loss for how to explain his way out of this one, so he shoves his underwear back into his duffel and zips it up with as much dignity as he can pull together at a time like this. He's almost disappointed the full BUZZ LIGHTYEAR OF STAR COMMAND hadn't been visible. If the universe is so keen on embarrassing the shit out of him today, the least it can do is not do it halfway.

"Yeah," he says slowly, facing the aisle again and pointing a thumb over his shoulder. "I'll be honest—I have those in, like, six different colors."

She purses her lips when she looks up from her manila folder, holding back a smile. "I'm Bennett, by the way."

"Bennett?" Teddy repeats in surprise, then wishes he hadn't. She raises her eyebrows at him, waiting for him to continue, and honestly? He's got nothing. "I mean, I've never met a girl Bennett before. Well, I don't think I've met a guy Bennett, either, but I like it. It's—yeah. It's a cool name."

Bennett appears to be somewhere between trying to figure out the angle he's working and trying not to laugh at him. Again.

"It's short for Mary Bennett?" she offers. "I don't think I look like a Mary."

Teddy gives her a quick once-over before he realizes what he's doing, then attempts to play it off by letting his eyes dart around the cabin for a moment. "So, you're from the south then?"

"What?" she laughs.

"I just figured since your accent, and, like, the double name and everything . . ." His awkwardness knows no bounds, apparently. "That's a southern thing, right?"

Bennett cocks an eyebrow. "Are you gonna ask why our tea is so sweet next? I can probably find you a *Buzzfeed* article or something that covers all this."

Teddy holds up his hands, pleasantly surprised by the sarcasm. "Hey now, cut me some slack here. I was born in Pittsburgh and grew up in California."

"Yeah? That's cool," Bennett says, looking around thoughtfully. Teddy wonders what the logo is on her hat. "But, yeah—I'm from North Carolina. I've lived in the same spot in North Carolina my entire life, actually. Kinda lame."

"I don't know, staying in the same place for a while sounds nice to me," he says, scratching the back of his neck. He bounces around filming on location so much that it's starting to feel like nowhere is home anymore.

She snorts. "I'm supposed to go to college there, too, though. Also kinda depressing."

"Really? What school?"

"Davidson College. . . . It's about thirty minutes north of Charlotte," she says, like she isn't expecting him to know where it is. (To her credit, he doesn't.)

"Nice. Do you know what you're gonna major in?"

"Negative." She shakes her head absently for a second, then says, "Hey, so how're you feeling about that audition this morning?"

Teddy stares at her.

"Whoa, how did you—" He stops midsentence as the pieces finally click together. "Hold on—I do know you. You were at my audition, weren't you?"

A hint of a smile flickers across her face.

"You totally were!" Teddy remembers now. She was sitting (sans baseball hat) with the group in the back corner. How the hell could he forget that? Teddy knows he has a tendency for tunnel vision when he's working, but he hadn't realized he'd gotten that oblivious.

"Are you like an intern or a PA or something?" he asks, wondering why she didn't say anything sooner.

She shakes her head. "The director really liked you, by the way."

"Are you serious?" Teddy resists the impulse to lean forward, hope surging in his chest. "It felt like an absolute train wreck on my end."

"Didn't seem like it from ours," she says, and Jesus, Teddy can't sit still now.

"So, like, what's the over-under on me getting the part?"

Bennett makes a face. "Come on, you know I'm not allowed to talk about it."

"You come on!" Teddy says, only half joking. "I'm dying over here. Not even a little hint?" He tries to give her his most charming smile, then worries he looks like a psychopath and stops.

"Sorry, Buzz," Bennett says. "But the good news is, you handled that takeoff way better than I was expecting."

"Wait, what—?" Teddy turns to look out the window. Sure enough, they're already thousands of feet in the air, still ascending, but the worst is over for now.

"Holy . . . ," he breathes out, then glances back across the aisle and finds Bennett watching him again. There's even a little grin at the corner of her mouth giving her away. "You sly dog," he says, slightly dazed with what he thinks is gratitude, but can't quite put the right word to it.

Bennett shrugs him off and turns back to the stack of papers in her lap. "It was the least I could do. You looked so nervous you were giving *me* anxiety."

Teddy watches her lower her tray table and fan the stack of papers out in front of her, the bill of her hat covering her face again. He wants to say something to get her to look up, but of course, he draws a blank—the one time he could actually use his talent for talking in circles. Maybe if he wasn't busy being so endeared, he'd be able to come up with something to say.

When the flight attendant appears after the captain turns off the seat belt sign, she asks Teddy if he wants to order a bourbon on the rocks now. Actually, *daring* him to order that bourbon on the rocks is a more accurate description. Teddy politely declines and settles for a soda. Bennett follows suit.

"So, random question," Teddy says once they're alone again, because he can't help himself. Desperate times, desperate measures. "You don't happen to know where Terminal E is in the Charlotte airport, do you?"

CHAPTER THREE

Teddy and Bennett talk for almost the entire flight.

Well, mainly Teddy talks. It starts out with not-so-discreetly prying for information on *Parachutes* (homegirl is like Fort Knox over there with her manila folder and indestructible poker face), and it kinda evolves from there. Teddy talks, and Bennett works on whatever those papers are, occasionally asking questions or offering snarky commentary on something dumb he says. It's a solid four-and-a-half-hour distraction.

"Sorry to interrupt, but we're preparing to land," the flight attendant says to Bennett, wedging herself into Teddy's dramatic retelling of a Fourth of July fireworks debacle he was involved in last year. "May I take your trash for you?"

"Yes, please." Bennett smiles up at her. "Thank you."

She reaches for Teddy's trash without a word.

"You're mannerly," he says to Bennett once the flight attendant is out of earshot. "Your mama must've raised you right."

"Bless your heart." Bennett presses a hand to her chest, exaggerating her own accent. "No wonder you've got one of them picture shows on the tee-vee."

Teddy laughs, despite the unease that shows up whenever

someone mentions his acting career. He hasn't been in the game long enough to be too paranoid about people's intentions, but the thought that maybe he should've kept his guard up a little more around Bennett creeps into his head anyway. He steals another glance at her—at the way she's meticulously evening the edges of her papers on her tray table, pen between her teeth and eyebrows furrowed in concentration—and feels like a complete douche.

"Ladies and gentlemen, if I could have your attention, please," the pilot crackles over the intercom. *"We'll be making our way into the gate in about twenty minutes; however, I do have an announcement to make, as I've been informed there are several passengers on board trying to catch connecting flights."*

Teddy's stomach drops.

"Flight 1123, nonstop to West Palm Beach, and Flight 1435, nonstop to Miami, have been delayed indefinitely due to inclement weather. We apologize for the inconvenience and will assist passengers in any way we can to help make other arrangements. On behalf of myself and the crew, thank you for flying with us tonight. Welcome to Charlotte."

Teddy presses his head back against his seat, and the word is out of his mouth before he can stop it. "Shit."

"Sounds like that was your flight," he hears across the aisle.

Rolling his head to the left, he nods at Bennett, and instead of panicking about landing, Teddy spends the rest of the flight trying not to look as pissed off as he feels.

* * *

"So, you got a game plan, Buzz?" Bennett asks on the way off the plane. Teddy's so distracted by his blossoming predicament and those damn jean shorts and being called Buzz that he doesn't realize when the strap on his duffel bag gets caught on an armrest until he's suddenly yanked backward.

"Uh—" He flails around to untangle himself, thankful Bennett doesn't turn back at the sound he makes. The flight attendant from earlier definitely watches all this go down, though. Teddy ducks his head and turns his phone off airplane mode for something to do underneath the unimpressed glare he receives. It chimes immediately with a voice mail from Chelsea. He pauses just inside the Jetway and presses the phone to his ear.

"Hey, Ted. I know you're on a flight right now, so this is kinda shitty, but I'm stuck in Vancouver for the weekend. Give me a call when you get this."

"You've gotta be kidding me," he mutters, because of course this is happening. Today's just one shade of awesome layered over another. He scowls at his voice-mail screen for a moment, trying to decide whether to call Chelsea back or throw his phone off the Jetway. He decides to catch up with Bennett instead. He needs to regroup. Or something. And he figures talking with a local would be more productive than anything. Except when he looks up to find her, she's nowhere in sight.

Continuing up the Jetway, Teddy finds an information desk and heads over, pulling himself out of the scene looping through his head—one that involves buying a ticket to Vancouver, showing up to Chelsea's set, and demanding an MLA-formatted explanation on exactly what the hell her deal has been lately.

Since the plane arrived around nine p.m., Teddy definitely isn't in the mood to turn around and hop on a red-eye back to LA tonight. He toys with the idea of catching a flight to Pittsburgh to see his grandparents, then thinks better of it. There's really no way around being stuck in Charlotte at this point, and

Teddy knows this isn't the lady behind the help desk's fault, but he isn't doing a good job of hiding his impatience as she lists off tomorrow's flight options.

"I've got a nonstop to LA tomorrow afternoon at two p.m.—I think it's the best option we've got for you. I could get you out earlier in the morning, but with the connections, you'll be arriving back in LA around the same time," she says, typing on her computer. She kind of reminds Teddy of the receptionist from his audition, and it only adds to his current sense of gloom.

"Let's just do that, then," he sighs, getting out his wallet and handing over his credit card. He's been standing at the service desk for a few minutes now and keeps glancing around the line that's formed behind him to check if Bennett's still nearby.

"All right, sir. You're all set for a two p.m. flight to Los Angeles tomorrow."

"Thanks," Teddy says, fumbling with his card and wallet as he steps aside. He uses his foot to drag his duffel along with him, and spots a girl in a baseball hat emerging from the bathroom across the way. He tucks his credit card into his wallet and almost trips over the bag at his feet to follow after her.

Bennett smiles when he walks up.

"Glad to see you didn't fall off the Jetway," she says, and under normal circumstances Teddy would appreciate the reference. She studies his face and adds, "You good? You're looking a little stressed out again."

Teddy snorts. "Yeah, well. The rest of my weekend plans just fell through, and I'm kind of stranded in Charlotte for the night."

"Yikes—I'm sorry." She pauses for a second, messing with the tied off end of her braid. "I mean, do you need a ride or anything? I have my car here."

Teddy feels his eyebrows lift, and he grins. "Look at you, all over this southern hospitality shtick already. I'm impressed."

She leaves the braid alone to readjust her backpack straps. "You should be. Even I'm impressed with how charitable I'm being."

"This is about my Buzz Lightyear briefs, isn't it?"

Bennett laughs. "Sure, we'll go with that—"

The last half of her comment is drowned out by a chorus of squeals coming from somewhere to their left. They both turn.

There's a group of teenage girls standing a few yards away, Starbucks drinks in hand and hearts in their eyes as they huddle together. One of them is even wearing a *Testing Wyatt* T-shirt.

"Sorry about this," Teddy mutters to Bennett. Then he waves, prompting the girls to rush over in a fit of Frappuccino-fueled enthusiasm.

There are only four of them, but they're all talking over one another about how much they love Teddy and his TV show. Teddy listens and grins and doles out hugs, and when the boldest of the group, a tall girl with bright red hair, asks if they can get pictures, Teddy pushes his luggage aside and tells them that he doesn't know how to work Instagram, but they're welcome to tag him if they want.

"We love you so much," the redhead gushes, clutching a hand over her heart like she's sure it's about to burst.

Honestly, Teddy loves meeting fans, but he still doesn't understand why they get this way around him. He's pretty much the most average-looking guy ever—dark hair, brown eyes, a little on the skinny side. And it'd be one thing if he were an actual movie star, but all he's done is a couple of indie movies and hold down a recurring (secondary) role on an MTV show. His acting résumé doesn't merit this kind of attention. . . .

Teddy throws a glance at Bennett. She's standing off to the side, watching it all go down with a hint a humor in her eyes. Teddy feels bad for making her wait, so he asks, "Actually, do you guys mind if we do a group picture? I've got an Uber coming soon."

It's a fib, yeah, but hey—occupational necessity sometimes.

"I'll take it for y'all," Bennett volunteers cheerfully, moving around the group and holding out a hand. "Which phone do you want to use?"

The girls squeal again, pushing all their phones toward her, and Teddy gives her a good-natured headshake before smiling for the camera.

Bennett turns out to be quite the accommodating photographer, having the girls switch places so they each get a turn to stand next to Teddy. She takes pictures on all their phones, then tells them to do one last goofy one, and Teddy ends up with the redhead hooking an arm around his shoulders and pretending to give him a noogie. Bennett has to retake the picture because the first one "supposedly" turns out blurry.

"Who knew you were such a good photographer, Bennett?" Teddy says once they're crossing through the airport again.

They step onto a moving sidewalk and Bennett throws him a smirk over her shoulder. "Who knew you were such a big deal, Buzz?"

Both of their bags are on the carousel by the time they make it to baggage claim. Teddy glances at the exit doors while Bennett searches the front pockets of her backpack for something.

"Sorry—looking for my valet ticket," she says.

"Oh, you fancy, huh?"

"Obviously." She grins up at him. "But I also promised my dad I wouldn't walk through long-term parking by myself."

"Touché," Teddy says, thinking about her offer from earlier. He doesn't want her to think he was blowing her off when he fibbed about having an Uber coming, but he also doesn't know how to bring it up again.

"So, cabs usually hang out here," Bennett tells him as they stand outside of arrivals. "And if you put your airline into your Uber request they find you pretty quickly. Where are you headed tomorrow?"

Teddy hikes his duffel bag up on his shoulder. "Back to LA, if I can make it through the night here. Speaking of—where's the closest hotel?"

"We're at an airport," Bennett says. "You could probably throw a rock and hit one from here."

Teddy pushes her with his elbow. "Okay, smartass." She steps sideways, grinning, looking like she might push back. But she doesn't.

"I guess hotels depend on how much you want to spend on an Uber," she says, then lists off a couple of places around Charlotte. Teddy nods along politely, watching multiple cabs whiz by. Before he can ask which one she recommends, Bennett readjusts her baseball hat and says, "Are you sure you don't want a ride? I know it's kinda weird, but yeah. Offer still stands."

Teddy's eyes cut back to hers. "Why would that be weird?"

She shrugs. "I mean, for all you know I could, like, run a Teddy Sharpe fan blog and want to take secret pictures of you to up my follower count." Teddy bursts out laughing. Bennett shrugs again. "Didn't know if it'd be weird or not for a complete stranger to offer you a ride."

Teddy wonders what her definition of "complete stranger" is, considering they just spent the better portion of the past six hours together.

"Do you run a fan blog for me?" he asks.

Bennett snorts. "Yes."

"You sure giving me a lift to a hotel isn't out of your way?"

"I have to go toward the highway regardless. And I'm pretty sure there are, like, eight hotels on the way." The guy working valet pulls up in a Jeep Cherokee. "Your call, Buzz," Bennett says, walking to the trunk and popping the liftgate.

There's a split-second hesitation; then Teddy replies with, "That'd be great, actually," and finds himself in the passenger's seat of Bennett's Jeep, reflecting again on how this is not the way he anticipated his day going.

"It's exceptionally clean in here," Teddy comments when Bennett hops into the driver's side. He watches her hesitate with her key fob, like it takes her a second to remember that it's not actually a car key, and adds, "New car smell, too. Nice. Graduation gift?"

"Yeah, just got it," she says, sounding a little distracted as they pull away from the curb. "Should you call ahead to some hotels?"

"Oh—yeah." Teddy props his elbow up on the center console and opens the map app on his phone.

Bennett drives past the first two hotels he finds, claiming, "They're for sketchballs." She actually pulls into the parking lot of the third one, but it ends up being at full occupancy because of a convention in town for the weekend.

"There are so many good hotels uptown," Bennett says when they're back on the road. She's been lobbying for wherever the hell *uptown* is for the past ten minutes. "We're already past the highway, anyway."

Teddy looks up from his phone and frowns. "Uptown sounds too far out of the way, so no. The next hotel looks promising."

"Promising to give you hepatitis."

"What do you think, *A*, *B*, or *C*?" he asks.

Bennett grins at the windshield. "Pick one."

Teddy can't decide if she's being stubborn or if she's really this concerned for his well-being. "Come on, Bennett," he says, lightly tapping her arm with the back of his hand. "I appreciate it, but it's not a big deal. Just drop me off somewhere and I'll figure it out."

Bennett stills for a second, and there's a long pause before she says anything—long enough for Teddy to think she's actually entertaining the idea of leaving him somewhere to fend for himself.

"You said you have to be back at the airport around noon tomorrow, right?" she asks.

"Yeah, but—"

"This is about to be so weird," she mutters, pressing a hand to her forehead and glancing out the driver's side window.

"What is?"

She hesitates before answering, "So, my older brother has to fly out tomorrow for some charity golf tournament he's playing in down in Fort Myers. If you don't mind getting there a little early, you could stay at our house tonight and ride with him to the airport tomorrow. . . ."

"And before you think I'm some humongous creep," she starts up again, talking ninety miles an hour and throwing nervous glances across the center console, "I'm only offering because I feel bad your weekend plans fell through and that you have no car and it would be so shitty to catch any of the hepatitises in the alphabet while stranded in Charlotte."

It's the longest monologue Teddy's heard from her so far, and it takes him a second to register what she's saying.

Bennett frowns at him when he doesn't respond, adding, "Hep-a-ti-tis. Hep-a-ti-tis-es—that doesn't sound right. The hell is the plural of hepatitis?"

Teddy starts cracking up.

Like, really cracking up—mouth hanging open, no sound coming out, having-to-clutch-his-stomach cracking up.

"Oh my God, this is hilarious," he says, then sees the expression on her face. "No, no—in a good way," he backpedals, still laughing. "I don't know how we got here, but that's really sweet of you to offer."

Bennett changes her grip on the steering wheel and checks her rearview.

"Yeah, well, I'm doing a great job of convincing you that I'm not some psycho stalker fangirl," she mumbles.

"But you are a fan of me, obviously," Teddy says.

"You know what, that was inappropriate; I shouldn't have said anything," she says, her face still flushed. "What's the next hotel on your list?"

A tiny shard of disappointment works its way into Teddy's stomach, and he has no idea why or where it's coming from. He and Bennett have only known each other for a few hours— maybe it is a little weird she's being this nice.

"Are you doing all this because I'm, like, kind of famous, or are you really this nice?" he asks, cringing as he says it.

Bennett doesn't even hesitate. "Because you're *kind of* famous."

Teddy's head snaps up. "Seriously?"

This time Bennett's the one to laugh. "Don't flatter yourself, superstar. I didn't even know who you were until a week ago."

"Hey, now—ouch." Her comment stings a little more than it should, but, ironically, it makes him feel better.

"See? I'm not that nice."

"Just to recap here." Teddy begins counting off on his fingers. "You took pity on me and talked me through our flight, you were a great sport about taking pictures earlier, you're currently chauffeuring me around on a hotel tour of Charlotte, and now you're offering me a free place to stay so I don't catch any of the hepatitises in the alphabet." He pauses, enjoying how hard Bennett's trying not to smile now. "I don't know who you've been hanging out with, Bennett, but I'd say that's pretty freaking nice."

"I can't help it—I just feel so bad for you. It's like the state of North Carolina is allergic to you," she says dryly.

Teddy laughs, letting his gaze slip over to the driver's side again. Bennett's in profile against the passing streetlights outside, all pleased smirks and genuine intentions, and honestly? Screw it. Chelsea bailed on him, his plans fell through, and the last thing he wants to do is sit in some hepatitis-ridden hotel room watching *SportsCenter* all night.

"You're killing me, Smalls," he says, eyes shifting away from her ball cap to the approaching stoplight up ahead. "Have you reinvited me to stay at your house yet? Because if I do end up getting hepatitis, it'll be on you."

Bennett bites back another grin and puts her turn signal on. "Staying at my house is a ballsy move, Buzz," she tells him as they drift into the left-turn lane. "I could actually be a psycho stalker. Or a serial killer."

"I think I'll take my odds against you rather than a virus that attacks my liver."

"A-plus famous last words," Bennett says, then pulls a U-turn around the median.

CHAPTER FOUR

It doesn't sink in that Teddy's going through with this until Bennett pulls onto the highway, heading north. Maybe he's being paranoid, but it feels like the atmosphere changes between them—and it doesn't help that at first Bennett busies herself with her phone instead of talking.

"Just so you know, I give great lectures on texting and driving," Teddy says.

"I know, I'm sorry." Her eyes dart between her phone screen and the windshield for a few more seconds before she puts it down. She starts messing with the radio next, settling on a scratchy Led Zeppelin song.

Teddy points at the dash. "What's up with this station?"

"It sounds better the closer you get to the lake. It's all we listen to there, so I apologize in advance if you're not a fan."

"Lake?"

"Oh—yeah." She throws him a quick glance. "We kind of live on a lake."

Oh. *Casual.*

"Anything else I need to know before you take me home to meet the fam?" Teddy asks.

Bennett pretends to mull it over. "As long as you don't mind dogs and you're not a picky eater, you should be good."

"How far away is your house from Charlotte?"

"Thirty minutes, tops."

"And, uh—how many people are going to be there?" he asks, but what he means is, does she have a younger sibling who watches a lot of MTV? Are her parents into movies and might recognize him from his? Does he need to call up Rita for another PR lesson on how to deal with the masses?

"Just my mom and my dad, and my older brother, Tanner," Bennett says. Teddy relaxes for a moment until she adds, "My aunt and uncle and cousins will be there tomorrow for dinner—actually, never mind. You're leaving tomorrow."

Teddy wonders what the rest of her family's going to be like.

"Should I just call your mom and dad, *Mom* and *Dad* then?" he asks.

Bennett snorts. "And you call me a smartass. Mr. and Mrs. Caldwell. Or Tom and Libby. Whatever you're comfortable with."

"Bennett Caldwell," Teddy says, trying it out.

She gives him a skeptical look. "Teddy Sharpe?"

"Correct. But do you know my *full* name?" he asks.

"Can't say I do."

"That at least proves you're not a psycho stalker fangirl. Any respectable Teddy Sharpe stan would know that it's Theodore Maxwell Sharpe."

Bennett laughs. "Yikes. And I thought Mary Bennett Caldwell was a mouthful."

Teddy's about to fire off another crack about her running a fan blog when something occurs to him, and it's like the world's biggest light bulb turns on over his head.

"Hold on a second," he mutters, his mouth barely keeping up with the jump his brain makes from Mary Bennett Caldwell to *M. B. Caldwell*. "What the—holy *FUCK*."

"What?!" she startles, gripping the steering wheel with both hands and looking over at him like he's nuts.

"You wrote the book the movie I just auditioned for is based on?" Teddy asks. "You're the author of *Parachutes*?"

Bennett blushes, confirming the answer, and it certainly all makes sense now: Why she was sitting with the director during his audition, why she's not allowed to talk about casting . . . Teddy's been casually hanging out with the creator of the YA film franchise he just auditioned for, and this is just now occurring to him.

"Jesus," Teddy says, rubbing a hand over his forehead. How *the hell* is this just now occurring to him? "How old are you?"

Bennett squirms a little in her seat. "Eighteen."

"You're a best-selling author. At eighteen." Teddy gapes, then adds (mostly to himself), "That's so freaking *cool*."

Even in the artificial dashboard light, he can still see Bennett blushing when she mumbles, "Thank you," and Teddy can't figure out why she looks so embarrassed.

"I mean, maybe I should start a fan blog about you, Bennett. Holy shit," he says.

Finally—*finally*—Bennett cracks a smile, and Teddy counts it as a monumental win for about three seconds until it dawns on him that Bennett's known since before they even took off today that he auditioned for her movie without reading the books first.

* * *

Teddy spends the rest of the car ride reeling over this M. B. Caldwell discovery, and it quickly becomes apparent that

Bennett's sticking to her You-Know-I-Can't-Talk-About-This policy, regardless of how many times Teddy tries to sweet talk his way into getting some answers. He has so many questions about the books and film adaptation that he can't keep his thoughts straight, but he also feels guilty that Bennett knows he hasn't read the series yet. The least he can do is rein in the peer pressure.

Once he and Bennett pull off the highway, they drive through a small town before getting onto some back roads that are more than a little terrifying. Teddy's used to being surrounded by traffic and city lights, so he gets a little restless as they cruise through the boonies and their lack of streetlamps. Particularly when they make another turn onto a dark road completely lined with trees. The moonlight and Bennett's high beams are the only sources of light for what looks like miles.

"Maybe you are a serial killer, Bennett," Teddy says, staring out the window. "You've definitely got the setting down."

Teddy's shoulders relax back into his seat when a well-lit neighborhood emerges up ahead, but the relief is short-lived. His phone vibrates in his pocket just before they turn in, and his heart sinks when he sees Chelsea's name on the screen. A text message shows up a few seconds after it goes to voice mail.

Thu, Jul 20, 10:14 p.m.

Why are you ignoring my calls? I know you have your phone. And it rang so your clearly not on a flight.

Call me back ok?

Teddy doesn't have the energy for this now. He'll text her back later.

"Well," Bennett says quietly. "We're here."

Teddy shoves his phone back in his pocket and glances through the windshield. He hadn't realized they'd stopped moving—they're parked behind a couple of other cars toward the bottom of a roundabout driveway.

"Oh, wow," he says, letting his eyes adjust. "This is beautiful."

The Caldwells' house looks like it's straight out of one of those home and garden magazines Teddy's mom keeps around his parents' house. It's all white brick and dark shutters, with stairs on the right side leading up to what Teddy assumes is a back deck with a great view, seeing as the lake they live on comes right up into their backyard.

Bennett shoulders open her car door and hops out; Teddy follows, meeting her at the trunk to grab their bags. She has the liftgate open and is reaching for her rolling suitcase by the time he gets there, and regardless of the unsettled feeling lingering in his stomach over Chelsea, Teddy at least remembers his manners.

"Here, I'll get those," he says, reaching for her luggage. He accidentally bumps into her as he leans in, and he pretends not to notice the way she jumps and steps sideways to give him more room.

"Thanks," Bennett says to the driveway, hiding behind her hat.

"No problem." Teddy straightens up and sets both of their rolling bags on the ground.

"I can get mine," she offers. Teddy's still fumbling with both telescoping handles, but he manages to steer hers out of reach.

"Hey—what kind of houseguest would I be if I made you carry your own luggage?" he asks, wanting to pump some of the easiness between them earlier into whatever's settled around them now. Bennett smiles but seems distracted, which in turn distracts Teddy.

She shuts the liftgate and locks her car, then falls into step next to him on their way up the driveway. They walk to the deck stairs off the side of the house instead of the front door.

"Just a heads-up, my family might be surprised to see you," she says quietly. "You're probably going to get bombarded with questions."

Teddy glances over and shrugs. He can handle questions. Occupational hazard.

"Hello?" Bennett calls out when they reach the top of the steps. It takes more effort to carry both rolling bags up than Teddy cares to admit, and he tries to be nonchalant about how winded he is when he sets them down to catch his breath.

"She's here!" someone yells back from the other side of the porch—right as a ginormous animal comes barreling around the corner.

"Hey, Buddy!" Bennett drawls, intercepting what Teddy thinks is a dog. She grabs the wiggling mass of brown-and-black fur by the collar before he can get to Teddy and says, "This—is Buddy."

"Is that a dog or a horse?" Teddy asks. Buddy's head comes up to Teddy's hip.

"He's a Saint Bernard–German shepherd mix," Bennett explains, letting go of his collar. The dog surges forward and smushes his face in between Teddy's leg and his duffel bag.

"So, a horse."

Bennett laughs and grabs the handle of her rolling bag before Teddy can protest, so Teddy resolves himself to scratching Buddy behind the ears with his free hand while he follows

Bennett around a bend in the deck. They come to a covered porch area where a chorus of greetings ring out. Bennett's mom is sitting in one of the four rocking chairs lined up, while her dad and her brother stand at a high table in the corner.

"Hey, guys!" Bennett says happily. She points back to Teddy as she hugs her mom. "I brought a stowaway."

All eyes shift to Teddy.

"Yeah? Who's this?" someone asks.

"I'm Teddy," he says, putting on his best smile and waving. His duffel slips off his shoulder by accident and drops to the ground before he can catch it.

Bennett sets her own bags by the deck doors and moves toward the middle of the porch. "This is Teddy," she repeats, then gestures to the blond woman sitting in the rocking chair. "Teddy, this is my mom, Libby."

Mrs. Caldwell smiles warmly at him when they shake hands and says, "It's very nice to meet you, Teddy."

Bennett points across the deck to her brother. "That's Tanner."

"How's it goin', man?" Tanner asks. Teddy isn't sure if Tanner looks older or younger than he is, but he does look a lot like Bennett. Just with a darker shade of blond hair, and scruff.

After Teddy shakes Tanner's hand, he looks to his right to find Bennett pulling back from hugging her dad.

"Mr. Caldwell," Teddy says, stepping forward. "Thanks so much for having me."

He claps Teddy on the shoulder when they shake hands. "Of course—the more the merrier."

"Are y'all hungry?" Mrs. Caldwell asks. "We've got pizza, or I can make you something if you want?"

"Oh no. Pizza's great with me," Teddy says quickly. "Where

is it? I can grab it—" But Mrs. Caldwell is already up and crossing the deck and Bennett's telling him to sit down. Teddy takes the rocking chair next to her and Buddy plops down on Teddy's feet. Literally. On his feet.

It's unsurprising that Bennett's family is just as welcoming and hilarious as she is. Between heated-up pizza and rapid-fire conversations, Teddy learns that Tanner is a year older than him and plays on his college's golf team. That Mrs. Caldwell has a slightly thicker variation of Bennett's accent, giving her a kind of *Steel Magnolias* vibe, and likes to brag about her kids as much as they'll let her (which is not a lot, in Bennett's case). And that Mr. Caldwell is definitely the person Bennett gets her sense of humor from—sarcasm and all. It's pretty similar to Teddy's own family dynamic, now that he's thinking about it. Minus the accents.

"Your house is beautiful, by the way, Mr. and Mrs. Caldwell," Teddy says between his second and third slice of pizza. Mrs. Caldwell keeps putting them on his plate, so Teddy keeps eating them. "You don't see a lot of houses like this out in California. I'm pumped to see what the lake looks like tomorrow."

"We appreciate that, Teddy," Mrs. Caldwell says. "Is that where you're from, then?"

Teddy nods. "Originally from Pittsburgh. My family moved out to LA right before I started junior high."

The cool thing about the Caldwells, Teddy finds, is that they ask plenty of questions, but only based on information Teddy volunteers first. He's been at their house for an hour now and it's sort of refreshing that he hasn't been asked about his career yet. Granted, they probably don't know who he is, but usually it's the first thing out of people's mouths when they meet him.

"The Braves got swept last week again. It's going to be a

problem in October," Mr. Caldwell says to Tanner at some point, and Teddy can't be expected to not invite himself into a conversation about baseball.

"Oh no," he says, "don't tell me I'm surrounded by Atlanta fans here."

Tanner comes back at him with, "Let me guess—Pirates fan?"

"*Die-hard* Pirates fan," Teddy says. He joins them at the high table and they launch into baseball, which turns out to be a great conversation despite Teddy getting distracted half the time by Bennett.

She and her mom are in the middle of their own chat, and Teddy's already heard *Parachutes* dropped at least twice. Now he's trying to pick up bits and pieces of what they're saying, which makes him a terrible person, yeah, but can you blame him?

The only problem is Bennett keeps making eye contact with him from across the porch like she knows he's trying to listen. Every time it happens, Teddy ducks his head and looks away, and then has to find his way back into the baseball conversation without making it obvious that he's only halfway paying attention.

"So, Teddy," Tanner says after the second or third time Teddy misses a question because he's looking over at Bennett. "How do you and Bennett know each other again?"

It's an inevitable question. Teddy should have been more prepared.

"I, uh—auditioned for the *Parachutes* movie earlier today, actually," he says, scratching the back of his neck. "We started talking on the flight to Charlotte, and when I found out my connecting flight got canceled, she helped me out a bit."

There's a pause, then Tanner's eyes widen. "What?"

"What?" Teddy repeats, combing back through his sentence

and finding nothing that would make Tanner look this alarmed. What?

"Mary Bennett Caldwell," Tanner calls out, leaning around Teddy to look at his sister. "What did he just say?"

"I didn't hear him," Bennett says, looking to Teddy. "What'd you say?"

But it appears Tanner already has the answer to whatever's going on inside his head, because a massive smile breaks out across his face. "Your movie had auditions? Does that mean it's, like, officially happening?"

Bennett hesitates, eyes darting between Teddy and Tanner. Then she gives her brother a rueful smile and says, "Surprise?"

Tanner jumps out of his chair and almost sends it toppling over. "WHAT?! Are you serious? This is fucking amazing, Bennett!"

"*Language,*" Mr. Caldwell snaps.

"When were auditions? Wait, *that's* why you were in LA? You told me it was for a book signing!" Tanner says, practically talking over himself. "When were you going to tell us? Wait—why aren't you guys freaking out about this, too?" Tanner glances back and forth between his parents, looking suddenly wounded. "Mom and Dad already knew? Not fair, Bennett—you promised you were gonna tell me first if it happened!"

Teddy's stomach is in his throat the entire time Bennett gets bombarded with questions. He has no idea why she hadn't told her brother yet, but he's absolutely mortified he blew her cover.

"I didn't want to say anything until a budget was set and first-round auditions were over," Bennett calmly explains. "Didn't want to jinx it."

To his credit, Tanner gets over it pretty quickly and goes straight back to interrogation mode. Question after question, and Teddy desperately tries to catch Bennett's eye to convey some kind of apology. When is it coming out? (In 2019, but they haven't set a date yet.) Are they doing movies for the whole series? (They need to get through this one first before they start thinking about that.) Does this mean she's moving to LA? (Nope.) Is Spielberg directing? (Again, nope.)

And when Bennett finally does take a second to glance Teddy's way, she throws him a subtle smirk and shakes her head at all the *I'm so sorry!*'s he mouths at her.

CHAPTER FIVE

Everyone decides to turn in around midnight (once Tanner calms down about Teddy's little revelation).

They all file through the deck doors and walk into a high-ceilinged, open living room that connects to the kitchen. A stone fireplace takes up most of the wall to the right, bracketed by shelves overflowing with books and picture frames. It's a trip to look at books under the same roof as someone who's actually written one—Teddy does a quick scan and spots *Parachutes* and its sequel on one of the top shelves.

There's a staircase leading down to the basement in the back corner and a hallway leading out of the kitchen opposite it. Mrs. Caldwell says Teddy can sleep downstairs in the guest room before she and Mr. Caldwell wave good night. Tanner follows suit, rounding out of the kitchen and disappearing down the hallway.

"Thanks again for having me, Mr. and Mrs. Caldwell," Teddy calls after them.

"Your room's down here," Bennett says, moving past him toward the back staircase.

Teddy follows her down the steps, careful not to bang the feet of his rolling bag against the hardwoods along the way.

His brain takes this time to remind him again of what an ass-hole he is for blowing Bennett's cover in front of her brother. As soon as they get to the bottom of the steps and round the banister, Teddy can't hold it in anymore.

"Okay, holy shit—I'm so sorry, Bennett," he grovels. "I didn't mean to—"

Bennett turns around immediately, like she'd been expecting it, and holds up a hand. "It's fine, I promise. I was going to tell Tanner this weekend anyway."

"But—"

"Teddy."

"No, I—"

"Seriously, it's okay," she says. There's humor in her eyes, but mostly *shut up and stop apologizing*. "I'd tell you if I were mad."

Would she, though? The girl is mystifying.

"You're over here," she says, waving for him to follow her around a corner.

Teddy's definitely not done talking about this yet, and he's expecting to have at least a hallway's length of time to collect his thoughts. Instead he walks straight into a bedroom with lime-green walls—a little lighter shade than what's used on film sets for special effects scenes, actually. Teddy can't help himself.

"Holy Chroma key," he laughs, looking around. "So, is this where *Parachutes* is gonna film special effects? Or is it gonna be more of a situational thing?"

"Movie jokes. You're funny," Bennett says, twirling the tied-off end of her braid around her finger. "Cell service is bad down here—I can give you the Wi-Fi password if you want. Bathroom's down the hall."

Teddy crosses the room and drops his bags at the foot of the bed, then takes a seat on the duvet cover to test it out.

"Your family's awesome, by the way," he says, standing up again.

Bennett grins. "They're a little ridiculous sometimes."

"You promise you're not mad at me for telling—okay, noted," he says when she shoots him a dirty look. He puts up his hands in defense and switches gears. "Are you guys doing anything else this weekend? Do you have a boat?"

"We do. We'll probably get out on the lake and float around. No concrete plans, though."

"Sounds nice," Teddy says, and he's a little surprised by how much he means it.

"Yeah." Bennett eyes the ceiling and takes a half step back toward the door. "Way nicer than LA, probably."

"Probably," he laughs, though there's more truth behind it than he wants to let on. Teddy hates flying back to an empty apartment to begin with, and it'll be even worse when he gets back and has to deal with Chelsea stuff. Maybe he'll go see his parents, now that he has no concrete plans, either. Actually wait, no—his parents are on vacation in San Francisco this weekend. Dammit.

"All right, I think I'm gonna call it a night," Bennett says, taking another step back.

The distance she keeps putting between them needles Teddy a bit. Probably because he's already thinking about how lonely LA's going to be when he gets back tomorrow.

"What time should I be up?" he asks.

Bennett shrugs. "Whenever you feel like it. My dad doesn't work Fridays in the summer and my mom has the summers off in general. Fridays are usually laid back for us."

Teddy perks up at an excuse to stall for time. "What do your parents do?"

"My dad's a lawyer and my mom's a teacher." Bennett starts playing with the end of her braid again and rocks back onto her heels. "My mom said something about cooking breakfast in the morning if that interests you."

"Yeah, absolutely."

"Cool. It'll probably be around nine or so."

A pause follows.

"Hey—um. Thanks again for inviting me, by the way." Teddy scratches the side of his face, then rubs his nose. "I probably would've spent the night watching *SportsCenter* by myself in some hepatitis-ridden hotel room if it weren't for you."

Bennett laughs and looks down, the bill of her hat covering her face again. "No problem. I'm just glad you don't think I'm some weirdo stalker for inviting you."

"I mean . . . I do think that, but I wasn't going to say anything."

"Fair enough," she says lightly. "Just do me a favor and don't out me and my Teddy Sharpe fan blog to my family at breakfast tomorrow. They're not ready to see that side of my life yet."

Teddy's jaw drops into an openmouthed grin.

"So, when are you gonna give me the URL to this fan blog? I'm pumped to see it."

Bennett wrinkles her nose at him. "Sorry, Buzz. I like the fourth wall too much."

Sounds about right.

"For the record," Teddy says (which is oddly difficult to do with his smile going all goofy from the nickname), "those briefs you saw in my bag were a Christmas gift."

She nods like she totally believes him. "Sure they were."

"They were! From my younger sister."

"This is gonna make an excellent blog post," Bennett says. "A complete guide to Teddy Sharpe's underwear preferences. Easily viral."

"Easily viral?" Teddy puts his hands on his hips and turns around, pushing his ass out a little—which no doubt looks anything but viral in his khakis. Doesn't stop him from cocking an eyebrow at Bennett over his shoulder and asking, "You think so?"

Bennett hums as she eyes him up and down with a less-than-impressed expression. "Maybe I'll forgo the underwear piece for a critical analysis on why Buzz Lightyear is your childhood hero."

"I can tell you exactly why and spare you the research," Teddy says. "I was a clumsy kid—I took the whole 'falling with style' thing to heart."

Bennett grins like this is the best news she's heard all week. "Stop it. You did not."

"My dad was the one who came up with it," Teddy goes on, shocked he's actually about to tell her this. "I was a clumsy kid and was pretty hard on myself about it—especially since all I wanted to do was play baseball, and I could barely make it around the bases without face-planting. *Toy Story* was my favorite movie growing up, so one day my dad was like, *Hey, Ted, you're just falling with style!* It made me feel better."

Teddy leaves out the part about how the whole "falling with style" epiphany had been a pivotal moment in his life, and that he still applies it to bad days on set and botched auditions and that one time he slipped in front of Emma Stone at a VMAs afterparty and took an entire champagne tower down with him. Luckily the glasses were plastic and Teddy's suit was rented.

Bennett stares at him, her face unreadable.

"What," Teddy asks.

"Nothing," she says, shaking her head.

Now Teddy's staring at her, trying to figure out what to do next. She looks amused at least. Apparently he thinks reaching out to poke her in the side is a good idea. Bennett jumps back before he can get there.

"Oh, man. You're ticklish, aren't you?" Teddy asks, walking toward her and trying to poke her again. "Or are you just this skittish around people?"

"What kind of—stop!" She laughs and shoves his hand away. "What the hell kind of question is that? Of course not."

"You sure? Seems like you are," Teddy says thoughtfully, taking a step forward for each one Bennett takes back. She tries to fake him out and bolt around him, but Teddy pokes her in the side twice before she can bat his hand away, getting a couple of squeals in response. "Come on, Caldwell, I thought you said you weren't ticklish," Teddy says, going after her again.

"Seriously, stop—!"

Teddy's phone chimes with a new text message. They both freeze, glancing at its spot on the nightstand.

"Nice, I guess you do have service down here," Bennett says.

"Guess so," Teddy says slowly, straightening up a bit and still watching his phone.

Bennett straightens up, too, but she keeps her hands raised between them, ready to fight him off again. It's a tiny bit adorable, even after Teddy's phone all but dumped an ice-cold bucket of your-girlfriend-is-texting-you over his head.

"I'm not gonna tackle you, Caldwell. Chill," Teddy jokes, walking past her just to prove a point. "I mean, I will if you want me to."

She snorts and drops her hands to her hips. "Don't flatter yourself, superstar."

"Such delightful manners. Speaking of—how can I help with breakfast tomorrow? I make killer toaster waffles," he says, wiggling his eyebrows.

Bennett laughs this time. "Don't worry about it—my mom loves to cook. You'll probably offend her if you ask to help."

"You sure?" He grins as she rolls her eyes and turns to leave. "I'm great with butter-to-syrup ratios—"

"Good night, *Teddy*," Bennett says, pulling the bedroom door shut behind her.

"Night," Teddy calls. After she's gone, he forgoes the new text on his phone from Chelsea, sets an alarm, and crawls into bed with his copy of *Parachutes*. He isn't putting a lot of stock into landing this role, but he figures why not read the book anyway.

You know, just in case.

CHAPTER SIX

Teddy wakes up well before his alarm the next morning.

The first thought to cross his mind is that all his efforts to get Bennett out from behind the brim of her baseball hat last night made for a pretty interesting end to the evening. He stretches himself out underneath the duvet cover, knees and ankles cracking, and tries not to squirm when the second thought to cross his mind puts a guilty pit in his stomach.

Chelsea.

Teddy doesn't know what's going on between him and Chelsea, hasn't for a while, but that doesn't give him the right to go around flirting with other girls. And yes, he can admit there was some low-key flirting going on last night, but it was more accidental than anything. . . .

Teddy opens his eyes and stares impassively at the ceiling fan and—okay. Maybe not so much accidental. He'll own up to that.

He should probably text Chelsea back today. It's not cool of him to ignore her like this. Teddy gropes for the nightstand until his hand lands on his phone—turns out he has five new text messages and a voice mail. All from Chelsea.

So much for calling me back

Seriously where the hell are you? Why is your phone off?

Ok I get your mad but this is kinda ridiculous

I'm going to bed. Call me if you want. Or don't. Whatever.

Fuck this. I'm done.

He doesn't even want to know what the voice mail says. Especially after the third time he reads the "Fuck this. I'm done" text. That's certainly a new one. Teddy tosses his phone onto the nightstand instead of responding and rips back the covers.

Showering doesn't bring much insight to the situation. It kind of makes it worse, actually. Teddy stands with his back turned to the spray, hot water hitting his neck and shoulders, and debates whether getting mad about the texts from Chelsea makes him a hypocrite. He's the one who ignored her and spent most of yesterday with a girl he met fewer than six hours beforehand . . . but Chelsea's the one who ditched him on the other side of the country and pretended like she didn't do anything wrong.

It's not like he hadn't seen this coming in the past few months, but it's a whole different ballgame when "Fuck this. I'm done" is actually staring you back in the face.

Does this mean they're broken up?

"Morning, Teddy," Mrs. Caldwell calls from the kitchen when Teddy reaches the top of the steps. His hair is still damp and his phone is in his pocket, but the whole house smells like bacon, and that at least makes things a little better.

"Morning," he says cheerfully, rounding the banister and crossing through the living room.

His eyes shift and land on Bennett. She's next to Tanner at the kitchen counter, and it's a nice change of pace to see her without a ball cap on. Her hair is a lot longer than he expected. And a lot wavier. She and Tanner turn to greet him, and Teddy is a tiny bit more grateful that he didn't wake up to those texts from Chelsea in some hepatitis-ridden hotel room.

"Smells great up here," Teddy says.

Bennett has a section of the newspaper in front of her and doesn't look up when he sits down next to her. Tanner, on the other hand, is perusing the sports page and says, "Yeah, we're just waiting for my dad to get out of the shower."

"How'd you sleep?" Bennett asks, turning the page of whatever section she's reading. She still won't fully look up at him, and Teddy isn't sure what to make of it.

"Really well—and wow, that looks amazing," he says, eyeing the breakfast spread Mrs. Caldwell is setting up on their kitchen island.

Then his phone chimes.

"Sorry," he mumbles, slipping it out of his pocket to switch it to vibrate. Chelsea's name glares back at him on the lock screen (which—yikes. It's just after six a.m. her time. Not the best sign). He'll text her back after breakfast. It's hard to deal with Chelsea on an empty stomach, anyway.

"So your flight's at two today, right, Teddy?" Mrs. Caldwell asks. In addition to tending to half a dozen pancakes on the electric griddle by the stove and frying up more bacon on a skillet, she's also in the middle of rinsing out an enormous silver pot. A breakfast ninja.

"Yes, ma'am," Teddy says, then turns to Tanner. "What time are you trying to leave here, man?"

"Maybe like eleven thirty-ish? My flight's at one ten."

Bennett looks up at Teddy for the first time that morning and asks, "Does that still work for you?"

Teddy manages to hold her gaze for a second. "Yeah, that sounds good," he lies.

* * *

Breakfast is so good that it takes an extraordinary display of self-control for Teddy to wait until someone else goes for seconds before filling up his plate up again. (He doesn't want to be *that houseguest*.) Finally Tanner makes the move, and Teddy almost loses his footing as he jumps up from his barstool.

He digs into his second stack of pancakes while the Caldwells talk about the cookout they're having later with their family—the one Bennett mentioned in the car yesterday. It sounds like it's going to be awesome. Teddy sits and listens and looks at the view of the Caldwells' dock from their kitchen windows. Whatever lake they're on is gorgeous—lined with pine trees and multicolored houses and double-decker docks. There isn't a cloud in the sky this morning, and Teddy isn't positive, but he's pretty sure what he's feeling right now is FOMO.

"Is the lake always this crowded?" he asks Bennett, nodding at all the boats already out.

"Yeah, but only in the summer," she replies.

Teddy's spent a good portion of breakfast trying to engage her in some kind of conversation. It's not like she's freezing him out or anything, but it's not like it was yesterday. Teddy can't decide if she's purposely being a little standoffish or if he's hypersensitive to everything this morning.

"Tanner, get off your damn phone at the table," Mr. Caldwell says on his way to refill his coffee. "You know better than that."

Tanner jumps and hides it under the bar. "Sorry, Dad—I just got an e-mail from the airline, though. I think my flight got canceled."

"Canceled?" Mr. Caldwell repeats, the coffeepot paused halfway toward his mug.

Tanner goes back to his phone and reads aloud, "Flight 1376, nonstop to Fort Myers, has been delayed indefinitely due to inclement weather in the Fort Myers area."

"That's exactly what happened to my flight to Miami yesterday," Teddy says, looking from Tanner to Mr. Caldwell.

Mr. Caldwell hums. "Bet it's that hurricane coming in. Last I heard it was heading for the Keys, though. Libby—pull up that radar app you have on your iPad for a sec, will you?"

Teddy wasn't even aware it's hurricane season, but it must be pretty bad if they're still canceling flights down in Florida.

That would have sucked had he and Chelsea actually gotten down there. He would have been stuck with her complaining about the weather the whole time, and then they probably would've broken up during the evacuation.

"Oh, wow," Mrs. Caldwell says, then shows everyone her iPad. It's a satellite image of the state of Florida, except the entire bottom half is splattered in green, yellow, orange, and red.

Mr. Caldwell's mouth pops open. "Good Lord—is all that rain?"

"Yeah," Tanner says. "Guess that means the charity tournament's canceled? I'm surprised I haven't gotten a call by now. . . ."

"Why don't you call the tournament director to see what's going on. Maybe call some of your buddies playing in it, too," Mr. Caldwell says. Tanner stands from his barstool.

"Yeah, good idea," he says, then heads out onto the deck.

"I'm surprised they didn't cancel it ahead of time— remember the tournament he played in Galveston a few years ago? They canceled that a week in advance because of a tropical storm," Bennett says to her parents.

"What's the verdict?" Mr. Caldwell asks when Tanner comes back a few minutes later.

"Whole tournament's off," he says, sitting down again. "The course is underwater."

"Sorry about that, bud," Mr. Caldwell says.

Tanner shrugs. "I have another one in two weeks before the semester starts, so I should be fine. But that means Teddy still needs a ride to the airport." He glances at Teddy. "Right?"

"Oh—well, I mean, yeah," Teddy stumbles out, not trying put anyone out here. "But don't worry about it, man. I can call an Uber or something."

"You just headed home, Teddy? Or somewhere else?"

Mr. Caldwell asks, leaning back and folding his hands behind his head.

"Heading home. I'm on break from filming until Wednesday." Teddy tries not to cringe at how douchey that sounds. "I was supposed to go to Miami for the weekend, but my flight got canceled yesterday and my plans fell through."

"You get a lot of breaks in your schedule?" Tanner asks. "It's gotta be pretty nuts."

Teddy nods. "Yeah, I've been pretty busy this year. But, like—*good* busy, you know? I have until Tuesday off, and then I have to be back on set in LA by Wednesday morning. Not sure what my schedule will be like after the holidays, but right now it's pretty slammed."

Pretty slammed is putting it lightly, but Teddy doesn't want to sound like he's complaining on top of already sounding like a Hollywood douche.

"You like it out in LA?" Tanner asks, and Teddy isn't sure how to answer that.

LA is basically where he grew up. On one hand, he can't imagine living anywhere else (or doing anything else). On the other hand . . . it's always nice to get away from the agents and the sixteen-hour workdays for a while. That's what Teddy was looking forward to the most about his trip to Miami.

"LA's great ninety-five percent of the time," Teddy admits with a rueful smile. "Definitely not as laid back as this place, though. Getting out for a bit and hanging here has been great," he says, pointing toward his view of the lake.

Mr. Caldwell nods and sips his coffee. "Well, if you don't have anywhere to be until Tuesday, you're welcome to stay if you want."

"St-stay here all weekend?" Teddy startles out.

Tanner's first to jump at the idea with, "You definitely should, man!"

"I think that's a great idea—but only if you want to, Teddy," Mrs. Caldwell adds, smiling as she puts down her iPad. "Don't feel obligated."

A bolt of indecision runs down Teddy's spine. It surprises him that his initial reaction is *Hell yeah, I want to stay,* and he has to remind himself that he literally met the Caldwells yesterday. Overstaying his welcome would be rude. And weird. And—Teddy's eyes shift to the windows across the kitchen for the thirty-seventh time—and *God,* the lake looks so inviting outside.

"This is crazy nice of you guys to offer," he starts, trying to come up with a way to stall for time that won't seem like he's stalling for time. It's not that he wants to say no—he just needs a second to process what's being said.

And what's *not* being said, in Bennett's case.

Teddy can't gauge her reaction, even when she turns to her brother and tells him to stop being so peer pressure-y.

"Y'all give him a second to breathe before you start bribing him," she says. She picks up her plate and asks Teddy if he's done with his, too.

Teddy nods absently before he realizes what he's doing. "Wait, no I'll get that—"

But Bennett's already rounding the end of the counter.

"I'm not peer pressuring," Tanner says with mock offense, holding up his hands. "I just firmly believe there's nothing better than a weekend on the lake. And a minute ago Teddy was talking about how nice it is to get out of town sometimes. . . ."

And he's got a point there. Given everything that's happened in the past twenty-four hours—his audition, his trip falling through, *Chelsea*—lying low with the Caldwells on the other side of the country sounds oddly enticing.

Mr. and Mrs. Caldwell chime in on Bennett's peer pressure comment, prompting some back-and-forth joking between them and Tanner that lends a little privacy to the other side of the kitchen. Teddy watches Bennett clear their plates to the sink, waiting to see if she'll show him some kind of indication that this isn't crazy or weird or awkward. Even if Bennett's not the biggest fan of him staying, Teddy has every intention of trying to make it up to her this weekend if she does give him the okay.

"Bennett," he says quietly. "Are you cool with this?"

Bennett's eyes flick to his as she rinses off their plates, and there's a tiny grin pulling at her lips. She raises her eyebrows and gives what Teddy wants to believe is a *Why not?* shrug, and maybe that's all the indication he needs for now.

"So what do you say, Teddy? You in or out?" Mr. Caldwell calls across the kitchen.

Teddy laughs. "You guys are, like, the nicest people I've ever met. You sure I'm not messing up your plans for the weekend if I stay?"

He gets a resounding, "Come on, it'll be fun" from three-fourths of the Caldwells.

"All right, I'll stay," Teddy says as he does a one last sweep of the kitchen, lingering on Bennett. "But only if I get to, like, do the dishes or something for the rest of the weekend so I don't feel like a total freeloader."

That earns him a resounding, "Absolutely not" and a big smile from Bennett.

Teddy decides to stay anyway.

* * *

After breakfast, Teddy gets a text from Rita saying to call her when he can. Bennett suggests he head down to the dock since it's more private, and there's apparently better service. Teddy walks to the dock's edge, taking another second to appreciate his view for the next three days, then calls Rita. She answers on the second ring.

"There you are," she says in lieu of a greeting. "What's goin' on, Ted? I heard you had some flight troubles yesterday."

"Hey, Rita—" Teddy starts, then feels his eyes go wide. "Whoa—how'd you know about that?"

"Chelsea called me."

"What? When?"

That's nowhere near the realm of Usual Chelsea Behavior. Teddy didn't even know she had his manager's number.

"Yesterday. She told me about your plans changing and that she couldn't get in touch with you," Rita says, hesitating before adding, "She did not sound thrilled about it."

Teddy clenches his jaw. "Yeah, well—"

"It's none of my business," Rita says, more than likely doing that nonchalant hand gesture thing she always does when she just *doesn't want to know*. Which is a lot. Bless her. "Where are you? I'm glad you're not down in Florida with that hurricane right now, at least."

"I stayed in Charlotte last night," he tells her. "I wasn't trying to catch a red-eye to LA right after flying from there to Charlotte."

"I don't blame you," she says lightly. "Sorry you got stuck in there overnight, though—I wish you would have called me. Where did you end up staying? Hopefully the hotel wasn't too shoddy. . . ."

"Nah, it's cool. And funny story, actually—I didn't end up staying in a hotel."

"Oh God," Rita says. "Please, Teddy, *please* tell me you didn't sleep in the airport. My conscience can't take it."

"No, no." He laughs. "It's actually pretty crazy, though. I kinda ran into Bennett Caldwell on the flight here last night."

There's a pause, and then Rita asks, "Bennett Caldwell, as in, like . . . M. B. Caldwell?"

"As in M. B. Caldwell," Teddy confirms, feeling a little smug. Another pause.

"You stayed with Bennett Caldwell last night," Rita says slowly. "The girl who basically wrote the movie you just auditioned for—that Bennett Caldwell."

"Yes, Rita, that Bennett Caldwell," Teddy says, his eyebrows knitting together. He's not sure what to make of her tone—it's deceptively calm and not at all on par with the reaction he was expecting. It makes him nervous, and Teddy tends to talk himself in circles when he's nervous. Which is exactly what he does when explaining the story to Rita.

To her credit, Rita patiently listens all the way through and doesn't interrupt, but when Teddy finally trails off talking about breakfast with the Caldwells this morning, the first question out of Rita's mouth is, "Nothing, like, happened between the two of you, did it?"

"Jesus, Rita. Are you serious?" Teddy bites out, his free hand jumping up to grip the back of his neck. He glances quickly over his shoulder to make sure he's still alone, then lowers his voice and says, "No. You know I'd never—"

"That's all I need to know," Rita says before he can finish his sentence. "The rest is not my business."

"You're the one who brought it up!"

"Because I'm your manager, and despite how much you and I don't like it, we both know I need to be in the loop about these things," she points out. "Preferably a loop that's made of the barest details possible."

"Fine," Teddy says, doing his best to ignore how quickly his pulse had doubled. He definitely shouldn't be blushing this hard, either.

"Can we go back to that minor little detail you failed to mention in the car yesterday," Rita says. "The one about Bennett Caldwell being at your audition? Because I'd like to hear more about that. Starting with why you failed to mention it."

"Honestly, I didn't figure out she was at my audition until last night," Teddy says, hoping she doesn't think he's a total space cadet for it. "But yeah, she was there. Which is kinda weird, right? Like, she and the director and a few other people were sitting off to the side the whole time. I didn't know authors were that involved during preproduction."

"They're usually not unless they help adapt the screenplay, which is the point I'm trying to make—*Teddy*," Rita says, excitement slipping into her tone. "I don't want to jump the gun here, but this is a good sign. Word is Burt Bridges brings his writers in during the audition process for role frontrunners because he likes to tailor the script to whomever he casts as his leads."

Teddy hears what Rita's saying, understands exactly what she's insinuating about his audition (which in reality makes no sense, given how last-minute his audition was scheduled). Yet his brain only wants to focus on the one part of that statement that isn't about him.

"Hold on, wait," he says, reeling for the second time in less than twenty-four hours about another M. B. Caldwell revelation. "Bennett worked on the screenplay? Since when?"

"I'm not sure," Rita says, sounding confused by his reaction. "Maybe a few weeks after the movie was green-lit? I don't know much outside of it causing some waves around town a few months ago."

"Why? It's not like an author helping adapt their book into a screenplay is unprecedented or anything."

Rita snorts. "It is when a director fires half a staff of seasoned writers and brings on a teenager with zero screenwriting background as a script consultant."

Teddy feels his jaw go slack, because holy shit.

From a logical standpoint, it's a little too hard to believe the director of a major film franchise would take a gamble like that, but Teddy's also heard Burt Bridges has a bit of a nonconformist reputation.

Rita hums thoughtfully. "Has Bennett said anything about your audition? Or the movie in general?"

"Not really."

"Have you asked?"

"I started to on the plane, yeah, but I don't want to come off, like, desperate or unprofessional or whatever. She and her family have already been so nice, I'm not trying to press anything here," he says, following it up with a disbelieving laugh. "I mean, they freaking invited me stay the whole weekend when they found out my Miami plans fell through. Who does that? The least I can do is act against my own self-interest while I'm here."

A long pause follows—long enough for Teddy to think the call dropped. "Rita?"

"Are you gonna stay, then?" she asks.

Teddy switches the phone to his left hand and rolls his shoulders. "I mean, I kinda just agreed to it, so . . ."

Rita takes another moment to clear her throat, then says, quite eloquently, "Goddamn, Teddy. I think you're the luckiest little punk I've ever represented," and it catches Teddy so off guard that he can't do anything about the guffaw that comes barreling out of his mouth.

"I'm being serious!" Rita insists. "Do you even realize what an opportunity this is?"

Her question sobers Teddy instantly. "What does *that* mean?"

She hesitates, probably searching for the best way to phrase whatever she's got planned next, but Teddy already knows where this is going. Rita isn't a fundamentally devious human being, but she *is* in the same business as he is. A mandatory sense of "by all means necessary" is written into any job description in Hollywood. What separates the people you want to work with from the people you don't is how much stock they put into it.

"I'm saying you've got a chance to do some networking here," she finally says.

Teddy laughs bitterly. "You mean kiss her ass, don't you."

"Jesus, Teddy. No. Well, maybe—" She groans, then starts over with, "Let me ask you something, and I want you to answer me honestly this time. Do you think your audition went well yesterday?"

Teddy's stomach bottoms out as he fumbles around for something to say.

"That's what I thought," Rita sighs when he doesn't answer. She doesn't sound angry at least, but Teddy still feels like the worst client in the world. "I could tell in the car yesterday. You're not a good liar, kid."

Teddy glances out across the lake in front of him, eyes following a speedboat in the distance.

"Yeah, I know," he mumbles. "I'm sor—"

"Don't apologize, Teddy. I'd be an awful manager if I expected you to land every audition you go to."

"Yeah, well. You guys worked so hard to get me that audition and then I completely blew it."

"Stop. No sulking," Rita says, switching back to all business. "Look. I'm just gonna lay this out for you. Do you want this *Parachutes* role?"

"Yes," Teddy says, because it's mostly true. Part of him is terrified of it, sure, but the rest of him—the hungry side of him—is screaming he'd be an idiot not to want it.

"Okay, then. You and I both know how this business works. Hollywood is tiny. You can be the next Meryl Streep, for God's sake, but if you don't know anyone, you're screwed," Rita tells him. "You're already in an incredibly advantageous position right now—you're talented, you're up and coming, and you've got an unprecedented fan base for the small amount of projects you've worked on."

Teddy's tempted to contradict her on a few of those points, just to give himself some control over how uncomfortable this makes him, but he knows she'll just tell him to shut up and stop being self-deprecating.

"I'm not saying you should be conniving or manipulative or anything," his manager continues, "and I know this is weird as hell—trust me, I'm still trying to wrap my mind around how this even happened—but Bennett Caldwell is possibly a direct line to the role you want."

Teddy scoffs. "You're acting like she's the casting director. . . ."

"She's someone working *with* the casting director. And the director. And probably the producers, since she's involved with the script," Rita points out. "And who knows? She might have no say in who gets cast, but honestly, when it comes down to the difference between two equally talented actors, the actor that's generally *liked more* by people working on the film gets the role nine times out of ten. You know what I mean?"

This is just . . . Teddy can't believe what he's hearing.

"So you're saying I should stay to sell myself," he says.

"I'm saying this could be your *Hunger Games*, Teddy. Remember?" Rita presses. "Would you be able to live with yourself if you didn't exhaust every resource you've been given to land a role like this?"

* * *

Bennett is sitting on the deck with her computer in her lap when Teddy walks back up from the dock. He climbs the stairs, still a little flustered from his phone call, and plops down in the rocking chair next to Bennett with a groan. He doesn't even realize how pathetic he probably sounds until Bennett says, "More flight troubles?"

And Teddy laughs, because at least that's the one thing in his life that's actually in order. Before he hung up he asked Rita to rebook his flight for Sunday and e-mail him the details.

"Nah. Just—stupid shit with my manager," he says, then wishes he hadn't. His eyes drop to her laptop. "What're you doing?"

"Answering e-mails." She gives a little headshake. "E-mails on e-mails on e-mails."

Teddy's eyes flick up to her profile. He takes in the

downward curve of her mouth and the slight hunch in her posture.

"Got a lot going on?" he asks. Which is a dumb question, all things considered. She nods, and Teddy can't help himself. "Anything I can do to help?"

Bennett purses her lips and tries not to smile. "Can you convince my literary agent that I don't need a personal assistant?"

"More than happy to try, if you'd like," he says lightly. "But first I'd like to point out that you're no longer allowed to call me a big deal."

"Not true," Bennett snorts.

"Who's getting a personal assistant here, Bennett, you or me?" he teases. But Bennett just sighs, and Teddy kicks himself for killing the repartee before it had the chance to gain traction. "Why do they think you need a personal assistant?"

She looks up, hesitating a second. "My agent wants some stuff taken off my plate, I guess."

"Well, do you need stuff off your plate?"

"I don't know, maybe," she says, her frown deepening. Teddy's already teeing up his next question, since getting information out of Bennett Caldwell basically requires the same amount of strategic planning as getting information out of the Pentagon, so he's a little surprised when she offers, "Everyone's all worried I'm not going to meet my deadline for the third *Parachutes* book because I'm going to Wilmington for filming. Apparently the solution is to hire a babysitter to make sure everything gets done."

So she is going to be on set in Wilmington. Teddy could've done without this information, because now everything Rita said to him on the phone is parading back to the foreground of his mind. And then some.

"When's your deadline?" he asks.

"March fifteenth."

"I mean, I'm not going to pretend like I know anything about novel writing, but that's, like, seven and a half months away."

"Yeah, but I technically haven't started writing the last book yet because of all the movie stuff," Bennett says, looking guiltily down at her laptop again. "Plus my agent knows I'm not the fastest writer in the world, so. Getting an assistant is probably the right thing to do . . . it just doesn't sit well with me."

"Sucks when you know something can help your career but it doesn't feel right," Teddy says dryly, staring through the pine trees in their backyard and out across the lake.

Bennett hums in agreement, and a quiet settles between them—one that brings back some of the unease from his phone call with Rita.

"You sure it's okay that I'm staying this weekend," Teddy says suddenly.

Bennett looks over at him, amused. "I'd tell you if I weren't, Buzz. Why?"

"Because . . ." He takes a moment to search for the right way to word this, then thinks screw it. There's no getting around what he needs to say, and candor is always better than fluff. "Because my manager just talked to me for ten minutes about how much of a networking opportunity staying this weekend is, and I'm feeling superweird about it now."

Bennett lurches forward and bursts out laughing. (Thank God.)

"I'm serious!" Teddy says. "I mean, this entire situation is so bizarro to begin with, right? And I don't know—you never actually *said* you were cool with me staying. I just don't want you to

- 68 -

think I'm, like, skulking around just to get the scoop on your movie."

"Did you just use the word 'bizarro'?"

"Yes—because this is."

It takes her a second to keep a straight face long enough to look him in the eye. "Look, Teddy. I'm glad you're staying, and it never occurred to me that you might want to stay to get the scoop on the movie. I honestly thought—well, I don't know what I thought the reason was, but it wasn't that."

Teddy's at least relieved that she didn't initially think the worst of him.

"I'm staying because I want to stay," he says.

"Good." Bennett stands, still giggling a little. "Then we're all on the same page here. Now go put your bathing suit on."

CHAPTER SEVEN

After drinking a couple of beers Tanner snuck them and sitting in the sun for most of the afternoon, there aren't enough words to describe how happy Teddy is when two p.m. rolls around and he isn't boarding a flight back to LA. Instead, he's lounging on the Caldwells' dock, a beer in one hand, a great mood in the other. The music is up. There isn't a cloud in the sky. And Teddy's only problem is his own guilty conscience.

"Want to get in the water?" Bennett asks from the chair to his left. She puts down the book she's reading and stands, and Teddy forces himself to look literally anywhere else but in her general direction.

First of all, everything was fine and under control after breakfast.

But then it all went sideways after lunch when Bennett said she wanted to go down to the dock to get some sun. Teddy and his conscience could do without the image of Bennett in her stupid little black bikini branded into the side of his brain. It takes the better half of the afternoon to convince himself that just because he's staying at the Caldwells' house this weekend doesn't mean he's cheating on his (ex?) girlfriend. But this is fine. Teddy is not in over his head.

"I'll get in, yeah," Teddy says, standing from his chair and watching with some amusement (but mostly misplaced frustration) as Bennett picks up a nearby life jacket and steps into the armholes. She pulls it up her legs like she's pulling on a pair of pants and starts clipping it across her stomach. It's obvious she isn't aware Teddy's watching her. He tries his best to keep quiet, but ends up busting out laughing anyway.

"Yeah, you think it's funny now," she says, grabbing another beer for herself before waddling over to the dock's edge. It looks like she's wearing a gigantic diaper, and Teddy's just about to start making fun of her when she jumps in the water. She bobs up to the surface, cracks her beer, and says, "Come on—just try it. It's the only sensible way to float on the lake."

Teddy can't argue with that, so he grabs the nearest life jacket and clips himself in the same way, then makes a pit stop at the cooler before waddling in after her. A moment later, they're floating a little ways from the dock.

"There does seem to be some logic behind this whole upside-down life jacket madness, and I fully support it," he comments happily.

Bennett nods. "Yeah, plus, it keeps you a little higher above the water than wearing it the right way does, so it's a lot easier to look out for alligators."

Teddy's in the middle of a long pull of his beer and chokes on it.

"What?!" he squawks, flapping at the water's surface and drawing his legs up as high as he can. He ends up tipping himself over backward and almost loses his beer. When he comes up for air, Bennett is laughing so hard he can't help laughing, too. They end up settling in like that for a while (once Teddy has confirmed three times that there are, in fact, no alligators in the lake).

"So, your family's coming over tonight," Teddy says after he's done telling a story about the time he slipped and got his foot stuck in a toilet his senior year of high school while trying to reach an air vent for a prank. "Who's coming and what should I call them?"

Bennett ducks underwater for a moment, holding her beer above her head so it doesn't get wet. She wipes her face when she pops back up and says, "Yeah. My aunt and uncle and cousins—so for you, that's Mr. and Mrs. McGeary, Liz, and Will."

"Sounds fun."

"Fun is a stretch," Bennett mutters absently, catching Teddy off guard. He studies her profile again and is about to ask what she means when she apparently remembers herself. "I mean—yeah, no, it'll be fun. They live on the lake, too, so they'll probably bring their boat over."

Teddy knows a backstroke when he sees one.

"What, you're not into family gatherings?" he asks, and judging by the look on her face, Bennett knows he's onto her. She wrinkles her nose and squints out over the water.

"They're just . . ." Her eyes flick to Teddy's for a moment as she searches for the words she wants. "They're just a lot."

"Aw, come on," he says, feeling robbed. He gives her a reassuring eyebrow wiggle. "I'm just as good at listening as I am talking, if that's any consolation."

She laughs, smoothing the hair on the top of her head.

"My cousin Liz and I aren't really getting along at the moment," she says.

"What happened?" he asks.

"It's a long story. Liz and I have never had the closest relationship to begin with—" Bennett stops short and shakes her head. "She just—I don't know. Things got weird when she found out about all the *Parachutes* stuff. She thought I was purposely not telling her things, even though I wasn't telling *anyone* at the time. So she just started acting . . . weird."

"What, like, jealous weird?"

Bennett's laugh has zero humor behind it. "It'd be stupid pretentious of me to think that, but I guess I don't know what else it could be? Even when it literally makes no sense."

"Sounds like it makes a lot of sense, actually," Teddy says, tracking a few water droplets running over her collarbone. He forces himself to stop.

"Nah, you just—you'd just have to know Liz. It doesn't make sense."

The only thing that doesn't make sense is Bennett thinking *this* doesn't make sense.

"Bennett," Teddy says, holding up both his palms like the human embodiment of the scale of justice. He pushes one palm higher and lowers the other as he says, *"New York Times–*best-selling author . . ."* He raises and lowers his hands again, switching their positions and wiggling his fingers. "And . . . what does Liz do?"

Bennett's watching him with an expression that says she doesn't approve of the direction he's taking this, but she still answers, "She's gonna be a freshman in college."

"Then of course it makes sense," he says, well aware that he doesn't actually know anything about the situation. "She has, like, nine million reasons to be jealous of you. And it's shitty of her to make you feel bad about it instead of just being happy for you."

Bennett stares at him with another one of those infuriatingly unreadable expressions, even after Teddy turns his scale of justice into jazz hands to try to make her laugh.

"You're definitely right about the shitty part," she admits after a moment. "And Liz has definitely pulled some shitty stunts recently, not gonna lie."

"Yeah? Like what?" he asks, keeping his tone light. He knows Bennett isn't exactly into first-person monologues, and he doesn't want to spook her in the middle of one.

"Just . . . stuff with our friends," Bennett says, trying to shrug it off. "I moved to the same high school as her in tenth grade, and she's always had this weird thing about how our friends were her friends first . . . I don't know. It's not that big of a deal, actually."

All this new information with no supporting details is making Teddy's imagination run a little wild with possible explanations.

"I mean . . . is it possible that she's worried your friends will like you better, so she tries to keep you in check by reminding you that she's the reason they're your friends in the first place?"

Bennett cocks her head to the side, studying him.

"Which makes for solid evidence that she's already jealous of you," Teddy adds thoughtfully. "So naturally she'd go all bat shit when it turns out you're this best-selling author with a movie deal happening. Sounds pretty consistent with her . . . character, I guess."

Teddy feels so lame dropping acting jargon into this, but it's the only way he knows how to get his point across.

Bennett's staring at him again when he looks back over. There's a tiny crease between her eyebrows, and Teddy isn't sure what to do about it, so he gives her jazz hands again.

"You're, like, not a real person. You know that?" she says, shaking her head, and Teddy is stupid proud of the smile he gets at the tail end of it.

"Obviously," he says. "*Such a big deal*, remember?"

"God, there's gotta be a 'Buzz Lightyear to the Rescue' joke in here somewhere," Bennett says, rubbing a hand over her face in a failed attempt to hide how hard she's trying not to laugh. Some anxiety creeps back into her expression when she pulls her hand away, though.

"What," Teddy prompts, letting himself drift close enough to give her leg an encouraging nudge underwater.

She nudges him back. "Nothing, it's just—Liz is gonna freak when she sees you here."

"Why?" he asks, even though he could take a wild guess.

Bennett hesitates, so Teddy nudges her again.

She tips her head back and smiles up at the sky. "God—okay. I have to give you some backstory here on how Liz is before I make my point, though."

"All ears," Teddy says.

"Long story short," she starts, still not looking at him, "I was kind of dating this guy last fall . . . who Liz claimed was cheating on me, and, like, only liked me because of all the *Parachutes* stuff happening. Liz kept telling me, and I just didn't believe her because, like, *it's Liz*. So fast forward to this party I went to over Christmas break . . . I ended up walking in on him and Liz together, and Liz literally climbed off him and said, 'See? Told you he was cheating.'"

When Teddy doesn't say anything, Bennett glances over at him and rolls her eyes. "It's fine. Seriously—just stupid high school drama."

Teddy immediately finds words again. "No, no. Don't do that. Don't play the high school drama card and let her off easy. What kind of person does that to their friend? To their *cousin*?" He gapes at her for a second. "I mean, seriously—*are you kidding me?*"

"It doesn't even matter anymore, though. The guy was only dating me because of the *Parachutes* stuff, especially since Liz made it her personal mission that year to tell everyone and their mother about my publishing deal. And he was cheating with more girls than just Liz, so it was better I found out when I did instead of later on, you know?" Bennett says, squinting out over the water. "Anyway, I only brought it up to give you some insight on what you're in for. Because she's gonna freak when she sees you."

"What, because I'm *kind of* famous?" Teddy says, already irritated by the prospect. And the only reason he bypasses the thing about Liz's personal mission is because he's not trying to bombard Bennett with questions about *Parachutes*. He does make a mental note to come back to it later, though.

"That you're kind of famous, yeah, and that I didn't tell her you're here," Bennett says. "She's gonna take it personally and think *I'm purposely not telling her* things again."

Awesome. Tonight should be fun.

"So when are they supposed to get here?" he asks.

"Probably soon," she says, squinting over at him. "Again, I'm not trying to be dramatic about this, but, like, they're all kind of a lot sometimes. Except Will. You'll love him. But just a heads-up—he's . . . sort of super into acting?"

"You make it sound like that's a bad thing," Teddy jokes.

"No, no—not at all. I just don't want you to, like, feel obligated to talk about anything you don't want if Will brings it up. Which he will."

Teddy shrugs. "No worries. I don't mind talking about it."

Just as long as it doesn't turn into the focal point of the evening, which he's now a little worried that it might. But at least

Teddy's prepared for it when the McGearys do show up half an hour later. What's the worst that can happen, right?

* * *

Teddy and Bennett are still floating in the lake when the sound of an approaching boat interrupts their conversation.

"Before I forget," Bennett says, "do you mind not saying anything about the movie around them? It needs to stay on the DL for now."

"Hey, Bennett!" someone yells before Teddy can answer.

Bennett swims over to the dock's edge and hoists herself out of the water, then gets to work removing her life jacket. Teddy follows after her, watching as a dark-haired guy at the front of the boat throws her a rope to tie up.

Teddy's got a bit of a trick shoulder (Little League mishap involving an unsuccessful slide into second base when he was twelve), so he has to swim over to the ladder off the opposite side of the dock to pull himself up. The boat is docked up by the time he's all the way out (sans diaper life jacket), and the first thing he sees is a large amount of dark brown hair draped over Bennett's shoulder. Some girl is hugging her.

A very tall girl. In a neon-pink bikini that doesn't leave much to the imagination.

She pulls back and her eyes immediately flicker to Teddy's.

Teddy makes his way toward them, grabbing his and Bennett's towels off their lounge chairs along the way. Bennett gives him a grateful smile when he hands hers to her, then turns to introduce him to everyone.

"Teddy, this is my aunt, Susan, and my uncle, Fletcher," she says, gesturing first toward a couple stepping off the back of the boat. The man holds the woman's hand as she tries to get her footing—they both look to be around the same age as Bennett's parents, though Mrs. McGeary is bundled up in a sweater despite it being ninety degrees out, and Mr. McGeary looks like he stole his getup off a Tommy Bahama mannequin.

"Hi there, Mr. and Mrs. McGeary. I'm Teddy Sharpe," Teddy says, making sure his game face is fully in place. Mrs. and Mr. McGeary return the greeting and shake his hand once they're safely on the dock, but they don't spare any time for small talk, continuing straight past and down the walkway. Yikes.

"This is Will," Bennett continues, gesturing toward the dark-haired guy. Will's been staring at Teddy in wide-eyed shock for the past minute or so. He surges forward to grip Teddy's hand before Teddy has a chance to properly introduce himself.

"I'm Will!" he says. He's a few inches shorter than Teddy, with a mess of black hair and a face full of freckles. When he shakes Teddy's hand, there's so much enthusiasm behind it it's almost cartoonish.

"Teddy," he says, trying not to laugh.

"Holy *shit*, it's cool to meet you." Will glances between Teddy and Bennett, an obvious question written in his expression. Before he can ask, though, another hand slides into Teddy's.

"I'm Liz," the brunette girl says, stepping closer than what feels necessary. Teddy opens his mouth to introduce himself but she cuts him off with, "It's so nice to meet you, Teddy."

Yep. Teddy knows the look she's giving him all too well—it's the same look the flight attendant gave him on the plane to Charlotte yesterday, except paired with a sly smile that makes Teddy ten times more uncomfortable.

"You too," he says, pulling his hand away as fast as he can without seeming impolite.

Liz's eyes never leave Teddy's face as she says, "Bennett, I'm just dying to know how you two know each other."

Teddy's not sure if she's trying to be intimidating or charming with it . . . not that it matters. All it comes off as is irritating.

"We were sitting in the same row on a flight into Charlotte yesterday," Bennett says, surprisingly. Teddy had been expecting some kind of deflection, or at least a vague enough response that could squash any follow-up questions.

"That's so cool!" Will says. "Random for sure, but still so cool."

"Superrandom," Liz agrees, cocking her head to the side and studying them with open suspicion.

"Yeah—I had a connecting flight down to Miami that got canceled," Teddy jumps in, since this is getting weird, fast. "So Bennett agreed to take me home with her after I practically got down on my knees and begged her to. Then I just invited myself to stay the whole weekend."

Bennett and Will laugh.

"That's so nice of you, Bennie," Liz says, grinning as she takes a step toward Teddy. Teddy, in turn, moves a little closer to Bennett. (Whether it's for his own protection or for hers, he's not sure.) Liz glances between them again and smirks.

"Liz, help me with the food in here," Will says, hopping back into their boat and rummaging around. Liz's face drops into a scowl as she turns toward her brother.

"I think you can handle that one on your own, Will," she says. Then she heads up the dock walkway, throwing another sly smile over her shoulder at Teddy, and yikes—this evening's definitely going to be fun.

CHAPTER EIGHT

Bennett pretty much goes AWOL after the McGeary landing, leaving Teddy stranded in a kitchen full of strangers. She disappeared to take a phone call after they all walked up from the dock, so Teddy hopped in the shower to kill some time while she was gone. Tanner told him she was still on the phone when he came back upstairs, but that was thirty minutes ago, and Bennett's still nowhere to be found now.

Since Mrs. Caldwell basically kicks Teddy out of the kitchen when he asks if there's anything he can help with (*Guests are not allowed to help, Teddy*), he and Tanner decide to head out onto the back deck to try to catch today's baseball highlights on their phones. (Mr. McGeary already called dibs on the living room TV to watch some MSNBC special before dinner....) Unfortunately, they only make it about twenty minutes before Liz descends upon them again.

"There you guys are," she says when she swings open the deck doors. She takes a seat at the high table in the corner, eyes on Teddy the whole time.

Will steps out onto the deck behind her and grabs an open rocking chair. "What're you guys up to?"

"Checking the baseball highlights from today," Tanner says. "The Braves swept—"

Liz cuts him off with one of the most theatrical sighs Teddy's ever heard. Even in show business. "God, do we have to talk about baseball? It's so *boring*."

"Do you have any other suggestions?" Tanner asks, the edge in his tone indicating that he's done with her, too.

She shrugs and pulls out her phone. "I don't care—just, anything else."

"So hey, Teddy, not to be weird or anything," Will starts after a moment, aiming for nonchalance and missing completely, "but you're from *Testing Wyatt*, right?"

Liz scoffs without looking up from her phone. "Way to be subtle, William."

"Yeah, I am," Teddy says to Will.

Will looks so excited he might jump out of his chair. "Nice! I loved your movie *Corduroy*, too. I'm a huge fan of the director."

"Really? Thanks, man. You a big movie buff of something?" Teddy asks. People naming off his acting résumé is never comfortable, so maybe Teddy can reroute the conversation.

"Yeah, definitely. I'm actually pretty into theater—"

"Pretty into theater *dudes*, you mean," Liz snickers under her breath, but it's just loud enough for everyone on the porch to hear.

Will freezes, and it takes about as long for Teddy to make sense of Liz's implication as it takes for most of the color to drain from Will's face.

"Jesus, Liz—are you serious with this again?" Tanner mutters, and just the fact that the word "again" is in his sentence is enough to put Will and Liz's relationship into clear focus.

"What? Aw, come on," Liz says with so much fake innocence behind it it's offensive. "It's not like it's a big secret anymore. Plus, it's 2018, Will! You should be *proud*."

Teddy steals a glance at Will, who looks like he's either going to take a swing at his sister or start to cry. Teddy had been expecting bad, but he hadn't expected *this*—what kind of asshole outs her own brother in front of a total stranger? Teddy wants to divert the conversation before it can get any more uncomfortable for Will.

"Hey, Will. If you're into acting, man, I'm definitely down to talk more about it," he says quickly. "I'm kind of a rookie in comparison to others, though, so try not to hold it against me."

It takes a few seconds, but a hint of a smile appears on Will's face. "Come on, man. You're killing it right now—don't try to tell me you're still a rookie."

Teddy laughs. "I am! For real. I didn't start acting until I auditioned for *Testing Wyatt*, and in retrospect I wish I'd taken some acting classes or something in high school."

"Ugh, acting classes are all Will does these days," Liz says, wedging herself back into the conversation. Teddy has never been so close to telling someone to shut the hell up in his life. "There's only so much you can learn before it becomes repetitive—"

"Yeah, that's not true. At all," Teddy cuts across her, surprising himself with how dismissive he sounds.

Liz scoffs, apparently offended by the shutdown. When no one jumps to defend her, she gets up from her spot at the high table and mutters something that Teddy doesn't catch on her way back inside. Will pretends like she isn't even there as she walks by, and Tanner throws up a half-hearted salute to her before going back to his phone.

Teddy turns to Will. "So, anyway, definitely keep taking as many classes as you can. I promise you'll be glad you did."

* * *

All right. Teddy knows Bennett probably isn't doing it on purpose, but this is getting a little ridiculous.

When the hell is she going to get off the phone?

"I'm gonna run inside for a sec," Teddy says after he finishes talking to Will about his stance on Method acting. (He's actually torn on it, honestly.) When Will starts to protest, Teddy says, "I'm just gonna go see where Bennett is. I'll be back in a sec."

In the kitchen, Mr. Caldwell is helping Mrs. Caldwell mix corn on the cob into the gigantic silver pot she'd washed out that morning, while Mrs. McGeary rearranges the platters on the kitchen island. Once again Teddy gets denied when he offers to help, but he does learn from Mr. Caldwell that Bennett's downstairs on the patio. Teddy takes the long way around the kitchen counter to avoid walking by Liz on his way to the basement stairs.

The back wall of the Caldwells' basement is mostly windows, so when Teddy reaches the bottom of the steps, he catches sight of Bennett outside with her phone clutched to her ear. She's pacing around as she talks, looking like she needs a few more minutes, so Teddy veers off down the hallway to grab his own phone out of his room. He still hasn't responded to any of Chelsea's texts or voice mails (which is pretty ironic, considering during the past year their relationship lived and breathed by their iPhones thanks to conflicting filming schedules).

Teddy sits on the edge of his bed and stares at the three new text message notifications on his home screen, feeling guilty about leaving his phone in his room all afternoon so he wouldn't have to deal with this. Sure, they've fought a lot, but not once has Chelsea ever said anything along the lines of "Fuck this, I'm done." Had she sent that text a week ago—hell, two days ago—Teddy probably would have been devastated. Now, he just feels . . . indifferent? Maybe he's finally maxed out on emotional whiplash and constantly worrying about never knowing where they stood with each other.

Teddy decides not to read the texts just yet. He's been thinking about how he wants to respond all day, but even now he still doesn't know how or where to start. He stands after another minute or so, pocketing his phone and straightening the duvet cover.

Then he turns to head back upstairs.

"Jesus *Christ*—" he yelps, pressing a hand to his forehead.

Liz is leaning against the doorframe, blocking his exit.

"Sorry," she giggles, covering her mouth with her hand. "I was looking for Bennett."

Teddy clears his throat. "Is she not out on the patio?"

Liz moseys into the room toward the windows. She peeks through the blinds for a second before turning back, a coy smile on her face.

"No, she is," she says. Which, what?

"Oh. Well. I'm gonna go grab her and head back upstairs—"

"So, like, you and Bennett just met each other, right?" Liz says, making no effort to be discreet as she eyes him up and down and waits for an answer.

"Um, yeah," Teddy says. "On the plane. Remember?"

Liz hums, strolling past the bed and dragging a finger lazily across the duvet cover.

"That's so crazy, right?" she says, and Teddy has no clue what to say to that. "Plus, it's *so* unlike Bennett to invite someone she barely knows to spend the weekend with her. So, so crazy."

Teddy rocks back onto his heels and shoves his hands in his pockets. "I mean, I wouldn't say we barely know each other. . . ."

"You're right, that was a little one-sided of me to assume." Liz pauses to smile innocently over at him again. "You're Teddy Sharpe—*obviously* she knew who you were beforehand, or else you wouldn't be here. Is she, like, trying to get you to do a promo thing for her books or something?"

"Are you—are you for real with this right now?" he laughs despite the heat creeping up the back of his neck and spreading to his cheeks and forehead. He's sure the look on his face would probably be considered rude by most people's standards, but he has no effing clue what Liz is even doing here, let alone talking about. "Bennett doesn't need my help with promo stuff, trust me. What are you even saying?"

Liz wanders toward him and takes her time gathering her hair over to one shoulder. "Okay, what's the deal, then? Why are you here?"

Teddy feels himself getting defensive for Bennett. Not that he's, like, this suave dude that everyone wants to be around, but why does Liz think he has to have some big reason to be here?

When Teddy doesn't respond again, Liz shoots him a nasty look and mutters, "God, this whole secrecy for attention thing she does is so extra."

"You clearly don't know Bennett if you think she's secretive for attention," Teddy snaps, folding his arms across his chest. "Maybe she just doesn't want people telling everyone and their mother her business."

Liz's eyes go wide.

"Sorry, I didn't mean to—" she starts, looking theatrically hurt. "I-I was just trying to figure out why a famous actor with a girlfriend would agree to spend the weekend with a random girl he met on the plane."

"You should ask her, then," Teddy says, starting for the door.

Liz gasps. "So it does have something to do with her books?"

"Or *maybe* Bennett and I are friends and I enjoy spending time with her?" he wheels around and says before he can stop himself. He realizes a moment too late that Liz is on his heels, so when he turns she's right there, up in his space and almost at eye level. She stares at him for a moment, even after he takes two gigantic steps back, and Teddy can practically see the synapses firing behind her eyes.

"Wait a second," she says, looking like she's too close to putting two and two together, and at this point, Teddy'll say just about anything to distract her from jumping to the correct conclusion—a movie-related conclusion.

"Fine, yeah—I'm here because I like Bennett, okay? We're kind of . . . you know . . ." He trails off, and he'll deal with the repercussions later (especially since it doesn't feel like a lie, which is as unexpected as it is nerve-racking).

Liz looks like nothing makes sense to her anymore.

"You and Bennett? Seriously?" she says, then she throws her head back and laughs, the sound ricocheting around the room. She pretends to wipe a nonexistent tear from her eye. "Oh, *God*, this is great. Does she know you have a girlfriend?"

"I don't—" Teddy starts, but he knows he can't technically finish that sentence. Not yet.

"Oh shit, she doesn't, does she?" Liz says, eyes lighting up, and it's sickening how much she's enjoying this. "Makes sense.

Bennett would never get involved with a guy with a girlfriend. I can't imagine her wanting any part of ruining somebody else's relationship, since, you know, she's had it done to her before."

"What, you mean when you did it to her?" Teddy shoots back, and Liz's expression goes completely blank for one quick, satisfying second.

Teddy decides not to stick around for the rest of her reaction, though. He's had enough of this for one night. Liz's words are still clattering around in his head as he rounds out of the bedroom and down the hall—only to skid to a halt at the bottom of the stairs, his stomach launching into his throat. Liz nearly smacks into the back of him a second later.

"What're you two weirdos doing?" Bennett asks. She's standing halfway up the steps, phone still clutched in her hand.

Liz doesn't even miss a beat.

"I was asking Teddy to let me borrow some contact solution— my allergies are going crazy right now," she says with a terrifying amount of ease.

"Yikes—I'm sorry," Bennett says. "I think I've got some eye drops upstairs if you need them later."

"Oh, perfect!" Liz heads up the stairs, dropping a hand on Bennett's shoulder as she steps around her. "Come on, guys! Dinner's going to be ready soon."

Bennett rolls her eyes and motions for Teddy to follow her. "Yeah—*come on*, Teddy!"

Teddy's not sure how to get his legs to work. He wants to say something to Bennett about what just happened for the sake of his own sanity, but where does he even start? That he just admitted to Liz that something's going on between them to make sure Liz didn't guess about Bennett's movie? And that it might be more truthful for him than he was expecting?

"Hey, do you think I have time to make a phone call before dinner?" Teddy asks instead, pointing a thumb over his shoulder toward the basement patio. At least one good thing came out of what just happened with Liz: the clarity that Teddy needs to sack up and handle this with Chelsea before it blows up in his face.

"Yeah, no worries," Bennett says, cocking her head to the side. "Is everything okay?"

"Definitely—just need to return a couple of messages. I'll be quick."

CHAPTER NINE

Teddy pulls his phone out of his pocket once he's down on the Caldwells' dock.

It's time to deal with this.

Chelsea doesn't deserve Teddy walking around saying there's something going on with him and another girl when they haven't talked yet (regardless of how nasty Chelsea was to him during the past twenty-four hours), and Bennett doesn't deserve this, either. Even if there is a possibility she might reciprocate what Teddy's apparently feeling, the last thing Teddy wants to do is string both girls along. He at least needs to let Chelsea know where his head is at first.

Fri, Jul 21, 2:20 p.m.

So this whole ignoring me thing is a little immature Ted

Fri, Jul 21, 4:57 p.m.

Seriously why is your phone off . . .

Are you back in LA?

Teddy's not trying to have this conversation over text—even if it has to be on the phone, Teddy still owes it to Chelsea to speak to her directly.

Fri, Jul 21, 7:47 p.m.

Hey - are you on set or can you talk on the phone?

Teddy's in the middle of typing out a follow-up message on how he needs to talk to her about why he's still in Charlotte when her response stops him short.

Jesus. About time you responded?? And yeah I'm on set. What's up

Teddy sighs. Text it is, then.

Having absolutely no idea where to start, he types out the first thing to pop into his head and hits send before he can change his mind.

Were you being serious when you said you were done?

The little typing ellipsis pops up immediately.

Idk. Kind of. Yeah. Things have been

> so fucking weird lately. That's one
> of the reasons why I wanted you to call
> me when you landed in Charlotte

Reading that is strange. It hurts she's being so cavalier about whatever their relationship is, and it's frustrating she's so quick to respond now after it basically took an act of Congress to get her to reply to him in recent, normal conversations.

Then the implications behind the last sentence of her text sink in.

> You wanted me to call to talk about how
> things have been weird lately or about
> how you were done?

The more Teddy mulls it over, the more he gets the feeling he already knows the answer. It would certainly be within the realm of Normal Chelsea Behavior. Without waiting for a response, he adds:

> You weren't really stuck in Vancouver this
> weekend were you?

A minute or so passes before she texts back.

> My director asked me to stay, so I did

> That didn't answer my question.

> Ok. Fine. I chose to stay and work on
> some extra scenes.

You said you wanted to meet up with some of your friends in Miami anyway. I figured you'd just do that.

That's pretty messed up Chelsea.

I'm sorry. You know I'm not good at shit like this.

Shit like this—seriously? Does she mean their relationship? It's amazing how three words can resolve most of Teddy's guilt. Here he is, genuinely worried about how he's handling everything, while Chelsea is probably posted up on set in Vancouver, relieved to have another weekend without having to deal with *shit like this*.

If by "shit like this" you mean actually putting some effort into our relationship, then yeah. You're not good at shit like this.

Don't start. You work just as much as I do but then turn around and get all butt hurt whenever my schedule conflicts with something. It's hypocritical

That's a joke right? Are you kidding me?

Just to recap here—this is the third time in a row you've canceled on me and YOU JUST SAID YOU CHOSE TO STAY ON SET TO WORK ON EXTRA SCENES

I chose to stay on set bc it was the right thing to do for my career. Chill out.

And tbh Ted we weren't gonna have fun in Miami anyway. We both know it. Let's not pretend like planning this trip was anything more than us feeling obligated to do something bc we haven't seen each other since I left for Vancouver

I told you everything's felt weird lately. It's like we're trying too hard or something

First of all, the irony behind "It's like we're trying too hard" is so hilariously hilarious it has Teddy questioning his own sanity, because second of all—Chelsea might actually be right about this. Teddy remembers looking forward to their trip down to Miami while on the plane in Charlotte, yeah, but he also remembers plenty of pop-up moments of relief that he and Chelsea never made it down. He just assumed it was because he was mad she bailed on him last second, but now? Now, not so much.

Fine. But honestly what do you expect me to say to this? I didn't push this trip because I felt obligated. I genuinely wanted to spend time with you. That's what people in relationships do. . . .

And what I'm gathering here is that wasn't the case for you. Am I wrong, or?

Come on Ted, you know how much I care about you. It's not that black and white

If you have to say stuff like "it's not that black and white" when it comes to wanting to spend time with me, then it actually does seem that black and white.

Maybe it is then.

Awesome. I guess we should save the rest of this inevitable conversation for when we're both back in LA. Unless you'd rather just end it now.

I guess your right. And no Teddy. I have too much respect for you to end it over text. Are you already back in LA? I can come down for a few days soon if you want.

So Chelsea will take a few days to come to LA to break up with him in person but she won't take a long weekend with him in Miami? Jesus. How the hell did this relationship make it two years?

Teddy wants to lash out. Wants Chelsea to feel as shitty as he feels right now. Sure, it'll sound petty and detached and sort of middle school-esque, but Teddy could not care less.

No. I'm staying in Charlotte <u>until Sunday</u> with a friend I met at my audition. Thanks for asking how it went btw. And don't worry about coming down since we both know you have such a demanding schedule. I'll see you around Chels

Chelsea's response is instantaneous.

What time's your flight on Sunday?

Teddy almost doesn't answer. He just wants this conversation to be done. He types out a quick message, taps send, and watches the little DELIVERED materialize underneath.

Sunday at 1

Then he turns his phone off with no intention of turning it back on until Sunday.

* * *

"Teddy, grab a plate, man," Mr. Caldwell says, clapping Teddy on the shoulders and shaking him out of his mental exhaustion long enough to remember he's standing in the middle of the kitchen. He looks around.

Everyone is already seated or hovering around the food on the kitchen island. The Caldwells and the McGearys clearly know how to do it right when it comes to cookouts, and calculating how much food Teddy can fit on one plate is a welcomed distraction from the current state of his personal life. Bennett picks up a plate after him and laughs as he piles up as much as he can get.

"What's this?" Teddy asks, pointing at the giant platter in

the middle of the other dishes. It has jumbo shrimp and corn on the cob and little red potatoes and—sausage, maybe?—and Teddy has never thought about smushing his face into a pile of food before, but at this point he wouldn't put it past himself.

"It's called Frogmore Stew," Bennett says, reaching for the salad. "You're gonna love it—"

"Oh no, Bennie, I'm so sorry!" Mrs. McGeary steps between them and takes the salad tongs out of Bennett's hand. "I completely forgot, I used walnuts in the salad. I feel terrible."

"Oh—that's okay, Aunt Susan," Bennett says, setting down her plate and walking to the kitchen sink. She washes her hands twice while Mrs. McGeary takes Bennett's place in line.

"What was that?" Teddy murmurs once Bennett's picked up her plate again.

She shrugs. "I'm allergic to tree nuts."

"Really?"

"Yeah, I can't get them anywhere near my mouth or eyes. I'll swell up and start wheezing and stuff. It's superattractive."

"Yikes, that sounds miserable," Teddy laughs, following her to the dining table.

Frogmore Stew ends up being one of the best things Teddy has ever tasted, and it's a shame he can't enjoy the full dining experience since Liz has chosen to sit directly across from him. She spends all dinner with a tiny little grin on her face and seems hell-bent on making sure everyone is paying attention to what she's saying.

Teddy doesn't wait for someone else to get up for seconds this time around. After enduring monopolized conversations all night, he's way past decorum. He piles up more Frogmore Stew and resolves himself to only speaking when spoken to. Which doesn't last.

"Right, Teddy?"

Teddy's eyes flick up from the jumbo shrimp to find Liz looking back at him expectantly. Again.

"Sorry, what was that?" he asks.

Bennett helps him out, her tone laced with humor no one else seems to pick up on. "Liz thinks social media's going to be the downfall of our generation."

Teddy raises his eyebrows in hopes it'll disguise the what-the-hell-does-this-have-to-do-with-me? trying to etch itself into his expression.

"I deleted myself off *all* social media this summer," Liz says, since apparently this is vital information for everyone to have. "And it's honestly the best decision I've ever made. There's so much more going on in the world than on the Internet."

"Then what're you doing on your phone all the time?" Will asks through a mouthful of garlic bread.

"I obviously still keep up with my friends," Liz says, looking at her brother like he's not even worth answering. "Plus my roommate from Clemson and I are trying to coordinate who's buying what for our dorm. Which reminds me—Bennie, have you figured out your little college roommate situation yet?"

"Still doing random as of now," Bennett says.

"Ugh. Are you sure you want to do that, though?" Liz's eyes go wide with faux sincerity. "What if you end up with, like, a psycho or something?"

Bennett wrinkles her nose as she sips her water. "I'm not worried about it."

"That's the one thing I did before deleting myself off the Internet—vetted my Clemson roommate to make sure she's suitable to live with." Liz shudders. "It was her idea to delete everything before rush. Supersmart."

"Why? Afraid all the sorority girls are gonna find out about your seventh-grade emo phase?" Will asks.

Liz throws a piece of sausage at him. He catches it and puts it down on the edge of his plate with distaste.

"*Manners*, William," Mrs. McGeary snaps from the adult side of the table, giving her son the same look her daughter gave him a minute ago. Will casts his eyes back down to his plate.

Pleased, Liz continues with, "But, yeah. So many of my friends have gotten in trouble because of all the stuff about them on the Internet. Bennett and I know this guy named Robbie, who almost got his basketball scholarship taken away because someone took Snapchat screenshots of him at a party and posted them on Facebook."

"Seriously?" Teddy turns to Bennett for confirmation, then gets completely distracted watching the way she puts down her silverware and reaches for the napkin in her lap. She balls it up in both fists, knuckles going white.

"Robbie deserved to get caught, though. The piece of shit." Liz sniffs. She looks directly at Bennett and says, "Right, Bennie?" and honestly, Teddy might be jumping the gun here, but if Robbie turns out to be the guy Bennett dated, then this is proof positive that Liz is actually evil.

"Is that why you think social media's going to be the downfall of our generation, then? The invasion of privacy?" Teddy asks, suddenly in the mood to partake in the conversation.

Liz considers it.

"I guess that's a more specific way to put it," she says. She takes in what Teddy can only assume is an annoyed expression on his face and adds, "What, you don't agree?"

"Not really."

"Interesting." Liz sips the glass of wine she demanded her parents let her have (*since Bennie and everyone else have been drinking beer all day*). "I thought you of all people would agree— what with all the stuff that's written on the Internet about you without your consent."

"He's a public figure," Bennett pipes up. "People don't need consent to put stuff about him on the Internet."

"Occupational hazard," Teddy adds, glad Bennett's come out of whatever was going on inside her head.

"I guess that's true." Liz smiles sweetly across the table at them in a way that has Teddy gritting his teeth. "A drawback to being one of Young Hollywood's brightest rising stars, right?"

Wow. She's quoting his own Encyclopeakia article at him. Bold move.

"I don't see it that way," Teddy says. "But I also don't go out of my way to read what people are saying about me on the Internet. Most of it's probably bullshit anyway."

"Really?" Liz gasps. "Not even to read all the amazing reviews you've gotten?"

Teddy shakes his head.

"That's too bad." Liz pouts. "I know that one movie you were in for Sundance definitely got some killer reviews. What was it called again, Teddy?"

And now she's gonna go *there*. Awesome. Bring it on.

"*Bistro on Fifth*," Teddy replies, looking Liz square in the eye. Daring her to keep going.

But then Bennett says, "Oh yeah—I really liked that one, actually," and now Teddy has to live with the knowledge that Bennett has not only seen the movie he and Chelsea worked on together, but specifically all the lovey-dovey parts and that one sex scene toward the end.

Liz grins over her wineglass. "I know, right, Bennie? Such a cute movie! What was the name of the actress again? Chelsea something . . . ?"

"Chelsea Bordeaux!" Will provides. "Y'all were both amazing in that movie, Teddy."

"Oh—thanks, man," Teddy says, hoping his expression isn't giving him away. He's still raw from his text conversation with Chelsea (and just from the past thirty-six hours of his life in general). It's hard to keep your game face on while being water boarded with your own emotions.

"For real, though. You should read your reviews, Teddy," Liz says, swirling her wine around in her glass. "Even though I still think the Internet and social media will be the downfall of our generation, it's *amazing* what you can find on there."

And Teddy's had just about enough of this.

"Definitely some amazing things," he agrees. "Like those superinsightful *Psychology Today* articles I use to research roles—you know, like the ones that talk about the differences between a psychopath and sociopath? Or help you figure out why you have so many deeply rooted insecurities? They're great. I can send you some links if you want, Liz."

Will snorts into his salad. Tanner, who's been participating in the adult half of the conversation most of the night, still muffles a guffaw with his napkin. Teddy can't see what Bennett's doing because he's too busy staring down Liz, but he's pretty confident Bennett got a kick out of it, too.

Meanwhile, Liz looks totally calm, though Teddy's willing to bet the wineglass in her hand might shatter at any moment.

"Oh, man," Tanner chimes in, leaning over and hooking an arm around Bennett's shoulders. "Don't you guys just love family cookouts? Who wants to go play Ping-Pong?"

* * *

"So, you any good at this?" Tanner asks when he and Teddy step down into the garage. The Ping-Pong table is already set up in the middle of the room.

"I'm all right," Teddy lies. Ping-Pong is his go-to pastime on set. And he was so thankful for a reason to get up from the dinner table that he only feels mildly guilty about leaving Bennett and Will back inside with Liz.

"We can definitely still play if you want," Tanner says, walking over to an old refrigerator on the back wall. He pulls out two beers and adds, "But I figured you could use a cold one after we forced you to sit through dinner with our extended family."

"No worries, man. Are your parents gonna be cool with this if they walk out here, though?" Teddy asks. He's actually been wondering about this since Tanner snuck him and Bennett a few this afternoon.

"Yeah—they're pretty lenient with us once we go to college, as long as we don't go, like, bat shit crazy or anything," Tanner says, snagging a couple of paddles off a shelf. He hands one and a beer to Teddy and asks, "Are you not twenty-one yet?"

"Almost. September."

Tanner walks to the end of the table. "Nice. Yeah, Bennett's got, like, another three years. But again, once college rolls around, our parents kind of mellow out."

"Speaking of—what do you think Bennett's going to do about college with the movie?" Teddy asks. It's nosey and probably overstepping a boundary, but Liz asking about her roommate situation at dinner had gotten Teddy thinking. If Bennett's going to be on set in Wilmington for filming, how is she going to go to school?

"No idea. I didn't even know the movie was happening until you blew her cover yesterday," Tanner says.

Teddy bursts out laughing as he positions himself on the other side of the Ping-Pong table. "I felt so bad about that. I thought you knew already or else I wouldn't have said anything."

"Don't worry about it," Tanner says. "I'm just glad they're finally making the movie so I don't have to read the books . . . shit—" He grins. "Don't tell her I said that."

"You're good." Teddy laughs again. "You should read them, though. I've only read a few chapters of the first one but I'm a big fan so far."

"Oh yeah! Congrats on getting the part, bro. That's awesome," Tanner says, knocking him a practice serve, and Teddy isn't sure if he's least prepared for the impressive top spin or for Tanner congratulating him on a role he hasn't landed. Either way, the ball ricochets off Teddy's paddle and bounces across the garage.

"Oh, well, thanks, man," he says, chasing after it. "But I just auditioned yesterday. I probably won't hear anything for another month or so."

"Wait, I thought Bennett said you were, like, slated to be in talks soon or some—what, why are you looking at me like that?" he asks when Teddy whips around. Then Tanner's eyes go wide and he curses under his breath.

"What?" Teddy says, which is surprising, considering it feels like he just lost all motor function capabilities.

"What? Nothing," Tanner spouts off, breaking eye contact. "She just said you auditioned."

Teddy can't breathe.

"Bullshit," he says as he bends down to pick up the Ping-Pong ball. It's the only thing he can think to do at this point.

Tanner still hasn't said anything by the time Teddy gets back to his side of the table.

"Tanner, come on, man," he prods, unconcerned with how desperate he sounds. "This could be the biggest movie of my career so far. You can't leave me hanging like this. I might die."

Tanner scratches the back of his neck, looking everywhere around the garage except at Teddy. "God, we all suck at keeping her secrets. No wonder she doesn't tell us anything."

That's probably true, and Teddy's going to feel so bad later about grilling her brother for information, but he has to know. Right now.

"Do *not* tell her I told you this," Tanner warns, pointing a finger across the table. "She was talking this morning about how they're, like, expediting the casting process because of scheduling, and my mom asked if you were gonna get the part you auditioned for. Bennett said she wasn't allowed to say, but, I mean, she still told us." His expression is a little remorseful, but it looks like he's biting back a grin. "She said they're gonna have to have more auditions for the girl lead, but that they're gonna approach you soon about a contract, or something? That's what 'in talks' means, right?"

Teddy stares at him for a moment.

"Oh, *FUCK YES*," he shrieks, throwing his arms over his head. He claps a hand over his mouth, panicked that everyone in the house just heard him, but he cannot be expected to hold it together right now. He's so balls-out excited he's about to start doing laps around the garage. "Holy—oh my *God*, Tanner!"

Tanner rolls his eyes and laughs. "Yeah, yeah. Congrats, man. That's sick."

Teddy has no idea how this is possible. Like, seriously—no idea. He's jumping around and fist pumping and he actually does a lap or two around the garage, but that's fine, because Rita's going to get a phone call about Teddy's contract soon, and Teddy might start tearing up if he doesn't watch himself.

Tanner's still laughing at him when he says, "Come on, man. Let's play before I give up more insider information."

Teddy stops dead in his tracks, grinning like a fool. "Wait, is there more?"

"Stop."

* * *

Teddy and Tanner play Ping-Pong until the McGearys announce they're leaving, and Teddy's secretly glad everyone decides to turn in early that night. He's still riding an adrenaline high about the *Parachutes* role when he climbs into bed, and it's upstaging every other emotion he's had to wrestle with today. It's been quite the thirty-six hours, to say the least, and the weekend doesn't look like it's going to slow down anytime soon. Apparently the Caldwells and the McGearys are all going to a big party tomorrow.

An hour of lying in bed later, though, Teddy's surprised to find himself so wired he can't get comfortable. He was banking on some kind of emotional crash considering he covered the entire spectrum today. Instead, he thrashes under the covers, kicking the sheets down to the end of the bed, and giving an exasperated sigh every time he has to sit up and pull them back to the top of the mattress.

He thinks about his *Parachutes* role. And about his text conversation with Chelsea (his *breakup* conversation with Chelsea). But mostly he thinks of Bennett. They spent almost the entire night together, but it still feels like he didn't see her at all.

And the conversation he had with Liz is still sitting heavily in the back of his mind.

Teddy finally throws the covers off and climbs out of bed. He already can't sit still, and after drinking a fair amount of beer today, he figures it'd probably be best to hydrate a little. He tiptoes up the stairs and he pauses on the landing when he hears a TV playing softly, thinking maybe he should just settle for faucet water from his bathroom. Against his better judgment, he continues up the rest of the steps and peeks over the railing.

Bennett is in the kitchen. She's sitting on the counter by the sink, legs dangling over the granite, and she jumps out of her skin when she sees Teddy.

"Boo," he whispers as he rounds the banister and pads through the living room.

"Jesus," Bennett breathes out, her shoulders sagging. "Give a girl a heart attack."

"Sorry." Teddy grins and strolls around the corner of the bar. "What're you doing?"

She holds up her glass of water. "Hydrating. You?"

"Same," he says casually. "Where are the cups?"

"Cabinet next to the microwave."

Teddy leans a hip against the kitchen island, and a few things register with him as he eyes the plastic tumbler in her hand: Bennett's wearing plaid pajama pants and a soft-looking T-shirt, her hair is piled messily on top of her head, and there's a pair of square, thick-rimmed glasses perched on her nose. And it's strangely adorable.

"Cute glasses, nerd," he teases.

"Real nice, Buzz. Make fun of the blind chick."

"That sounds like a bit of an exaggeration."

"Blind as a bat, honest." Bennett shrugs. "Glasses since fifth, contacts since sixth."

Teddy shudders. "Yikes. The idea of putting something in my eye every day wigs me out—I'm glad I don't have to wear them. No offense."

Bennett levels her gaze with his over her tumbler. "None taken," she says after a long sip.

"So, like, exactly how bad is your vision, then?" Teddy asks.

"I'm nearsighted, and if you were standing three feet away from me and I wasn't wearing glasses or contacts, I still wouldn't be able to see your face."

"There's no way it's that bad." Teddy moves to stand directly in front of her—what he thinks is about three feet away. "Take them off and tell me how many fingers I'm holding up."

"Wow, *didn't see that one coming*," Bennett says, and sets her tumbler down on the counter next to her. Her pun clicks with Teddy as she slides the frames off her face, and it takes a conscious effort to not reach out and ruffle the bun on top of her head. Instead, he holds up four fingers and watches as she squints hard at them.

"Four?" she says after a moment.

"See? A bit of an exaggeration." But when Teddy sticks his tongue out at her to prove his point, she just stares in his general direction, eyes unfocused.

Maybe she is blind.

She squints again. "Are you sticking your tongue out at me?"

Teddy hums and moves closer, sticking his tongue out again.

"You're a real charmer, Sharpe," Bennett says, pushing her glasses on again. Teddy wonders just how off her depth perception is without them, because he can see the exact moment when she registers the amount of space that's no longer between them. She shifts back a little on the counter, and it doesn't matter if it's just a subconscious movement or something else, because either way Teddy's not about that life.

"Hey," he says softly, taking another step toward her and hoping he won't scare her off. He brings a hand up to grip the back of his neck, thinking about how much he wishes he could ask her about the *Parachutes* role. "Thanks again for letting me stay this weekend. Seriously."

"No worries," Bennett says to her hands, then she meets his eyes and grins. "I'm glad you did."

"Yeah?" Teddy grins back. "Me too."

"Now that I'm thinking about it, though," she says, her tone light, "I never stopped to consider the possibility of you being the psycho stalker fanboy type. Maybe you're the real criminal mastermind here."

"Have you noticed we talk about stalking each other a lot for two people who met yesterday," Teddy says. "Not that it matters, since my odds against you are better than yours are against me."

Her mouth drops open. "Hey, watch it."

"What, you think you can take down all this?" He gestures down his body. "All this—solid muscle and pure athleticism? You don't stand a chance."

Bennett bursts out laughing.

"So I gotta tell you something," Teddy says after a moment, just because he wants to get this out of the way now so he won't feel guilty about his shameless attempts at flirting later. Bennett's smile vanishes as soon as he says it, though, and the unease that shows up on her face puts a knot where Teddy's heart is supposed to be. "I mean, it isn't anything bad," he adds quickly. "I just had a weird conversation with Liz tonight while you were on the phone."

Bennett keeps her gaze steady, eyes giving nothing away. "Oh yeah? About what?"

"Honestly? I'm not even sure," Teddy hedges, rubbing a hand over the top of his head. "She kept asking for the real reason why I'm here, and then things kinda went off the rails. . . ."

"And ended up where?" Bennett asks.

"Well, I was afraid she was somehow going to guess something about your movie, so I kind of told her . . . there was something going on between us? To distract her?" Teddy says ruefully, eyes dropping to the granite countertop.

"I see," she says, and when Teddy finally works up the nerve to steal a glance at her, he's pleasantly surprised by the way the corner of her mouth is quirked up.

Teddy scuffs the ball of his foot on the kitchen floor. "Yeah— so I just wanted to give you a heads-up, in case she says something. Which I'm sure she will."

Bennett hums and waits a few seconds before asking, "So, does that mean there is, then?"

Teddy freezes, eyes flicking up to hers. "There's what?"

But instead of answering him, she reaches for her water and downs what's left in a few quick gulps. Teddy steps closer to her when she's done and slips the cup from her hand, now actively ignoring the stutter step in his pulse. Bennett doesn't move as he refills it at the sink, or when he steps right into her space again to give it back.

"Nah, you drink that. I need you on your day-party A-game tomorrow," she says, pushing the water toward him.

"Ah yes. Good lookin' out, Caldwell. Cheers," Teddy says,

and it sounds surprisingly smoother than he'd been expecting. He throws her a wink in between swigs for good measure, then sets the cup down and leaves his hand splayed next to her thigh on the counter. "So what were you asking a second ago? Does that mean there's what?"

There's not much room between them, and Teddy can practically feel it when she sits up a little straighter and shrugs innocently.

"Can I offer you a pointer?" she asks, her voice slung low in a murmur that has Teddy leaning toward it.

"Hmm?"

"If you're planning on making a move here, now's probably a good time," she says, and God bless. For all Teddy knows his heart could have been beating this fast the whole time he's been in the kitchen, but he's certainly aware of it now.

"Really? What kind of move, Caldwell?" he asks, grinning like an idiot. In a heroic display of confidence, Teddy reaches down and lightly grips the backs of both of Bennett's knees. Her pajama bottoms hold no traction against the granite as he drags her forward. He pulls her right into him so she's straddling his waist now.

"Not bad," she teases, tipping her head from side to side.

"Oh, just not bad?" Teddy says, smoothing his hands along the outsides of her thighs. Then, just to prove his point, he ducks his head and presses his lips to a spot on her neck just below her jaw, and the giggles he gets in return are honestly the best thing to happen to him all night. When one of Bennett's hands ends up at the nape of Teddy's own neck, he draws back just enough to smirk at her.

"You know, I've kind of been thinking about doing this all day," he says.

Bennett looks unconvinced. "Yeah, right."

"I'm serious." He traces a thumb along her collarbone. She squirms a little, clearly ticklish, and Teddy wiggles his eyebrows at her. "Don't pretend like you weren't thinking about it, either, Caldwell."

"Don't flatter yourself there, superstar," she murmurs, smiling into it as she leans a tiny bit closer.

Teddy tips his head back and groans, "I hate it when you say that," even though the massive smile on his face suggests otherwise.

And just as he's meeting her gaze again, Bennett's leaning all the way forward and telling him he's taking too long and suddenly she's kissing him, and Teddy's not sure what he'd been expecting here, but he's smiling so much that he actually has to stop for a second to try to wrap his mind around what's happening.

"Jesus," he mutters, then tilts his head the other way and presses his lips to hers again. He kisses her slowly at first, but after a few seconds, Teddy can't help upping the tempo a bit. Bennett grazes his bottom lip with her teeth, and things get a little overwhelming after that.

"Teddy," she sighs against his mouth, which only encourages him more. He wraps an arm around her lower back, hauling her even closer, still feeling like he can't get close enough.

"*Teddy,*" she whispers again, gripping a fistful of hair and wrenching his head back. It takes a second for him to focus on her face, and he smiles lazily at her when she has to straighten her glasses. "I'm scared someone's gonna walk in on this."

"Fine." Teddy grins, then leans back in and whispers, "Come downstairs with me, then."

CHAPTER TEN

"Teddy."

"Mmm . . ."

"Teddy," Bennett whispers again, and in his half-asleep state, Teddy reaches across the sheets to pull her closer to him.

He comes up empty-handed.

Confused, he lifts his head and peeks open an eye, and it takes him a second to remember that, sadly, no one slept on the left side of his bed last night. He rolls over and finds Bennett smirking down at him.

"Morning, Buzz. Sleep well?"

"Hmm—yep," Teddy croaks, rubbing his eyes. Bennett laughs. "What could possibly be amusing to you right now?"

"You. Looking like a goofball when you wake up."

"Careful, those are fighting words," Teddy says. He wonders if he looks as groggy as he sounds. "Wanna come in here and say them to my face?"

"Is that how you normally get a girl into bed with you?" she snarks.

"No." Snaking a hand out from under the comforter, Teddy wraps his fingers around her wrist and yanks her forward. She squeals as she topples across his chest, landing on her back in the spot next to him. "That's how I get a girl into bed with me."

Bennett's cracking up now, and her leaving her legs sprawled across Teddy's knees is the equivalent of about nine espresso shots.

"You've got some serious game, Buzz."

"You've got an unsettling amount of energy this morning, Caldwell."

Bennett laughs again, prompting Teddy to roll all the way over until he's straddling her. She squeals and tries to push him off, but he grabs both her wrists and pins them down on either side of her head.

"You're a little *giggle puss* this morning, Caldwell."

Bennett seems to find that even more hilarious. "Someone fan me. I'm swooning."

"Well, I had to up my game somehow after, and I quote"— Teddy lets go of one of her hands and counts off the words on his fingers—"Not. Tonight. Buzz."

"I didn't hurt your feelings, did I?"

"What, when you decided not to come downstairs with me last night?" Teddy pretends to be wounded. "You cut deep, Caldwell."

Bennett uses his moment of theatrics to break the hold he has on her by buckling his elbow with her free hand and pushing him off. Teddy manages to get a grip on her forearm as she shoves him, though, causing them to roll and switch places.

"Guess I should probably make that up to you, then," she says, flashing him a grin, and Teddy becomes acutely aware of the compromising position he's in. Fortunately (and also unfortunately), Bennett doesn't give him time to react before she pushes herself up and jumps off the bed, heading for the door.

"Boat's leaving in thirty minutes!" she calls over her shoulder.

Teddy presses his head back into the pillows and honestly doesn't even know where to start.

* * *

The Caldwells, Teddy quickly learns, have a raging social life.

After breakfast, they all pile into the boat and head to this day party everyone's been talking about this morning. Apparently the guy throwing it has one once a month during the summer. Bennett tries to give Teddy the rundown over the roar of the boat's propeller.

"So, just a heads-up," she adds. "The house where we're going? Lots of kids will be there."

"As in, lots of kids who might watch MTV?" Teddy asks, trying not to laugh while Bennett attempts to keep her hair under control.

"I'd say there's a good chance," she says. "But they'll make it a big deal for, like, the first fifteen minutes, and then it'll be over. And you don't have to, like, pose for a million pictures or anything if you don't want to—that goes for autographs, too. Do people still sign autographs who aren't authors?"

Teddy's never seen the nervous chatter side of Bennett, but he's kinda here for it. Bennett's been extra chatty all morning, actually.

"Oh—and Liz will be there." Her eyes shift to Teddy's as she says it, but the knowing smirk speaks the loudest.

Teddy rubs a hand over the back of his neck. "Yeah, she made a point to tell me before they left last night."

"No surprise there."

Ten minutes later, Mr. Caldwell slows the boat as they turn into a cove off the main channel. Teddy has no idea how anyone can navigate such a huge lake—especially since everywhere looks the exact same. The only way Teddy knows they've arrived at the party is when a man calls out to them from a nearby dock.

"About time y'all got here!"

"What's goin' on, Paul?" Mr. Caldwell yells back. "You guys started without us!"

Bennett waves at the man, then leans over to Teddy and says, "That's Pontoon Paul—he's the coolest guy you'll meet today."

Pontoon Paul is sporting tie-dyed Hawaiian swim trunks, what appears to be a retro lacrosse jersey, and a pair of club-master sunglasses. He has a Bloody Mary in one hand and a half-eaten hot dog in the other, and his graying five o'clock shadow frames one of the most genuine smiles Teddy has ever seen. This guy might be Teddy's new hero.

"He likes to buy old pontoon boats and rebuild them into floating tiki bars," Bennett explains.

"That's freaking awesome."

"Yep. This is his house. He's got three daughters who will definitely lose their minds when they see you, so again, just a heads-up," she says.

When they reach the dock, Tanner hops out to help tie up, while Bennett and Teddy help her parents unload all the food and coolers they brought for the party. Teddy's never seen a family that shoves food at other people the way the Caldwells do, but he fully endorses it.

"Who's the new guy?" Paul asks, extending a hand to Teddy once he hops out of the boat.

"Teddy Sharpe, sir. Great to meet you."

Recognition weaves its way into Paul's grin. "Ah, right, right, right. You're the kid my girls have been throwing a fit over all morning. Figured you must be a hell of a guy, you know, being the first one I've seen Bennett bring around—"

"Whoa, all right, Mr. Paul. None of that," Bennett says, reaching up to hug him. Teddy can see the slightest shade of pink creeping into her cheeks.

The party is set up in Pontoon Paul's backyard, and there are probably fifty people already in attendance. There are hot dogs and burgers on the grill; games of cornhole going on, kids running around playing football. . . . People are everywhere—some lining the dock's walkway, more in the lake swimming and throwing tennis balls for a couple of dogs on the shore. But the majority of the party is up in the yard and hanging out on the wraparound porch.

Paul has just handed Teddy a beer (which at first Teddy is hesitant to accept) when he hears a chorus of squeaks and giggles erupt behind him. Paul and the rest of the Caldwells take that as their cue to wade deeper into the party, leaving Teddy and Bennett with a decently sized group of teenage girls heading right for them.

"Bennett!"

"It's true! Oh my God!"

"Are you sure? I don't think it is—"

"It so is! Liz was right!"

Bennett intercepts them halfway, since at first it seems like the group is too shy to come all the way over. Bennett throws a grin back at Teddy as they all surround her, asking a million questions over one another.

"Oh my God, where did you meet him?"

"Do you know how gorgeous he is?"

"Are you sure that's him?"

"Hi, girls—it's nice to meet you," Teddy says, stepping up to

Bennett's side, and the squeals that follow are just shy of deafening.

"These are Paul's daughters and their friends," Bennett explains, and there are hugs and *Thanks so much*'s and *I'm so glad you like the show*'s and a few tears (but not on Teddy's end). Overall the enthusiasm is a bit contagious, until one of Paul's daughters pulls Bennett aside for a second to gush to her about how lucky she is. Bennett tries to tell her that it's not like that . . . that she and Teddy just met. And Teddy would be lying if it didn't sting a little, but he doesn't exactly blame her for deflecting.

"I just can't believe he's actually here. I mean—Liz said he would be, but we were all kind of, like, not sure if we could believe her," Paul's daughter tells Bennett while a few of the other girls in the group talk to Teddy about one of his character arcs in season three of *Testing Wyatt*. Teddy's having a hard time multitasking. . . .

Bennett gives her a noncommittal shrug and says, "We all had dinner last night. She and Will met Teddy then."

"Oh, *we know*," Paul's daughter says, subtly rolling her eyes.

"Can we take some pictures with you? If you don't mind?" one girl asks, yanking Teddy back to the group in front of him.

"Don't mind at all," he says cheerfully, still distracted.

Six different iPhones and fifty pictures later, the majority of the people at the party are watching them now, including Liz, who has the same smug smile on her face from the night before. Now that Teddy knows she's the one who spread the word he was coming to the party, he can't help himself when an idea pops in his head to throw this back in her face a little. So in the midst of the photo shoot, he tells all the girls to yell, "Thanks, Liz!" right before the next picture is taken.

Teddy adds his own thanks by waving overzealously at her, and for one brief, satisfying moment, the rest of the party looks questioningly at her—and for once she looks like she doesn't enjoy her spotlight.

* * *

Bennett was right about Teddy's arrival being a big deal for about fifteen minutes, because the rest of the afternoon at Pontoon Paul's is nothing but laid back. Paul apparently has no qualms about most of the kids drinking at his party (except for his daughters and their friends). Tanner keeps handing Bennett and Teddy beers, and Teddy's pretty sure he's a little buzzed, but Bennett seems like she is, too, so it's all good.

They spend a good portion of the afternoon locked in a heated cornhole tournament someone organized, and after losing in the semifinals to two fourteen-year-old boys (who Bennett congratulated for peaking early with "non-exertional sports"), they find a couple of spots at a picnic table with Tanner. Most of the people they sit with are kids of guests and friends of friends, and despite a few of them making some jokes about the photo shoot Teddy was in earlier, no one else brings up anything Hollywood-related, surprisingly. Not even Liz when she walks over to try to join them.

"What're you guys up to?" Liz asks, coming to stand at the head of the table. She has her hand wrapped around a hot-pink koozie containing some kind of fruity hard lemonade drink. Her gaze flicks to a dark-haired guy sitting at the other end of the table and she says, "Oh, Matt! How are you? Will is going to be *so bummed* when he hears he missed you today!"

Bennett goes completely still next to Teddy, and across the

table Tanner stops his beer bottle halfway up to his mouth, glowering at Liz.

"Where is Will, Liz?" Teddy asks suddenly.

"Another one of those lame acting workshops," she sniffs, and examines her cuticles in such a cliché way that Teddy almost tells her *she* could benefit from "one of those lame acting workshops."

"Yeah? That's cool he's so dedicated. I was telling him last night that I wish I'd taken acting classes in high school," Teddy says instead, sipping his beer and glancing around the picnic table. "I got thrown through the gauntlet when I first started auditioning—classes definitely would've helped keep me from looking like an idiot my first few times around."

(Teddy knows he sounds like such a Hollywood douche for bringing up his career like this, but at this point he's okay with sounding like a tool as long as it shuts Liz up.)

To his complete relief, everyone at the table laughs.

"I'm serious," Teddy insists, grinning. "I wish they'd play my first audition tape at beginner's acting classes to show what *not* to do. I was such a spaz. Still am."

More laughter. And out of the corner of his eye, Teddy sees Liz motion for someone on her side of the table to scoot over. He (along with everyone else) pretends not to notice and starts into another story about a train-wreck audition just to ensure the subject stays changed. Liz stands awkwardly at the head of the table for about half of Teddy's story before stalking off. At least she (somewhat) knows when to quit. Once she's gone, though, Teddy's ready to talk about literally anything else.

Half an hour later of hot dogs, surprisingly good country music, and Teddy attempting to convince everyone at the picnic table that they should all become Pirates fans, Teddy feels

Bennett nudge his leg under the table. She leans in a little bit closer than he anticipates, grinning as she asks him if he wants to walk down on the dock with her. The sun is starting to set, and Teddy's inner romantic cheeseball side isn't about to pass that up.

"So," Bennett says once they're strolling down the pier.

Teddy waits for her to continue and thinks about putting his arm around her. He dips his body and gently knocks their shoulders together instead. "So?"

Bennett smiles out over the lake. "So. Having a good time?"

"I'm having a great time. You?"

She stops at the edge of the dock and sits down, dipping her feet in the water.

"You really aren't a real person, you know that?" she says from left field.

Teddy takes a seat next to her and tries not to laugh. "Yeah? What makes you say that?"

She looks at him like she can see straight through his attempt to fish for compliments, then points a thumb back at the house. "You just sat up there all afternoon with a bunch of strangers and you got every single one of them to love you."

"You flatter me."

"I'm not," Bennett insists, raising her feet out of the water and letting them drop again. "Not to mention distracting everyone from what Liz was trying to say about Will. . . ."

"Nah, I was just making conversation—"

"Shut up, you were not. You never bring up your acting career unsolicited." She looks up at him then. "And for real, you don't know how cool that was. So, thank you."

There's a seriousness in her expression that makes Teddy finally ask a question that's been in the back of his mind since last night. "What is her deal with that, anyway? What kind of asshole tries to out her brother all the time?"

"That's just Liz," Bennett says, rolling her eyes. "She likes to collect things about people she thinks she can use to make herself look better."

"Like telling everyone at the party that I was coming with you?" Teddy asks.

Bennett's eyes flick to his, and she looks caught between surprised and impressed.

"Yep. And even when you don't tell her anything," she continues, shaking her head, "she even holds *that* over your head."

"Sounds about right," Teddy says dryly.

"But anyway. Liz would love it if she knew we were down here talking about her, so let's talk about how awesome it is that you've been a good sport about everything my family's thrown at you this weekend."

"What, all the other dudes before me didn't fare well against Pontoon Paul?"

"Still fishing, I see." Bennett raises an eyebrow. "You heard Paul. You're kinda unprecedented, Buzz. Don't go getting all cocky about it."

Teddy is definitely getting all cocky about it, though. He glances out over the water and has to bite down on his bottom lip to keep his smile from getting any bigger.

Bennett looks over, catches him, and says, "Oh, God. Stop it."

He laughs again, and she keeps her eyes on his longer than what Teddy's used to. Her brows furrow for a second, but then she breaks eye contact with an apologetic smile and turns her attention back toward the lake.

"What," Teddy says.

"Nada."

"Come on, Caldwell. What?"

"Seriously, nothing." She shrugs. "I'm just—you just make me a little nervous."

Teddy finds that a little hard to believe, all things considered. "Oh, please. I'm, like, the least intimidating guy ever."

Bennett's eyes get big.

"Seriously? Have you met yourself? You waltz in here like you're everybody's new best friend and not some famous actor from Hollywood and you're just . . . I don't know." She sighs and rolls her head back to look at the sky. Teddy gets a great view of the subtle little marks he left on her neck the night before. They're only visible if he looks hard enough, but they're definitely there, and they're definitely a bit of a turn-on.

"Oh no. That's not gonna cut it, Caldwell," Teddy says, refusing to let himself get distracted. "I'm what?"

Bennett smirks. "Well, for starters, you're a hell of a kisser."

Jesus, maybe he will let himself get distracted.

"Is that you talking or all those beers you were knocking back during cornhole?"

"And you're funny. And sweet. And stupid observant, and honestly?" Bennett says. "It's a little outrageous how hard it is to *not* like you."

Teddy leans toward her. "So you're saying you *kind of* like me then, huh?"

She pauses to consider it, bobbing her head from side to side and wrinkling her nose. "Yeah, but only because you're *kind of* famous."

Teddy grabs her by the shoulders and pretends to try to push her off the dock.

"Such a smartass," he mutters, slipping his arms around her and squeezing. Then he murmurs in her ear, "But just to be clear . . . there's nothing *kind of* about the way I like you."

And you know what? It might seem fast and it might be too convenient and the universe might secretly be planning the spectacular downfall of Teddy Sharpe, but right now . . . Teddy means it. He has no idea how the hell he got here so soon, but he's definitely glad he has.

Bennett's grin is blinding.

"So, I have a secret for you," she says, swirling her feet around in the water, "and you have to swear you won't tell anyone."

Teddy knocks their shoulders together again. "Swear."

"You're gonna get cast as Jack, if you want the role."

She says it so matter-of-factly, so straightforward, it catches Teddy on heels. He starts to pretend he's surprised but stops, because he realizes no matter what he does, it's probably going to come off unconvincing. "I—uh," he says, a huge grin pulling at his lips. "I heard."

Confusion flickers across her face for a split second before understanding takes over.

"Dammit," she groans. "Tanner can't keep his mouth just to save his life."

"It wasn't his fault! He accidentally mentioned something when we were playing Ping-Pong and I hounded him for details."

"I guess I can't blame you," she says. "I just—sort of wanted to be the one to tell you."

"You know, the fact that you wanted to is just as good," he says. Bennett's staring down at her feet in the water again, fingers now tucked underneath her legs. Teddy slides a hand over the nape of her neck, and Bennett hesitates when she looks up, eyes shifting to something behind him.

"Pretty sure Liz is watching us right now."

"Good," Teddy says, pulling her toward him. Bennett smiles into the kiss, and it's just the right kind of overwhelming—like Teddy's either going to launch into space forever or completely collapse in on himself.

They break apart after who knows how long, with Teddy grinning like an idiot as Bennett tries to hide the blush working its way across her cheeks. They wander back up to the house to rejoin the party, and Teddy's so blissfully dazed he almost doesn't catch when Liz makes a side comment about how she didn't know Bennett was *so into PDA.* Teddy can't get himself to care, though—not with the way Bennett keeps smiling over at him like he's the only person worth smiling at.

The party begins to slow just after it gets dark. A long day of drinking in the sun seems to take its toll on everyone at once, and people begin to trickle back to their boats to call it a night. The Caldwells are saying bye to the McGearys down at the dock when Liz looks pointedly at Teddy and says, "It was *so* nice to meet you, Teddy. Have a safe trip back to LA tomorrow!"

"Uh, thanks," he says, hoping the smile plastered on his face is somewhere close to being sincere. How the hell does she know he's flying back tomorrow? "It was nice to meet you, too. Tell Will I said bye, will you?"

"Uh-huh," she says before turning and hugging Bennett. "I'll text you later, Bennie!"

It's a long boat ride back to the Caldwells' house—longer than it felt on the way to the party. Mrs. Caldwell and Tanner both fall asleep in the front of the boat before they get back.

Bennett leans into Teddy with one leg crossed over the other, her knee pressing into his. Teddy sneaks his arm around her to pull her closer, and they stay like that until the boat slows and Mr. Caldwell quietly guides them back into their dock slip.

"Bennett, can you get the lift?" Mr. Caldwell asks, and Teddy hates the chill that replaces her when Bennett stands and climbs out. She unlatches the gray box on one of the dock's support beams and the lift roars to life, waking up everyone in the process.

"What time is it?" Tanner yawns.

"After ten," Mrs. Caldwell says. "We're all gonna sleep well tonight."

Teddy nods in agreement, even though he isn't so sure.

Liz mentioning his flight back to LA earlier left a pit in his stomach—one he isn't equipped to deal with as Bennett leads him up the boardwalk, their fingers playfully hooking and rehooking, but never fully coming together.

CHAPTER ELEVEN

Once everyone gets back up to the house, the Caldwells say good night while Tanner toys with the idea of staying up a little while longer. He ultimately decides against it. He grabs a water from the fridge and wanders off to his room, leaving Teddy and Bennett alone in the kitchen.

"Tired?" Bennett asks.

"No." Teddy tries to poke her in the side. "Are you?"

She bats his hand away, and he could swear he sees her eyes dart toward the basement steps before looking back at him. "What do you want to do?"

And, well. There are a few answers to that question.

"Wait, what time's your flight tomorrow?" she asks.

"At one," Teddy sighs, running a hand over his forehead.

"Are you packed?"

Teddy's bag is never not packed (a habit from traveling so much), but at this point he'll lunge at an opportunity to get Bennett downstairs with him.

"Not really. Wanna come help me?"

She hesitates, and it feels like the longest two seconds of his life . . . until she nods. Teddy ignores the spasm of nerves that hits him and grabs her hand, pulling her toward the stairs.

Bennett lets him lead her all the way down to his room, but she lets go and puts a few feet between them when she sees his bags by the closet.

"You liar, you're totally packed. And you made your bed this morning," she snickers.

"I always make my bed. Don't hate."

"You're ridiculous."

"Now, now, Caldwell," Teddy says, watching her mosey around the room. "Fess up—what you mean is I'm actually devastatingly handsome and/or refreshingly good company."

"Real talk, I couldn't hear you over all the adverbs you just threw at me," Bennett says.

"You *would* use a comeback about grammar."

"Well, you *would* have the temperament of a romantic comedy."

"Oh my God," Teddy guffaws. "What does that even mean?"

Bennett's straight up giggling now. "That's exactly what you are: a portable romantic comedy."

"No, no—see, if I actually had the temperament of a romantic comedy, I would have thought of something a lot wittier to say a minute ago; you would have swooned, and then I would've kissed you with a full three-sixty panoramic shot of the whole thing while a nineties one-hit wonder played in the background."

"You've clearly thought this through."

"I'm an actor. It's my job."

"Yeah, except the only problem with this is, I don't actually swoon."

Teddy cocks an eyebrow at her. "Yeah, right. All girls swoon. All dudes swoon, too—we're just better at hiding it."

Thank God for that.

Bennett looks like she's not buying it.

"I bet I can get you to swoon right now if I wanted to," Teddy adds, feeling a surge of confidence coming on as he walks toward her. She puts her hands up between them and steps back, but Teddy reaches out and catches her around the waist with one hand, splaying the other across her hip so she can't wiggle away.

"Now, if this were, indeed, a romantic comedy, this would be the part where I explain how adorable I think you are by naming off all the little quirks you have that both delight and infuriate me," Teddy says, smiling down at her. "Which would include all that freaking sarcasm you've got going on, how you somehow always manage to come up with something funny to say at my expense, and how you're actually a gigantic nerd who's completely oblivious to how hot you are."

Before she can protest, Teddy moves his hands down to the backs of her thighs and lifts, hoisting her legs up around his waist. She squeals and grips his shoulders.

"After that," he goes on, feeling brave, "I'd start talking about how at first I wasn't sure if you wanted me to stay the weekend because I couldn't gauge your reaction, and how I made it my mission to make it up to you somehow before the weekend was over."

She leans back, looking unconvinced. "Are you kidding me? I told you I—"

"No, no," Teddy interrupts. "I'm talking; you're supposed to be swooning, remember? Roll with me here."

He takes Bennett sliding her arms around his neck as his cue to continue.

"So, anyway. You'd respond with something cute and a little bit self-deprecating, to which I would again remind you of how gorgeous and smart and *wonderful* I think you are, before finally telling you my true feelings. The camera would spin around us, the music would surge, and then I'd true-love's-first-kiss you and we'd live happily ever after. The end."

Bennett stares at him for a minute, eyes locked on his. "That's some serious Academy Award material there, Buzz. Nice work."

Teddy nods seriously at her. "But all that depended on whether or not we were actually in a romantic comedy, and since we're not, I'm gonna go ahead and do this—"

He barely gets the last part of his sentence out before he crushes their mouths together, nearly dropping her in the process. That certainly gets another squeal out of her, but a second later she's kissing him back—actually, full-on making out with him is probably a better way to describe it. It's nothing like their kiss on the dock earlier. It's wild and rushed, and soon Teddy's walking them back toward the bed. His kneecaps nudge the mattress and he turns to sit down, positioning Bennett in his lap before scooting back. Bennett has a fistful of his hair, right behind his ear, and Teddy can't do anything about the groan that escapes his mouth when she gives it a little tug, tipping his head and snickering in between kisses.

"The hell are you laughing at, Caldwell?" he asks with no intention of letting her answer. Instead he bites down on her bottom lip and lies all the way back, taking her down with him. Bennett stretches out on top of him, tangling their legs together, and Teddy uses it as an opportunity to slide his hands low over her jean shorts, just to test the waters a bit.

These damn jean shorts.

Teddy rolls them over after a moment, reaching down to shift her shirt up just enough to expose a little ribbon of skin. Then he traces the length of the top of her shorts all the way across her stomach with his thumb, grinning when she has to stop midkiss to catch her breath.

He goes for the button next.

"Jesus—wait." Bennett freezes.

Alarmed, Teddy leans back to give her some air and catches the expression on her face. "What? What's wrong?"

"This is such a bad idea," Bennett mutters, pressing a hand to her forehead.

"What, why?"

"Because you're leaving tomorrow."

"So?"

"So?" Her gaze snaps to his. "And I've only known you, like, two days."

"Okay, but—"

"Holy *shit*." She pushes him all the way off so she can sit up. "And I don't know if or when I'm gonna see you after I drop you off at the airport tomorrow—January's a long-ass time away."

"Jesus, Bennett, hang on a sec." Teddy sits up with her and smooths his hands over her shoulders. It's meant to be consoling, to shake her out of whatever's going on inside her head, but instead she shrugs him off. And that stings. Teddy waits another moment to let her get her bearings, then tries again with, "Hey—talk to me here. It's okay, okay? Everything's good."

"Sorry, I—this is all . . ." She shakes her head. "God, I don't even know what to say."

"Wow, Bennett Caldwell at a loss for words?" he teases gently. "Would it help if I did another hypothetical romantic comedy monologue?"

It doesn't work. Instead, Bennett exhales a slow, ragged breath, and Teddy's heart drops a little.

"Bennett," he says, trying to calm himself down now. "There's absolutely no way I'd ever ask you do anything you're uncomfortable with, okay? But can you at least talk to me here?"

Bennett stays quiet and picks at the duvet, and after one of the most agonizing awkward silences Teddy's ever experienced, she finally puts him out of his misery.

"Definitely lied about swooning," she says, and once again, it's all the way from left field.

"Huh?"

"You heard me." She gives him a tiny smile. "That whole romantic comedy thing you just went on? Yeah. Loved every second of it. And before you go and get all smug about it, just remember that I've been writing full-length novels since I was thirteen. I'm biologically wired to romanticize everything."

Teddy smirks to hide how relieved he is. "And you tell me not to be smug?"

"Just being honest."

"Okay," he says slowly, wanting to reach for her but worrying he might scare her off again. "Well, while you're at it, want to tell me what else is going through your head?"

Bennett eyes shift away from him. "I don't know—this whole situation just makes me nervous, I guess."

"Why, though?"

She shoots him a look like the answer should be obvious.

"Because . . ." She covers her face with her hands. "Because there's nothing *kind of* about the way I like you, either, and I hate that you're flying back to LA tomorrow."

Teddy's heart has an unhealthy reaction to that, but the warmth that starts in his chest and spreads all the way out to his fingertips makes up for it. Bennett might as well have wrapped him around her finger, right then and there.

"And despite how much I'd like to continue what we were just doing," she says, her words muffled by her hands, "I don't know when I'll see you next, and it doesn't sit right with me."

"Bennett."

She still won't look at him.

"Bennett," Teddy repeats, figuring it'd be okay to gently pull her hands away from her face. He gives her a soft smile when their eyes meet and says, "I mean, I can't say I'm not a little bummed out over here . . . but for real, I get it. And I respect that. It scares me, too."

"Sorry to disappoint," she says, looking down at the duvet again.

"You didn't," he insists, and he hates she's even thinking it. He scoots closer. "But you will if you don't stay and snuggle with me at least."

* * *

It's still dark outside when Teddy wakes up to Bennett trying to wriggle out of his arms. Even half asleep he still registers what's happening, so he pulls her right back in and ruins all the progress she'd made.

"I have to go upstairs," she whispers in the dark, pressing a kiss to his cheek. "My parents will kill me if they catch me down here."

"Mmm—the bigger the risk, the bigger the reward, am I right?" Teddy says. His eyes aren't open, but he can still picture the look he probably earned for that one.

"I'll come back and get you in a few hours."

"Hey." Teddy sleepily catches her arm as she slides off the

bed. Maybe it's because he's half asleep and warm and already missing her next to him, but he feels like he needs to say something big and important and charming here.

What comes out is, "You know you're kind of stuck with me now, right?"

Bennett chuckles softly. "I know. Go back to sleep, Teddy."

CHAPTER TWELVE

"You ready to go?"

"No."

"Come on. Cheer up, Buzz."

Bennett grins at him from his bedroom doorway later that morning, but Teddy can tell this is bothering her just as much as it's bothering him. He stands from the bed and shoulders his duffel bag, then holds up his phone, which he forced himself to turn back on when he woke up. "Will you put your number in?"

"I *guess*." She sighs, pretending like it's an inconvenience as she crosses the room toward him. Teddy studies her while her head is bowed over his phone. It's easier to look at her this morning when she's not looking back. He doesn't have to worry about her seeing anything in his expression that might give away how dramatically dejected he is. She hands his phone back when she's done but doesn't meet his eyes. "Come on. Time to go."

"Fine," he says, and he tries not to drag his feet as he follows her upstairs.

"Heading out now, Teddy?" Mr. Caldwell calls across the kitchen. He and the rest of the Caldwell clan are seated at the counter eating breakfast and watching TV.

"Yes, sir. Time for me to get outta here," Teddy says, forcing a smile.

Mr. Caldwell claps him on the back when he shakes his hand. "Glad you stayed, man. Come back the next time you're out this way."

The prospect pulls a genuine smile from Teddy. "Absolutely."

Mrs. Caldwell comes over and gives him a hug next, reiterating what her husband said and asking if he needs anything for his flight. Teddy shakes his head, thanking her anyway.

"Tanner, you better up your Ping-Pong game for the next time I'm here," Teddy says, giving him a high-five.

Tanner scoffs. "Whatever, dude. Any time, any place."

"Bye, guys. Thanks again for having me." Teddy waves one last time before he and Bennett head out through the garage. Saying bye to her family just makes him feel worse as he trudges down the driveway, his rolling bag hitting every rock or crack along the way.

Bennett pops the liftgate to her Jeep, and the look on Teddy's face must be particularly pathetic, because a second later she grips his wrist and pulls him toward her.

"Teddy."

He tosses his duffel in. "Hmm?"

"Look at me."

And he does. For the first time since she came to his room this morning.

"Quit moping. You're bumming me out," Bennett says, grinning up at him like she knows how much of a sucker Teddy is.

Teddy tries to even the playing field by nudging her back against the trunk of her car and ducking his head toward her. Once his mouth is almost touching hers, he replies, "Sorry,

Caldwell. Won't happen again." He pulls back to watch her reaction.

"It better not," she says, gripping the front of his T-shirt and tugging him back toward her. "But now you owe me."

Teddy doesn't even hesitate, and after a small kiss he wishes was longer, Bennett wiggles away and opens the driver's side door.

The trip to the airport is just as miserable as Teddy expects it to be. He and Bennett keep the conversation light and about anything that doesn't involve the three thousand miles Teddy's about to put between them, but somehow not talking about it feels worse.

They're in the car for about twenty minutes when Teddy's phone vibrates in his pocket. Thinking it's one of his parents calling to check in on him, he digs into his shorts pocket, pulling out his phone and wallet at the same time. Then sees the name on the screen and accidentally drops everything he's holding onto the floorboard.

"Easy there, Buzz," Bennett says as Teddy scrambles to pick up his phone again.

He taps the ignore button and shoves it back into his pocket. "Sorry. Preflight jitters."

Bennett easily accepts that lie, which only mixes guilt into the massive amount of unease building up inside Teddy's rib cage. He steals a quick glance across the center console at her. She has her elbow resting on the windowsill, head leaning against her fist, and today's prop to hide behind is a pair of black wayfarers.

"You're making me self-conscious," Bennett comments, still watching the road.

"Er—sorry," Teddy startles, his voice cracking as he redirects his gaze through the windshield. "How much longer until we get to the airport?"

"About ten minutes."

Dammit.

Teddy nods. "So, what're you going to be up to for the next couple of months?"

"Just *Parachutes* stuff and writing the last book in the series," she says. "You?"

"Shooting another season of *Testing Wyatt*. When do you think they'll get the *Parachutes* filming schedule out?" he asks.

"Not sure. They'll probably wait to get an idea until they figure out who we're casting as the female lead . . . so maybe, like, September? I don't know when they're gonna approach you about negotiations yet, but it'll probably be soon. The director's getting antsy."

"Cool," Teddy says. "So, uh—do you think you'll be too busy in the next few months to make a trip back out to LA?"

Bennett grins. "Wasn't aware there was an invitation."

"You let me stay at your house for a weekend. . . ." He hopes he at least sounds like he's maintaining some cool here. "I think it's only fair for me to return the favor."

"I guess I could pencil it in somewhere," Bennett says, and Teddy's about to call her a smartass for the forty billionth time when she adds, "Your schedule's probably way more demanding than mine—why don't you figure out some times that are good for you and I'll make something work."

Teddy lunges at the opportunity and thinks back over his upcoming work schedule. "I've got another month of *Testing Wyatt* coming up, so August probably isn't the best." He hums as an idea pops in his head. "My birthday's at the beginning of September, though?"

"What day?"

"The third."

"I'll keep that in mind," she says, and the idea of Bennett coming to visit him for his birthday is almost enough to put him in a better mood about his trip back. Almost.

"At least we have plenty of time between now and January to figure out our schedules," Teddy adds dryly. "But now that I have your number, you can expect constant scheduling updates. With lots of emojis. And gifs."

Bennett grins at the windshield. "I can only imagine how creative you get with emojis."

"It will shock and awe you."

Five minutes later, they exit off the highway and Teddy's almost-good mood is nowhere to be found. The only sound inside the car now is the same staticky radio station they listened to on the way up.

"What airline are you flying?" Bennett asks.

"American."

Silence.

Airport signs are becoming more and more frequent, giving out directions to overnight parking and the cell phone lot. Bennett steers them into the far left lane running under another giant sign labeled DEPARTURES. She readjusts her grip on the steering wheel for the seventh time, and that's when Teddy finally loses his cool.

"God*dammit*, Bennett," he bites out suddenly, and he knows he's being so dramatic now, but it feels like they're never going to see each other again.

Bennett jumps, gripping the steering wheel with both hands. *"Jesus—*what?"

"This is so shitty," Teddy whines.

"You just scared me half to death." She presses a hand to her chest. Then, for reasons unbeknownst to Teddy, she bursts out laughing.

"The hell are you giggling at right now, Caldwell?"

"God, we're a mess," she says.

"We're?" Teddy repeats. Bennett looks the exact opposite of a mess right now. In fact, she's sitting about as still as Teddy's ever seen her, composure fully intact.

"I told you last night I wasn't a fan of you flying back to LA today, remember?" she says, wrinkling her nose at the windshield. She readjusts her sunglasses and Teddy feels the car slow as they approach the airport's drop-off area.

"Welp. Here we are," she says, pulling to the curb and shifting into park.

"Are you gonna get out and hug me good-bye, or are you gonna make me pull you across the center console?" Teddy asks, and he's not even kidding.

Bennett waits to let some of the airport traffic pass before shouldering open her door. When she meets Teddy around at the trunk, she leans a hip against her taillight and pops the liftgate for him, hiding behind her sunglasses the whole time. Teddy pulls out his bags, drops them on the ground, and plasters a half smile on his face.

"Come on, get over here," he says, opening his arms.

At this point, it doesn't even matter how shitty he feels about leaving—all that matters is the little grin Bennett gives him before he wraps her up in a hug.

"Call you when I land?" he says, kissing the top of her head.

"Don't let your arms get tired."

"A-plus advice, Caldwell," Teddy says. When Bennett starts to pull away from him, he takes her face in his hands and presses a slow kiss to her lips. "I'll see you soon," he murmurs, more as reassurance for him than anything.

"Soon," she agrees, hands coming up to squeeze his wrists. "You're starring in my movie, remember?"

Ah, yes. A silver lining.

"Try not to miss me too much," Teddy calls as she rounds her car and climbs into the driver's seat.

She rolls down the passenger's side window and says, "Don't flatter yourself, superstar."

Teddy grins, waving as Bennett pulls back out into traffic . . . then he groans and scrubs a hand over his face. He needs to get a grip. This was inevitable. He and Bennett both have stuff to do before filming starts for *Parachutes*. He needs to stop being such a wuss about it.

Before heading inside, Teddy pulls out his favorite Pirates hat and tips the bill down lower than he likes. (The last thing he wants to deal with right now is someone recognizing him and asking him why he looks so sad.) He walks toward the automatic doors, getting out his phone to see what time it is—and stops dead in his tracks when he finds not one, but four missed calls. And just like clockwork, the fifth one comes through.

Something has to be up. Even at their best, she never call-bombed him like this.

"Chelsea?" he answers, walking inside. "Is everything okay?"

"Hey, Ted—yeah, why wouldn't it be?" her voice rings out. Teddy has to pull the phone away from his ear for a second.

"Because you called me, like, five times in a row."

"I wanted to make sure I caught you before you got through security."

"Well, you succeeded," Teddy says, then winces at how irritated he sounds. "I mean—no. I'm not through security yet."

"You're flying out of American Airlines, right?"

Teddy balks. "How the hell do you know that?"

The Caldwells had a printer at their house, so Teddy was able to print his boarding pass before he left. He breezes past the check-in desks, weaving through the crowd. On top of trying to figure out why the hell he's on the phone with Chelsea right now, the airport is overwhelmingly crowded. People are whizzing by in all different directions, and he gets so distracted he doesn't hear what Chelsea says in response.

"What?"

"I *said*," Chelsea starts, already sounding agitated, "I looked up your flight online."

What the— "That's creepy, Chels."

"No it's not!" she yells, and Teddy almost drops his phone for the second time that day. Not that it matters.

Chelsea's voice hadn't come from the phone's speaker.

Teddy looks to his left, his stomach rolling up into his throat. Chelsea is standing about twenty feet away, bags in hand. She smiles at him and lowers her phone from her ear. Then she starts toward him, and for just a second it has Teddy seriously considering the current state of his mental health.

Chelsea is here.

In the Charlotte airport.

"Surprise!" She launches herself at him.

What.

"You're supposed to be in Vancouver," is all he can think to say, bracing himself. His duffel bag slips off his shoulder right before she throws her arms around him.

Chelsea looks the exact same as she did the last time they saw each other (more than a month ago). Teddy can't explain why he was expecting anything different. Her dark hair is hairsprayed into curls that scratch the side of his neck as she hugs him. She's wearing a sundress he's never seen before and, when she pulls back, an expectant expression he's come to know all too well.

"Wow, thanks for the warm greeting, there," she says.

Teddy registers that his arms are still hanging by his sides. "Okay, but . . ." He gestures at the Charlotte airport around him to help get his point across. "Why?"

"I came to surprise you! Are you surprised?" she presses.

Teddy just keeps staring, mouth hanging open. Chelsea doesn't appreciate it, apparently.

"The least you could do is *pretend* to be excited," she snaps, which—no. Absolutely not.

"Are you kidding me, Chelsea?" Teddy says, finally locating the words he was looking for a second ago. "The last time we talked we were breaking up. I'm a little too freaked out to be excited right now."

She pouts at him. "I know. And I feel bad about how it ended. I wanted to make it up to you, so I caught a flight out after we wrapped on set yesterday and got in last night—you literally won't *believe* what I had to go through to get a decent hotel here."

Teddy scrubs a hand over the top of his head and glares at the floor. "How did you even find me?"

"Jesus—I already told you I looked up your flight. It's not

that weird," she says, looking more and more upset. "Why are you being like this?"

And again, no. Absolutely not. She's not allowed to make him feel that shitty and unwanted and then turn around and pretend like he's the bad guy here. Or like everything's fine because she showed up out of the blue today. No.

"Seriously, Chels. Help me out here," Teddy says, his tone cold. "After Friday night, why the hell would you fly all the way here from Canada, just to fly right back to Vancouver, or LA, or—wherever the hell you're going after this?"

A huge smile spreads across Chelsea's face, and it's as confusing as it is irritating.

"Actually, it's where *we're* going," she says.

"What?"

"Here, hang on," she says, digging through her purse. She pulls out an envelope and hands it to him. He stares impassively at it.

"I don't know what I'm supposed to do with this."

Chelsea scowls again. "Why don't you try opening it."

Teddy's hands shake as he pulls out the envelope's contents, but Chelsea's already going into detail before he can read over everything.

"I booked us two seats on a flight to Miami at 3:30! I felt so bad about this weekend, so this is me making it up to you. We're booked through the week because I couldn't remember when you said you needed to be back for *Testing Wyatt*, but I figured you can get a flight out whenever."

This is not happening.

"What about your movie?" he asks.

She smiles wider. "I told my director I need the week off for creative development, since I've already been working so many extra weekends."

"Chelsea, I can't—"

"I know this means we have a couple of hours to kill at the airport, but I'm sure we can find a place near our gate that won't card you," she says excitedly, bouncing up and down. "Get some alcohol in your system before the flight?"

There is no fucking *way* this is happening.

"I already paid for my flight back to LA," Teddy says, and Chelsea rolls her eyes.

"Please, Teddy. You're a professional actor. Don't pretend like that's an issue here. Come on." She lifts up onto her toes and leans into his space. Before he can react, she kisses him on the cheek—dangerously close to the corner of his mouth—and says, "Let's just get to the gate and then we can figure it out."

She walks away then, heading for security, and Teddy watches her go. It's not like he has a choice other than following in the same general direction, but this is all just too much. How is he supposed to get her to understand there's no way he's getting on a plane to Miami with her? That's one tantrum he doesn't feel like dealing with before flying anywhere.

"Teddy."

Teddy freezes, every single muscle in his body tensing. He can't breathe—can't do anything other than pray whoever just called his name isn't who he thinks it is. He turns around.

It is.

Bennett's standing a couple of yards away, smirking at him. But it's nowhere near her usual number. If looks could kill, this one would definitely make sure there'd be nothing left of Teddy to find.

"Bennett, I—"

"You left this in my floorboard," she says, tossing something to him.

His wallet.

Teddy catches it against his chest, glancing down at it and then back to her, but she's already disappearing into the crowd, heading for the automatic exit doors.

Fuck.

Fuck, fuck, fuck. *SHIT.*

Teddy bolts after her, too panicked to watch where he's going. He bumps into a few people as he scrambles through the masses with his bags in tow, throwing half-hearted apologies over his shoulder as he goes.

"Bennett!" he yells, and it seems like Bennett's the only person in the airport who doesn't turn to look at him. He freezes again, realizing his mistake a second too late.

"Hey, is that—is that Teddy Sharpe?" he hears somewhere to his right.

"Oh my God, it is!"

"Teddy!"

"Bae!"

It happens so fast—faster than Teddy's ever been swarmed before. Suddenly there are more people in front of him, looking and smiling and giggling and Jesus Christ in heaven, this cannot be happening. iPhones are already pointed at him from every direction, girls are squealing and yelling his name, and Teddy needs to keep moving but it's like everyone's moving with him now.

"Hey, guys," he manages to get out, straining to look over the crowd for Bennett.

"Teddy! Can we get a picture?"

"Teddy! I love you. Teddy, please!"

Someone shoves a pen and a piece of paper in his hand. Another person is already trying to take a selfie with him. He can't breathe again. Can't form coherent sentences. He tries to dodge them but more people step in his way. And just when he's seriously considering bowling over a twelve-year-old to break the circle they've formed around him, a familiar voice cuts through the crowd. Not the familiar voice he wants to hear, though.

"Hey, guys! How's it going?" Chelsea says, pushing herself through to get to Teddy's side. More squeals and iPhone flashes follow. Chelsea curls a hand around Teddy's bicep and pulls herself next to him. She takes the pen out of his hand and says, "Of course we'll take a picture, no worries! Do you guys mind backing up a little, though?"

Teddy didn't think he could feel the tiniest bit of relief at this point, but for the first time that day, he's thankful Chelsea's here—only because she brought an airport security guard with her, who's now helping herd the crowd back.

"Teddy, they want to take a picture of us together," Chelsea says, wrapping an arm around his back. Teddy puts his arm around her shoulders out of reflex as he stares wide-eyed at everything and nothing in front of him.

"We love you guys so much!"

Teddy doesn't know what phone to look at so he doesn't look at any of them. Instead, he finally finds a break in the crowd that lets him see the airport exit doors, but Bennett is nowhere to be found.

Parachutes (series)

Parachutes is a three-book series of <u>young adult</u> action-romance novels written by American author <u>M. B. Caldwell</u>. It follows the story of seventeen-year-old Katherine Rawlins and her recruitment to a special operations unit known as The Company, as well as her complicated relationship with fellow training recruit Jack O'Heinessey.

Since the release of the first book, *Parachutes*, in 2017, the series has found immense popularity and commercial success, most notably in the North America, and has begun the process of translation into several languages. The series' second book, *Safety Net*, was released in April 2018, with the third and final installment, *Off the Grid*, slated to be released in early 2020.

Film rights to the series were purchased before its publication in 2017. Production was initially delayed due to several factors surrounding the script, but was eventually <u>green-lit</u> in late spring 2018. It is rumored that <u>Burt Bridges</u> has signed on as the director, and the first film adaptation is set to begin production in January 2019.

CHAPTER THIRTEEN

Sun, Jul 22, 12:51 p.m.

Hey Bennett it's Teddy

Just got on the plane-I really need to talk to you. I have to turn my phone off soon . . . Please call me back if you can?

Sun, Jul 22, 6:08 p.m.

Just landed in LA and just tried to call. The flight attendant yelled at me for getting my phone out while the plane was still moving. . . .

Sun, Jul 22, 9:37 p.m.

Please answer

Hey

Mon, Jul 23, 3:01 p.m.

Bennett please let me explain. That wasn't what it looked like in the airport I promise.

I tried to find you after you gave me my wallet but I got mobbed.

Tue, Jul 24, 4:34 p.m.

If I hear "your call has been forwarded to an automated voice message system" one more time I might die.

Wed, Jul 25, 5:02 p.m.

Look. I get it. You don't want to talk to me. But could you please at least check your voice mail if you haven't?

Please?

Thu, Jul 26, 1:48 p.m.

Did you check your voice mail? Also, what's your address? I'm trying to get a thank-you note to your parents.

Look. I'm shitty at explaining things in writing but since I can't get you on the phone, you at least need to hear this somehow.

The girl you saw in the airport was my ex-girlfriend Chelsea. I was supposed to go to Miami with her but then she bailed and that's when I knew things were done with us. I mean, deep down I guess. She and I officially broke up the night your family was over. And in retrospect I know that was such a dick move on my part but the only reason the break up didn't happen sooner was bc I thought we should at least have the conversation in person. We were together for two years-I thought we at least owed it to each other to not do it over text message, but that's exactly what we ended up doing. Then she showed up in Charlotte saying she wanted to make it up to me, and after we got mobbed I told her I was done. She got on a plane to Vancouver and I got on a plane to LA and we haven't spoken since. None of what you saw in the airport was planned. I'd never do that to you, Caldwell. Or any girl, actually. It was fucked up yeah but I didn't know it was gonna happen. Not that that's an excuse.

I just really want you to understand.

Please call me back.

Fri, Jul 27, 7:16 p.m.

And SURPRISE call number 23098445 goes unanswered. I'm starting to feel like a psycho Bennett. Please call me back.

Sat, Jul 28, 10:26 p.m.

Just giving you a heads-up that your voice mail box is full.

And that I'm going to try not to bother you anymore.

Mon, Aug 6, 1:56 a.m.

It's been two weeks, Caldwell.

I tried to stop, but I can't fucking think straight anymore.

Tue, Aug 7, 12:19 p.m.

Hey. I'm sure you probably already know,

but I'm officially in negotiations for Parachutes now. Regardless of how much of a dick I've been, I want you to know how excited I am for it.

Your voice mail box is still full.

I miss toy. It's killing me

You**********

Not toy. I beg ur pardon that was disrespectful

And to answer your question no I am not drunk

K maybe a little drubk

Hey remember that time you told me I was a hell or a kisser heheheheh

I think abut that weekend all the ducking time man. I wish you eould just talk to me

Even if it's to tell me to fuck off

I just miss you

Sry I'm celebrating my bday early since I didn't get my actual bday off bc my exec producer is a big duck

But now everyone's passed out

I wish you were here to celebrate w me

Sat, Aug 25, 3:01 p.m.

Your voice mail is still full. And I apologize for drunkenly blowing up your phone last night, but not for anything I said.

Mon, Sep 3, 10:02 a.m.

Guess what day it issssssssss?

Guess. What. Day. It. Is.

Mon, Sep 3, 1:17 p.m.

(I'll give you a hint: it's my birthday)

Mon, Sep 3, 3:32 p.m.

Hope you're doing well-I'd love to hear from you.

Mon, Sep 3, 11:08 p.m.

Still wish you were here to celebrate with me.

Tue, Sep 25, 12:22 p.m.

I'm pretty impressed with myself that I've managed to leave you alone for the past three weeks. But now I'm caving big time and wanted to let you know that I'm still thinking about you.

Hope you're doing well

Wed, Oct 10, 1:09 p.m.

Caldwell-I've come to terms with you not wanting to talk to me, and I get it. But I just heard from my manager about the

Parachutes schedule and wanted to tell you I'm really excited for it.

I'll see you <u>January 16th.</u>

CHAPTER FOURTEEN

Bennett's gotten her morning routine down for the most part. It helps with the nerves.

1. Wake up.
2. Go for a run.
3. Shower.
4. Breakfast.
5. Read the newspaper.
6. Attempt to mentally prepare herself for the possible devastation of her entire career as a writer.
7. Convince herself that everything's fine.
8. Start her day.

She's still working on what comes after the *start her day* part.

And, well, the whole mental preparation part, too, but she likes to think that she's getting better about it. Kind of. (Not really.)

She's been on the *Parachutes* set in Wilmington, North

Carolina, for a week now, and between production meetings and trailer assignments and last-minute coffee-stained script rewrites, she's still secretly waiting for someone to jump out at her and yell, "*Surprise! We're just messing with you, Bennett. Your books actually suck. Get off the set.*"

Despite how self-deprecating that is, Bennett knows sitting back and watching one of her childhood dreams come true merits a certain level of apprehension. Something so close to the heart always comes with the prospect of collateral damage if it ends up falling short of expectations. That's supposed to be the point of her routine: to keep her distracted from everything that can go wrong by compartmentalizing all that gut-wrenching anxiety into organized, scheduled, daily activities. It's all very Zen.

Actually, it's all still absolutely terrifying.

Especially since today happens to be the day Bennett has been dreading for five months now.

Her run on the beach this morning was colder than usual. The warmth of the hotel lobby hits her as soon as she walks through the automatic doors, her sweatshirt and leggings clinging damply to her skin as she waits for the elevator.

Emmy is already in Bennett's room, tapping away on her iPad, when Bennett keys in.

"Morning, B," her assistant says, smiling warmly when she glances up. "You doin' all right?"

"Good," Bennett replies, and they both know it's a lie.

Emmy Akers is the sole reason Bennett hasn't completely lost her mind yet. For real. Bennett had been so against the idea of getting a personal assistant when her literary agent suggested it to her last summer, but she'll be the first to admit now how much of a mess her life would be had her literary agent not flown Emmy to Charlotte in August for an interview. After talking with her for only ten minutes, Bennett hired her on the spot and hasn't looked back since.

"Your e-mail's a little crazy this morning—you want the rundown now?" Emmy asks.

Five minutes later, she sits on the bathroom counter while Bennett showers, reading out all the new e-mails from lit agents and editors and producers and publishers. Bennett does her best to answer questions about how the final chapters for *Off the Grid* are coming and whether she'll be available this summer to go on another book tour . . . but mainly, she tries not to hyperventilate under the shower spray.

Today is January sixteenth. But that's the only acknowledgment she's allowing herself.

"One of the producers e-mailed and said your trailer is ready—we can pick up the keys whenever," Emmy says absently, then adds, "Oh, and Burt said he already has a fresh copy of the script for you to take notes on for the first table-read this morning, so no need to bring one."

Bennett leans her head against the shower wall and squeezes her eyes shut, and Emmy segues into some logistical stuff about a big book signing they're having here next month, during which Bennett may or may not zone out a bit. . . . She gives herself a pass, though, since she's starting to feel nauseous.

"B? Still with me?" Emmy says after a moment.

Bennett can't remember if she's washed her hair yet, so she reaches for her shampoo. "Yep. What's next?"

"I think that's about it for now," her assistant says. There's a tiny trace of hesitation there before she asks, "So—um. You wanna talk about it?"

Bennett's fingers are still in her hair, suds running down

her forehead and almost into her eyes. She knows exactly where this is going, but there's no way anyone's going to see any cracks in her facade today. Not even Emmy.

"Talk about what?" she asks, peeking out from behind the shower curtain.

Emmy gathers her dirty-blond hair up into a ponytail, then lets it drop past her shoulders again. "The actors getting here today?" she says gently, looking a little uncomfortable. The steam from the shower is fogging up the lenses of her glasses. "I wasn't sure if you wanted to, like, talk about it before we go to the meeting this morning, or . . ."

Bennett closes the shower curtain. "I'm good. No worries."

Emmy doesn't say anything else, and Bennett knows it's because she doesn't want to overstep. Emmy's a top-notch assistant and an even better person to confide in. Bennett doesn't like shutting her out like this, but she's terrified that if she actually does bring herself to talk about what Emmy's hinting at, it'll just solidify that Bennett is in no way, shape, or form prepared to deal with it.

She shuts the water off and reaches for a towel. "Did we get today's newspaper?"

* * *

They stop to get coffee on the way to set, even though Bennett pumping caffeine into her system probably isn't the best call given the meeting she's about to attend. Emmy rides shotgun, skimming through Bennett's social media accounts instead of talking, so Bennett downs half her latte and actively tries to keep her thoughts away from what's coming.

This is fine. Everything is fine. Bennett will not freak out.

So what if the actors are arriving on set today? Bennett

already hates herself for getting this worked up about it—all the effort she made toward *not caring* during the past five months feels like it's working against her now.

"So, you've only got a few events to attend over the next eight weeks," Emmy says while Bennett parks her car. "I wanted to keep your schedule as open as possible so you can be on set as much as you can. Should any conflicts come up, we'll work around them."

Bennett takes a deep breath, pushing back against the staticky nerves filling up her heart and lungs. "We'll figure it out, Em. It's not like they need me around for filming."

"But, Burt wants you here! And it's so important that you be as involved as you can, you know?" Emmy insists. "I know I keep saying it, but you getting to be this hands-on is so, so unprecedented."

Unprecedented.

"No, you're right," Bennett says, shouldering open the driver's side door. Every inch of her is already alive and electric with anxiety, and she just doesn't have it in her to debate this with Emmy right now, regardless of how much she wants to disagree.

Film sets, Bennett has learned, are just a random assortment of warehouses, trailers, and parking lots. Their set's meetings trailer sits between the cast trailers and what Bennett has been told is going to be a cafeteria. There are always people hanging around outside, either on the phone or smoking cigarettes, but there are noticeably more people milling around this morning—people Bennett doesn't recognize from around set during the past week.

Bennett will *not* freak out. She's a professional. She can handle this.

She forces herself to walk up the trailer steps and pull open the door, letting Emmy go in ahead of her.

A few producers are already sitting around the makeshift table in the middle of the trailer—it's actually four smaller tables pushed together to make an even bigger one. *It seems too bright inside.* Too bright and too warm. Bennett won't allow herself to look at anything but the floor while she gets her bearings, and she's just psyched herself up enough to walk around the table to her usual spot next to Burt when she realizes someone is already in her seat. He's slumped in his chair, head down as he sifts through the pile of papers in front of him, and Bennett barely has time to think *Please, God, please no* before the guy looks up.

She stops walking altogether.

All the madness Bennett's wrestled with for the past five months finally comes crashing down on her in the half second their eyes meet. Every available emotion calibrates to the sudden influx of proximity, with Bennett's heart climbing up into her throat like it's preset to close as much distance between it and him as possible. It's hard to breathe. And when he smiles at her, Bennett can't decide what's more infuriating: that he looks way too happy to see her, or that all the goddamned butterflies she managed to chase off from that weekend in July have come swarming back in triple the numbers.

Bennett manages to get her legs working again. She makes a hard right toward the opposite side of the table, aiming for the farthest seat away.

"Bennett," Burt calls out, just as she's pulling out the chair caddy-corner from him. "I need you over here with us."

Three days. This is all because of *three days* back in July.

God, catching feelings for someone is a fucking nightmare.

"You remember Teddy from auditions over the summer, right?" Burt asks when Bennett sits down next to him. The director leans back in his chair, and Bennett finally comes face-to-face with the scruffy-haired bane of her existence on the other side.

"Great to see you again, Bennett," Teddy says, and his grin widens like he can sense how much her heart jumps when he says her name. Bennett glares at him.

God . . . he looks good.

Like—*really* good. Bennett despises herself for admitting it.

His hair is longer than the last time she saw him, and the angles in his jaw and around his face are sharper, like he spent the last few months getting cut for his *Parachutes* role instead of doing whatever, with whomever . . . Bennett stops herself there.

"Good to see you, too," she says, switching her attention to the new copy of the script Burt pushes in front of her. There's absolutely no way she's going to give him the satisfaction of knowing how easily he can get under her skin. And if her game face has to start with fake-smiling at the wall behind him instead of looking him in the eye, then so be it.

"I was just telling Teddy about our script approach," Burt says, oblivious to the tension ricocheting back and forth in front of him. Even inside, Burt still wears a pair of black Ray-Bans. They're completely at odds with his white hair and mustache. "Since today's the first table-read, I think it should be the most improv-oriented so we can make notes and adjust accordingly."

"Sounds good," Bennett says—thinks she says, at least. She can't hear herself over her own pulse roaring in her eardrums.

This is so unfair. Teddy Sharpe isn't allowed to still have this kind of control over her emotions.

"All right, people, take a seat if you haven't. I don't think everyone's here yet, but we can get introductions out of the way in the meantime," Burt says, standing to address the room. "I'm Burt Bridges, the director. I've directed a few indie movies over the past few years and had a couple go to Sundance. This is my fourth major picture, and I'm excited to get started."

He sits back down and, unfortunately, looks to his right, meaning Bennett has to go last.

"Oh, yeah," Teddy says after a moment. "What's going on, guys—I'm Teddy Sharpe. I'm playing the role of Jack, which I'm superstoked about."

Bennett stares at the cover page of her script as they go around the room. Most of the people sitting at the table are either different types of producers or members of the crew. They give similar introductions to Burt's, with some of them name-dropping a few of the bigger movies they've worked on in the past. It's all ridiculously intimidating, and they get a little more than halfway around the table when the trailer door flies open.

"I'm so sorry I'm late!" a tall brunette huffs, sweeping into the room and shrugging out of her winter coat.

"That's all right, Olivia. Come on in," Burt says. "How about you introduce yourself before you get seated?"

An award-winning, megawatt, million-dollar smile appears on her face.

"Oh, I'd love to! Hi, everyone—I'm Olivia Katsaros and I will be playing the role of Katherine Rawlins, the lead female pro-tagonist." She announces it like she's doing everyone a favor, then sits down in the only open seat left at the table.

Bennett sits very still for a moment.

That's the girl who's supposed to be playing Katherine. . . .

Katherine, who's going to be involved in plenty of heavy make-out scenes with Jack . . .

Bennett didn't think there was any room left on her emotional tab, but apparently exceptions can always be made for jealousy. Seeing Olivia in person is the perfect reminder that the next two months are going to be such a blast—and it's all Bennett's fault. She couldn't attend the auditions for Katherine in August because she had a small book promo tour already scheduled. When Burt sent her a headshot of Olivia Katsaros, Bennett almost told him she looked nothing like Katherine's character, and that's still true now.

Katherine is supposed to be relatively plain-looking, with short brown hair and somewhat boyish features. Real-life Olivia is even more stunning in person. She's probably at least half a foot taller than Bennett, with gorgeously thick brown hair and *legs*. Based on the olive skin and the accent she used pronouncing her last name, Bennett figures Olivia's just a notch of mortality below Greek Goddess Barbie. And that's a massive issue.

Burt had insisted Olivia was the right person to cast.

Bennett had trusted him on that decision.

Now, Bennett's stuck somewhere between wishing she said something to Burt about his casting choices sooner and absolutely hating herself for getting jealous over this. Of course she'd thought about what would happen on the days when they have to film those intimate scenes—the reality of the situation just hadn't sunken in until Olivia Katsaros walked into the meetings trailer. Bennett is not down for girl-on-girl rivalries—way too cliché, especially over a guy—but Jesus Christ. The playing field is so uneven now it might as well be a cliff.

It's only a playing field if Bennett chooses to participate, though, and she made the decision to take herself out of the game months ago.

Burt's elbow digs into her forearm. Bennett glances up to find everyone at the table looking back at her. "Right, sorry," she stammers out, going hot around the ears. "Hey, everyone. I'm Bennett Caldwell. I wrote the Parachutes book series, and I've also been helping out with the script."

She stops short from thanking everyone for being there, wishing she had the guts right now to say something like, *Hey, thanks for uprooting your lives to come work on this story with us. It means more to me than you'll ever know.* She already feels childish and out of place as it is.

"Now, filming begins Friday, and the scene Teddy and Olivia are going to read through today is one of the first ones we'll be shooting," Burt says, pulling out a legal pad. "Today's focus is going to be more on getting the actors comfortable with each other and the script. . . ."

Speaking of childish—Bennett tries to listen during the next few minutes of the meeting. She really does. But when Burt stands to walk around for a bit, leaving a huge, gaping mess of empty space next to her, it's hard not to think about what's happening on the other side of that space.

It's like Teddy's *trying* to get her to look over.

Tapping his fingers on the table. Clearing his throat every two seconds. Ruffling the pages of his script. . . . Bennett already knows the dude fidgets like nobody's business, but *God*, he's basically flailing all over the place.

"I thought we could start the read at the top of page fifty-four," Burt says, eventually taking his seat back and opening his script. "The altercation scene between Katherine and Jack, when they're reunited after Katherine sneaks away for an assignment without telling anyone. You guys cool with that?"

No objections.

Bennett, on the other hand, wonders what she did in a past life to deserve this, because of course Burt picked this scene for the read—the one scene in the entire movie involving a tension-filled reunion between the male and female leads, fueled by the fact that neither of them is willing to admit the feelings they have for the other.

"Oh, I love this scene! So much emotional and sexual tension. It's fabulous," Olivia says, clapping her hands. Which— she *would*.

"We left a lot of room in the script's structure for improvisation," Burt explains while everyone flips to the right page. "But—and I'll say this to the other actors as well, Teddy and Olivia—while improv is welcomed and encouraged, we want you to mostly build on the original dialogue to fit preferred speech patterns. Plot points need to stay as is, please. Any questions?"

"Yes, actually." Olivia speaks up. "I saw a note in my script that you'd prefer Katherine to come off more subdued than how she is in the book? I'm not sure I agree with that approach."

Burt replies, "Most of her personality is projected through her first-person narration, which we had trouble translating into the script, since her actual dialogue in the book is more reserved."

"Yeah, but that's no reason to cut out one of her key characteristics," Olivia argues. "One of the reasons I wanted this role so badly was because of Katherine's robust personality. I think it'd be a bit of a disservice to both the character and her author if we don't at least try to bring in that element."

Bennett takes a time-out from her pending anxiety attack and raises her eyebrows.

Maybe Greek Goddess Barbie isn't as bad as she thought?

Burt presses a finger to his mustache. "How about you read Katherine the way you pictured her for now, I'll make a few notes, and then you, Bennett, and I schedule a time to sit down and talk about it before Friday?"

Olivia looks pleased with that answer.

"Okay. Teddy, you wanna start at the top of fifty-four for me?" Burt asks after jotting something down on his legal pad.

"*Katherine,*" he begins, before Bennett has time to prepare. "*Were you even going to tell me you were back? Or were you going to let me find out on my own, like when you left to go on this suicide heist by yourself?*"

Olivia sighs dramatically. "*I've been back twenty minutes— nineteen of which were spent getting chewed out by Commander Mitchell. At least gimme a sec before you start into yours.*"

"*Did you ever stop to think that maybe you wouldn't have gotten chewed out by Mitchell had you told someone where you were going?*"

"*Guess not. Didn't think anyone would be up for it, anyway.*"

"*I would have, had you told me. It's protocol—*"

"*Protocol,*" Olivia snaps, pointing across the table, "*is exactly why I didn't tell you.*"

"*Why, because you thought it wouldn't look as cool if you let someone help you on this? Seriously, Katherine? I don't get whatever fixation you have on being a badass, because nowhere in the job description does it say 'Must be badass at all times.'*"

Olivia chuckles.

"*But it does say how you need to be smart and rational above everything else, and you were being stupid,*" Teddy bites out.

"I was stepping up and doing what needed to be done instead of waiting around for something to happen like everyone else in The Company."

"No, had you looked at the bigger picture, you would have realized how irresponsible it was to go off the grid on a rogue mission without telling anyone where you were going or what you were doing," Teddy shoots back; then he adds, "I don't know why you have such a problem with letting people in, Katherine."

Bennett stares at her script.

The line is supposed to read, "Letting people help you."

"I don't have a problem with that. What I do have a problem with is taking unnecessary precautions," Olivia says, adjusting the first part of her line to fit Teddy's deviation. "And it's not like you didn't know I was thinking about it. I told you I wanted to do this as a solo gig a while ago. You didn't have a problem with it then."

"You told me that two months ago and then never mentioned it again! And just because you wanted to do it solo doesn't mean you should have, Katherine!" Teddy grinds out with a little more intensity than Bennett thinks necessary.

"Are you going to wrap this up soon, or are you gonna drag it out?" Olivia asks. "I need to go file my report."

"Nice, Kat. Glad to see you didn't lose your knack for pissing me off while you were gone."

"And I'm glad to see you didn't lose your knack for blowing everything out of proportion while I was gone, either."

"You think me privately reprimanding you about one of the biggest transgressions you've pulled since you were recruited for The Company is 'blowing everything out of proportion'?" He pretends to laugh, even though the script specifies it's supposed to be a serious question.

"I'd say yelling at me about something that's kind of none of your business is pretty close."

"I was assigned to be your partner. Everything you do is my business," he snaps. *"Nothing kind of about that."*

That last line is not in the script, and to Bennett, it *kind of* feels like a slap in the face.

"Oh, I like that little addition there; what do you guys think?" Burt says, looking around to the rest of the producers. Again, no objections. "Let's keep it going, Teddy."

Teddy reads the next few lines, with Olivia following along, while Bennett forces herself to believe it was a coincidence. Nothing more.

"Do you have any idea what would have happened had you not made it back?" Teddy asks.

"Here I am, aren't I?"

"Sure, here you are, and you haven't even looked me in the eye yet."

That isn't in the script, either.

"I spent four years in training, Jack. I don't need a bodyguard."

"And those four years of training couldn't help prevent that nice little shiner you're sporting right now, huh?"

"You're clearly upset because I managed to make it to the headquarters and back without your help," Olivia says.

"No, I'm freaking livid *because not only did you go without telling me, you also ignored every attempt I made to get in touch with you!"*

And just where the hell does he think he's going with that?

"Jack—"

"If you're going to disappear on some solo gig because you think it makes you look like the hero, then at least act like you've

- 168 -

done it before and follow the protocol for solo missions—which includes checking in with The Company so people won't think you're dead."

Olivia tries to start her next line, but Teddy cuts her off again.

"You know how that made me feel? Completely shutting me out like that? Every call and text going unanswered? We couldn't even leave you voice mails anymore because it was full with all the other voice mails you ignored!"

What the fu—no. Bennett is imagining this. She's being paranoid.

But this is all wrong. So wrong. Yeah, Katherine ignores their attempts to get in touch with her in the script, but Jack is supposed to understand Katherine doesn't want anything traced back to The Company. Jack isn't supposed to be dwelling on this at all. . . . Why the hell isn't Burt stepping in?

Olivia frowns. *"Clearly I was a little preoccupied at the time, and I didn't want to have any contact because they could've traced me back to you and The Company."*

Damn. Despite everything, Bennett has to admit Olivia's good with improv.

"Yeah, right, Katherine. You didn't want to give me a chance to talk to you because you were afraid of what I had to say, and you know it."

"What was there to talk about? This solo gig had nothing to do with you!"

"There was a lot to talk about," Teddy says defensively. *"And you wouldn't even hear me out—you disappeared and pretended not to notice how it would affect everyone."*

"Can you blame me?" Olivia asks, getting back to the script.

"Jesus, Jack! I needed to do this, and I didn't tell you because I knew you'd go running off to tell Mitchell I was violating protocol the first chance you got. Don't try to tell me you wouldn't have."

"You act like I'm some tattletale that's out to get you all the time."

"Well, then, stop acting like you are, and maybe I'd trust you more. Constantly using protocol against me is a high-horse move, and you know it."

Teddy groans. "There's a reason we have protocol, Katherine. Get used to it."

"Fine. You wanna talk about protocol? What's the protocol on separating yourself from your work, huh? Approaching everything objectively instead of letting your emotions interfere? Because you're certainly going against that little part of protocol right now."

"I don't know what you're talking about."

"Oh, you don't? So, you freaking out about this has nothing to do with anything other than protocol?" Olivia asks, and Bennett exhales slowly. They're coming up on the end of the scene, and for a second there she thought . . .

"What, you think it has to do with something else?" Teddy shoots back.

"I don't see you getting this worked up when other agents go against protocol—which, by the way, is all the time."

"I'm just doing my job," Teddy scoffs. "Don't flatter yourself, superstar."

Bennett tries to convince herself she didn't hear that correctly—that that didn't just come out of Teddy's mouth—but she can't pretend the calm demeanor she's been clinging to all morning didn't just crack beyond repair.

"Why don't we stop there for a moment and discuss?" Burt says, and Bennett can't move. Her hands are numb. Her shoulders are up by her ears. And since she definitely isn't getting enough oxygen circulation to keep her brain from short-circuiting, all she can do is switch to autopilot and hope to God her face isn't giving her away.

Another producer says, "Even though some of that was a little more unscripted than I'd like, I'd say it still worked nicely. I like the idea of Jack's character getting more upset about not being able to get in touch with Katherine."

"Thanks, man," Teddy says. "I don't know, after getting to know Jack's character more, I kind of pictured him reacting that way."

"I'd be careful about coming off too forward, Teddy. Jack's character isn't the type to admit to pining over a girl, no matter how much he loves her," Olivia throws out.

"That's true, too. I guess that's just what I personally would've done in a situation like that. It seemed more organic."

Burt folds his hands behind his head and says, "I could definitely see us being able to work that in, Teddy. It's a good idea."

"Yeah?" Teddy says innocently. "Hey, Bennett—what do you think about it?"

And you know what? That's enough. Teddy messing with her during the table-read was one thing, but throwing it in her face while everyone else is blissfully unaware of what he's doing is a whole different ballgame. And it's exactly the motivation Bennett needs to snap out of the anxiety-induced paralysis she had going on a minute ago.

This is how Teddy wants to play it? Fine. Bennett will bite.

"Yeah, I like it," she says after pretending to clear her throat. "I think it works well with Jack's complete inability to take a hint."

Burt turns all the way toward her in his chair, eyebrows raised. "Inability to take a hint?"

Bennett shrugs. "Jack's character isn't stupid. If he knows Katherine as well as he says he does, he would understand she had legitimate reasons for not responding to him on the mission—that's why we wrote it that way in the script. But Jack's also pretty fragile. I could see him getting worked up over being ignored, even if it makes him look a little desperate."

"Or maybe it's his *refusal* to take a hint instead of *inability*," Teddy mutters, and Bennett presses a hand to her mouth to hide her grin.

"I feel like Jack trusts Katherine's judgment, regardless of how many times she goes against protocol," Olivia points out thoughtfully. "But again, I still don't think it's in his nature to pine over a girl, regardless of how desperately in love he is with her."

"The refusal to take a hint component could appeal more to our target audience, though. It looks more romantic," one of the producers says.

"I agree," Teddy cuts in. "Plus, once I got to know Katherine's character—you know, from reading the books and stuff—it seemed like she wanted Jack to put in more effort instead of waiting around for her to come back. She spends the entire book trying to prove she doesn't need anyone else, almost to the point of overcompensating. It fits."

Olivia considers it, pushing out her bottom lip and tipping her head to the side. "That's true. I did sense Kat secretly wanting someone to chase her through all the stunts she pulled. Maybe she likes the reassurance of Jack being so persistent? She's already proven she's insecure like that," she says, and Bennett gets so irrationally defensive that it takes her a second to remember Olivia's actually talking about the character.

"Definitely likes the reassurance," Teddy says. "Katherine's not exactly one to hold her tongue when it matters. If she wanted Jack to stop, I think she would've told him to."

Bennett isn't sure who he thinks he's talking about now, because if he seriously thinks Bennett ignored him for the past five months for *reassurance*, then he's not as observant as she used to give him credit for.

"I dunno—I agree with what you guys are saying, but I also think there could be more to this for Katherine than the reassurance," Burt says.

"Like what?" another producer asks.

"Like Olivia said when she was improvising, Katherine knew the risks of contacting anyone from The Company while she was on such a critical mission," Burt explains. "Ignoring Jack could correlate with how much she cares for him."

"And maybe correlate with her not wanting to look vulnerable, especially after everything that went down between, uh—them." Teddy hesitates before adding, "I mean, with the unspoken mutual attraction they had before she left."

And what would Teddy Sharpe know about being vulnerable?

Burt nods. "Exactly. This scene is already important because it solidifies what's going on between them. This new factor could take it to the next level if we play it right."

"I think we need to be careful," Bennett says suddenly, unaware of when she decided to speak. She has to work hard to keep her tone even. "I mean, it's safe to assume the majority of the audience has read the books, so they probably already have an idea of Jack in their heads."

"So?" a producer says.

Bennett leans forward to rest her elbows on the table. "I

wouldn't want people to end up confused or disappointed if Jack doesn't turn out to be the person they thought he was. We don't want to give anyone the wrong idea."

Sure, it's not her most eloquent response, but it's enough to get her point across. Out of the corner of her eye, Bennett watches the jackass who started this shift in his seat, sighing loudly through his nose.

Screw looking vulnerable.

CHAPTER FIFTEEN

The table-read meeting comes to an end, and once everyone passes their newly noted scripts back to the producers, Burt thanks them for coming and gives a special shout-out to the actors for making the first table-read so successful. Bennett's in the middle of holding back an eye roll when Burt asks if she can stay after the meeting.

"It'll only take a few minutes," Burt insists as people file out. "You don't mind, do you?"

Bennett feels someone drop a hand on the back of her chair as she and Burt wait for the room to empty out. When she turns to see who it is, she watches the reason this meeting shaved off a few years of her life continue around the table to introduce himself to Greek Goddess Barbie.

Actually—it's unfair for Bennett to call her that. After seeing how the table-read went, Bennett's sort of looking forward to meeting Olivia. That doesn't mean Bennett enjoys seeing her smile her megawatt, million-dollar smile at Teddy, though. They shake hands, then Teddy holds the door for her and they both disappear from the trailer, leaving Bennett behind to sulk over all her conflicting emotions.

"I'll meet you at your car, B," Emmy says before heading out herself.

Burt stretches his arms over his head once everyone's gone. "Wanted to touch base to see where your head's at about the first read. What'd you think?"

"I thought it went well," Bennett hedges.

"Really? I couldn't tell if you liked the improvisations or not."

"I was just . . . engrossed."

Burt hums, then finally removes his sunglasses. "You sure? Maybe I was just misreading. You haven't changed your mind about casting any of the leads, right?"

What a loaded question.

"No, I haven't," she tells him, and it's surprisingly the truth. Bennett's just changed her mind about a few other things when it comes to one of the leads. . . .

"Good," Burt says, then he launches into a ten minute analysis on the table-read and how he thought the actors meshed well together. Bennett's just fine with sitting back and letting him talk. She knows the longer she sits here, the less likely she'll run into anyone after they're done.

"I know this has been a lot to put on you, so I appreciate you taking everything in stride," Burt says as they gather up a few stray scripts and notes left around the table.

"It hasn't felt like too much," Bennett says.

"Good. The industry doesn't need another overprocessed young adult book adaptation that fizzles out after opening weekend. I want this to be next wave," Burt tells her, which isn't the first time he's made a comment like this. "Although, it helps your book was already so adaptable," he adds, swinging open the trailer door so Bennett can walk out first.

Her eyebrows knit together as she descends the trailer steps.

"I thought the whole reason you wanted me working on the script was to bridge the gap between all the parts of *Parachutes* that *weren't* adaptable. . . ."

"No, I wanted you working on the script because of how you write dialogue," Burt says casually. "I figured you wouldn't have trouble with the transition because your book already read more like a script than a novel, anyway."

Bennett frowns.

"That's a good thing, by the way," he says when he catches her expression. "Most of the YA adaptations during the past five years either tanked because they deviated too much from the original storyline or they stayed so close it created plot holes for people who didn't read the books. *Parachutes* had a few things that wouldn't adapt, yeah, but it has more potential to find the Goldilocks medium here than any other series I've seen optioned for film recently."

Bennett isn't sure why Burt's telling her this, but now it's got her thinking about expectations—the black hole of Bennett's doubts about everything. Burt veers off toward one of the buildings on the far side of set, calling over his shoulder, "See you later. I'll consolidate all the script notes and e-mail them out to the writers tonight."

Bennett's still frowning as she crosses through the parking lot toward her car. She never considered the idea of *Parachutes* reading more like a script than a novel. She spent the past three and a half years trying to pass off *Parachutes* as a decent piece of prose, and now Burt's saying she still might not have pulled it off. . . .

"Hey, Bennett!"

Bennett's head whips up from the parking lot gravel. Emmy is standing by Bennett's Jeep, waving her over. And she isn't alone.

Seriously, what the hell is this?

Teddy hasn't been on set for more than three hours and he's already *everywhere*. Which is so typical Bennett can't stand it. She fishes around in her bag for her sunglasses, unconcerned that it's cloudy out.

"Hey," is all Teddy says when Bennett reaches them. She doesn't look at him, but she knows he's looking at her.

"What's up?" she says, because it's safe and she can't think of anything better.

"I was just telling Teddy about the hotel we're staying in," Emmy replies.

"Yeah," Teddy says, scratching the back of his neck. "I, uh—got dropped off straight from the airport this morning, so I haven't seen it yet."

Bennett nods, wondering how bitchy she'd sound if she asked if there's a point to him informing her of this.

"His manager is running a little late right now," Emmy provides, folding her arms across her chest. "I said we could give him a ride back to the hotel if he needs it."

"Only if that's cool with you, though, Bennett," Teddy's quick to add.

Of course. This is all just too perfect.

"Sure," Bennett says, her voice an octave too high. She presses the unlock button on her car key and steps around both of them, making a mental note to have a word with her assistant later about the definition of *betrayal*.

"So, Teddy, are you excited to start shooting? Sounds like the schedule is going to be a little intense," Emmy says on the way back the hotel. She at least had the decency to take shotgun on this little carpool adventure, which was great until Teddy climbed into the seat directly behind the driver's side.

Now every time Bennett glances in the rearview mirror, she's forced to look at at least half of Teddy's face. How's that for irony.

"Yeah, I'm stoked, but kinda nervous," he says. "It's been a while since I've been on a movie set."

"I thought the table-read went well today. Don't you guys think?" Emmy says, moving right along. Bennett tightens her grip on the steering wheel and her eyes find Teddy's in the rearview, though she isn't sure if he knows it or not. Her sunglasses are the only thing helping her keep her composure.

"Yeah, I felt pretty good about it," Teddy says. Then, because he's a little shit, he asks, "What'd you think, Bennett?"

"Same," she says, and what she means is: *You're a real dick for asking me that.*

"By the way, B—you got a weird spam e-mail during the read this morning. I went ahead and changed your e-mail password just in case," Emmy says, tapping Bennett's arm with the back of her hand. "Want me to go ahead and change it on your work phone while I'm thinking about it?"

"Sure," Bennett says, forcing her eyes to stay on the road instead of shooting her assistant a scathing look. Her fingers are probably leaving dents around the steering wheel—she pries one away and digs into her coat pocket for her work phone, knowing it's the only way to save face. She passes it across the center console and pretends like the reason she has a work phone in the first place isn't watching from the backseat.

"Work phone, eh?" Teddy says. "You fancy."

Emmy beams. "First order of business when Bennett brought me on as an assistant back in August. It's pretty much the only phone you can get her on these days."

Teddy chuckles. "Oh yeah?"

"Yeah," Emmy sighs dramatically. "Thank goodness she has me. She'd be lost otherwise."

"Yeah, thank *goodness*," Bennett says, checking her rearview again.

Teddy's biting down on his thumbnail and smiling out the window.

They pull into the hotel parking lot ten minutes (of mostly Emmy talking) later. As soon as Bennett cuts the engine, Teddy unbuckles his seat belt and hops out, appearing at the driver's side window to open Bennett's door for her.

"Um—thanks," she says, startled by how much she likes the gesture.

"No problem." He grins and keeps a hand on the top of the doorframe as Bennett gets out. "Thanks for the ride."

The parallels happening right now hurt Bennett's heart.

"What's on your agenda for the rest of the day, Teddy?" Emmy asks when they fall into step across the parking lot.

"I guess just getting settled in," Teddy says, shrugging. "My busy stuff starts tomorrow. What about you guys?"

"We've got a conference call with Bennett's editor this afternoon," Emmy says. Bennett's been so busy being borderline traumatized this morning that she completely forgot she has other things to do later.

They breeze through the almost empty lobby. Teddy pushes the up button for the elevators and asks, "What floor are you guys on?"

"Eight. You?" Emmy says.

"Nice. I think I'm on eleven. Hope my manager's still up there because I definitely don't have a room key yet," he says, following them into the elevator.

Emmy suddenly curses under her breath.

"Whoops—forgot I need to stop by the front desk," she calls over her shoulder, darting back out into the lobby. "I'll be up in a minute!"

Bennett's stomach barrels up into her throat. "What? Why?" But Emmy disappears around the corner, right as the doors close, and she doesn't get an answer.

There's an excruciating pause before the elevator starts moving, but it's fine. Bennett is trapped in a small space alone with Teddy for the next eight floors, but really. It's fine. She presses back against the railing along the wall, mentally grasping for things to say but determined not to speak first. Teddy seems cool with the silence for a little while, scuffing the sole of his shoe against the floor. It's disturbing how it feels like it takes thirty minutes to go up four floors. They get to the sixth before Teddy finally clears his throat.

"It's, uh—it's really great to see you, Bennett," he says.

Bennett has zero idea what to say to that.

"I mean, not trying to make this weird or anything. I just . . ." He jerks a hand up to the back of his neck and clears his throat again, pointing up at the illuminated floor number. "Um, I guess this is you, right?"

The elevator lurches to a halt on the eighth floor, and even after extensive brainstorming, Bennett still can't come up with anything to say back. Her eyes flick to the illuminated eight above the buttons as Teddy drops his hands and shakes them out by his sides.

The doors slide open.

"So, I'll see you later, then. Right?" he says, giving her a shy smile.

Bennett needs to leave. Immediately.

"Yeah," she manages, shrugging away from the elevator wall.

The second she starts moving, Teddy rocks onto the balls of his feet and steps toward her. Bennett isn't sure what he's trying to do, but the possibility of him giving her a hug pops into her head and she reflexively flinches away from him.

"Er—yeah," Bennett repeats, her shoulder clipping the elevator doorframe on her way out.

"See ya, Caldwell," Teddy says, and Bennett hates herself for slipping up and meeting his eyes. He gives her a small wave right before the doors close.

CHAPTER SIXTEEN

"Emmy Akers."

Emmy hesitates in the doorframe, clutching Bennett's spare key card.

"What exactly was that urgent front desk business?" Bennett asks, lying on the bed and staring up at the hotel room ceiling. She's been like this for the past ten minutes, contemplating the state of her life.

"I wanted to ask if the phones in our rooms were able to make conference calls." Emmy crosses into the room and drops her bag on the desk. "We have that call with your editor later, remember?"

"Don't we normally FaceTime for those?"

"Well—I wanted to make sure we had a backup plan in case someone has a bad Internet connection or something. Your deadline for *Off the Grid* is coming up. You know how important these calls are."

Bennett sits up on the bed and cocks an eyebrow. "You're so full of shit."

Then Bennett bursts out laughing, and she continues to laugh as she crosses her legs up underneath her, because she just had one of the most awkward elevator rides in the history of awkward elevator rides, and somewhere between the little wave she got before the doors closed and the walk down the hall to her room, Bennett came to the conclusion that laughing about how utterly and indisputably screwed she is, is the only way to actually *deal* with how utterly and indisputably screwed she is.

Look at all those adverbs. Bennett is unhinged.

"Bennett . . . ?"

"Oh, man," Bennett chokes out, rubbing her eyes. "I wish you'd been there to see it, Em. It was so awkward."

"What was?" she asks.

The confusion in her voice makes Bennett laugh harder.

Emmy waits another moment before saying, "Okay, still missing what's funny here."

But that's the point: Nothing about this Teddy situation is funny. And because nothing about it is funny, it's actually all hilarious. Why can't Emmy see that?

It takes about four deep breaths before Bennett can keep her face straight enough to say, "Freaking Buzz Lightyear, man. He has me so wound up I almost died getting off the elevator."

Emmy's now looking at Bennett like she's going to start fitting her for a straitjacket.

"Buzz Lightyear? Is that code name for Teddy?" she asks.

Hearing his name out loud jolts Bennett for a second, but it's long enough to shake her out of her little giggle fest. "Yeah. Him."

"Well, I'm glad you're finally admitting to it now," her assistant says. "What happened in the elevator?"

Bennett tries not to zero in on her use of "finally," but it's already grating on her nerves and draining all the humor from the conversation. "Nothing. He just told me it's good to see me and that he's not trying to make things weird. Then I was getting off the elevator and almost popped my shoulder out of the socket trying to run away from the dude."

Emmy hesitates. "And by 'dude,' you mean Teddy."

Bennett's eyes lock with hers. "Yes, Emmy."

"Just making sure." She shrugs. "Because I'm pretty sure I haven't actually heard you say his name since we got here."

"Because this is, like, the second time he's come up."

Emmy raises an eyebrow. "Okay, so say his name now, then."

"What? No."

"Why not?"

"I don't see why I need to," Bennett counters, officially (irrationally) crossing the line between defensive and circling the wagons.

"I don't understand why you won't," Emmy presses.

"Because I don't think I need to say his name to prove anything to you."

"I didn't say you did—"

"What're you saying, then, Emmy?" Bennett snaps, holding her hands up. "Since this is any of your business."

Bennett regrets it as soon as she says it, because one, she's acting like a disrespectful brat right now, and two, a second later, Emmy's eyes go wide, changing her entire demeanor from pushy assistant to kicked puppy.

"Oh, God—I'm so sorry, Bennett," Emmy says. "I'm completely butting into your personal life and making things worse."

"No, you're not—"

"No, this is so, so unprofessional of me," Emmy says. Which makes Bennett feel even more like an asshole (especially since she already finds it inappropriate to be the boss of a twenty-six-year-old who has plenty of better things she could be doing outside of personal assisting a teenager).

"Emmy—"

"I just, I don't like seeing how much this bothers you! Not that it's, you know, obvious it's bothering you. . . . You're actually really good at hiding it. . . ." She's babbling now. "The only reason I ditched you in the elevator was because I thought it'd be better for you to maybe deal with it head-on instead of having time to stress about it beforehand, you know? I—"

"Jesus, *EMMY.*"

Emmy's mouth snaps shut.

"I gave you an open-ended invitation into all my dramatic bullshit after I hired you, remember?" Bennett says.

Specifically, a Saturday morning in August a few weeks after Emmy started. Bennett had woken up to a slew of drunk texts from the night before, and it was the only time she ever let herself cry over this ridiculous mess. Emmy happened to call to check in on something (Bennett can't remember what it was about) right at the peak of her meltdown. Bennett ended up spilling the entire story to her, since Bennett can't separate her work life and her personal life, apparently. She was stunned Emmy still wanted to work with her after that.

Before Emmy can start groveling again now, Bennett adds, "I'm sorry—I didn't mean to snap at you. And you're right. I should probably be thanking you, actually. . . ."

Emmy balks. "For what? I could have at least tried to make today easier for you."

"You've pointed out how pathetic I am, so that's helpful," Bennett says, and she means it.

"You're not path—"

"I can't even say the guy's name, Em," Bennett cuts her off. And that, by definition, is pathetic. Bennett hadn't even realized she was doing it, either, which makes it worse. "*Anyway.* What's the conference call this afternoon about again?"

Emmy opens and closes her mouth, clearly thrown by the subject change. Bennett looks at her expectantly, hoping she won't press it anymore. Truth is, on top of already being annoyed with herself for talking about this as long as they have, Bennett is too embarrassed to continue the conversation.

"Er—it's just another touch base about where you are with *Off the Grid.* If you want, I can reschedule and tell them you're spending the afternoon writing. That's probably more productive anyway," she says, and Bennett makes a mental note to check to see if she can give Emmy her Christmas bonus for Easter this year.

* * *

It's 9:43 p.m. and Bennett is already in bed. Contacts out, glasses on, retainers in.

Emmy wanted to go see a movie after they had dinner in the hotel restaurant earlier. Bennett suggested a rain check and has been hiding in her room watching *Friends* since. Well, watching *Friends* and getting more work done on *Off the Grid.*

She's just gotten into a groove when her phone vibrates on the bedside table. Thinking it's Emmy sending another complaint text about how they're both losers for being in bed so early, Bennett grabs it without looking away from the paragraph she's working on and thumbs open the lock screen. It's a text from a number with a vaguely familiar area code.

I'd say don't flatter yourself superstar-

but this is well deserved.

http://tinyurl.com/prk9w8g

Bennett freezes, thumb still hovering over the screen, and the turnaround time it takes to start panicking is impressive. She has no idea how long she stares at the little text bubbles, but she's still staring when the little typing ellipsis appears again.

P.S. You left me on read

FREAKING TECHNOLOGY.

Bennett mashes the home button down, then accidentally taps the camera icon as she scrambles to pull up her message settings. Once she finally gets to the right place, there aren't enough words to describe her relief when she sees her read receipts are, in fact, not on. Her phone vibrates again.

Just kidding. But if you are reading these texts right now, I bet you just checked your settings on your fancy new work phone to make sure ☺

What a little asshole. How did he even get her work number?

Bennett clicks whatever link he had the nerve to send her. Partly out of curiosity, but mostly out of spite. A page from *The Hollywood Reporter* pops up, and five minutes later, she's sobbing.

The article is fourteen paragraphs of praise for *Parachutes*, and major hype for the upcoming film adaptation. There are even a few additional notes about the *"Promising young author, from whom the readers can expect more best-sellers very, very soon."* It also mentions the adaptation is about to start filming, and it's already slated to be one of the biggest movies set for release in 2019. Which only makes Bennett more upset. The only thing worse than unrealistic expectations is having them amplified in print.

Still, it's a flattering article. There's even a brief moment about two-thirds into reading when Bennett registers a tiny bit of pride peeking out of the shadows in the back of her mind. It's been MIA for a while now, but she's glad to know it's still alive back there.

Bennett sniffs and takes off her glasses, wiping underneath her eyes with the collar of her T-shirt. Then she does something incredibly stupid.

> Yikes. That was quite the article.

The regret is instantaneous. Bennett's in the middle of swearing she won't text him back again when another message comes through. You give Teddy Sharpe an inch . . .

> What?! I thought it was great!! I'm sorry 🙁

God. Bennett can just picture him pouting at his phone. She's such a sucker.

> No no. It is. Thank you for sending it to me.

Maybe—maybe Emmy's right—maybe in the long run it'll be better to just deal with this head-on instead of being such a wimp about it. They're going to be spending the next two months together, regardless. . . . But Bennett needs to proceed with caution here. She can already feel herself getting restless when he doesn't respond right away. If she doesn't watch herself, she'll slip right back in over her head again. And she can't have that.

You're very welcome

So now that I have your attention and the best number to reach you

How many little whale emoticons is it gonna take to convince you to come downstairs and have a drink with me at the hotel bar? 🐳

Thank God Bennett actually has a real-life, legitimate reason to say no to this instead of having to come up with some lame and totally transparent excuse to turn it down.

Save the whales for a better cause that isn't against the law

No it's cool-I'm boys with the bartender. He's a Pirates fan and therefore my new best friend

Of course he is, because Teddy has this insane, superhuman

ability to be everyone's best friend. Bennett's never seen anything like it, and it's so annoyingly cute it makes her want to push him off a cliff into a vat of thirty-seven crocodiles that's also on fire. Except then he'd probably figure out a way to emerge unscathed and with thirty-seven new friends.

> Why the whale emoticon?

Bc it's adorable and felt right in the moment. Are you coming or not?

> They're not gonna let me drink I look like I'm 12

Stop peer pressuring me.

Look at that whole pod of peer pressure whales now you really can't say no

Goddammit.

See this? This is exactly the kind of thing that happens when you're too quick to lift the Teddy Sharpe texting embargo. He goes and does something ridiculous that makes it hard to remember why an embargo is such a necessary precaution.

I'm already in bed, sorry dude

It's barely 10! Don't be lame Caldwell
👎 👎 👎

Early day <u>tomorrow</u> 😴

We don't even have to drink

And you say I'm lame?

So is that a yes?!

No, that was a rhetorical question.

You're killing me smalls COME ON

The little ellipsis of death pops up again before Bennett can think of another excuse.

I'm coming to see you either way . . .
Meeting me downstairs would just save
me the embarrassment from having to
knock on every door on the 8th floor

Since I know you probably won't give me
your room number. . . .

God. Bennett rereads *I'm coming to see you either way* five times before she finally acknowledges that she can't force herself to feel indifferent about it. She does the only safe thing she can think of at a time like this.

She calls his bluff.

> Would you mind asking whoever's in 8123 to turn down their tv?

Bennett taps send and tosses her phone aside, feeling pretty pleased with herself.

That feeling lasts for the first ten minutes to go by without getting another response. After that, her mood sours. She picks up her phone again to check what time she'd sent the last message, then tosses it back to the end of the bed. All guys have their limits, and Bennett certainly hasn't given Teddy a reason to push his. . . .

Her phone vibrates again, and she almost falls off the side of the bed trying to get to it.

Her heart sinks when she sees it's from Emmy.

> Are you still up? Might as well marathon Friends together. 😊

Apparently her assistant has already made the decision to crash, because the sound of three quick knocks comes a minute later. Bennett pads over to her door, ready to fire off a joke about the five extra key cards Emmy had made earlier this week—a joke that gets lodged in the back of her throat the second she swings open the door to not-Emmy standing in the entryway.

Teddy grins.

"Hi. Do you mind turning down your TV?" he asks, pointing a thumb over his shoulder. "Some chick on your floor is being superlame and keeps complaining about it."

Bennett stands there for a second with two thoughts on her mind: First—this is her own fault for texting him back. And second—her mouth is hanging wide open, meaning the clunky, plastic-and-metal retainers she's worn every night since getting her braces off in tenth grade are currently on display.

Bennett snaps her mouth shut, turns to her right, and walks straight into the bathroom, unconcerned with the possibility of the door slamming in Teddy's face. Only after she's pried her retainers out of her mouth and shoved them back into their case does it occur to her she probably just gave him a good excuse to leave.

But then she hears him snicker, "Cute glasses, nerd," and her eyes cut to her reflection in the mirror. That smug little shit shows up at her door looking dressed for a night out, and here Bennett is in well-worn pajama pants and an arguably see-through T-shirt. With no bra on. He's not allowed to pull the trigger on a stunt like this and not expect some kickback here.

Bennett moseys out of her bathroom and finds him leaning against the door to keep it propped open, arms crossed over his chest.

"Makes sense you picked acting," she says, mimicking his stance against the bathroom doorway. "You've got such a talent for repeating lines."

Teddy rolls his head back, grinning up at the ceiling. "Every single time, man," he murmurs, then he looks at Bennett and his grin turns smug again. "You know, using your own room number in that text was a cheeky little move, Caldwell. You can imagine how thrown off I was when I went to the front desk to ask what room you're staying in."

"Payback for the read receipts."

Teddy fist pumps. "Knew you'd fall for that. *God*, I'm good."

"Right," Bennett says, pretending she doesn't notice his gaze dropping to where her arms are crossed over her lack of bra situation.

Teddy shrugs, eyes flicking back to hers. "Not my fault you're gullible."

Bennett has to catch herself before she yells, *Clearly*, with as much implication behind it as she can. Instead, she goes with the classic, "I am not."

"Please," Teddy says. "I'll bet you a drink at the hotel bar I could get you again just as easily."

"Excuse me?"

"You heard me." He cocks his head to the side and gives her a wicked grin. "I already got you once; I'll bet you a drink at the hotel bar I could get you again."

Bennett blinks at him, because God—what is she supposed to do with that?

"Hi, by the way," she stalls, gesturing out in front of her. "Welcome to my entryway."

"Thank you, ma'am. Your southern hospitality never disappoints. You're dodging my bet, though," he says.

But then of course he follows it up with that *look*—the same look from last summer that doubled as a constant reminder that in addition to Teddy Sharpe having an insane, superhuman ability to be everyone's best friend, he also has the terrifying capability to see straight through Bennett's bullshit facades, all the way to the fine print written on her heart that says NOT AS TOUGH AS IT APPEARS, HANDLE WITH CARE.

And you know what? Teddy Sharpe is not going to throw her off her game like this. Bennett straightens up and plasters on the best smirk she can manage.

"Fine. What do I get if I win?" she asks.

Teddy bites down on his bottom lip to keep his grin from getting bigger (which, *Christ*—he has to know how hot that is, right? It's so unfair). "I dunno," he says thoughtfully, dropping his gaze to where Bennett's arms are folded across her chest again. "Either way, I saw this ending with us getting a drink, so . . ."

Bennett glares at him.

"Okay, okay," he laughs. "What do you want?"

What she wants is to not have the urge to self-incinerate every time he smiles at her like that.

"You have to actually knock on every door on this floor and ask them to turn their TVs down," she says after giving it some thought. It's not her best work, but whatever.

Teddy groans. "Fine, deal. Shake on it?"

Bennett shakes her head instead. She might look composed, but there's no way she can handle touching him in any capacity right now.

He frowns. "How do I know you'll stick to your word, then?"

"How do I know you'll stick to *yours*?" she shoots back before she can stop herself, this time with plenty of implication behind it.

Teddy's eyes flick to hers and hold her there.

"Easy now, Caldwell. I always stick to my word," he says, his tone calm but laced with tension. "Don't want to give anyone the wrong idea about me."

Bennett didn't need confirmation about Teddy's intentions at the table-read this morning, but his words hang heavy between them anyway. Something stops her from calling him out on it, though. She already made the decision to deal with this head-on—it's not fair to be so abrasive about it, especially since she's the one who initiated it just now.

"Nope, wouldn't want that," she says. Teddy's shoulders visibly sag. "So, what are—"

"Hang on a sec, sorry," Teddy interrupts, stepping into the room toward her. "What is that?"

"What is what?" she panics, too afraid to move as he closes the space between them.

Teddy half smiles and points a finger to the left of her sternum. "*That*—what is that?"

Bennett tips her head down, trying to remember if she's wearing a necklace or something. "What, is there something on my shirt? Is that what you've been looking at?"

Her mistake dawns on her a half a second later.

"WAIT—" she shrieks, trying to bat Teddy's hand away, but it's too late. His finger flicks the tip of her nose, and Bennett Caldwell has officially fallen for the oldest trick in the book.

"YES!" Teddy howls, jumping around and fist pumping.

Bennett stares at him impassively. He would act like a five-year-old on Christmas morning over a practical joke. Teddy Sharpe has two personality settings: Portable Romantic Comedy or Five-Year-Old on Christmas Morning. There is no in between. And, honestly, Bennett would probably find all the cinnamon-roll enthusiasm irritating if she weren't already so charmed by it. Teddy somehow keeps her door propped open during the entire scene, and Bennett watches an elderly couple shoot him a nasty look as they walk by. He's too busy dancing to notice.

"Oh, man. It was just too easy, Caldwell," he says, switching to ridiculous hip gyrations.

"That was so cheap." Bennett sulks.

Teddy stops dancing immediately and looks down at her, his expression dropping to something far more serious than Bennett thinks should be possible for a guy who was doing the disco point three seconds ago. "No, no. Don't do that. Don't be a bad sport, Caldwell—it's unbecoming."

Bennett starts to tell him that *he's* unbecoming, but Teddy changes gears on her with: "Come on, nerd. Time to settle your debt. We're getting champagne to celebrate that article I sent you."

He reaches for her hand, and Bennett ignores both the nervous jump in her stomach and the look that crosses his face when she shies away from it.

"It's too late tonight," she says. "Rain check."

Teddy snorts. "That's not gonna fly. Change your clothes— I'll meet you at the elevator."

CHAPTER SEVENTEEN

Pro tip: Champagne is just bubbles and truth serum hidden by a fancy French name, and Bennett hates whoever decided it was a good idea to distribute it to the masses.

Sure, at first drinking it was flirty and exciting and a little bit dangerous since Bennett is definitely underage and Teddy's bartender friend definitely knew. . . .

But now it's morning and Bennett's hungover.

She already skipped her run this morning. And she has like five meetings to go to. And she's still in bed and hasn't showered yet. And she has to figure out how to deal with all this today in addition to dodging Teddy Sharpe until she can piece together what the hell happened last night.

"So you never came to visit me on my birthday," Teddy had said at one point when they both were on their second glass. They'd somehow managed to keep the conversation light up until then.

"Yeah, well, you didn't tell me you had a girlfriend," Bennett had replied, meaning for it to sound breezy and playful.

It did not come out that way.

"Dude, I told you, she wasn't my girlfriend at the time! Technically."

"Yeah, well, technically *doesn't cut it.*"

It all went downhill after that. Bennett already acts like a moron when she's had too much to drink, so when emotionally unstable is thrown into the mix, it turns into a fiasco.

"*Did, uh—did you ever tell your family about what happened that weekend?*"

"*Why does that matter?*"

"*Because it does.*"

"*No, I didn't.*"

"*Why not?*"

"*They were already asking me so many questions about you, I figured telling them would only make it worse.*"

"*Probably better that way, I guess.*"

Bennett pulls the comforter up over her face and groans as more pieces of last night's conversation rush back to her. Teddy had asked, "*You want another?*" at least four times, and each time the conversation was steered into more dangerous territory.

"*Liz told me.*"

"*Liz is a terrible person.*"

"*At least she can keep her lies straight.*"

"*Hey, what the hell is that supposed to mean?*"

"*Nothing. It just means I don't wanna talk about what happened at the airport, all right? Stop bringing it up.*"

"*But I—*"

"*No.*"

"*Can we just—*"

"*Is this why you brought me down here?*"

"*No. Kind of. One of the reasons.*"

Bennett finally forces herself out of bed and into the shower. She doesn't have any Advil, and her headache only gets worse when she remembers that the subject of *feelings* had come up more than once last night, though most of what was said is still under review. If the knot in her stomach is any indication, she probably said some things that will land her in a compromising position sooner rather than later.

Thus, the reason to dodge Teddy Sharpe like it's her day job.

"I'm not drunk."

"Me neither."

"Bullshit."

"I want to finish this conversation, though."

"Well, we need to go before they kick us out."

At least today's going to keep her busy. She has three table-reads to attend (that don't involve the leads), a final production meeting, and a sit-down with Burt and Olivia, so there's a solid, solid chance her and Teddy's schedules won't overlap at all in the next twenty-four hours. The only possibility she has to worry about is running into him at the hotel. . . .

Bennett stands in front of her tiny little hotel room closet and contemplates if it's going to be a leggings day or a jeans day. She needs caffeine. And twenty-seven Gatorades.

"You didn't have to walk me back to my room, you weirdo."

"Don't try to act like you didn't want me to."

"Yeah, well—don't try to act like that's a line that's gonna get you inside."

Plus, the reality that she let herself drink enough last night to entertain the idea of letting Teddy into her room after the bar . . . well. Let's just say the moral hangover is worse than the physical one.

Half an hour later, Bennett's in her car heading to set. (It's definitely a leggings day.) Her first meeting is at nine thirty, and it's one she can probably coast through unnoticed. She shows up a few minutes early with wet hair and a latte, and she's just about to pull the meetings trailer door open when her phone goes off.

Her personal phone.

It's silly for her to tense the way she does, particularly since, as he pointed out multiple times last night, Teddy has both of her numbers now. (He admitted to getting her work number off Burt yesterday.) The good news is the person calling her personal phone is Will.

"You're up early," Bennett answers in lieu of a greeting.

"Bennett! What's up?"

Naturally, the McGearys finding out about the movie turned out to be just as much of a disaster as Bennett had expected. Liz did some online digging after seeing Teddy that weekend and pieced it together on her own. Three of the four McGearys pretended to be "so hurt" that Bennett kept it from them. Will, on the other hand, was so happy for Bennett he cried. Since then, he and Bennett have spoken a few times a week about how everything's going.

"About to go into a production meeting," Bennett says, switching the phone to her left hand so she can untwist one of her backpack straps. "What're you doing?"

"Just at school. I have an early study hall on Thursdays. I was calling because I thought shooting started today and was going to wish you luck! But I definitely got the days mixed up, didn't I."

Bennett grins and tells him they start tomorrow. Then she gives a rundown of the past three days and what the schedule is supposed to be like for shooting. She does not say anything about Teddy. And Will—bless him—never brings him up, despite how much she knows he wants to.

"Olivia Katsaros is the lead, right?" Will asks.

"Yeah."

"She'll kill it. She's killed it in everything she's done so far. I actually can't believe this is her first franchise—someone should've picked her up years ago."

Out of the corner of her eye, Bennett sees a couple of producers heading her way.

"Hey, Will—lemme give you a call later. I gotta go into this meeting," she says.

"Word. Call me when you can."

They hang up and Bennett heads inside the meetings trailer, reminding herself again to sort out a good time to have Will come visit set. She's had this idea since he told her over Christmas that Liz signed herself up for the same acting workshops he's been taking for the past three years. Will is stuck surrounded by semi-unsupportive parents and a sister who's made it her life's mission to personally steal any spotlight that might point in his direction. Setting up a day on set is the least Bennett can do.

The rest of the day passes in a blur once production meetings start. It's a lot of tying up loose ends and making sure everyone knows where they need to be tomorrow morning. Bennett wonders if Burt's drinking coffee or rocket fuel out of the thermos he carries around, because the dude is a force of nature today. Just watching him makes Bennett feel even more tired than she already is. By the time he and Bennett sit down with Olivia later that afternoon to discuss how Olivia wants to portray Katherine, Burt's so jittery he might jet pack out of his chair, and Bennett's so tired she might fall off hers.

Olivia Katsaros is not what Bennett had been expecting, and she feels guilty for jumping the first-impression gun. Olivia's incredibly educated on the acting techniques she wants to bring in, and she's unwavering on making Katherine's character as robust as she reads in the books. Olivia's so passionate it's hard to disagree with her. Even for Burt. They all end up walking out of the meetings trailer in agreement with everything Olivia suggested, and Bennett one-eighties from worrying that Olivia was wrong for the part.

So when Bennett finally does crawl into bed later that night, she lies there for a minute and takes a moment to appreciate the exhausted satisfaction she feels from a productive day (despite the hangover). She's strangely calm—even with the few anxious butterflies she has floating around inside her rib cage— and she doesn't initially panic when she sees a text message from Teddy pop up on her work phone.

Thurs, Jan 17, 11:03 p.m.

> FIRST DAY OF FILMING TOMORROW. GET EXCITED. 🎬

Bennett doesn't respond.

She didn't have much time today to piece together more of what was said between her and Teddy over illegal champagne last night, but she remembers enough to remind herself that she still needs to keep some perspective here. Teddy fell right back into the role of the guy Bennett had difficulty breathing around in July—back when it took him less than seventy-two hours to get enough of a grip on her heart to absolutely shatter it.

"Fuck you—I don't still have feelings for you."

"Then why are you smiling like that, Caldwell?"

Imagine what he could do in two months?

* * *

The atmosphere on set the next day feels a lot like the first day of school, if the first day of school were also the Super Bowl and held on New Year's Eve.

Bennett and Emmy arrive half an hour before anything is supposed to start, and it almost feels like they're late. Production assistants are flying around, bouncing off one another and calling out orders using set jargon Bennett doesn't understand. Crewmembers are running through lighting cues and sound checks and equipment logging. And Burt is standing at the helm of it all, looking every inch a movie director in his ball cap and Ray-Bans.

Bennett is a little overwhelmed as she blindly follows Emmy over to one of the PA tables to put their bags down. She pulls out her copy of the script for something to do, making sure none of her sticky notes were dislodged or lost, and of course Teddy is the first person she sees when she turns back to face the set. He's with a few other actors in a cluster of director's chairs about thirty feet away. His elbows are propped up on his knees with his own script open in his hands, and even though he's bent over the pages in front of him, his head is up, his neck is craned, and he's looking right at Bennett.

Bennett watches Olivia tug playfully on Teddy's sleeve when he stands. (She can't do anything about the pang of insecurity it brings on, either—she's only human.) Olivia laughs at whatever Teddy says when he puts his script down in the seat of his director's chair, but her smile wanes in confusion when he turns and sets off across set.

Meanwhile, Bennett resists the urge to use Emmy as shield, because Teddy is heading straight for them and Bennett apparently has the emotional maturity of a six-year-old.

"Ladies," Teddy says, sauntering right up to them like the

ridiculous person that he is. He stops just close enough in front of Bennett to make her accidentally take a step backward into the PA table.

"Morning, Teddy," Emmy says brightly. "Doin' all right?"

He jerks his jacket zipper up and down a few times and says, "Doin' well, thank you. A little cracked out on caffeine, but doing well. You?"

Emmy laughs. "I know what you mean. Bennett and I stopped for coffee this morning and we both finished our lattes before we got here."

Bennett should have contributed something to the conversation by now, but every time she opens her mouth nothing comes out.

"Yeah, Caldwell and I had a big night the other night—I feel like I'm still recovering," Teddy says, giving Bennett a lazy smile. Bennett wants to ask him if it gets exhausting, being this extra.

Emmy throws a smug glance between them. "I heard."

A PA appears and tells Teddy he's needed in makeup.

"Okay—I'll see you two later," he says, letting himself be steered away to one of the standby stations. He throws one last grin over his shoulder and waves, and Bennett's hand swings back to her side before she even registers making the decision to wave back.

Emmy sighs and covers the bottom half of her face with her iPad. "He's so cute."

"Not helping," Bennett mutters, walking away. Burt told her he wants her behind the camera with him today to get a feel for how shooting works, and Bennett plans on taking cover there until someone tells her to move.

Twenty minutes later, Burt's on the bullhorn announcing

for everyone to get to their places, and Teddy and Olivia are running through blocking one last time before the camera rolls, and Bennett might be sweating through her shirt. The scene Burt chose to film first is supposed to be a quick, easy scene to get everyone back into the ebbs and flows of a movie set, but just because it's quick and easy doesn't mean it feels that way. It actually feels like sensory overload pandemonium. Especially when Burt takes his seat behind the camera and jokingly tells Bennett to "gird her loins."

There's a dramatic, collective pause right before Burt calls action when the entire cast and crew stills, almost like they're taking a moment of silence for the last few seconds of normalcy before their lives become nothing but *this* for the next eight weeks. The energy crackles across set in the quiet. The excitement is raw. And the importance of it all is intimidating as hell.

"And—*action*."

The scene plays out almost identically to how Bennett pictured it when she and Burt wrote it into the script. It's just some casual dialogue between a few secondary characters in front of a green screen, but as Burt works with the production team to get the best angles and shots, Bennett finds herself at a loss for words for the second time that morning.

This is, without a doubt, the coolest thing she's ever seen.

"Are you still breathing? I can't tell," Burt leans over and says after who knows how long. Bennett thinks she nods. Hopefully.

Burt calls cut at the end of the scene and the set breaks into a frenzy. PAs run around offering people water. A makeup artist yells about not having enough translucent setting powder. Burt gets swept away by at least five crewmembers. Even parts of the set are in the process of being changed out, and Bennett doesn't understand how all this chaos lasts for only thirty seconds before coming to a halt as quickly as it started.

Burt calls action again.

Teddy walks into the frame on the camera monitor in front of Bennett, his entire demeanor changed.

Bennett did her research on Teddy the week before his audition (which, in retrospect, makes her feel exceptionally creepy), so she thought she had at least a decent idea of what to expect coming into this. She marathoned his show, watched his movies, worked her way through an embarrassing number of YouTube interviews . . . and now, two minutes into filming his first *Parachutes* scene, Bennett realizes she could not have been less prepared.

Watching Teddy act on TV and in movies was one thing. Watching him act in real life is entirely different. At one point Bennett actually sits up and leans around the camera to see it happening live, and it goes without saying that despite all the drama and bullshit over the past five months, it was hands-down one of the best decisions of preproduction to cast Teddy Sharpe in this movie.

Bennett catches Teddy's eye in the middle of a decently long monologue. He doesn't even miss a syllable before glancing away.

CHAPTER EIGHTEEN

The first three days of filming are so chaotic it's like the movie is operating on its own space-time continuum. A fifteen-hour day on set feels like it passes in thirty minutes, and for every shot they get, ten more spring up in the queue. How is it mathematically possible for films to be created in such a small window? How do people have time to sleep and eat and not die?

By the end of the fourth day, Bennett is convinced her internal clock isn't cut out for life in the industry. Burt made a set rule that he'll always call for an early wrap the Monday after a weekend shoot, and Bennett almost cried when she saw the seven p.m. wrap time on the schedule this morning.

Emmy left set after lunch today to finalize some things for the book signing here in a few weeks. She took Bennett's car back to the hotel and promised to pick her up on set at seven p.m. sharp, which seemed like a solid plan until filming wrapped for the day at six thirty.

As the set is clearing out, Bennett tries to drag out a conversation with Burt about the scenes they shot today, but after about three minutes he gets distracted by one of the producers and cuts the conversation short. Thinking she can at least hide out in the cafeteria warehouse until Emmy comes to get her,

Bennett heads off toward the set door as fast as she can with-out looking conspicuous.

She almost makes it, too.

"You're not avoiding me, are you?" Teddy asks, jumping out of nowhere and blocking her escape route. Like, there's an actual hop-skip and some bouncing involved.

Bennett skids to a halt and says, "Nope," because yep, that's exactly what she's doing. It's a miracle she made it through the weekend, honestly—what with all the random texts from him that went unanswered and the attempts to chat her up between takes on set. Bennett's proud of her acquired talent for looking busy when everyone knows she doesn't actually serve a purpose on set. It helps keep her sane—helps her avoid situations like this.

Teddy raises an eyebrow when Bennett starts past him. His fingers wrap around her arm, right below her elbow, and stop her from getting too far away. The shock of it has Bennett angling back toward him without thinking, and he brushes his hand all the way down her forearm until his fingertips press into her palm. Which—not acceptable.

"Hey, you sure about that?" he asks.

Bennett glances down at their hands, like, four times before her brain finally figures out what to do about this. She isn't sure if it's the way he's running a thumb over her knuckles or the look in his eye, but she ends up pulling her hand away and blurting out, "Maybe a little."

Teddy laughs and studies her for a moment, taking a half step into her space. Which, again—not acceptable.

"Okay, so I know you're maybe avoiding me a little and stuff, but I feel like I haven't seen you in days." He leans in just a frac-tion closer and says, "Wanted to see if you had any interest in finishing that conversation we started Thursday?"

No. There is no interest.

"I mean, from what I can remember, we touched on some key points that definitely need some follow-up," he says lightly, and he *would* be smug about this while Bennett's trying so hard to keep herself upright. She can't even think of something sarcastic and safe to say back, because now she's got it in her head that it's likely Teddy remembers more about that night than she does.

"So what do you think?" Teddy asks, jerking his head toward the exit door. "I heard there's a restaurant, like, five minutes from our hotel that's supposed to be good. Are you hungry?"

"Er—I'm fine," Bennett stammers out, because *nope*. "Emmy's picking me up."

Needless to say, Teddy sees straight through that poor attempt of an excuse. He digs into his pocket and pulls out his phone, tapping the screen a few times.

"What're you doing?" Bennett asks when he presses it to his ear.

He ignores her.

"Hey, Emmy? Yeah—it's Teddy."

Bennett lunges at him.

"Yeah," he laughs, leaning away to keep his phone out of reach. "Hey, have you left the hotel yet?"

Bennett's mouth drops open and she lunges again. This time, though, Teddy gets ahold of her shoulder and spins her around, crossing a forearm over her sternum and pinning her back against him. Bennett stamps on his foot.

"Yeah, don't worry, I'll give her a ride back—*ow!*" Teddy howls, half laughing, half cringing. He finally lets go, but by then he's off the phone and glaring at her. "That was so uncalled for, Caldwell."

"And canceling my ride wasn't?" she asks, more irritated by the smile trying to creep across her face than the actual context of the situation.

"Hey, you gotta do what you gotta do when people are avoiding you."

Bennett scoffs. "Cool rhyme."

Teddy grins. "Yeah. Thought you might like that."

* * *

So this is apparently how Bennett's life is going to be now—a random assortment of pop-up moments of Teddy Sharpe that leave her wondering if she's always been this pathetically tractable when a hot guy gives her attention, or if it's just specific to tall, lanky, and infuriatingly endearing ones.

"The dealership just *gave* you this for the next two months?" she asks skeptically as Teddy drives them to dinner.

"Yeah, my manager set it up for me." He shrugs. And he looks damn good doing it in the driver's seat of his fancy new car. Bennett wants to throw herself out. "The dealership probably wants me to be seen in it or something."

He turns on the radio, settling on a station playing an Allman Brothers song.

"I found this station the other day when I was driving to set," he says, pulling his hand back and splaying it on the center console. "It's not as good as the one you guys listen to on the lake, but it's not bad."

"Where are we going?" Bennett asks, staring through the windshield. She will not allow the conversation anywhere near that weekend on the lake. She's had no time to prepare.

"This cool seafood spot a PA told me about. I got takeout from there for lunch yesterday," he says, then steals a nervous glance at her. "Shit, I didn't even ask if you like seafood. We can go somewhere else if you don't—"

"It's fine, Teddy."

Ten minutes later, a hostess shows them to their table, and Bennett busies herself with a menu as soon as they're seated. It's better than focusing on how stupidly intimate the atmosphere is at this restaurant. The few people around them are talking too softly; there are too many Edison-style light bulbs hanging from the ceiling; and there's too much of *something* charging the mood lighting around their table. There should be health code regulations against making guests feel this romantically victimized.

"Hell yes." Teddy fist pumps. He points to something on the menu and says, "We have to get this shrimp appetizer. It's amazing."

Bennett waits until after the waitress has left with their drink and appetizer orders to ask, "So, was this a spur-of-the-moment kidnapping, or premeditated?"

He laughs. "There might have been a little premeditation involved, yeah. You've been actively avoiding me, Caldwell, remember?"

"Actively avoiding is a stretch," she says.

"Bullshit. And don't try to tell me to not flatter myself, either."

Bennett shrugs. "Not my fault we've had different schedules."

"True," he says thoughtfully. "You're not getting producing credits for this movie, are you?"

"No? Why would I?"

Teddy sips his water. "I mean, with all the production meetings you go to and the work you did on adapting the script and, like, how involved Burt has you . . . it seems like you do just as much work and maybe even have more influence than some of the producers."

Bennett raises an eyebrow. "Keeping tabs on me?"

Teddy eyes her for a moment, pressing his tongue to the inside of his cheek. Then he leans forward, rests his elbow on the table, and says, "Don't flatter yourself, superstar." And he looks so pleased with himself that Bennett has to smile.

The waitress comes back a few minutes later with an elaborate-looking appetizer plate. There are four different kinds of dipping sauces surrounded by enough shrimp to feed the world's hungry. Teddy looks like this is all he really needs in life.

"Oh my *God*," he groans, popping two shrimp in his mouth and reaching for a third. "My mom would be so distraught I didn't offer you some first, but I'm kind of an ill-mannered barbarian when seafood is involved. Don't let it gross you out."

"Ill-mannered barbarian is redundant," Bennett says, and Teddy snorts into his water glass. "What's your mom like?"

"Literally the best person on the planet. Same with my dad. And my younger sister, Amanda, most of the time," he tells her. "Speaking of—how's your family?"

"Everyone's good. Tanner's freaking out about graduation. My parents are pretending they're not freaking out, too. The usual."

"What about Will?"

Bennett grins. "He's losing his mind over the movie."

"We should for sure hook him up with a set visit," Teddy says through a mouthful of shrimp. Bennett wants to smush his face.

"Working on it," she says instead.

"How did the rest of the McGearys take the news?"

Bennett thinks of Liz and how she always manages to make everything big to happen in Bennett's life about herself. "They . . . were surprised."

Teddy stops eating. "Don't tell me Liz pulled some more shitty stunts. I'll break a bitch in half—"

That startles a genuine laugh out of Bennett.

If by "shitty stunts" he means Internet stalking all the actors cast in the *Parachutes* movie and constantly giving Bennett updates about one in particular, then yeah—she's pulled some more shitty stunts. It wasn't enough that Bennett already had to deal with Teddy blowing up her phone in the fall. She also had Liz's constant stream of texts asking how she's "holding up" when she pieced together more about the result of that weekend than Bennett wanted to let on. She even had the nerve to tell Bennett she knew Teddy had a girlfriend when he was there in July, and she was trying to do Bennett a favor by not saying anything, since she "didn't want Bennett to get hurt."

Liz and her fucking favors.

Bennett doesn't have the emotional funds available at the moment to handle talking about Liz while she knows Teddy's biding his time before he brings up Thursday again, so she reaches for a shrimp and asks which dipping sauce is his favorite.

Teddy's eyes light up.

"Try this one." He points to the one that sorta looks like honey, which freaks Bennett out a little.

"Not bad," she says, wiping her mouth with a napkin.

Teddy's eaten almost half the plate by the time Bennett tries out the other three. One of the sauces is spicier than she anticipated, and even after chugging most of her water, it's still tickling the back of her throat.

"Caldwell, you good?"

Bennett coughs, pushing her hair back from her face. "Yeah—that last one was just a little hotter than I thought."

But there must have been some spice or something left on her fingers, because it feels like she'd gotten some near her eye when she pushed her hair back. She picks up her napkin and dabs at the spot just below her tear duct. As soon as she makes contact, it's like someone has thrown itching powder in her face.

And she's still coughing.

And her heart's starting to race.

"Seriously Bennett, are you okay?"

The concern flickering across Teddy's face is what ultimately reminds Bennett of what an idiot she is. Panic slams into her a half second later—which, as her doctor told her when she was eight years old, is something she needs to avoid at all costs during an allergic reaction. God. Bennett's usually so careful about what she eats at restaurants, too. How the hell did she let herself get distracted enough to forget to check ingredients?

Bennett can feel her eyes and tongue already starting to swell, and she knows her throat's on deck. Panic, in its purest form, is settling in for the show now.

Teddy curses and jumps up suddenly, almost tackling one of the waiters walking by.

"Are there tree nuts in these sauces?" he demands, pointing back at their table. Bennett laughs, even as she thumbs at the hives popping up on her neck. Her left eye is almost swollen shut and Teddy still needs to ask if tree nuts are in the food?

She catches something the waiter says to Teddy about spiced walnut shavings, and yep—that'll do it.

"We need to go," she says as calmly as she can. This does

not need to be made into a scene. Of course, by now her right eye has almost caught up with her left. She can only imagine what she looks like. There's a gasp from somewhere to her right, and a hand hooks around her arm a second later.

"Do you have an EpiPen?" Teddy asks, helping her stand.

"Er—no," Bennett admits as he leads her through the tables (and all the people who are probably staring).

"Are you kidding me? You're this allergic to something and you don't carry an EpiPen?" Teddy snaps, and no, Bennett does not need that attitude right now. She wants to snap back at him that she hasn't had an allergic reaction in years, but it sounds like he might be panicking more than she is, so she lets it slide. She also doesn't mention she's supposed to avoid anything that increases her heart rate during anaphylaxis, and that he either needs to move the hand he has splayed across her rib cage or stop lacing and relacing their fingers together. Something.

"Are you breathing okay?"

His mouth this close to her ear isn't helping, either.

"Yeah," she says, but it probably won't be the case much longer. "Did you ask the restaurant if they've got an EpiPen?"

"No. We're going to the hospital."

The abrupt change in temperature is the only way Bennett knows they aren't inside the restaurant anymore, reminding her that her jacket and bag are still on the back of her chair.

"Shit—I left my stuff inside," she says. She hears a car door open and Teddy starts shoving her into the passenger's seat. Then, after he buckles her seat belt for her, she feels her bag slide into her lap.

"No, you didn't."

* * *

Bennett tries to tell Teddy it's unnecessary to take her to the hospital—that all they need to do is find a drugstore that stockpiles Benadryl.

Teddy doesn't listen to her.

And as it turns out, it's probably a good thing he doesn't, regardless of the three wrecks they almost get into on the way there. The ER doctor says Bennett had been well on her way to anaphylactic shock, and had they arrived a few minutes later, it might have been a lot worse. He also tells her, after hooking her up to an IV, that he'd like her to stay at the hospital overnight to monitor her reaction as a precaution.

Bennett tells him there's no way in hell that's happening.

"Seriously—I'm fine now," she argues. "The swelling and the hives are almost gone, and it's not like y'all haven't pumped me full of antihistamines and epinephrine and shit to last me into next year."

"It's just a precaution," he repeats for the third time.

"But this is ridiculous. I've never had to stay in the hospital because of a reaction!"

"Based on the severity of your reaction, you'll probably be asleep in a few minutes anyway, now that the adrenaline is wearing off," the doctor says, undeterred by her hostility. Which only agitates Bennett more. She isn't about to admit it, but she can already feel her eyelids drooping.

"Fuck that," she says. "Actually—fuck *this*. I'm leaving."

Teddy slides a hand over her shoulder to keep her from getting up. "Bennett . . . it's already late. You need to stay and get some sleep."

Bennett still isn't sure how Buzz Lightyear over here sweet-talked his way into the family-only area of the ER, but it's infuriating.

"How the hell are you in here, anyway?" she snaps.

"Irritability is a side effect of adrenaline wearing off," the doctor comments, and Bennett wants to tell him it's also a side effect of being surrounded by assholes. Lying back on the hospital bed and shutting her eyes for a second seems like a better plan, though.

"Whatever. I'll sleep for an hour and then I'm going home."

CHAPTER NINETEEN

Bennett told Teddy multiple times to wake her up after an hour, so she's more than a little irritated when she wakes up on her own and he's asleep in the armchair next to her bed. She does a sweep of the hospital room before finding her phone on the bedside table.

She has thirteen missed calls and twenty-three new text messages.

"Holy—" She looks back at Teddy curled up in the corner, his mouth hanging slightly open, and the window behind him catches her attention. The curtains are half closed, but daylight is streaming in through the slits in the blinds. Panicked, she checks her phone again.

9:23
Tuesday, January 22

Teddy and Bennett had definitely gone to dinner on a Monday. Bennett had definitely had an allergic reaction on a Monday. She had definitely fallen asleep in a hospital bed on a Monday. And they were definitely supposed to be on set two hours ago.

"Are you kidding me?" she hisses, ripping the covers back and jumping out of bed.

This turns out to be a horrible idea.

Bennett is standing for about two seconds before dizziness pours over her, making the edges of her vision go black. She reaches out to grab the first thing she can find to steady herself—which ends up being the IV pole stand. Another horrible idea. It wheels forward as soon as she puts her weight into it, and she's caught so off-balance she can do nothing but look on helplessly as she stumbles forward. She smacks into something hard and there's a pinch in the crease of her elbow. She squeezes her eyes shut as the IV pole crashes to the floor.

Everything is quiet then, and despite not knowing how she ended up on the ground, Bennett is pleasantly surprised to find that whatever she ran into didn't hurt as much as it should have. The downside is the scene she made attracts some unwanted attention from across the room. She doesn't understand how Teddy got over to her so fast, and she definitely doesn't understand why he's shaking her and yelling her name so much. It isn't helping how sick she's starting to feel.

"Holy shit, Bennett! Are you okay?"

He says something else but it's too muffled by the ringing in her ears to hear. Bennett groans and rolls over onto her stomach, pressing her cheek into the floor. The tile is cold enough to keep the waves of nausea somewhat under control. Now if she could just get Teddy to leave her alone.

"Bennett? *Bennett*, look at me!"

He sounds so frantic. Why does he sound so frantic?

A hand slides over Bennett's forehead—a gesture that probably would be nice under different circumstances. But everything is too warm. And Bennett is way too close to puking.

"No," she breathes, cringing away from him. "Go away."

"Oh, shit, you're blee—hey, excuse me!" Teddy calls out and pushes away from Bennett. Not having his body heat pressed to her back ultimately keeps her from throwing up. "Yeah, my girlfriend needs help—we need a nurse in here!"

Girlfriend . . . wait a minute.

What.

Bennett doesn't have time to start freaking the hell out over that; the sound of footsteps hurrying into the room is too distracting.

"Oh my—sweetheart, are you okay? Did you hit your head?" a new voice asks.

"I'm fine," Bennett says, her voice cracking as she tries again to push away the closest person. Two sets of hands are now trying to get her to roll back over and sit up, and Bennett is not cool with that. "But I'm gonna be sick if you guys don't stop touching me."

The hands disappear, but Bennett can still feel them hovering.

"Sweetie, what happened?"

"Got up too fast."

"Why were you getting out of bed? Did you need to use the restroom?"

"Jesus," Bennett mutters, finally opening her eyes and shifting onto her back. Some nurse and Teddy are looking down at her—one with a little too much sympathy, the other with a little too much concern. "No. I got up because this dude"—she points a thumb at Teddy—"didn't wake me up, and we're two hours late to set."

"You needed to sleep, you almost went into anaphylactic

shock last night!" Teddy says, just as pieces of the conversation the night before with the ER doctor start coming back. . . . Including the colorful strain of profanity she used when told she had to stay overnight.

"Yikes. I was a delight to be around last night," she mumbles.

"You're okay," the nurse assures her. "You're not the first person to get like that when the adrenaline starts to wear off, and you certainly weren't the worst we've seen."

The nurse and Teddy give Bennett some space as she sits up, and they both stay quiet while she tries to gauge if she's going to be sick.

"Feeling okay?" the nurse asks. "Think you can stand and get back into bed?"

Bennett nods, and the nurse and Teddy take her by the elbows to keep her steady. That's when she realizes how sweaty she is.

"What the—ew, sorry," she grumbles, trying to pull away. They both tighten their grips.

"Not your fault. Just your body's natural reaction to passing out."

Bennett sits down on the edge of the bed. That's not right— she lost her balance and fell. Afraid they might keep her in the ER longer because of it, Bennett explains to the nurse what happened as the nurse digs into one of the bedside table drawers.

"Um. Bennett?" Teddy says, looking at her like she'd spoken a different language. "Bennett, you were out cold for at least ten seconds."

"What?"

He nods. "Yeah. Scared the absolute shit out of me, too."

"There's no way—" Bennett starts, only to be interrupted by

the nurse coming in close with a piece of gauze in her hand. She dabs at a spot above Bennett's eyebrow and a bolt of pain shoots across the crown of her head. Bennett curses so loudly the entire hospital probably hears her.

"Sorry, sweetie," the nurse says. "Looks like you've got quite the spot there. Do you know what you hit your head on?"

"Not sure," Bennett says, gripping the back of her neck.

After the nurse is done with the gauze, she shines a flashlight in both of Bennett's eyes and checks the rest of her vitals. Teddy hovers nervously in the background, his eyes searching Bennett's. She isn't exactly sure what he's looking for, but it's getting a little too intense for her.

Bennett points at him and smirks. "This is your fault."

Teddy stays unnervingly still. Like, he doesn't even blink.

"I know," he says.

Teddy can't stay still to save his life.

"I was kidding," Bennett backpedals.

He digs a hand into his pocket and halfway turns toward the window as he checks his phone, hiding whatever look is on his face. Bennett can't decide if she's annoyed or worried by how he's acting, and the nurse caps off the awkwardness by smoothing a ginormous bandage over the spot above Bennett's eyebrow. She goes on to explain the check-out procedures, mentioning that Bennett needs to wait for clearance from the ER doctor before she will get her release paperwork.

"I do hope you feel better, sweetie," the nurse says; then she turns to Teddy and smiles fondly at him. "That was so sweet of you to stay here with your girlfriend all night. Good luck with the rest of shooting your movie—I know my girls can't wait to see it."

Teddy blushes heroically and thanks her.

Bennett watches him, waiting for the nurse to leave them

alone with all the awkwardness building up between them. As soon as she's out of the room, Bennett opens her mouth to ask Teddy what's wrong, but he beats her to the punch.

"So, I, uh—I called Emmy after you fell asleep last night," he says, standing over by the armchair again. Eyes on the floor. "She called your parents and then your parents called me and—yeah. That's why you probably have a million messages on your phone. I told them you were fine but that you're in the ER. And your mom wanted to know if you had your insurance card, so I had to go through your wallet . . ." He trails off with a nervous shrug, scrubbing a hand at the back of his head. His go-to tell.

"What's wrong," Bennett says.

"What?"

"You're acting weird."

"I'm good," he says, starting for the door. "But, yeah. Last time I talked to your parents was at, like, eleven o'clock last night, and they asked me to tell you to call them as soon as you woke up. So, yeah. I'm gonna go find some coffee while you talk to the ER doctor." He keeps his eyes down as he all but speed walks out of the room, stuffing his hands into his pockets along the way.

Bennett spends the next hour and a half stressed the hell out about what is going on.

After reassuring phone calls to her parents and Emmy, follow-up procedures and a crazy amount of paperwork, Bennett rides shotgun as Teddy drives them back to the hotel.

In dead silence.

Like, the radio isn't even on.

Something must have happened last night. Bennett has no idea what . . . but it had to have been last night. Teddy had been so sweet, though—grabbing Bennett's jacket and bag for her and buckling her seat belt . . . Constantly asking about her breathing . . . Promising not to crack any jokes about how swollen her face got. (He did make one about a scene from the movie *Hitch*, but swore he was done after that.) And once they'd gotten to the hospital, he somehow convinced the staff that he was her boyfriend so he could stay with her overnight . . . Wait a second.

Is that why he's being weird? Bennett stares out the window at a line of palm trees whizzing by, anxiety rolling through her stomach. She didn't ask him to do that—to pretend to be her boyfriend so he could go back in the ER with her (which doesn't even make sense, since it's supposed to be family only). Maybe he's worried about how she'd react? Because that'd totally be something Teddy Sharpe would worry about. He's a subclass of boy so atypical *National Geographic* should give him a cover story.

By the time they pull up to the hotel, Bennett's worked herself up so much she doesn't immediately register Teddy bypassing the parking lot for the portico. He drives under the awning and pulls to the curb, keeping the car in drive. They sit in silence for a moment, with Bennett waiting to see if he has anything he wants to share with the class.

He doesn't.

"Are you heading to set now?" Bennett asks—which is dumb, considering he's still in his clothes from last night and probably hasn't eaten anything since.

"No, I'm gonna shower first. Thought I'd drop you off before I parked so you'd have less of a walk."

Bennett narrows her eyes at him and considers the two possibilities here: He's either being overly considerate, or he's hiding something behind being overly considerate. Bennett's heart wants to believe the former. Her gut's telling her she's being an idiot.

"Yeah. That would've been an awful fifty extra feet to walk," she says, prodding for some kind of reaction. He keeps his face straight and his gaze through the windshield, which only pisses her off more. "Welp, thanks for the ride, Buzz," she says as she wrenches the car door open. Against her better judgment, she turns around and leans back through the doorframe, adding, "And for pretending to be my boyfriend all night."

"Anytime," he says to the windshield, biting his knuckle. "I'm, uh—" He clears his throat. "I'm glad you're okay."

There's a tiny moment, a little window of opportunity that follows when their eyes meet, and it's the perfect time for one of them to say something. It'd be so easy. Bennett could gently say, *Hey, Teddy, for real. What's going on? You're freaking me out a little.* And then Teddy would respond with a truthful and detailed explanation for why he's been acting like a zombie all morning. And then they'd have a mature, adult conversation that eases the frustrated knot that's currently in the place of Bennett's heart.

But instead the moment passes.

Teddy pulls away, and Bennett somehow manages to make it through the lobby, on the elevator, off the elevator, and down the hall to Emmy's room before she can process how she's feeling about this.

"Holy *balls*, Emmy. I'm about to go out of my freaking mind," she says the second she keys in. "I—"

Olivia Katsaros is sitting at Emmy's desk in the far corner, stopping Bennett halfway through the doorframe.

"Oh my God, Bennett!" Emmy comes running out of the bathroom to hug her. When she pulls away, she takes Bennett's face in her hands and turns her head from side to side. "Are you okay? What happened? What's this?" Emmy pokes at the bandage over her eyebrow.

"Ow—Jesus, Emmy." Bennett winces. She has to smack her hand away to keep from smacking her assistant instead.

"Sorry!" Emmy takes a step back. "What happened there?"

"Long story," Bennett says, not wanting to get into it in front of Olivia. The less people who know about all this, the better. "Hey, Olivia."

"Oh, Bennett! So glad you're okay," Olivia says, crossing the room and pulling Bennett into an exceptionally unexpected hug. Olivia towers over her, so Bennett ends up being yanked face-first into her cleavage.

"Thanks." Bennett pulls back, trying to keep her smile sincere.

"Emmy told me what happened—I can't believe you had to spend the night in the hospital!"

"Yeah. It's not as bad as it sounds, though."

Emmy snorts. "Bennett, they don't keep you in the hospital overnight for the hell of it. Good thing Teddy was there to make sure you stayed. . . ." She trails off when Bennett shoots her a warning glance.

"So true—Teddy is such a sweetheart," Olivia says, plopping down on the bed.

Bennett ignores her and asks Emmy, "Why aren't y'all on set right now?"

"Burt gave us a long lunch today. I took your car to set this morning and Olivia needed a ride back, so here we are," she says, going to sit at her desk.

Meanwhile, Olivia is still going on about Teddy.

"—so talented. And such a cutie, too. You two are precious together."

"That's not like Burt at all," Bennett says suspiciously, trying to get Emmy to elaborate. Then Olivia's comment registers and Bennett turns toward her, adding, "Teddy and I are not together."

"Wait, really?" Olivia pouts. "That was the rumor floating around set today—must have heard wrong, then. Still, you guys would be so cute together."

"I'm sorry—*what*?"

Olivia's eyes go wide, and Bennett realizes her question came out harsher than she intended. But when Olivia doesn't say anything, Bennett turns to Emmy so fast her assistant actually flinches.

"A rumor?" Bennett repeats. "Floating around set?"

Emmy cuts right to the chase and starts talking ninety miles an hour. "Burt was irritated that you didn't show on set today without telling him, so I had to tell him the truth—which, you know, ultimately led to why Teddy wasn't on set, either . . . and I, I told him he was with you at the hospital."

"So?"

"So . . . there were a lot of people around." Her gaze drops to the floor again. "And, well, to the people who aren't familiar with the situation, the context of the conversation kind of hinted at you two, sort of—I don't know—being involved, somehow?"

Oh, God.

This *situation* is going to give Bennett heart problems before she makes it to her twenties. Emmy starts to apologize, but Bennett's not here for that.

"That's not your fault," she says, dragging a hand over the

side of her face and wincing when her fingers hit the bandage above her eyebrow. "I'm sorry I put you in that position in the first place. I should've called. Was Burt pissed?"

Neither Emmy nor Olivia respond, and Bennett takes in both of their expressions.

"Oh, God. What else?"

"On the contrary," Olivia says, looking like she wants to smile but isn't sure if it's appropriate. "Burt seemed pretty happy about it. Especially after he saw the pictures of you guys at the restaurant. We shot some scenes this morning, then he let us go and called a meeting with the marketing team."

Bennett's brain is rejecting this information. Surely she's hearing things.

"Bennett?" Emmy says. "B, what's wrong? Are you okay?"

"Pictures?" Bennett repeats.

Emmy's eyes slowly close for a second, and that's all the confirmation Bennett needs.

"Yeah . . . " her assistant says, crossing her arms uncomfortably. "There are pictures of you and Teddy on Twitter at some restaurant?"

This is not happening.

And for some reason Olivia looks angry about it.

"God. I love my fans, but I hate it when people take pictures of celebrities without their knowledge or consent. *So* inconsiderate," she says.

"Someone took pictures of me and Teddy at the restaurant," Bennett says.

Emmy nods.

"And posted them on Twitter."

Emmy nods again. "And Instagram."

"Is Burt calling a marketing meeting to do damage control?"

Bennett asks, because she's naive and still hopes for the best from people.

It looks like it hurts when Emmy shakes her head.

Bennett's about to cry. She feels violated. And taken advantage of. And freaked the hell out that she had no clue someone was taking pictures last night.

"So what does that mean, then?" she asks.

Emmy sighs. "It means Burt's probably going to try to convince you to use whatever's going on between you and Teddy as a marketing angle for the movie."

"Is that a joke?" Bennett looks at Olivia, who shrugs, and then back to Emmy, who sighs again. "Are you serious?"

This is when Bennett gets confirmation that she's having an out-of-body experience or something, because Emmy says, "It might not be as bad as you think," and Bennett knows her assistant would never say that.

"How is this not as bad as I think?"

"Think about it, Bennett," Olivia says. Bennett almost tells her to stay out of it. "You've got the fan base. He's got the fan base. The movie's got the hype. . . . What's the harm in adding as much fuel to the fire as you can?"

"How about because it's not true?" Bennett snaps, eyes burning.

Olivia looks offensively unconvinced. "You sure about that? Because I've definitely noticed some stuff going on between you two since the first table-read. I mean, even if you guys aren't involved, would it really be such a bad thing to let people think you are?"

Bennett starts to say something completely unnecessary, catching herself at the last second. There's no point in lashing out at Olivia over this—it would only prove Bennett's upset because whatever rumor is floating around on set holds more truth than she's comfortable with. Which . . . it does . . . but definitely not enough for a damn marketing campaign.

Bennett needs to figure out how to squash this as quickly and as discreetly as possible.

"Hmm," she says instead of arguing or freaking out like she wants. She forces her shoulders to relax while she's at it. "That'll be an interesting conversation with Burt. I'm gonna go shower. When were y'all thinking about going back to set?"

"What—um." Olivia pauses, confusion flickering across her face. "Probably in like half an hour?"

"Cool. I'll ride back with you then," Bennett says, heading for the door.

She does not acknowledge the pitying look she gets from Emmy on her way out. She does not sink to the floor of the shower and put her head between her knees underneath the spray. And she does not think about the looming shit storm waiting for her on set.

CHAPTER TWENTY

It's raining by the time they get to set, and in true North Carolina fashion, the temperature is hovering somewhere in the forties—cold enough to make you miserable, but not cold enough to snow. Bennett has on two jackets under her raincoat, and her Bean Boots are so old they have worn-in holes in the sides that sop up half the puddles she steps in.

No one says anything on the drive over about the puffy red circles under Bennett's eyes. Emmy busies herself with what she says is new paperwork from Bennett's publisher. Olivia live-tweets Wilmington's shitty weather. And once again, Bennett is left alone with her thoughts, and once again, that has proved to be bad for her mental health. She goes back and forth for so long about who she's going to talk to first—Burt or Teddy—that the idea of talking to either of them starts to feel abstract.

Bennett hums into the rain and glances off toward the cast trailers as they cross through the parking lot. Her publisher arranged for her to have a writing trailer to use during downtime on set to finish *Off the Grid*—Bennett's only been inside a few times so far (it doesn't feel right that she has her own trailer) . . . but right now it's the only place on set that can give her some space to pull her thoughts together.

"Emmy, do you have your copy of the key to my trailer?" she asks.

Emmy tugs on the sides of her hood, then reaches into her raincoat pocket. "You trying to get some writing done this afternoon?" she asks, handing Bennett a key ring. "I can let Burt know for you."

"No, it's fine," Bennett says quickly. "I'm just gonna stop in there real quick and then find y'all on set."

Emmy gives her a questioning look.

"I'll catch up with you later," Bennett says, veering off across the parking lot.

Bennett just needs another minute or two to get her head on straight and decide how to approach this situation. If she talks to Teddy first, it'll give them the opportunity to get on the same page before telling Burt this marketing plan isn't going to happen. But if she talks to Burt first, maybe she can bypass getting Teddy involved altogether. . . .

Bennett wonders if Teddy already knows what's going on, if that's why he was acting so weird this morning. And if that's the case, it's bullshit he didn't give her a heads-up about it.

Now Bennett's leaning toward touching base with Teddy before she talks to Burt. It feels like it might give her some . . . what exactly? Comfort? Reassurance? Mental stability? Who knows. But hopefully he'll have her back on this. He's said before he likes to keep his personal life on the DL.

The rain upgrades itself from a steady drizzle to a complete downpour by the time Bennett gets to her trailer. Her fingers have stopped cooperating in the chill, so it takes her a second to get it unlocked. The inside is warm and just as sparsely decorated as Bennett had left it. (It reminds her of the inside of an

RV a family would take on vacation cross-country.) There are a few stray scripts scattered across the kitchen table. A vase of wilting flowers from her agent sits on the coffee table in front of the green pleather couch and matching armchair.

Shivering, Bennett shrugs out of her raincoat and the wet jacket underneath, slapping them both down onto the kitchen table. Then she pulls out her phone, and her stomach somersaults when she sees the text from Teddy sent seven minutes ago.

Tues, Jan 22, 1:56 p.m.

Where are you

Bennett frowns. Whoever said text messages can't portray emotions has clearly never tried to decipher the linguistic implications behind lack of punctuation usage.

My trailer

She tosses her phone onto the armchair after tapping send. It hits the surface just as two quick knocks come from outside the trailer door. It swings open a second later, and Bennett very literally almost falls back over the coffee table.

"Jesus—" She stumbles sideways and catches herself, splaying her other hand on her chest. When she glances back at the doorway, she doesn't need any punctuation—or lack thereof—to decipher the emotions written all over Teddy Sharpe's face. He's standing soaking wet in the doorway and looking like he's keeping it together but not for much longer, and Bennett does her best to stay calm.

"That was quick," she says.

He doesn't say anything.

So she doesn't say anything else.

After a moment, Teddy continues into the trailer, shedding his raincoat along the way. He drapes it onto the back of one of the kitchen chairs and walks right up into her space.

"Dude—what the hell is going on with you?" Bennett asks, holding up her hands and subtly taking a step back.

Teddy ignores her. "Do you believe me about the airport last summer?"

"What?"

"Do you—" He looks down at her and his face crumples for a second. "Look, I know we still haven't talked about this yet, but I gotta know right now, before all this shit blows up—is there a chance this is gonna happen again? You and me, for real this time? Even if I haven't fixed it all the way yet, are you gonna let me try?"

Bennett doesn't know what to do. She's lost feeling in her face.

And maybe it's because she's overwhelmed. Or the intensity behind the look in his eyes. Or that Bennett has always known, deep down, that what she thought happened at the airport back in July wasn't the full story, regardless of how much it had hurt to watch. . . . Whatever it is, it has her nodding at him helplessly before she realizes what she's doing.

Teddy's expression goes blank for about a second, and then he's closing the gap between them and backing Bennett into the trailer's fake wooden paneling. He braces one hand on the wall by her shoulder, bringing the other up to her neck and pressing his thumb underneath her chin to tilt her head back.

Bennett barely has time to think *Oh God, this is it—this is how it ends* before he crashes their lips together.

He kisses her hard and steady, with the type of conviction that leaves no room for misinterpretation. It's assertive and demanding and so terrifyingly honest that, despite knowing how bad the fallout could be, Bennett gives in to him instantly, sliding a hand around the nape of his neck and letting him press her back into the wall of her own trailer.

This. This is what Bennett's been so afraid of—the confirmation that no matter what she does, she's always going to get pulled right back in. Teddy's got his hands in her hair and his tongue in her mouth and there's exactly zero space left between them, and Bennett knows she's never going to recover.

It's embarrassing how audibly she sighs when he finds that spot on underneath her jaw that sets her off all the way down to her toes, and it's even more embarrassing when she feels him smile against her neck like he knows exactly what's he doing to her. He reaches down and wraps an arm tightly around the arch in her lower back, and Bennett might as well wrap her legs around his waist when he hoists her up, because it's not like she's going anywhere now that he officially has her pinned.

"Jesus," he mutters, dragging his lips over hers and moving his hands to the back of her thighs to support her. "You scared the absolute shit out of me this morning at the hospital. You know that?"

"I—what?" Bennett says, a little dazed and clutching the shirt fabric stretched over his collarbone.

"I woke up to a crash and you on the ground. Don't ever do that to me again."

"Is that why you were acting so weird?" she breathes.

Teddy kisses her again, slower this time, then pulls back just enough to lean his forehead against hers, away from the bandage above her eyebrow. "You believe me about the airport, right?" he asks instead, just as he finds that spot on her neck again.

And yeah, Bennett does.

"That text you sent me explaining it—was it all true?" she asks, trying so hard to concentrate on what she's saying and not on the way his teeth are grazing over her skin.

Teddy pulls back again and looks her in the eye, nodding frantically. "Every bit of it. God, I'm so sorry. I had no idea she was coming and I—"

"Then yes, I believe you," Bennett cuts him off. She's terrified of the repercussions that come with second chances, but now that she's openly acknowledging how much she's missed him since July, she might as well own up to it face-to-face.

"I—"

There's another knock on the door, then the sound of the pouring rain outside is suddenly louder and the moment Bennett realizes it's because the trailer door is opening, she forces her feet to the ground and pushes Teddy away so hard he stumbles backward and has to catch himself on one of the kitchen table chairs.

"*Shit*—"

"Hey, Burt." Bennett panics. She smooths her hair and crosses her arms over her chest as she leans back against the wooden paneling again. She's aiming for nonchalance, but she knows she's flushed and her lips are swollen and she might as well be screaming that she and Teddy were just making out against the trailer wall. Thankfully Teddy's far enough away now that it at least eliminates some level of suspicion, even if Bennett had to shove him.

Burt's head whips up like he'd been expecting her trailer to be empty.

"Hey, Bennett," he says. His gaze shifts and he grins. "And Teddy. Exactly the two people I was looking to catch before I left." He takes his raincoat off and shakes out his umbrella as he wades deeper into the trailer. "I apologize—I didn't think you'd be in here. I came to get those extra scripts from the production meeting the other day."

"Oh. They're right there," Bennett says, pointing at the kitchen table. She isn't sure what to do now, but she's positive she's being awkward about it.

"You're heading out for the day, Burt?" Teddy asks. He's sitting in the kitchen chair Bennett practically shoved him into, looking casual as ever and not like he had Bennett's legs wrapped around his waist ten seconds ago. Bennett blushes hard just thinking about it.

"We can't get any more filming done because of the rain. I sent everyone home early," Burt says, then looks directly at Bennett. "Sit down, will ya? I want to talk with both of you."

Bennett pushes away from the wall and chooses to sit on the couch instead of at the kitchen table with Teddy. Burt eyes the space between them before sitting down in the armchair in the corner.

"Sorry about the rain, man," Teddy says after an awkward pause.

Bennett almost laughs at him.

"All good. And I'm glad to see you're feeling better, Bennett, though that spot on your forehead looks like it hurts," Burt says. "Good thing Teddy was there to make sure you were taken care of."

Jesus—is he serious with that wording?

"Yeah," Bennett says dryly. *"Samesies."*

"Teddy filled me in on some of the details—you should really carry an EpiPen if you're that allergic to something."

"Agreed," she says, and what she means is, she could really do without the condescending lecture here.

Burt shifts in his seat, eyes still darting between her and Teddy. "Well, I'll get right to it, then. I'm sure you know by now some pictures of you two popped up on the Internet last night."

No one says anything.

"Teddy and I had a nice little conversation about it this morning," Burt says, propping his elbows up on the armrests and steepling his fingers. "We were brainstorming the possibilities of some friendly midproduction marketing for the two of you."

Bennett blinks. Teddy's already talked to Burt about this?

"So what does that have to do with the pictures?" she asks, lobbing it up there for him to take. The idea of this conversation is already weird enough—and the faster Burt gets on with it, the faster Bennett can tell him no. She needs to save her energy for calling Teddy out for not giving her a heads-up beforehand.

"He wants us to keep spending time together," Teddy cuts in, and there's a bitterness in his tone that makes Bennett tense. "And if we happen to be seen together, then we should milk the hell out of it."

Burt grins and holds up his hands. "I never said 'milk the hell out of it.' I said you should let people think what they want.

Get 'em talking about it. The added hype—especially with your fan base, Bennett—would be huge."

"Especially with my fan base?" Bennett growls.

"Exactly—think about it," Burt says. "You write YA fiction. Teddy stars in a TV show aimed at relatively the same age group. There's a good chance that your fan bases overlap already. Even Teddy agreed that if there were a few whispers going around about the two of you possibly dating, it'd be like the clash of the fandoms. Uniting fans like this is exactly what we want to be doing during production for movie hype. It'll sell itself."

Even Teddy agreed.

As if he can read her mind, Teddy immediately jumps in to defend himself. "I only agreed that getting as much hype as possible during production is one of the best things we can do right now," he says. Bennett refuses to look at him. "Bennett, think about that article I sent you—people are already talking. Imagine if we could somehow, like, amplify that to the point of people counting down the days until the first teaser trailer comes out? Think about how much that would reflect in ticket sales."

"*New York Times*–best-selling author of *Parachutes* steps out with lead actor of upcoming movie adaptation after long day of filming," Burt says wistfully, sweeping a hand out in front of him like he can already see the headline. "Get it out all over the Internet on fan sites, Twitter, Tumblr—*especially* Tumblr. You name it. Fans will take this shit and run with it, then they'll get online and research the movie that brought you guys together."

Bennett has a million unnecessary comments streaming through her head, but she can't get herself to say any of them yet.

"You're being quiet," Burt says when she doesn't chime in. "Why are you being quiet?"

Bennett rolls her lips back between her teeth to make sure she doesn't say the first reason that pops in her head. "Just letting it all sink in," she says.

"Well, what do you think so far?"

That this is a bunch of bullshit.

"That this is a bunch of information to process."

Burt snorts. "I mean, it's kind of a no-brainer, wouldn't you say? Teddy?"

"I guess, unless it makes her uncomfortable," Teddy says. "And if it does, then I'm definitely not doing it."

How chivalrous.

"Guys, level with me here," Burt says. "This is a marketing dream! It's not like I'm asking you to marry each other. Teddy, you even said that everyone at the hospital didn't question it when you told them you were Bennett's boyfriend. That's how these rumors get started! And with all that speculation comes people searching for answers, which will ultimately lead them back to this movie."

Bennett frowns. As the author, she should be on board with anything that will help the story reach as many people as possible. But this is offering up courtside seats to anyone who wants to watch whatever's going on between her and Teddy, and Bennett doesn't even *know* what's going on between her and Teddy.

"I want people to see this movie because they're interested in the storyline," she says, irritated that she has to speak over a lump forming in her throat. "Not because they think I'm hooking up with the lead actor thanks to some cheap marketing ploy."

"You mean *free* marketing ploy, Bennett. That's the point," Burt argues. "And so what if it's cheap? It doesn't matter what gets asses in those movie seats opening weekend. As long as people are there, who cares?"

Bennett can't believe what she's hearing. "Are you kidding? It matters because—"

"Bennett," Teddy cuts across her, his tone pleading. "I know it sounds bad between the lines, but you gotta look at the bigger picture here. This works. I've seen it done before. Regardless of how shitty it sounds, Burt's onto something, and at the end of the day it can only help, you know?"

Bennett looks directly at Teddy.

"I'm surprised you're even on board with this, Teddy, since we all know how much you love to be secretive about this type of shit," she snaps, and she expects some kind of recoil from him—*wants* some kind of recoil, actually—but all she gets is a slow, disappointed expression that makes her want to throw more cheap shots until she gets what she's looking for.

Burt shakes his head. "You're being a little irrational right now, Bennett. I don't know why you're so against this, but I think we should talk about it again after you've had a day or two to think about it."

Bennett sits there and glares at the top of the table for what seems like an unnecessarily long amount of time. It's childish, yeah, but so is the reason they're having this talk in the first place. And the fact that Teddy agrees with it makes it a million times worse.

"God," she finally exhales, dragging a hand across her forehead and hitting the damn bandage over her eyebrow again. "You seriously think this will work."

Burt nods. "Yeah, I do, Bennett. And I'm asking you to consider it."

"Fine, yeah, I'll consider it," she says. She'll say just about anything at this point to end the conversation.

"Good. I'll talk to you about it in a couple of days, then." He stands and stretches. "And now that that's been—discussed, kind of, I need to get the rest of these scripts to one of the producers. Either of you guys need a ride back to the hotel or anything?"

Bennett says no, and Burt collects up the spare scripts from the kitchen table. The second he's gone, Bennett aims her scowl at Teddy. She's about to ask him what the hell that was all about, but one glance at him brings her up short. He's slumped in his chair, arms folded across his lap. He doesn't even have to be looking up for her to see the emotions on his face.

They sit in silence.

"So, obviously this is the real reason why you were acting weird this morning," Bennett says. "A heads-up would've been nice, instead of me having to hear it from Emmy and Burt first."

"I didn't deserve that," Teddy says.

"What?"

He finally looks at her. "I didn't deserve to be snapped at like that in front of Burt, and I definitely didn't deserve what you said," he says quietly. "I was on your side that entire conversation and you bit my head off the first chance you got. Like you were just waiting for it."

"What are you—I wasn't *waiting* for anything," Bennett says.

Teddy shakes his head. "You know, I at least thought after what we were doing five minutes ago things were changing a little bit. But it's like this entire time you've just been waiting for me to once again prove to you that I'm an asshole and to give you another reason to go all radio silent on me again. And it's bullshit, Bennett."

"Sounds like you're being a little paranoid, there," Bennett says, and even she's surprised by how clipped her tone is.

"Can you blame me?" he asks. "Not only did you shut me out the second you left the airport last July, you didn't even give me a chance to explain myself. You know how that made me feel?"

"Probably similar to how I felt when I watched you meet up with some other girl two seconds after you kissed me good-bye outside of departures."

Teddy glares at her.

"See? There it is again," he says. "You've obviously got all kinds of passive aggressive comments like that stockpiled somewhere to use as, like, ammunition or something. What the hell was that a second ago? *I love to be secretive about shit?* Last time I checked, you're the only one being secretive about anything these days, so don't you dare put that on me."

Bennett snickers. "*I'm* being secretive and passive aggressive? You wanna talk about the first table-read last week while we're at it?"

Teddy scrubs both hands through his hair, letting out a frustrated groan. "I didn't know how else to get you to hear me out, and I still don't, Bennett," he says, clenching his jaw. "You just said you believed me about the airport, then made out with me like everything was fine, then turned around and used it against me in front of Burt. The only reason I even considered this stupid marketing thing is because I've seen it work and I want this movie to be as successful as you deserve it to be, Bennett. Don't paint me as the bad guy here."

"Don't get all self-righteous, then," she fires back, because of course he's playing that card right now. But then she zeroes back in on how he's seen this work before—how he's said it twice now—and she scoffs. "What, are you speaking from experience here? You've seen this work because you've done it before?"

It's meant to be half joking, half rhetorical until she sees the way Teddy freezes, guilt writing itself across his face. The realization hits her like a 747.

"Oh my God," she says, a disbelieving smile following it up despite the way her heart almost sinks through the floor. How had she not put this together already? "You have done it before— with the girl from the airport, right?"

Teddy pushes his hair back off his forehead, holding it there for a second before letting it drop back into place. "She and I were already dating by the time the director approached us about it," he says quietly. Like that's supposed to help.

Logically, Bennett has no justifiable reason to be this upset. And that's what's most frustrating about it.

"I mean, we knew people were going to find out eventually. Occupational hazard. So we just went along with it," Teddy adds, throwing her nervous glances now. "I don't see why it would be any different with us—"

"I'm not splashing my private life across the Internet just to sell a few extra movie tickets," she snaps, leaning back on the couch. It's only then that she realizes how rigidly she'd been sitting. Her lower back is stiff. "It's not an occupational hazard for me, and I refuse to make it one."

Teddy looks more confused than disappointed now. "Why, though?"

Bennett balks. "Why would I ever be okay with allowing that many people to know my business? Nothing's worth that."

Teddy leans forward in his chair, resting his elbows on his

knees and rubbing a hand over his mouth. He looks at her for a long time, and the longer he looks, the more he shakes his head.

"You know people finding out about who I'm involved with is inevitable, Bennett. Regardless of who I'm dating or some stupid marketing scheme," he says slowly, forcing her to meet his eye. "And if that's going to be a problem for you, then you need to let me know. Right now."

Bennett doesn't know what to say, but apparently her silence is enough.

Teddy gets up and puts on his rain jacket.

"Got it," he says, crossing the trailer and giving her a thumbs-up.

Bennett still can't bring herself to speak, and by the time she opens her mouth to say something to fix this, the moment has passed and her trailer door has already slammed shut.

* * *

Bennett doesn't know how much time passes before Emmy and Olivia come find her in her trailer. They walk in to Bennett lying on the couch, and neither of them ask questions about why she has her face mashed into a throw pillow. Bennett stays quiet as she drives them back to the hotel, and Emmy and Olivia tell her they made plans to meet a couple of the production assistants for dinner in the hotel restaurant later—that Bennett's more than welcome to join them.

Bennett tells them she's tired, even though it's only mid-afternoon, but maybe she'll meet up with them afterward.

By the time she gets back into her room, the past twenty-four hours finally catch up with her—the dinner kidnapping, the hospital last night, the hospital this morning, the conversation with Burt . . . but the only reason she draws the blackout curtains and crawls into bed at five p.m. is because she basically just told Teddy that a relationship with him isn't worth the trouble, and she's just now starting to feel the weight of what that really means. Bennett can admit she should've handled it better, but first she needs to figure out *why* she handled it the way she did.

The conversation with Burt was one thing, and Bennett will never be okay with a marketing scheme like he suggested . . . but why did she let the conversation go that far with Teddy afterward?

CHAPTER TWENTY-ONE

When Olivia Katsaros asks Bennett after the first week of filming if she can catch a ride to set with her and Emmy in the
mornings, Bennett can't really tell her no. One, because that'd
be insanely rude, and two, because Bennett has no reason to.
Bennett might be protective of her morning routine, but despite
first impressions—Olivia Katsaros is fucking awesome.

Not only is she as nice as she is considerate of everyone on
set, she also has one of those infectious personalities that makes
even the worst day of filming a little more enjoyable (which has
become a bit of a theme recently). Needless to say it doesn't
take long for their morning commute together to become an
integral part of Bennett's new morning routine:

1. Wake up.
2. Go for a run.
3. Shower.
4. Carpool to set with Emmy and Olivia.
5. Raid the set's daily breakfast buffet.
6. Pretend to not care that Teddy hasn't looked in
    her general direction since their blowup in her
    trailer.

7. Acknowledge that she's too much of a stubborn asshole to apologize to him, despite how much she knows she should.
8. Attempt to get some writing done in her trailer/get distracted by all the things that went down in said trailer.
9. Avoid Burt Bridges for the rest of the day by any and all means necessary.

One of Bennett's favorite tactics for number nine on the list involves pushing the limits of what is considered taking only an hour for lunch off-set with Emmy and Olivia. Usually Olivia's assistant or some members of the production team tag along, but today it's just them, and Emmy has barely finished ordering her salad when she decides to ruin the first somewhat-decent mood Bennett's been in all week.

"You know you need to talk to him at least one more time about next Saturday, Bennett. It's professional courtesy," she says, handing her menu to the waitress. Bennett waits for her to walk away before starting into her excuses.

"We've already talked a million times about it. There's nothing left to tell him."

"Tell who, what?" Olivia pipes up.

Emmy frowns. "Come on, Bennett. The whole point of next Saturday is film promotion. The director needs to be kept in the loop with everything going on."

"What's going on next Saturday?" Olivia asks.

"Let's e-mail him an outline and the itinerary, then," Bennett says, sipping her drink and pretending not to pout.

"Bennett, you know he needs more than that—"

"Stop ignoring me!" Olivia snaps, effectively commandeering

the attention of the table. Then she asks, with a little too much enthusiasm for Bennett's taste, "Does this have to do with that whole dating-Teddy-marketing-thing with Burt?"

"Not directly," Bennett mumbles.

"We're talking about Bennett's book signing next Saturday," Emmy says. "And how Bennett needs to have at least one more sit-down with Burt to go over all the logistics leading up to it."

"The publisher always handles this, though," Bennett says, and it's such a weak argument it might as well be working against her. Truth is, she doesn't want to sit down with Burt and talk logistics because she doesn't want to give him the chance to talk to her about convincing the entire Internet that she and Teddy are an item.

"Your publisher is handling it from their end," Emmy presses. "But this is the first signing that's tied with the film adaptation. And you're the publisher's only representative in Wilmington right now. You have to be the liaison."

"Can't you just talk to Burt about it instead?" she whines.

Emmy sighs and massages her temples. "Look, B, I get you're uncomfortable with Burt right now, but Burt's the one who went to bat to get you involved in this movie. I know it's weird with the whole PR thing, but this is business, and you've gotta show some respect here."

Bennett knows she's already lost this argument, so it doesn't help when Olivia chimes in.

"Bennett, this is your first experience with filming a movie, right?" Olivia asks.

She nods.

"And is Burt expecting you to talk with him more about the book signing?"

Bennett nods again. Reluctantly.

"All right, so—filming a movie doesn't work unless everyone involved is kept in the same loop and on the same page," Olivia says, sitting up a little straighter and lacing her fingers together on the table. "Everyone is sensitive as fuck in this industry, too. If Burt's expecting you to follow up with him and you blow him off because you guys aren't on the best terms right now—and believe me, that's exactly the conclusion he'll jump to—then not only does that make it look like this film isn't a priority for you, but it also makes you look unreliable, and honestly, a little ungrateful.

"All you have is your reputation in this industry—that's it," Olivia adds when Bennett refuses to meet her eye. "So if you want any type of film future for your upcoming books, then you need to make sure people know you're good to work with. All it takes is for one person to tell another person that they had a bad experience with you, and bam, you're done. Trust me."

"Agreed," Emmy says. "And it goes both ways, too. I don't think Burt's trying to make this personal. I think he's genuinely trying to give this movie the best shot he can. Even if his tactics are a little . . . questionable."

Bennett would be lying if she said she isn't taking this so personally because she thought she and Burt had a strong enough working relationship that he wouldn't try to exploit her for the sake of the movie. Olivia and Emmy are right, though. How Bennett handles every situation when it comes to this movie, no matter how big or small, reflects directly back on her. It's not like she's expecting to have the film rights for every book she writes in the future sold like *Parachutes*, but it's definitely something she's interested in pursuing.

"Fine," Bennett concedes. "You're both right."

Olivia gives her a megawatt, million-dollar smile. "Good.

And it's not like Emmy and I are going to leave you out to dry with this whole PR thing. If Burt tries to be an asshole about it, we've got your back."

"Good," Bennett says, "because I have a feeling he's probably going to try."

* * *

When they arrive back to set, Bennett works up enough nerve to sit next to Burt behind one of the cameras—it's the first time in a few days she's come within five feet of him. Unfortunately, filming moves at glacial speed all afternoon, and Bennett gets more anxious with each take.

"Teddy," Burt snaps, making the knot in Bennett's stomach twist. "We're close to the last scene of the day—I need you to stop fidgeting and pay attention, please."

Teddy's shoulders tense as he apologizes and walks back to his blocking place. Burt has a habit of coming off like an angry schoolteacher reprimanding his students sometimes, and Bennett doesn't like it when it's directed at Teddy, who's done nothing today but kill it as usual.

"Hey, Burt?" Bennett says, just as Burt's about to bark something else at the actors.

The director glances sideways at her, apparently surprised that she's talking to him at all. "What's up?"

Bennett inhales slowly and hopes it doesn't look like she's trying to psych herself up here. "When today's filming is over, do you want to set a time to sit down and go over next Saturday's book signing again?"

"Yeah—I'm glad you mentioned it, actually," he says. "I've got some things to discuss with you about it."

"Cool. We can talk more about it when this scene's over."

"You got it," Burt says, then stands to address the crew. "All right—everyone ready?"

Bennett glances at the camera monitor to see if all the actors are in place—and she startles a little when she finds two big brown eyes looking back at her for the first time in what feels like way too long. Granted, Teddy's looking at the camera and probably doesn't know Bennett is watching him, but it still counts . . . right?

Feeling brave, Bennett subtly leans around all the equipment in front of her, and Teddy's gaze meets her there, too.

"All right, people, let's get rolling," Burt calls, but Teddy is still looking at Bennett. She lets her eyes flicker away for a moment, worried she looks like a total creep. When she chances another peek at him, he's glancing down again, but there's the tiniest hint of a smile on his face that wasn't there before. Bennett tries hard not to get her hopes up that it might have something to do with her. She goes back to hiding behind the camera monitor just as Burt calls action.

Filming wraps for the day about thirty minutes later, and Burt spends another fifteen after that slinging around end-of-day orders from his director's chair. Bennett waits it out, trying to not let her imagination run wild with all the different ways he could bring up the PR scheme. She goes back over everything Olivia and Emmy said at lunch today, just to keep from chickening out.

"Okay, so, the signing next Saturday," Burt says, turning away from a herd of PAs crowded around him. He's still wearing his Ray-Bans, even though they're inside. And it's pretty much dark outside. "You wanna just talk now? Or schedule a time? Actually, now's probably best, since I talked to a rep from your publisher this morning."

This is news to Bennett. "What?"

"Yeah—just about logistics. I wanted to run a few ideas by them," he tells her, then takes in her reaction (or lack thereof) and says, "Look, Bennett. I know you're not on board with the PR thing with Teddy yet, but you gotta big-picture this here."

Oh, God. Oh, no. He's not—

"Your publisher seems to be on board with it, though," Burt says. "We discussed the possibility of getting Teddy to come to the signing with you."

And there it is. This is too perfect.

"You went to my publisher?" Bennett asks. It's the only thing she can think to do that doesn't involve demanding to know what gives him the right to go behind her back like this. At least Burt seems to pick up on some of the vibes radiating off her and has the decency to acknowledge what a dick move this is.

"I know it wasn't cool of me to do, Bennett, but this is a good idea even separately from you and Teddy," he explains. "All the actors are already in Wilmington—I don't know why someone didn't think of this sooner, actually. . . ."

"Because it's a logistical nightmare on such short notice," someone says. Bennett jumps and turns around to find Emmy standing behind her, Olivia by her side. "The actors have separate third-party contracts with talent agencies and managers in addition to the parent production company, and it's a whole mess of paperwork to get everyone to agree to scheduled appearances outside of the allotted time for promotional work."

"True," Burt says thoughtfully. "But it's not impossible to get everyone to agree, right?"

"Technically not, I guess," Emmy says reluctantly.

Burt hums, and Bennett can all but hear the gears turning in his head. Then, to her complete and utter horror, he leans back in his chair so he can see around Emmy and Olivia and calls out, "Hey, Teddy! Could you come over here for a minute?"

Bennett's eyes lock with the director's. "Burt? What're you doing?"

"Seeing what Teddy thinks about this," he says, which makes this the second time today he's decided to go over her head.

An excruciatingly long moment later, Teddy comes over to join them. "Yeah? What's up?"

Burt claps him on the back. "Did you know Bennett's publisher set up a big promotional book signing here in Wilmington for the Parachutes series next Saturday?"

Teddy hesitates. "Um. I did, actually. Yeah."

"How much begging and paperwork would it take for you to make a cameo?" Burt asks.

Teddy scratches the back of his head. "I don't know, man. You'd have to talk with my manager about it."

"All right. Let's say I do and we somehow expedite the process. Would you be open to doing it?" Burt asks, and it pisses Bennett off to no end that he's asking Teddy if it's okay but didn't extend the same courtesy to her before ganging up on her with her publisher.

"I mean, I guess I'd be as long as it's okay with Bennett and her publisher?" Teddy says, and he's more than likely trying to be tactful about it, but he pretty much just gave Burt the opening he'd been looking for. It takes active effort for Bennett to not tip her head back and groan.

"I've already spoken with Bennett's publisher—they're on board." When Teddy doesn't initially say anything else, Burt adds, "Sounds like a great opportunity for some PR work, yeah?"

Silence.

"What?" Burt asks when no one jumps at the idea. "Why are

you looking at me like that? This would be good for promo in general, guys—not just for what Teddy, Bennett, and I talked about."

More silence.

"What a wonderful idea, Burt," Olivia says suddenly, and Bennett has just started to panic that she's jumping ship when she adds, "I'd also love to attend an event like this."

Burt's expression is unreadable, giving Bennett a tiny shred of hope he's possibly bluffing. But then he sighs. "You're right, Olivia. I guess having both lead actors there would be pretty beneficial."

Olivia pretends to pout. "You guess? You mean we'll basically blow the lid off this thing! You said you want promo work, right? Think of all the promo two of us can generate instead of just one?"

Bennett has to bite back a grin, because again, contrary to first impressions, Olivia Katsaros is fucking awesome.

"Well, that's not necessarily what—" Burt starts.

"I'm in," Teddy interrupts. "I'll call my manager right now to see if we can make this work."

"Me too," Olivia adds.

"I think it's a great idea, actually," Bennett admits. "If my publisher's already on board with it, then I am, too."

Burt stands and picks up his jacket slung over the back of his chair. "All right. I'll send out an e-mail about it to everyone tonight and a calendar invite to set up meetings to get all this taken care of."

And Jesus, you'd think for a dude so worried about midproduction PR he'd at least have a little more enthusiasm about it, even if it is a watered-down variation of what he originally wanted. Burt heads across set, shouldering on his jacket as more crewmembers scurry up to him for last-minute touch-bases for the day.

Bennett waits until she's sure he's completely out of earshot before saying, "God, I cannot *believe* he went to my publisher." She looks at Olivia. "I told you he was gonna do this."

Olivia nods, though it doesn't look like she fully agrees. "Yeah—I'll admit that wasn't the best way for him to go about it, but I still don't think his intentions are disingenuous, B. It sucks, but at least the signing will be good, right?"

Bennett feels her eyes go wide, and they only get bigger when Teddy joins in.

"Yeah, I'm not sure he understands exactly what he's asking," Teddy says absently, rocking back on his heels and looking at something across set. Then he nudges Bennett with his elbow. "Still shitty of him, though."

Bennett's heart leaps into her throat, the unexpected gesture completely disarming her. Teddy seems startled by it, too, stepping away a moment later and casting his eyes down.

"Well, anyway . . ." He clears his throat. "I'm, uh—I'm gonna head out. I'll see you guys later." He turns and walks about three steps away, realizes he's heading straight for the dead-end side of the set warehouse, and turns back and walks past them. He points a finger toward the exit doors and says again, "Yeah. See you guys later."

Bennett watches him go, wondering if he actually somewhat agrees with all this, or if he's just good at putting up a front.

"God, can't you guys just kiss and make up already?" Olivia says, ruining her pout with a shit-eating grin when Bennett scowls at her.

"You are a ridiculous human being, Olivia," Bennett says. "But you just saved the day with Burt, so I owe you big-time."

Olivia beams and curtsies. "No worries. It's what I'm here for."

"Hey—Bennett?"

Bennett looks over at Emmy and realizes it's the first time she's contributed to the conversation in a while.

"Yeah?" she says, registering the unease in her assistant's expression.

"I wasn't supposed to tell you this because it's supposed to be a surprise, but given the possible change in plans here . . ."

"Okay, what's up?" Bennett prompts cautiously.

"Your—um," Emmy hesitates, looking more and more like she might throw up. Bennett might join her, depending on what she says next. "Your entire family is planning on coming to the book signing to surprise you."

Bennett freezes. "What?"

Emmy nods. "And when I talked to your mom a couple of days ago to finalize plans, she said your aunt and uncle and cousins are coming, too."

CHAPTER TWENTY-TWO

Teddy, Bennett, and Olivia have three meetings over the course of the week with Burt and some of the PR reps to go over the logistics for the signing. The new itinerary now involves a Q&A panel in addition to Bennett's reading, then the actual signing, and Bennett wants to murder whoever came up with the genius idea to give fans an allotted space to ask whatever questions they want—about whatever subject matter they want—during a signing that's supposed to double as PR relationship bait.

And bonus, Liz is going to be in attendance.

Bennett needs a hell of a contingency plan here.

"This is so *excessive*," she complains for the third time that morning. It's the only thing giving her a sense of control in the chaos that is her life now.

Olivia bursts out laughing and kicks her heeled boots up onto the limo's leather seat. "I don't even know whose idea the limo was, but I don't hate it."

Bennett glances at Emmy, who's next to Olivia and checking her e-mail on her iPad; then she subtly looks over at Teddy, who is sitting in the seat opposite her and scrolling through something on his phone. His eyes casually flick to hers, and Bennett's stomach twists up into her rib cage when she realizes he's probably smirking because he'd caught her staring at him.

Everyone involved with the signing has spent a lot of time with one another since Burt decided to put together this little field trip, and even though Bennett and Teddy haven't spoken very much during that time, it still feels like something has changed between them again. This time, for the better. Kind of.

It isn't so much the way she and Teddy act toward each other as it is the atmosphere change between them. The two weeks after the whole trailer debacle were full of this palpable tension that made Bennett feel guilty every time she and Teddy were in the same room together. But the closer they got to the book signing, the more it felt like someone had taken that tension and scrubbed away at it until there was nothing left but some kind of shy, unspoken olive branch for one of them to take.

Now it's up to one of them to take it. And Bennett knows it should be her. Teddy at least deserves the conversation/explanation he's been asking for since he arrived on set. Fighting with him is exhausting; avoiding him is exhausting; everything that involves going against the obvious feelings Bennett has for him is exhausting.

Bennett jumps when her personal phone rings.

"Hey, Mom," she says after checking the caller ID.

"You're not supposed to know they're coming, remember?" Emmy whispers. Bennett nods, and her eyes accidentally shift to Teddy again. He's biting down on his thumbnail and grinning at the floorboard.

"Sorry, Mom—what'd you say?"

"I said," her mom's voice rings out a second later, "'Hi, honey, how are you?'"

"I'm good. What're you doing?"

Bennett holds back a grin when her mom replies with, "Oh, you know, doing a few things around the house. Are you excited for your book signing?"

"Yeah. Should be . . . eventful," Bennett says, immediately regretting it.

"Why do you say that?" her mom asks.

"Just bec-because—" she stammers, then decides to just go with it, since her mom is going to find out sooner or later. "Some of the cast of the movie is coming with me, so it'll probably get a little crazy with the fans."

"Oh!" her mom squeals. "Is Teddy going?"

The only person who loved hosting Teddy that weekend back in July more than Bennett's brother (and Will, for that matter) is Bennett's mother. Listening to everyone go on about how cool and funny and smart and *amazing* Teddy is almost had Bennett rethinking deferring college for a year, just so she'd have somewhere else to live.

Bennett's eyes flick to Teddy again. "Yep, he'll be there."

He looks up, but she drops her gaze to her lap before they can make eye contact.

"That's so exciting! You think you'll have a big crowd?" her mom asks.

Ha. "I'd say it's a safe bet."

"Well, that sounds great," her mom replies. "I hope y'all have a great time."

"Thanks, Mom."

"Call me when it's over; I want to hear about it."

"Okay." Bennett tries not to laugh.

"Love you."

"Love you, too."

Bennett hangs up and can feel everyone looking at her.

"What?" she asks, self-conscious.

Olivia snickers and sits up, putting her feet back on the floor. "Were you aware that you get quite the little southern drawl when you're talking to your family?"

"What are you—"

"And when she drinks," Teddy pipes up, smirking.

"And when she's angry or yelling about something," Emmy adds.

"Wow. Cool, guys," Bennett says, trying to ward off the blush taking over her face. They just laugh at her. "Well, if y'all think mine is bad, wait until you meet the rest of my family."

"Who else is coming again?" Olivia asks.

Bennett refuses to look anywhere near Teddy when she replies, "My parents, my brother, my aunt and uncle, and my two cousins."

Olivia smiles. "Oh, how awesome—"

"Liz is coming?"

Bennett knows Teddy's question is for her, but Emmy is the one to answer him.

"She'll be there," she says.

Silence.

Teddy looks like he's close to saying something disapproving but hasn't fully committed yet.

Olivia sighs. "Okay, now what?"

"Nothing. Just—some stuff's happened between Liz and me over the past few years. No big deal." Bennett shrugs. This is the last thing she wants to get into today. Emmy and Olivia are eyeing her though, expecting her to elaborate, and she can practically feel Teddy's gaze pinning her to her seat.

"Jesus, okay, fine." Bennett drags a hand across her forehead.

No bandage today, but the cut is still there. She throws a quick apology to Teddy for making him listen to this story twice now, then says to Emmy and Olivia, "I dated a guy in high school that Liz said was cheating on me and, like, only liked me because of all the *Parachutes* stuff happening. Turns out he was cheating with *Liz* and half the other girls at our school. And somehow Liz convinced our friend group afterward that it was *my* fault for not listening to her in the first place."

And God, Bennett can't stand how cliché it is. Her face burns all the way through the awkward pause that follows.

Olivia frowns. "What a psycho—"

"It's fine," Bennett insists. "Liz actually did me a favor."

"How the hell can you say that was doing you a favor?" Teddy snaps, smacking his hand down on the leather seat next to him. Apparently he registers it might have been a bit of an overreaction, because a second later he clears his throat and adds, "For real, though?"

"Because the guy really was a scumbag who wasn't actually interested in me. Liz went out of her way to make sure I was *well* aware of that," Bennett says, reaching up to mess with the sunroof buttons. "He and I broke up, and now here I am in much better company."

She wishes she was brave enough to say who she really means by "better company."

"God," Olivia says. "Sounds like this girl has some serious issues, starting with being obsessed with Bennett."

"Okay, wait a sec—"

"That's what I said!" Teddy interrupts.

A slow smile spreads across Olivia's face. "Well, I can't wait to meet her now."

* * *

Book signings are intimidating enough as it is, and the added pressure of being flanked by two actors is almost enough to make Bennett second-guess her career choice here.

As soon as they arrive, they're informed of the million things to get done before doors open. A rep from Bennett's publisher has flown in and is already making the bookstore rearrange the panel setup (because it has to be both easily accessible but not too visible from the outside). The bookstore staff is doing all the heavy lifting and placing boxes of fresh copies of *Parachutes* out for sale. The bookstore's owner tells them Burt sent over a few of the makeup artists from set, free of charge. For some reason, Bennett wants to be irritated by this, but she can't quite get there.

Bennett's sitting in a chair with a makeup artist in her face and some kind of wrap from the lunch buffet in her hand when someone taps her shoulder. She's in the middle of having eye shadow caked on so she doesn't know who it is until Emmy's talking ninety miles an hour a second later.

"Bennett, we're doing seating arrangements at the panel table right now and we need to know where you'd like to be seated," she says.

"What do you think's best?" Bennett asks, keeping her eyes closed and trying not to flinch when the makeup artist begins to apply eyeliner.

"Well, seeing as it's going to be the same seating arrangement for the book signing after . . ." Emmy trails off.

Bennett smirks. "You think if the actors are the first ones people see in line then there won't be any incentive to stay in line after that, right? But if I'm the first person in line, then there's also a good chance I'll get jumped?"

"Well . . ." Emmy hesitates.

"Em, it's fine. Most of the people who come to this are only coming to see Buzz and Olivia, so it's not a big deal," Bennett says, then freezes for a second. That little nickname hasn't accidentally slipped out in weeks, and now she's going to spend all afternoon embarrassed about it.

"We came up with a plan for that, though," Emmy answers, and bless her for only honing in on the important parts of Bennett's statement.

"Who's we?"

"Emmy and Buzz," a new voice says.

Goddammit.

Bennett winces, and the makeup artist curses under her breath.

"Hang on, I've got to find my makeup remover towelettes," she says.

Bennett opens her eyes and apologizes to her for messing up her eyeliner, then has to work up the nerve to look at Emmy. Lo and behold, Teddy is standing right next to her assistant. He bites down on the grin pulling at the corner of his mouth and gives Bennett a little wave when their eyes met.

"Hey, Teddy," Bennett says in an attempt to keep a matching grin off her face. It doesn't work. "Okay, so what's the plan?"

Emmy launches into something about having one actor on either side of Bennett with Olivia greeting people first. Which sounds fine to Bennett until she says it'd be a good idea for Bennett to come out alone for her reading and bring the actors out afterward.

"What's the point of that?" Bennett asks. She's actually banking on the majority of the crowd getting distracted by Teddy and Olivia so they won't notice Bennett sweating through her dress.

Teddy scratches the side of his face and says, "To, like, . . . keep anyone from being upstaged, I guess?"

Bennett smirks at how embarrassed he sounds. "It'll make me feel better to not be standing up there by myself as I stumble through a five-page excerpt."

"But this signing was originally for just you," Teddy argues. "The least we can do is make sure people know you're the reason we're all here."

"No, this book signing was for movie promotion, originally."

Emmy gives an exasperated sigh. "Okay, this is getting us nowhere; if you two don't decide I'm going to go ask Olivia."

"I'm making the decision," Bennett says. "Olivia on my right. Teddy on my left. We all go out at the same time. Okay? That's what I want. Let's make it happen."

They both start to argue again, but the makeup artist returns just in time to bail Bennett out.

"Fine," Emmy concedes before heading back to where the signing table is set up.

Teddy stands there for a second, watching Bennett.

"What," she says.

He gives her a half smile. "Do you always call me Buzz when you're talking about me?"

Of course he'd ask that.

"No." Bennett leans back in her chair and closes her eyes again. "For about five months after July, I had a lot of different names I used. Be glad Buzz is the one that stuck."

He doesn't respond, but when she peeks open an eye at him,

she catches a spectacular glimpse of the smile on his face before he turns to walk away.

* * *

It's 1:58 p.m. and there's a line wrapped all the way around the outside of the bookstore.

Or, at least, that's what Emmy tells Bennett. Her assistant keeps running back and forth from the front windows to give them updates through the curtain set up behind the panel table. Olivia is telling jokes to the bookstore staff. The security guys are standing awkwardly off to the side and trying to look important. Teddy is snapping his fingers and swinging his arms as he whistles "Take Me Out to the Ball Game," and Bennett is just trying to keep converting oxygen to carbon dioxide.

The few minutes just before a signing starts are always the most intense. Bennett hears the front doors open and tries to take another deep breath, but it sounds more like a shudder than anything else. She feels someone poke her shoulder and she looks to her left.

"You all right over there?" Teddy whispers.

Bennett nods.

"Really? Because you kinda look like you're about to throw up."

She rolls her eyes before glancing up at him.

"You really are good at repeating lines, you know that?" she says, and the proud little grin she receives is almost enough to get rid of the nerves welling up in her throat.

"It's the least I could do—"

"All right, guys. Everyone's filing into seats now, but I'm pretty sure we're gonna end up with a lot of people standing in the back," Emmy says, bursting through the curtain again. "You guys will walk out together, Bennett will do her reading, and then the rep from the publisher will mediate the panel. After about an hour we'll get to the signing, and then we'll be golden. Good?"

Would it matter if Bennett said no?

Suddenly it's time to go onstage, and Bennett almost forgets the pages for her reading. The crowd is still screaming over Olivia and Teddy and the lights set up on top of some bookshelves are a bit disorienting, but Bennett's just glad she makes it to the podium without falling on her face. She's so nervous she trips up on the second line and thinks it's a good idea to start it from the top again. . . . And she's still shaking a little when she sits back down in the middle of the panel table. The only good thing about readings is getting the worst part over first.

Except Bennett's never had a Q&A panel with two famous actors before.

She thinks everything is fine at first, since all the questions are for Olivia and Teddy. What do they like most about the characters they're playing? Would Teddy rather go on a secret heist with the entire Pirates batting lineup or Jason Bourne? Is Olivia doing her own stunts? What scenes have they already filmed? What scenes are they looking forward to filming the most? Honestly, it goes on long enough to lure Bennett into a false sense of hope that she won't actually have to speak.

Then their moderator throws in a question about the book series to change gears, and okay, that's to be expected. Totally fine. Bennett has never been one for lengthy monologues, but she knows there are at least a few people in the audience wanting answers, so she tries to give as much information as her publisher will allow while talking about what to expect in the ending of *Off the Grid*.

"Now we're going to open it up for audience questions," the moderator says. "We only have a few more minutes before the signing. Who's got a question they'd like to ask?"

A redheaded girl gets called on.

"My question isn't actually about the book series. It's for Teddy and Bennett," she says, voice wobbling just barely over the standing speakers. She's grinning like a loon, though. "First of all, Shardwell is life," she says, and does kind of a half-salute maneuver that Bennett would normally wonder about if she wasn't already so distracted by the context. "And secondly—so I actually met you guys in the Charlotte airport last summer, and I was wondering if this time I can get a selfie with both of you?"

Jesus Christ. Shardwell is *what*?

Teddy, ever the media-trained machine, rushes in to save the day by laughing it off and telling her of course she can. Even Olivia jumps in and jokes about photobombing. The crowd laughs, and everything seems fine, except it's not. Especially when someone deep in the crowd waits for a lull in the buzz to yell out, "Shardwell is real!"

What the hell is *Shardwell*?

CHAPTER TWENTY-THREE

Bennett finds out exactly what *Shardwell* is when the book signing starts. Granted, she had an idea after she first heard it, but she'd hoped to God she was wrong.

The redhead who asked the question earlier is one of the first people in line to get her book signed, and she repeats it so many times in casual conversation that Olivia finally asks what she's talking about.

"It's their ship name," the redhead giggles, confirming Bennett's fears and holding her phone as high as she can to get Teddy and Bennett in the shot with her. Bennett has to force herself to smile instead of grimacing.

Shardwell is the result of a few blurry pictures floating around on Twitter? Jesus, Burt's going to lose his mind when he finds out.

"I love you guys so much," the redhead gushes as Olivia, Teddy, and Bennett take turns signing her book. Teddy takes everything in stride, smiling and laughing and indulging her. Bennett half expects Olivia to say she ships *Shardwell*, too, but she actually gets the redheaded girl talking about the book series until it's the next person in line's turn, bless her.

The signing only gets more chaotic, though.

The only other time Bennett's seen this many screaming fangirls in one place is when she went to New York Comic Con last year. It's exciting, but also a little terrifying. Up until this point, all her signings have been relatively low-key in comparison, but talking with so many people at once at least makes the time fly.

Bennett isn't sure how long it's been when Emmy squats down next to her.

"Okay. So. Your family will be here soon, and I told them it'll probably be better to surprise you in the back office," her assistant says as Bennett finishes signing another book. "They wanted to surprise you in line, but I told them that with the amount of people still here it'd be better for you to go to them."

Bennett pauses as another cluster of girls beelines past for Teddy's end of the table. So many people showed to see the actors (more Teddy than Olivia, honestly) that they had to get the security team to start policing how many can come up to the table at a time.

"Probably a good call," Bennett says, even though seeing her family in line would've been a nice excuse to get up from the table. "Thanks, Em—"

The last part of Bennett's response is drowned out by more eardrum-splitting squeaks. She feels another little push under the table from Teddy. He's given her so many apologetic nudges since the signing began that eventually he decided to keep his knee pressed against the outside of her leg. Bennett isn't sure when that started happening, but it's making it hard to concentrate on anything else.

"No problem. There's only about thirty minutes left." Emmy frowns and glances around the bookstore, adding, "It's still pretty nuts in here; I don't think we're going to be able to end it right at six."

Teddy shifts in his seat and his knee inches higher up Bennett's thigh.

"Um." She jumps. "It'll be fine. We'll be fine."

Emmy cocks her head and gives her a questioning look, just as Olivia leans over and asks, "What's up?"

Emmy switched sides behind Bennett so she can tell her privately.

"Oh, *hell* yes—the Caldwell clan's almost here? I can't wait to meet this Liz girl."

Bennett frowns. "Be nice."

Olivia sticks out her bottom lip in a mock pout, but it curls back into a smirk a second later. "Of course I'll be nice. I'm delightful to be around."

"Right," Bennett says, but as tempting as the idea is to unleash Olivia on an unsuspecting Liz, it doesn't sit right with Bennett. Sure, Liz is far from her favorite person on the planet, but she's still family. Bennett feels morally obligated to stay on manageable terms with her despite everything Liz has pulled over the years. . . .

Olivia's smirk deepens but she doesn't push it, and Bennett lets her eyes wander left again. Teddy's in the process of trying to take a selfie with the current group of girls at the table without leaving his seat—a rule the security guys had to establish earlier in the signing when the crowd began to multiply. Bennett still has all this Shardwell business clattering around inside her head to sort through in addition to watching Teddy interact with all his adoring fans, and it's been nothing but a distraction all day.

An idea pops in her head and she grins to herself. The signing is almost over, anyway. . . . This is too easy to pass up.

"Hey, I'll take the picture for y'all if you want," Bennett

offers, having to basically yell to get the group of girls in front of Teddy to hear her. "Why don't y'all get together in front of the table?"

Teddy's knee immediately digs harder into Bennett's thigh, and they all almost go deaf from the girls' reactions.

"Oh my GOD, PLEASE?"

"YAAAASSSSSS."

"PLEASE, I love you so much—please!"

Totally worth it.

The girls are screaming over one another so much that Teddy finally agrees—probably to spare the rest of them the hearing loss.

Sixteen different phones are shoved across the table a moment later.

"That was cruel," Olivia leans over and murmurs, sounding like she approves. Bennett has to roll her lips back between her teeth to keep from laughing.

Once Bennett manages to get to every phone, she places them all at the front of the table for the girls and watches Teddy give out good-bye hugs. He acts like each one of them is his new best friend—patting their backs before pulling away, telling them how cute they are and how happy he is they're there . . . reminding them to have their books signed before they leave.

Bennett's heart squeezes.

"Hey, Bennett?" Emmy taps her on the shoulder, and she turns around just in time to watch Olivia smack her assistant in the arm.

"Emmy, don't interrupt her when she's checking out bae!"

"Bae?" Emmy repeats so loudly that Teddy and the group of girls stops to look over.

Bennett wants to crawl under the signing table and die.

"Yes, *bae*—'before anyone else,'" Olivia says once the group has gone back to fangirling. Then she counts off on her fingers, "Bae . . . boyfriend . . . *lover* . . . whatever you want to call it."

Bennett's mouth drops open. "Oh, God. Stop."

"Oh, don't try to deny it, B," Olivia dismisses her. "PR scheme or not—you know exactly what I'm talking about. And honestly, I don't think I could stand being around the two of you and all that suffocating sexual tension if I didn't already ship you guys. OTP status 'n' shit."

"This is a whole subclass of linguistics that wasn't covered in grad school," Emmy comments dryly.

Olivia smirks and starts to say something else, but then her gaze shifts to behind Bennett and she closes her mouth. Someone grips the back of Bennett's chair a second later. Bennett doesn't need to look to know who it is.

"You can expect some serious payback for that one, Caldwell." Teddy leans in close and growls in her ear.

An involuntary grin spreads across Bennett's face at all the possibilities that could entail. She already owes him some payback for the little oldest-trick-in-the-book stunt he pulled, so the idea of the two of them getting into some kind of comeuppance war causes more than a few sarcastic comments to headline her thoughts. She turns toward him to fire one of them off.

Teddy ends up being a lot closer to her than she anticipated.

"Oh, real—" She stops short when she registers the way his head is angled toward hers, separating them by a few inches. They both still, watching the other, and Bennett's entire train of thought derails.

The memory of how good it feels to have him this close slams into Bennett so hard and so unexpectedly she sits there and just lets it level her. Teddy leans back just enough to drop his gaze to her mouth (which is still open from whatever snarky response Bennett had planned a minute ago), then his eyes flick back to hers.

"Very, *very* soon," he adds, and there's an edge to his voice, all throaty and playful and disarmingly hot. . . .

But then he's gone, moving to sit down next to her. By the time his knee finds its spot against her thigh again, Bennett realizes how quiet it's gotten. She looks across the table to find the majority of the group of girls with their phones pointed in Bennett and Teddy's direction. The rest are staring.

Olivia at least has the decency to wait until the group has moved on before leaning over and whispering, "Shardwell is *real.*"

Then, right on cue—like he can hear all the thoughts screaming through her head—Bennett feels another little nudge under the table. She isn't sure that one's meant to be apologetic, though.

The next group of girls to approach can't be older than thirteen—each sporting her own flower crown and carrying a copy of *Parachutes*. Olivia greets them as they crowd around the signing table. The giggles and nervous glances they keep directing at Teddy have Bennett smiling to herself. Again, they're all talking over one another about movies Olivia has been in and Teddy's MTV show. After a few minutes of signing their books and taking pictures, the girls go along their way. That's when Bennett sees the girl standing behind them.

"Wait, we've got one more." Bennett grins at her, hoping to make her a little more comfortable. The girl is hugging her book to her chest and staring down at her shoes.

Olivia joins in with, "Hi, sweetheart. Would you like us to sign your book?"

The girl glances up nervously, but she isn't looking at the actors.

"Bennett—I mean, Ms. Caldwell." She winces and takes a nervous step away from the table.

"Bennett's totally fine," Bennett says. "What's your name?"

"Um—it's Maggie," she answers, moving toward them again and setting her book in front of Bennett. It's the paperback version, and the spine has several pieces of duct tape holding it together. "I w-wanted to tell you how much I love your writing. You've already inspired me to write my own novels, and . . . " She trails off, pushing her glasses up to wipe underneath her eyes.

Bennett gapes at her, and it takes both Olivia and Teddy kicking her under the table to remind her that she needs to keep talking.

"No, please don't cry," Bennett says, laughing and already feeling her throat constrict. "I'll start crying, too."

Maggie sniffs. "Do you mind signing this? I know it's falling apart, but I've read it so many times, I—I don't want to buy another copy."

"I'd love to." Bennett reaches for her book, already knowing what to write inside.

Olivia and Teddy keep up small talk with Maggie while she waits for her book. When Bennett is done, she closes the cover carefully, hands it back to her, and thanks her twice for coming. Maggie takes it back without asking for any more signatures, and once she's away from the table, Teddy leans over and asks, "Do you normally write, like, a paragraph on the insides of people's books?"

Bennett shakes her head, still watching Maggie as she heads toward the exit. She stops dead in her tracks and turns around, the front cover to her copy open in her hands. At the risk of sounding cheesier than Bennett can even stand—the grin on Maggie's face is something Bennett knows all too well, and it's the reason she began writing in the first place.

"Nope," she says to Teddy. "Only certain ones."

* * *

They finally have to get the bookstore's owner to announce that the signing is officially over when it gets to be half past six.

The hundred or so people still in line aren't happy. If the panel hadn't already been sitting there for almost five hours straight, Bennett would stay longer. She (and everyone else for that matter) is so antsy to get up that she isn't bothered by the few angry shouts they get when the security team closes off the front of the line.

That's when Bennett notices the crack in their well-planned setup.

Emmy sent her parents and the McGearys to the owner's office toward the back of the bookstore. In order to get there, they have to follow the line that snakes all the way around the contour of the bookstore. There are ropes set up to keep the line organized, creating a narrow alley of people along the wall on one side and tall bookshelves on the other. Basically, a gauntlet of excited, somewhat annoyed Teddy Sharpe and Olivia Katsaros fans.

Bennett lets out a shaky breath as they stand and file out from behind the table. People are clearly agitated about the signing ending, but at least the majority of them don't say anything about it as they pass. They're all mostly interested in fangirling or getting a high five from the actors.

Bennett stays back to let Olivia and Teddy walk ahead so

they can get to as many fans as they can (and to sort of use them as camouflage). It works for the most part—every now and then someone calls out to Bennett over a few screaming fans to ask her to sign something, but it isn't anywhere near the attention Teddy and Olivia get. Bennett stays behind in their wake with one of the security guys, far enough back to give them space but close enough to keep up.

They're about three-fourths of the way to the back office when Bennett notices a group of guys huddled as close to the section ropes as they can get. A few of them are leaning on it like they're daring the security team to say something.

"Heyoooo, there she is!" one of them calls out over the dull roar of the crowd. They look like a bunch of college kids who are probably skipping class at the moment. The one who's yelling now is wearing a UNCW shirt. The group perks up at his words and plaster nasty looks on their faces.

"Yo, Olivia!" another yells. "Come'ere, baby!"

Bennett watches Olivia bristle as she finishes signing a picture for a fan.

"Aye, Olivia! I'm your biggest fan," UNCW shirt sneers.

"Yeah, he is." His friend pushes his shoulder. "You're not going to ignore your biggest fan, are you, baby?"

Olivia and Teddy are only a few yards away from the group now, and the jackasses yelling are about to spill over into their path.

"Off the ropes, fellas," one of the security guys barks.

A couple of the guys hold their hands up innocently.

"Bennett!" someone calls out in the crowd. Two girls wave her over.

"Please, Bennett, will you sign our books? We love you so much!" the other squeals.

Despite the situation with Olivia unfolding, Bennett smiles and walks over; but not before throwing a few wide-eyed looks at some of the security guys, hoping they'll get the hint. Teddy and Olivia are about to pass that group and things are probably about to get weird.

"Olivia, baby, can I get a pic?"

"No? What about a kiss?"

"Ow, ow!" UNCW shirt whoops.

Bennett can't concentrate on signing anything with all these comments flying around. She looks at both of the girls in front of her and says, "Please stay away from those guys."

They nod, nervously side-eyeing the group.

Bennett has just given the girls' books back when Teddy and Olivia finally reach the idiots—she actually holds her breath as they pass by, waiting for some dickhead to make another comment. To everyone's surprise, however, the guys only leer as they pass.

Bennett sighs.

Then someone yells, "Show us your tits!"

"Are you kidding me?" Teddy bites out, whipping around. Olivia steps in his way and shakes her head. Bennett doesn't hear what she says, but she does hear the reaction from the group. It looks like more words are exchanged, but after a moment Teddy places a hand on Olivia's back to guide her the rest of the way past them. One of the security guards escorting Olivia steps up to the ropes and points to the exit. Several guys send a few more jabs after Teddy, but the others are already going on about something else.

"Guys, guys!" one says. "What've we got here?"

"Who the hell is that?" another calls out.

Bennett looks around, trying to figure out to whom they're referring, only to realize that most of the security team is busy either keeping people in line (literally) or escorting Teddy and Olivia away. Bennett is just standing there. By herself. In the middle of the makeshift gauntlet, with that entire group of douchebags leering at her.

"She's the author, you idiot," says one particularly annoyed woman next to them.

"Author? Of what?"

"Oh *shit*," another singsongs. "Pretty hot—I'd get with that."

Bennett's eyes cut ahead to Teddy and Olivia. Teddy is busy signing someone's phone case, but he's angled back toward Bennett and glowering at UNCW shirt and all his friends. Bennett keeps her head down as she makes her way closer to the security team—inching toward the nearest bookshelf to put as much space between herself and the line as possible. All she has to do is get past these idiots. . . .

"Aye, sweetheart?" UNCW shirt says. "Why don't you head this way? I'll give you somethin' *big* to write about—"

"The *fuck* did you just say, bro?"

Bennett's head whips up at Teddy's voice ringing out, just in time to watch him storm over to the group of guys. Bennett bolts toward them, too.

"Guys, wait—" She grits her teeth, getting there at the same time as Teddy. He wedges himself between Bennett and the section ropes, while a member of the security team wedges himself between the group and Teddy. Bennett clamps down on Teddy's shoulder to pull him back—he looks like he's dangerously close to throwing a punch. The last thing Bennett needs to add to the list today is a brawl.

"I'm *sick* of your mouth, asshole. Back off," Teddy snaps with so much venom behind it Bennett almost takes a step back herself.

"Aw, sticking up for all the ladies now, Hollywood?" UNCW shirt says, then points toward Bennett. "You hittin' that, too? How is she?"

"That's *enough*," the security guy growls. He grips the collar of UNCW's shirt. "I gave you the option to leave on your own. Get the hell outta here or I'll throw you out myself."

One of the quieter guys of the group pops up from behind UNCW shirt. "Hey, man, we're leaving." He holds up his hands before trying to get his friend to follow suit.

The security guard glares as he tightens his grip on UNCW shirt. Without looking away, he says, "Keep it moving, Mr. Sharpe."

"Thanks, Howard," Teddy mutters, grabbing Bennett by the wrist and pulling her away with him.

Bennett thinks they're in the clear until someone behind them lets out an Oscar-worthy wolf whistle. Teddy turns back toward them so fast Bennett barely has time to react. She somehow jumps in front of him, though she doesn't think he even notices.

"Jesus *Christ*, Teddy," she bites out, digging her fingernails into his rib cage to get his attention. "They just want a reaction— quit giving it to them!"

Teddy glowers at the group over Bennett's head and takes hold of one of her wrists again. For a second, she thinks he's going to push her away, but instead he smooths his hand over hers and intertwines their fingers, taking a deliberate step backward. Bennett grips his hand and stalks past him, pulling him with her.

"Fucking disgusting," Teddy says under his breath.

They ignore the fans the rest of the way to the back office. A few of the security guards have to section off a space in line so they can get through to a side hallway that leads to the back office. Once she's confident they're far enough away from the crowd, Bennett turns around and yanks Teddy closer to her to make sure he sees the look on her face.

"Are you good?" she asks, letting more than a little attitude seep into her tone.

Teddy jerks a hand to the back of his neck, squinting at a spot on the wall behind her. He nods.

"Good," Bennett huffs, dropping his hand. She doesn't even know why she's so irritated right now. She can't say she has experience with being heckled like that by complete strangers. Olivia had handled the situation like a professional—like she was used to it—and it makes Bennett sick to think that something like that might happen to her regularly.

Teddy reaches out and catches Bennett's wrist before she can walk away. "Are *you* good?"

"Yeah? Why?" she asks, sounding more hassled than she should. She tries to pull her hand away but Teddy tightens his grip. God. Teddy had stood up for her out there—for her and Olivia. And it was really sweet. She shouldn't treat him like this, but just because she likes the idea of him standing up for her like that doesn't mean she appreciates the scene it caused. . . .

"Caldwell . . ." Teddy says, eyes searching hers. The intensity in his expression is putting her more on edge. "Those guys were dicks. Are you sure you're okay?"

"I'm fine, Teddy. And we need to go—my family's here," she says, trying to continue down the hallway. Teddy still doesn't let her go yet. "Dude, what?"

"Nothing, I just—" He shakes his head like he's trying to decide on something. "I just really want to do this."

Slowly, cautiously, he steps toward Bennett and leans down. Bennett tenses at first, unsure of what he's doing.

"I'm giving you a hug. Calm down," he says, dipping low and pulling her in. Bennett's arms wrap around his neck out of reflex and her chin rests on his shoulder, and for a second she thinks she's not up for this—too restless and strained from the day they've all had. But Teddy still hasn't let her go yet, and he smells like fresh laundry, and the warmth and sincerity behind the gesture is so overwhelming that Bennett suddenly realizes this is everything she didn't know she needed until now. She arches into him and squeezes.

"Oh, man," Teddy says after who knows how long, picking her up and setting her back down again. "You have no idea how much I've been wanting to do that lately."

Bennett isn't ready for the hug to be over but her shoulders are starting to burn from reaching up so high. Teddy makes a slight noise in protest when she unwinds her arms from his neck; then he gives a satisfied hum when she wraps them back around his rib cage. Her ear is pressed to his chest and she notes with a touch of self-regard that his heart is beating as fast as hers.

"Well, I mean—this and a few other things," he says. "Six months is a long-ass time, Caldwell."

She smiles into his sweater, completely overindulging in the way he's rubbing absentminded circles into her back. A million different clichés are running through her mind: how her heart feels like it's bursting; how she'd probably float away if he wasn't holding her down; how head over heels in lo—

And then her eyes snap open and every emotion she's feeling is upstaged by a new kind of anxiety.

"Caldwell," Teddy says after she accidentally exhales a frustrated sigh. "I can literally hear your brain freaking out right now."

Bennett snorts, but she doesn't want to ruin the fragility behind this with talking about what is going on inside her head.

"You smell good," she says, hoping to distract him.

"As long as you're overanalyzing what type of laundry detergent I use, instead of . . . anything else, then I'm cool," he says, and who even has a response like that ready to use whenever needed?

Bennett finally does pull back so she can look up at him.

"I'm a big fan of whatever detergent you use," she says, since she sure as hell isn't going to say anything else right now. Not yet.

Teddy laughs and lets her lead him down the hallway, while Bennett refuses to ruin one of the sweetest moments she's ever had with all the drama and bullshit of being emotionally inept. She stops in front of the back office's door and takes a deep breath. She can handle this. She can keep her feelings in check. This doesn't need to be a big deal, right?

She twists the doorknob and steps inside with Teddy right behind her.

And a second later they both come face-to-face with Liz McGeary.

CHAPTER TWENTY-FOUR

Bennett was wrong. This is sensory overload.

That's the only way to describe walking into the back office. An onslaught of emotions slam into Bennett all at once—sort of like how Liz slams into her before she can even get through the doorframe, screeching something over her shoulder as she hugs her. It's too much.

Thankfully Bennett's parents and brother appear in her field of vision after Liz pushes her aside to get to Teddy. At this point, Bennett's fine with letting Teddy fend for himself. She goes to hug her family and hopes her face isn't giving away the level of overwhelmed she's reached. Her mom asks if she was surprised over and over while Tanner and their dad stand off to the side, giving Bennett a few subtle, reassuring looks to balance things out.

Like mother like daughter, Aunt Susan wedges herself in next and holds Bennett at arm's length, making a big show of telling her to take deep, cleansing breaths—that they're all here for her and she shouldn't look so stressed out. Uncle Fletcher waves, not bothering to put down his iPhone. Will is the only one of his family to seem genuinely excited to be here—Bennett even catches herself smiling at the starstruck look in his eyes when Olivia introduces herself.

The only person to look more starstruck than Will is Bennett's mother, but that's only because Teddy manages to get away from Liz and walk over to say hi. Bennett watches him greet her parents, then watches his and Tanner's animated bro-hug of a reunion like no time has passed, and she's suddenly very aware of how tight her chest is—how it feels like she can't take a deep enough breath.

Eventually Emmy announces that they have dinner reservations at eight thirty across town, and that they all need to start heading that way. Liz throws a hand in the air, calling a spot in the limo like she's daring someone to tell her no. Bennett doesn't even know how she knew about the limo to begin with. Emmy explains that those involved in the book signing need to stay a few more minutes to go over some things with the owner (which is total bullshit), so it's probably best that Liz goes ahead with everyone to the restaurant. Emmy is a saint.

Bennett expects Liz to throw a tantrum. To the surprise of everyone in the room who knows her, though, Liz smiles sweetly and says she'll see everyone there then. Emmy gives Bennett's parents the name and address of the restaurant and a moment later everyone files out of the room except for Bennett, Emmy, Teddy, and Olivia.

Everything except Bennett's thoughts finally still.

* * *

"Bennett, are you gonna speak, like, at all?"

Bennett's gaze shifts from the back windshield to the concerned look on her assistant's face.

"Cut her some slack, Em," Olivia says, stretching out across her seat. "She's had a *day*."

Emmy isn't having it. Bennett doesn't blame her. Outside of thanking the owner for putting on the signing for them, Bennett hasn't spoken a word since leaving the bookstore. She isn't trying to be dramatic about it—it just feels like she has ninety million things to sort through in her head before she can attempt to do anything else.

And it sure as hell doesn't help that Teddy is pressed right up next to her with his arm slung casually across the seat behind her head.

It shouldn't have surprised Bennett that he'd sit next to her in the limo. And despite being a bit freaked out by how quickly her feelings escalated today, she really does want him there. But Liz being here is throwing her off. Her cousin already makes her cautious and protective of the important things in her life, and now that Teddy is included in that, Bennett's starting to worry how long it'll take before she catches herself teetering toward insecure as well.

"Bennett." Emmy tries again. "Would you like to tell us what you thought of the signing?" And what she's really saying is that Bennett needs to snap out of it. Now.

"It was—" Bennett starts, but her gaze shifts to the window behind Emmy's head. The limo is slowing to pull up to the curb of some building, but there's no way this is the restaurant. Surely Bennett's publisher would've picked a place with less of a crowd . . . right? Bennett nods toward the window. "Em, is this where we're eating?"

"I think so . . ." Emmy turns around. "Wait, what the fuck is *that*?"

"Did Emmy Akers just say fuck?" Olivia perks up happily,

but her smile disappears when she leans forward to look out the window. "Are those people?"

Even though it's dark, Bennett can definitely see a crowd—maybe fifty or so—outside on the restaurant's front patio. They're all standing in little groups, most with their heads bowed over what Bennett assumes is some generation of the iPhone. Maybe it's a trick of the streetlights, but most of them look like girls. . . . Teenage girls. And a limo pulling up in front of the restaurant is certainly exciting enough to snag their attention away from their screens.

Teddy shifts away, clearly having the same epiphany as Bennett. She watches him lean across the large amount of seat space next to him to knock on the limo's partition.

"Hey, man," he greets the driver as the screen lowers. "Is there a back way into this place?"

The driver says something that Bennett doesn't catch, then the limo slowly pulls away from the curb and out into traffic. Teddy draws back from the partition, propping his arm up again on the same spot behind Bennett's head. The outside of his leg is flush against hers and he's bouncing his knee wildly. Bennett finally lets herself steal a glance at his face. He's biting his thumbnail; and when his eyes flick to hers, he lowers his hand almost guiltily and gives her a tiny smile.

"Good call, Ted," Olivia says as they circle the block. Teddy's knee stops bouncing. "If those people are here for us, how the hell did they find out?"

Emmy is already tapping furiously on her iPad. "I have no idea, but we can find another place to go if you guys are uncomfortable. This is absolutely ridiculous; I cannot believe—"

"Em."

"—this. The restaurant assured me that there wouldn't be—"

"Emmy—"

"—an issue and guaranteed their discretion. Which means a waitress or someone blabbed and I'm not trying to get anyone fired but—"

Bennett groans, "Oh my *God*, EMMY."

"I—" Emmy knits her eyebrows together and glances up. "I'm sorry. The publisher and I have been planning this for a while, and after how well everything went today, I'd be really angry if the one thing to mess it up is some waitress who can't keep her mouth shut."

Teddy's knee goes back to bouncing against Bennett's as they listen to Emmy call and inform the restaurant's hostess that they will be coming in the back way due to the crowd on the front patio.

"Yes, well, this is unacceptable," Emmy says, her tone curt. "Even if no one there had anything to do with it, they're still out there. . . . Yes, we'll be arriving shortly. . . . No, I need you to make sure that someone is out there to escort us in. . . . Yes, thank you."

"Dropping F bombs, being rude to hostesses." Olivia gives a nod of approval when Emmy hangs up. "I'm digging this new side of you, Em."

* * *

The driver drops them off at the restaurant's loading dock.

Bennett climbs out of the limo after Emmy and Olivia and pauses for a second to look around. The restaurant is right on the beach, and the moon is abnormally bright and hanging low over the horizon. If Bennett ever decides to move to Wilmington, she'd definitely become a regular here.

"Hey, Caldwell, as much as I'm enjoying the view here, you mind if I hop out?"

"Oh, whoops—" Bennett jumps out of the way.

At first she thinks Teddy is talking about the same view she'd been admiring; then she realizes she'd been standing right outside of the limo's doorframe and was blocking him from seeing anything past her. She turns around and narrows her eyes at him once he's out.

"What?" he asks innocently, shutting the door. "I like the dress you're wearing; can you blame me?"

Yes, she *can* blame him.

Which makes her a total hypocrite, seeing as she'd spent the majority of the book signing getting distracted by all the wonders his sweater does for his shoulder-to-waist ratio. Now the sleeves are pushed up to his elbows and the black fabric is blending in with the night around him. He looks . . . mischievous. But that has more to do with the change in his demeanor than a well-tailored sweater. Especially when he smirks at her like that.

Bennett shakes her head and walks past him, trying to exude some form of composure, but the back of her neck and the tops of her ears are burning bright red, and the teasing chuckle she hears behind her indicates Teddy is well aware he's the reason for it.

A waiter has the restaurant's side door propped open for them. Bennett manages a friendly smile as she thanks the guy and joins Emmy and Olivia in a dark hallway off the kitchen. Once Teddy is inside, too, the waiter leads them out into the dining area. It's hard to ignore how crowded the place is, and it's even harder to ignore the gasps and squeals that echo around the restaurant when they walk in. The waiter takes them to a private room behind the bar and gestures for everyone to walk ahead of him. Bennett's family and the McGearys greet them as they look up from their menus.

"About damn time y'all got here!" Liz says, and points to the end of the table. "Bennett, you're at the head of the table so everyone can see you; and Olivia, my brother, Will, is *dying* to sit next to you."

Bennett snorts. Of the four empty seats left at the table, there's one open next to Liz, one next to that at the head, and two on the other side next to Will. Bennett knows exactly what Liz is trying to do here.

Olivia catches on, too, because she claps her hands and replies, "Oh, good, because I've been *dying* to sit next to Will too."

Will's smile takes over his entire face as the waiter pulls out Olivia's chair for her.

"You guys sit wherever you like," Bennett's dad says. "We've only ordered drinks so we can switch seats up if you guys want."

Bennett knows the only thing worse than obeying seating arrangement orders from Liz is making everyone get up and move around just to spite her.

The waiter pulls out Emmy's chair for her, then Bennett's at the head of the table. Teddy takes his seat between Bennett and an all-too-pleased Liz, and he barely has time to throw Bennett a soft smile before Liz's arm snakes around his shoulders.

"So, Teddy, tell me everything about filming," Liz says, yanking him toward her. "I'm *dying* to know."

* * *

On a scale of *Slightly Awkward* to *Excruciatingly Unbearable*, dinner has fallen somewhere near *Full of Overwhelming Second-hand Embarrassment*.

Aunt Susan and Uncle Fletcher think it's appropriate to

order drinks for their daughter (and reprimand the waitress for asking to see her ID), so Liz is drunk by the time they get through the appetizer. Only her parents seem to find it amusing. She monopolizes the conversation, orders the poor waitress around, demands to know all the details of filming (even after the third time they explain it to her), and somehow manages to keep a hand somewhere on Teddy at all times. As a writer, even Bennett couldn't have imagined this much of a train wreck.

And as an eighteen-year-old girl with a crush, Bennett wants to reach over and throw Liz's drink in her face.

"So, I mean, Bennett's book was good and all, but I'm so excited about the movie that I just—I can't even sit still!" Liz slurs, sloshing part of her third vodka and soda into Teddy's lap. "Oh, God; I'm so sorry, Ted. Let me help you."

"I've got it, thanks," Teddy mutters, carefully batting Liz's napkin away from his crotch.

If anyone deserves MVP for the evening, it's Teddy. The only time he's had a second to himself all night sans Liz was when he got up to use the bathroom halfway through dinner. Bennett had used it as an opportunity to hook a foot around the leg of his chair and subtly slide it closer to her end of the table.

Once everyone's finished with their meal, Emmy stands up with her drink in hand and clears her throat.

"First, I wanted to thank everyone for making today so great, despite a couple of changes in the original plan." Emmy smiles apologetically. "We didn't anticipate that many people coming out, so I appreciate you guys going along with it."

"You know, Emmy," Liz interrupts. "You can never be too careful when two famous actors are involved. Trials and tribulations of being a celebrity."

Emmy gives her a tight smile. "Yes, well, speaking of the actors—I have an announcement for everyone."

Tanner shoots Bennett a questioning glance from the other end of the table. She shrugs.

"Bennett and I have already been talking a little about setting up a set tour for Will, so I went ahead and arranged one for everyone tomorrow morning at ten. That way you all can see what we've been doing so far."

"What a great thought, Emmy," Bennett's mom says excitedly.

"Yes, how wonderful!" Aunt Susan chimes in, leaning over the table to look down at her daughter. "Liz, honey, now you can get a feel for what a real set looks like!"

"Oh, I'm so excited!" Liz practically screeches.

"Elizabeth has really taken to acting these days. Seeing a real set will be a great experience," Uncle Fletcher provides, and it's almost like a record scratches somewhere across the room. Everyone falls silent.

"Wait, Will," Olivia cuts in, shifting her gaze away from glaring at Liz. "I thought you were the one who's interested in acting?"

Will's slumped in his chair, his arms folded across his chest, and it looks like he's trying hard to keep his expression neutral. He'd made a couple of comments over the past few months to Bennett about Liz coming to his acting workshops, sure, but Bennett had chalked it up to Liz being bored with her life. She hadn't realized it'd come to *this*.

"Oh, I'm still interested in it—" he starts.

"Will took me with him to one of his acting workshops last fall and the instructor said it would be a *travesty* if I didn't pursue it as well," Liz interrupts in between polishing off her drink and almost missing the table when she sets the glass down.

Then she starts into all the details of the acting classes she'd started taking at Clemson so she can commit more time to *learning her craft*.

Emmy slowly sits back down and Bennett gives her an apologetic smile for her announcement getting hijacked. Jesus. Just when the McGearys couldn't get any more typical, they go and pull this. It's just—Bennett will never understand.

"Hey, Emmy?"

Bennett and Emmy look down the table to see Bennett's dad with his glass raised to her. "This has been really great, thank you." Bennett's mom and Tanner nod to her as well.

Emmy smiles and cheers them back, then she mutters to Bennett, "I do not understand how your family is so polar opposite."

"Ohmehga—!" Liz squeals, gripping Teddy's forearm. "I'm so excited for tomorrow. I can't even."

"Is there anything you *can even* with, Liz?" Olivia asks.

And Bennett isn't sure if it's because she's had to watch Liz drape herself all over Teddy all night, or the sad look on Will's face, or that she feels bad she subjected Teddy, Olivia, and Emmy to an evening with her extended family . . . maybe all the above. But either way, it's been the Liz McGeary Show since her family got here, and Bennett can't sit here and watch it anymore.

Bennett stands at the head of the table, clinking her water glass with the end of her fork. "I'd also like to thank you guys for coming today to surprise me," she says, only looking at her parents and her brother. "It really meant a lot that—"

"Oh, Bennie, stop. You know we just *love* coming to your—"

"Just two minutes, Liz. I promise," Bennett cuts clean across her cousin, holding up her hand (which is far more polite than what she wanted to say). Liz looks more taken aback than offended. "Anyway. It really means a lot to have you here. And I'm really excited for you guys to see the set tomorrow. I was thinking y'all could come a bit early and we can have breakfast beforehand? What do you think, Em?"

"Definitely a good plan," Emmy says, and Bennett knows she's itching to pull out her iPad to check what the breakfast buffet is going to be. "How about everyone gets to set around 9:15, 9:30?"

Everyone agrees, and Bennett raises her water glass. She knows she's probably going to sound so lame, but at this point, what the hell.

"And cheers to Teddy and Olivia," she says, "for choosing to be a part of this movie. I couldn't have asked for more talented actors to play these characters, and I can't wait for y'all to see the amazing work they do every day."

"Hear, hear!" Olivia says, clinking her glass with Will's first.

Bennett catches Teddy's eye as she sits back down, and she doesn't know how to describe the way he's looking at her, but it makes a blush creep up the back of her neck.

"And here's to Bennett Caldwell," Teddy says suddenly, his voice loud enough to carry over the McGeary chatter happening to his left. He raises his glass to the table but holds Bennett's gaze. "For being the reason we're all here in the first place."

* * *

As dinner is wrapping up, the same waiter from earlier appears at the door and offers to lead them out to their cars again. He says the restaurant staff tried to minimize the crowd that had gathered but there are still quite a few people left outside.

Bennett's parents and the McGearys valeted their cars, so the good-byes begin before they head up to the front of the restaurant. The McGearys waste no time with formalities, giving out curt good-byes and making sure Liz doesn't fall over when she stands from the table.

"Do y'all know where your hotel is?" Bennett asks, pulling back from hugging her mom.

"Your dad has the address so we should be good," she says.

"Okay, cool. As long as you know where you're going," Bennett worries. "And what about tomorrow? Do you know where to go for the tour?"

Tanner steps in and swallows Bennett into a hug. "Relax, Ben. We'll figure it out."

Bennett says bye to the rest of the clan, with Liz stepping on her toe as she yanks her in for another suffocating hug. Will sends Bennett an apologetic glance; Bennett sends one right back for him having to deal with a belligerent Liz for the rest of the night.

"Hey, kiddo," Bennett's dad says, walking over to her. "Tonight was great."

"Yeah." She nods, distracted by a wrinkled white envelope in his hand. "What's that?"

He holds it up. "Your boy Teddy gave it to me. I think it's a thank-you note for last July."

"A what?"

"Yeah. He said he meant to get it to us earlier. Better late than never, right?"

"Did he say why he's just now getting it to you?" Bennett asks, trying to keep her voice down. One particular text message she received (and ignored) last July about their address flashes in her mind.

"Nope. Just that he's sorry it's so late." He shrugs, adding, "He seems like a good kid, Bennett."

"He is," she says, eyeing the envelope again.

"We should get going, but we'll see you tomorrow." Her dad kisses the top of her head as he gives her a hug.

"Miss Caldwell." The waiter approaches after Bennett's family leaves. "Apparently a crowd has gathered at the loading door, too. You guys should probably get going before it gets worse."

Teddy appears at Bennett's side and says, "We can figure out another way if this is uncomfortable."

"Why would it be uncomfortable for me? They're here for you guys."

He reaches up and grips the back of his neck. "Sorry—you looked a little, I don't know, freaked out there for a second."

"Is there anyone else on staff that can help escort us out?" Emmy asks the waiter.

"I've got a couple of the barbacks waiting," he says, throwing a thumb over his shoulder.

Emmy's surprised expression is quickly rearranged back to neutral. "Very well, thank you. Bennett? Olivia? You both make sure a bouncer is with you at all times. I don't want a repeat of whatever happened out in line at the signing today."

Olivia is already heading for the door, sporting a gigantic pair of sunglasses.

"Oh, the trials and tribulations of being a *celebrity*," she sighs dramatically, pressing the back of her hand to her forehead and sweeping out of the room.

* * *

They end up spending almost an hour at the loading dock by accident.

Signing a few autographs turns into signing about fifty, and there are so many selfies taken Bennett thinks people are going to have retina damage from all the flashes. Olivia and Teddy handle themselves flawlessly. Not once are they rude; not once do they complain. And it gets to be so much that Emmy takes it upon herself to act as a step-in publicist.

"Okay, thank you, ladies," she repeats for the hundredth time. "Teddy and Olivia have filming early tomorrow. We have to get going."

Teddy and Olivia are posing with a group of six girls, one using a selfie stick to take the picture. An audible groan rings out.

"Wait! One more?"

"Teddy, I love you so much!"

"Teddy!"

"Please stay!"

Emmy nods at the barbacks.

"Please clear a path, ladies. They have to get to their car," one announces as they herd everyone back.

A few girls in front look like they're about to start mouthing off but stand down when they see how big each barback is. More muttering among themselves breaks out as Teddy, Olivia, Bennett, and Emmy pass them to get to the limo. Emmy and Bennett let Teddy and Olivia go ahead of them so they can get out of the line of fire first. Bennett is about to pass one girl with her phone pointed in Teddy's direction when something she says catches her attention.

"I can't believe Tumblr actually got something right for once," she says to her friend.

The other girl replies, "I can't believe more people didn't show. That post got, like, a thousand notes in the first thirty minutes. I just want to know how the person knew exactly where they'd be, you know? Stalker much?"

Bennett hesitates in the limo's doorframe, contemplating if

she should go back and ask what they're talking about. She decides against it at the last second and slides inside. A barback shuts the door behind her.

"I'm so sorry, you guys," Emmy jumps straight into apologizing. "I tried so hard to avoid that happening."

"Emmy, stop being ridiculous," Olivia says, removing her sunglasses.

"Yeah, it's not like you could have controlled that," Teddy adds. "I'm pretty curious about how they found out, though."

"Apparently some Tumblr post was involved," Bennett offers, sliding into the seat next to him. She crosses her legs and this time she's the one to press up against him. Teddy smiles and props his arm up on the seat behind her.

"Wait, what?" Olivia asks, amused. "How do you know that?"

"I heard two girls say it before I got in the limo."

"That wouldn't surprise me one bit," Olivia says, "especially with how much Tumblr loves some Teddy Sharpe."

He grimaces. "God, I hate Tumblr."

"What, you don't follow all your fan blogs, *Theodore*?" Bennett asks.

Teddy tries not to laugh. "I can barely handle Twitter. I looked at Tumblr once and was traumatized."

"There are so many fan fictions that you star in floating around the Internet, Teddy," Olivia joins in. "I read one the other day—I'll try to find the link again. It was called, like, 'HOV Lane' or something. . . ."

"All right, all right," Teddy interrupts. He shudders. "I'm not even going to start on how creepy it is that you read fan fiction about me, Olivia."

"Aw, come on. You should feel honored to be somebody's muse!" Olivia insists, megawatt smiling. "I read fics about me all the time. It's entertaining as hell." She grabs her phone out of her purse. "Here, name any celeb or character and a random fetish and I'll bet I can find a Teddy Sharpe pairing fic about it with at least fifty thousand reads—"

"And we're done with this conversation," Teddy says, failing to keep a grin off his face when they all start cracking up again.

The rest of the car ride is passed with Olivia going into elaborate detail about one of her fan blogs she found last year. She even admits to submitting anonymous messages about herself to rile things up. Bennett is laughing so hard by the time they get to the hotel that she's almost back to normal after the little sensory-overload spell she had earlier. But by the time they've crossed through the lobby, the exhaustion from such a long day seems to sink in with everybody.

"God, I cannot wait to go to bed," Olivia yawns after punching the elevator's up button.

The elevator arrives and Teddy holds the door while the girls step on. He gets on a second later, throwing Bennett a couple of eyebrow wiggles as he moves to stand next to her.

"Em, do you know what time we need to be on set tomorrow?" Olivia yawns again.

"The schedule has you and Teddy down for blocking at seven thirty. Filming at eight." When Olivia groans, Emmy adds, "Yeah, not that this will help, but tomorrow's got some intense shooting involved."

The elevator slows to a stop at the eighth floor and Bennett tries not to pout that for the first time in almost twelve hours, Teddy is going to be more than fifteen feet away from her. (Pathetic.)

"We'll see you guys tomorrow," Emmy calls, stepping off and rounding out of view.

Bennett follows suit, keeping her eyes down. "Bye, guys."

"Bye, Bennett. Today was awesome," Olivia says.

"See ya, Caldwell."

Just as Bennett turns around to wave, Teddy gives her *that look* again—except this time it has some implications behind it that leave her a little breathless there in the midst of the closing elevator doors. He knows exactly what he's doing, too, because he adds a heartbreaking smile at the tail end of it, and Bennett is this close to asking who the hell he thinks he is with that. When the doors finally do shut, she rolls her head back and groans at the ceiling.

There's an ear-to-ear grin on Emmy's face when Bennett looks over.

"Don't," Bennett says, trying to be stern. A gigantic smile breaks out on her own face instead.

Emmy holds up her hands. "I wasn't going to say anything."

"Yeah. Right."

"Well, I mean, other than make a comment about how you're glowing right now."

"My entire family showed up to surprise me at my book signing today," Bennett says defensively. "It has nothing to do with—"

"I didn't say it had anything to do with anyone," Emmy replies.

Bennett frowns. "I know exactly what you're saying. And thinking."

Emmy shrugs and starts walking away. "Well, at the moment I'm thinking I'm exhausted, so I'm going straight to bed. And also that Teddy is staying on the eleventh floor."

She throws Bennett a smirk before setting off down the hallway.

"Real subtle, Em," Bennett calls after her, waiting to hear Emmy's door close. She glances back at the up button on the wall and pretends that the only reason she's toying with the idea of getting back on the elevator is so she can ask Teddy the real question that's been on her mind since leaving the restaurant earlier:

Did he write that thank-you note last summer and hold on to it since then or did he write it when he realized he'd see her parents again?

"God," she exhales.

She presses the up button.

It occurs to Bennett as she watches the floor numbers tick up from eight to eleven that she has no idea what room he's in. She has no idea what she's doing in general, actually.

The eleventh floor is an exact replica of the eighth floor except for the painting that hangs over a small table outside the elevators. Bennett stops just outside the little room and pulls out her phone. She scrolls through her texts, thumb hovering over the last one she got from Teddy, but the sound of a door opening and closing somewhere down the hall makes her almost jump out of her skin.

Teddy Sharpe is strolling down the hallway toward her. His hands are in his pockets and he's staring at the floor as he walks, adding a little shuffle in between every other step like he's in a hurry but trying not to look conspicuous. Bennett's so caught off guard by the coincidence she can't think of anything to say to get him to look up. Instead, she manages to imitate a loud wolf whistle, exactly like the one from the book signing. Teddy's head whips up.

"Whoa—hey," he says through a smile.

Bennett starts toward him. "What are you doing?"

"What am I doing? This is my floor, Caldwell. What're *you* doing?"

"Oh, you know . . ." Bennett trails off. His grin widens when he stops in front of her, throwing her off her game even more. "I came to ask if you've had that thank-you note for my parents this entire time, or if you wrote a new one."

"I've had it the entire time," he says. No elaboration. No explanation. Just a slightly amused undertone in his voice. "If I recall correctly, I tried to get you to send me your address last summer."

"This *entire time*," Bennett repeats, just for good measure.

"Yeah. I was eventually going to give it to you during filming to give to them, but then we found out they were coming to the book signing so I figured I should give it to them in person since it's so late."

Her heart.

"Well, that was . . . thoughtful," is all she can get out. The only perk of staring down at the floor is being able to tell when he steps closer to her.

"Yeah. So, like, what're you really doing up here, Caldwell?"

"I—" She hesitates, trying to come up with another excuse. Whatever. She's already there. No point in playing hard to get now. "I was trying to decide which door to knock on first."

There's a pause, and then Teddy takes another step into her space. Except this time he reaches out and slips a hand around her lower back.

"So . . . you were coming to see me?" he asks, tugging her against him. Bennett's hands end up on his biceps, and she's hyperaware of the way his belt buckle is pressing into her stomach.

She scoffs casually, leaning back to get a better look at him (and to give herself time to reel some poise back into her stance). He apparently takes this as her trying to wiggle away, because he sneaks his other hand out of his pocket and gets a possessive grip on the fabric of her dress.

"You definitely were," he says.

Bennett has to redirect her gaze to anywhere but at him. "Yeah, so?" she challenges.

Teddy raises his eyebrows, looking absolutely delighted. "I would have bet a million dollars that you were going to say 'Don't flatter yourself, superstar.'"

"Figured I'd maxed that one out by now."

His grin fades a bit and is replaced with something a little more serious.

"I was coming to see you, too," he says.

"Yeah?"

He nods, leaning down and bumping their noses together. Bennett sucks in a breath. Today's been a good day, and she wants nothing more than for Teddy to kiss her right now, but the voice of reason in the back of her head thinks now is a good time to remind her that she still owes Teddy an apology.

"I'm sorry for what I said in front of Burt," she breathes, bringing a hand up to the nape of his neck. "I'm not good with handling these things."

Teddy chuckles. "Being asked to fake date someone for a PR stunt isn't exactly a normal circumstance."

"Well, it wouldn't have had to be fake if I wasn't such an asshole about it," Bennett says.

"True," he teases, smoothing his hand over her hip. He leans in close and adds, "But it also doesn't have to be fake now, right?"

Bennett laughs. "We'd probably have to talk logistics first."

Teddy considers it. "You too tired to talk now?"

"Not even close."

He pulls away from her instantly, grabbing her hand. "Now it is, then."

Teddy starts tugging her back down the hallway toward his room, dropping her hand when they get to his door to fumble with his key card. He accidentally knocks off the Do Not Disturb sign on the door handle and jumps to hang it back on. Bennett tries not to smile at the rosy splotches starting to appear on his cheeks.

He finally swings open the door and holds it so she can walk in first. Bennett steps into the room, waiting for him to turn on the lights.

"Did you make your own bed this morning?" Bennett snickers softly.

The sliver of hallway light cast across the duvet disappears when the door clicks shut.

"Caldwell," Teddy murmurs from somewhere behind her in the dark, and Bennett knows exactly what he's asking.

She turns around and reaches out until she finds him, hooking her fingers under the hem of his sweater to pull him toward to her.

And that's all it really takes before he has her in his arms and pressed back against the bathroom door.

CHAPTER TWENTY-FIVE

Bennett needs to brush her teeth.

She needs to brush her teeth and see if Teddy has any contact solution in his bathroom, even though she knows he doesn't wear them. Her contacts feel like they're a few blinks away from edging themselves out of her eyes.

What she needs to do first, however, is figure out how to pry herself out of Teddy's grasp so she can get up and start getting her life back together. She wiggles a tiny bit, trying not to wake him up in the process. Her heart melts a little as she starts taking inventory.

The guy is literally *everywhere*. Again.

His legs are tangled with Bennett's. One of his arms is curled around her rib cage. And she isn't sure how he's even breathing with his face mashed into the crook of her neck. He'd spent a lot of time there the night before, actually, and Bennett blushes thinking about all the kisses he pressed into the skin underneath her jaw.

She slowly starts working on the leg situation first; it seems like the most logical. The trickiest part isn't in the untangling, but in the attempt to shift her right thigh out from underneath his knee. She thinks she's doing a somewhat decent job until he shifts in his sleep, readjusting the grip he had across her rib cage and ruining all the progress she'd made. She finally gets too impatient to worry about waking him and uses enough force to shift herself out from under him. He stirs as she slides off the side of the bed.

"Hey," he mumbles, his voice groggy with sleep. He reaches out toward her and whines, "Come back."

"I'm going to brush my teeth," she whispers, but his hand catches her wrist when she rounds his side of the bed toward the bathroom. She's more than happy to let him pull her back in with him.

A second later, he's pressing kisses underneath her jaw again. Between the warmth of him on top of her and the way his hand is splayed playfully low on her hip, there's no way she can find the strength to put up a fight.

"We should just not go in today," Teddy murmurs into her collarbone, grazing it with his teeth for emphasis.

Bennett grins and tugs on the hair at the nape of his neck. "You know Burt will show up here and drag us out. And that would be mortifying."

"We'll push the desk in front of the door."

"That's not a good idea."

Teddy growls into the hollow of her throat and rocks his hips down into hers. "I don't recall you saying anything like that last night—"

"*Hey.*" Bennett smacks his shoulder.

"Just saying," he snickers.

"Seriously, though. Do you have an extra toothbrush?"

"Slow down, Caldwell. I don't know if I'm ready for that step in our relationship yet."

"Oh, God." She shoves him off. "I'm using yours if you don't."

Bennett finally manages to get out of bed, even with Teddy making it as difficult as possible. She took one of his T-shirts hostage last night and self-consciously pulls it down once she's on her feet. She pads toward the bathroom and accidentally steps on something cold along the way. Is it more impressive or embarrassing that it turns out to be her phone? She has no idea how it got there. She carries it into the bathroom with her, shuts the door, and turns on the lights.

Temporarily blinded, Bennett staggers around with her eyes squeezed shut as she tries to locate the bathroom counter. She finds his toiletry bag under the sink after she gets her vision back and rummages through it until she finds a toothbrush and toothpaste. No contact solution, unfortunately.

Bennett startles when she pops back up and catches her reflection in the mirror. She can't even look at the goofy-ass grin on her face, and she's probably going to be blushing for the next nine years.

As she's brushing her teeth, she picks up her phone again. The first thing she notices when her screen lights up is that she has a solid 3 percent of battery left. The second thing she notices is the time: 6:07 am. Then she sees the two text messages from Emmy, sent twenty-one minutes ago.

Sun, Feb 3, 5:46 a.m.

You and Teddy trended on Twitter last night

For 8 hours.

Bennett frowns.

Eight hours?

Against her better judgment, she pulls up the Twitter app on her phone and taps the notifications icon, taking a moment to scroll through the first few. . . .

Bennett stops brushing her teeth.

> OMG MY FAVORITE AUTHOR MIGHT BE
> DATING MY FAVORITE ACTOR IM D Y I N G
> SEND HELP #MBCALDWELL
> #TEDDYSHARPE @TeddySharpe97
> @mbcaldwellbooks

> You guys. #Shardwell IS REAL. . . .
> #ICANTHANDLETHIS 🖤 🖤 🖤 🖤

> .@MBCALDWELLBOOKS WHO WROTE
> PARACHUTES IS OUT TO DINNER WITH
> @TEDDYSHARPE97 RIGHT NOW WHO'S
> PLAYING JACK ALSDSKD WHAT IS LIFE

> Teddy & Bennett 4EVER<333 #CUTIES
> #PARACHUTES #BAES
> #MBCALDWELLBOOKS #SHARDWELL
> @mbcaldwellbooks @TeddySharpe97

> GUYS THIS IS THE GREATEST SHIP SINCE
> EVER @mbcaldwellbooks @TeddySharpe97
> #SHARDWELL #SHARDWELLFOREVER

PEOPLE I SAW THEM TOGETHER AT HER
SIGNING TODAY AND IT WAS MAGIC
#SHARDWELL IS REAL
@mbcaldwellbooks @TeddySharpe97

"What the—" Bennett breathes, one particular hashtag catching her eye. She searches #Shardwell. (Seriously? That's still the best they can come up with?) That's when the more vicious tweets start flooding in.

At least we know now that unless ur tiny &
pretty & can help his career,
@TeddySharpe97 wont date u 🙄 #Shardwell
#FandomWank

Who the hell is this #shardwell chick like why is
she even relevant enough for @TeddySharpe97
to date I don't understand

.@TeddySharpe97 doesn't waste time at all.
@mbcaldwellbooks is pretty & whatever but
come on, you had @lovecbordeaux
#downgrade #shardwell

@TeddySharpe97 rebounding from
@lovecbordeaux with @mbcaldwellbooks wtf
is this the apocalypse 😂 #downgrade

Everyone needs to calm down with all this
hate on Teddy and who he's dating. Let him
live his own life!!! #shardwell #shordeaux

#CheddyForever #TeamCheddy
#TeamShordeaux #JustSayin
#ShardwellisNotAGoodShipNameAnyways
#Shardwell

Chelsea Bordeaux >>>>>>>> Bennett
Caldwell. Not even a competition.
#shardwell #shordeaux

y'all acting like this #shardwell thing is the end
of the world pls u know it's not gonna last he'll
find some1 better

r u fuckin kidding me #shardwell is the
dumbest thing twitter has ever come
up w/ #killmenow

.@mbcaldwellbooks and @TeddySharpe97
together is a joke. Wtf who would believe he
would date her? #shardwell
#stoptryingtomakeshardwellhappen

Bennett's screen goes black before she can search anymore.
She curses under her breath.

"Bennett?" Teddy peeks into the bathroom, squinting at her.
She recoils away so he can't see her face.

"Be out in a sec," she says.

Teddy opens the door wider and walks in. "You mind if I
shower?"

She tries not to panic and glances down at the foamy toothbrush in her hand. Avoiding his gaze, she shakes her head and

stares at the sink while he reaches into the shower and turns on the water. She finishes brushing her teeth as fast as she can and heads for the door.

"All yours," she calls over her shoulder, right as Teddy is hooking his thumbs in the waistband of his briefs. His freaking Buzz Lightyear briefs.

He smirks and asks, "Why are you in such a hurry to run off?"

"I need to plug in my phone," Bennett says. It's a weak excuse, but it works. Once she closes the bathroom door behind her, she digs the heels of her hands into her eyes and tries to collect herself.

This isn't a big deal, right? They're just people on Twitter . . . a lot of people on Twitter, talking about Teddy and Bennett's business for a long-ass time. . . .

There are spots in her vision when she pulls her hands away. She sits down on the bed, then stands up again and goes looking for an iPhone charger. Teddy comes out of the bathroom a few minutes later, clutching a towel to his hips. Bennett does her best to keep her eyes on anything else but him.

"Did you find my charger?" he asks as he crosses the room to the dresser. After pulling out a T-shirt and a pair of khakis, he looks back and eyes Bennett expectantly.

"Oh—yeah. Thanks," she says.

He nods before disappearing into the bathroom again.

Bennett lets out another shaky breath. She needs to calm down. Twitter gossip doesn't change anything, and it isn't like Teddy's the one fueling the Internet fire. Maybe this will turn out the way Burt says it will? Helping the movie reach as many people as possible? The idea still doesn't sit well with Bennett, but she can't really do anything about it now, right?

The bathroom door swings open. Teddy is fully dressed again

and in the middle of brushing his teeth, and there's something so easy about the way he's casually going about his business that it yanks on Bennett's heartstrings.

"So, you pumped for your family to see the set today?" he asks around all the toothpaste in his mouth. "It's gonna be an awesome day of shooting to watch."

"Yeah, should be good," Bennett says, deciding that locating the rest of her belongings is the most important thing in the world at the moment. She just needs some space for a sec—physically and mentally—to get her head back on straight. "I should probably head out now, though. We need to be on set soon."

Teddy looks over at her, but Bennett can't bring herself to fully look at him.

"Okay," he says slowly as Bennett flits around the room. "You wanna carpool or something? Olivia and Emmy can ride, too."

"Do you know where my other shoe is?" she asks as she checks under the desk in the far corner. There's no way it's under there, but it's somewhere to *look*.

"Bennett," Teddy says.

Bennett finds her other shoe beside the nightstand and her tights near the bedskirt.

"I'll probably take my car on set today—I was planning on going to a coffee shop later in the afternoon to get some writing done," Bennett says. She gathers up the rest of her clothes and heads back into the bathroom, still not looking at him. "I'm going to get changed."

There's a sharp exhale behind her as she closes the door.

Bennett presses her palms to the bathroom counter and checks her reflection in the mirror again. She still looks absolutely wrecked—except this time it's from the looming anxiety courtesy of #Shardwell. Her hands feel numb.

Once she's fully dressed, she comes back out to find Teddy sitting on the bed with his head in his hands. He looks up, and the expression on his face stops her dead in the doorframe.

"What's wrong?" she starts.

His eyes are cold, his mouth a thin line.

"I don't know, Bennett," he says. "You tell me."

"What? Nothing is—"

"Bullshit," he cuts her off.

Bennett's stomach twists uncomfortably. Why can't Bennett just act normally and wait until she gets back to her room to have her meltdown? What is it about Teddy that makes her wear her heart on her sleeve, out where God and everyone on Twitter can see it?

"I'm gonna ask one more time, Caldwell," Teddy says, his tone almost pleading. "What's wrong? I need you to talk to me here."

"Seriously, I'm fine," she forces herself to say, refolding his T-shirt she borrowed and setting it on the nightstand. "I didn't mean—"

"Oh, *bullshit*, Bennett," Teddy snaps, and the outburst makes her jump back. "Everything was fine ten minutes ago, what the hell happened? Why are you acting like this?"

"Acting like what—"

"Like you're going to start ignoring my calls and texts and disappear again!" he says, scrubbing a hand through his wet hair.

Bennett flinches. "Teddy, I was literally just going back to my room."

"God, this is so fucking classic Bennett Caldwell," he growls under his breath.

His tone sets her enough on edge to straighten her spine and look him in the eye.

"Do *not* talk to me like that," she says.

"Then why don't you start talking to me for a change then, huh?" he says, standing and pacing the room. "Literally every time I think things are good again, you freak out over something and shut me out instead of talking to me about it—"

"Did you know we trended on Twitter last night?" she asks.

Teddy's face goes blank for a second. Only a second.

"Oh, lemme guess," he scoffs. "You're freaking out because you found some hashtag and read all the tweets about how I only like to date pretty chicks who can help my career?"

"Yeah, you *nailed it*," Bennett says, matching his sarcasm even though he's half right.

"Then what? You came across a shipping war between Team Chelsea and Team Bennett? Read all the Twitter hate directed at you for being romantically linked to me? Had little fourteen-year-old girls tell you that you're not even that pretty? I can go all day, Bennett—am I getting close here?"

Pretty damn close. But Bennett isn't about to let him know how insecure she is for buying into it.

"I wasn't freaking out," she says, and it sounds weak and frail even to her own ears. "I was just . . . surprised by it."

Teddy shakes his head. "Oh, don't feed me that. I know a classic Bennett Caldwell freak-out when I see one. I've become quite familiar with them, thanks."

And what the hell does he think he means by that?

She looks him dead in the eye and says, "And whose fault is that?"

Her words hang there between them, long enough to regret saying them, but not long enough for her to apologize for them.

"You know what, man," Teddy says mostly to himself. He starts across the room, widening the gap between them. "If this is all I'm gonna get when I've been trying so hard here, then I have to get ready to be on set, and you should go."

He opens his hotel room door and won't meet her eyes.

Bennett stands there for a moment.

"I can't keep doing this, Bennett," he says. "I can't keep getting my hopes up with you that everything's fine and then have the rug pulled out over stupid things like Twitter. Yeah, it sucks that my job brings in weird factors like PR schemes and people gossiping about us on the Internet, but it's the reality we've got. And if you're gonna freak out on me every time without even trying to explain, then I'm not gonna keep putting in the effort. I'm sure you appreciate the self-preservation."

His words sink down into Bennett's heart and harden along with the resolve already there. Yeah, she had picked this fight, but she doesn't know how things went sideways so quickly. If he wants to play the self-preservation card, fine. He can watch the pro. With as much dignity as she can muster, she picks up her bag, unplugs her phone from his charger, and starts for the door.

"So, I guess that's that, then, huh?" she says as she steps past him and out into the hallway. She doesn't bother to turn around. He's already closing the door before she's even through the doorframe.

The door clicks shut behind her and a loud thud from the inside immediately follows.

So do the tears.

CHAPTER TWENTY-SIX

Burt Bridges has no chill.

Bennett was late to set this morning—the first time ever—and he won't let her hear the end of it. But that's not what's irritating her the most. It's the constant, machine-gun fire questions about the book signing. Even during takes he's only halfway paying attention to the scene. Apparently finding out if his little PR stunt is a go is more important than actually filming the movie.

"Jesus Christ, Burt, why don't you check Twitter yourself?" Bennett finally snaps after the eighth time the director asks if she thought people caught on. He throws her a nasty look before turning back to the monitor in front of him.

"A little subtlety, Bennett," Emmy murmurs.

Bennett shrugs her off. She isn't in the mood for subtlety. She isn't even in the mood to be on set. The only reason she's here is because her family is going to show up for their tour soon.

"Hey—are you okay?" Emmy tries again. "You're looking a little off right now."

Bennett barks out a laugh and stands up from her chair. "You have no idea."

She knows she looks like she's come unhinged. She's wearing an oversized, wrinkled T-shirt under a fleece pullover, leggings, and her worn out Bean Boots. Her hair is a frizzy mess; and even though it's cloudy and looks like it could start pouring rain at any second, Bennett makes sure her sunglasses are on at all times.

"You wanna talk about it?" Emmy asks.

They start walking back toward the production assistant tables, away from the cast and crew.

"What time is it?" Bennett asks instead. It feels like she's been on set for hours, and it doesn't help that they're filming some of the more tender scenes between Jack and Katherine this morning. Watching Teddy and Olivia huddle together and pretend like they're in love is chipping away at Bennett's sanity.

"Nine seventeen," Emmy says. "Everyone will be here soon."

"Fan*tastic*. I'm gonna go to my trailer until then."

Bennett sees the hurt flash in her assistant's eyes before she replies with, "I'll come get you when everyone's here."

Awesome. Now Bennett's lashing out at everyone.

* * *

Her cheek is mashed against the top of her kitchen table when someone finally comes looking for her. Bennett hears the door open but she can't find the urge to lift her head to see who it is.

"Jesus, Bennett."

She definitely hadn't been expecting Will. Bennett twists around to look at him and readjusts her sunglasses. "Hey."

"What're you doing? Emmy told me to come find you."

"Just . . . collecting my thoughts," she says, sitting up straighter. When she stands, Will gives her a once-over.

"You look like hell."

"You look like you're late for a poetry reading," Bennett says. He's sporting black skinny jeans, a gray V-neck sweater, and a pair of square, black-rimmed glasses.

Will laughs—a good-natured, genuine laugh. It's enough to thaw some of the ice that's been building up in Bennett's chest all morning.

"This set is insane, Bennett," he says. "I can't believe you guys get to come here every day."

"Have you met the director yet?" she asks.

"No, not yet. Emmy said he was finishing up a scene and then he'd come meet us."

"We should probably head back there, then."

Will hesitates for a second, watching her carefully. "Are you okay? You seem—I don't know—a little off today."

"I'm fine."

"Well, I mean, compared to last night . . ." he presses.

Bennett starts for the door. "Seriously, we should go find everyone else. Don't want to be late for the set tour."

"Does this have anything to do with Teddy?" Will asks.

She stops, making sure there's a neutral expression on her face before she turns to face him again. "No? Why?"

"Because he looks a little off today, too."

"He's fine," Bennett grumbles. "He gets to cozy up with Olivia all day today."

She knows as soon as she says it it's confirmation Teddy is the reason she seems off. Will catches on, too, but thankfully he doesn't question her more about it. He nods, and they leave the trailer, heading off across the parking lot toward set.

"Fair warning: Liz is a bit hungover this morning," Will says.

Bennett almost laughs.

"What's her deal with acting now?" she asks. "I know you kinda told me, but I didn't realize how bad it'd gotten." Will doesn't answer right away. When Bennett looks back up at him, she slows their pace to a stop. "Hey, are you okay?"

Will looks like he's teetering between wanting to scream and wanting to cry.

"Yeah—no," he finally says, shaking his head. "It just sucks, you know?"

"What, having to deal with your older sister encroaching on your life even more than usual?"

"That, and my parents pretending like I was never into acting in the first place," he says bitterly.

"How did this even happen?"

He sighs. "I'm in a pretty exclusive acting class back home—one you have to get recommendations to get into. Liz kept hounding me after that weekend in July to help her get a spot. I finally did just to get her to shut up about it. Next thing I know, she's *found her passion* and is considering changing her major to theater."

Sounds like Liz.

Will adds, "And it's complete bullshit because I had to beg my parents to let me take those classes—like, I'm talking full-on groveling—and they acted like it was the biggest inconvenience. But the second Liz decided she wanted to start acting, they were all about it. Now it's 'Oh, Liz is studying to be an actress; she and Will sometimes take the same class together, but it's more of a hobby for Will.'"

Sounds like the McGearys. Bennett's always wondered how Will wound up with a family of complete assholes. It isn't fair.

"I don't understand why, though," Bennett says. "Liz used to make fun of you all the time for acting. It's so random that she suddenly got interested in it."

Will scoffs, digging his hands into his pockets and kicking at some loose gravel on the ground. "It wasn't random. Like, at all."

"What?"

He kicks more gravel. Harder this time. "Think about it, Bennett. She became obsessed with the idea of acting in *July*." He waits for her to catch on. When she cocks her head to the side, he sighs and says, "Otherwise known as, the weekend she saw you with Teddy Sharpe."

Bennett's mouth pops open.

"Are you serious?" she says, her anger mixing with a shot of guilt. "That's it? *That's* the reason? She's literally trying to steal your dream because of Teddy?"

"Teddy was definitely a factor, but he wasn't the main reason."

Bennett scrunches her eyebrows together. "So what was?"

"Come on, B." He gives her a look like it's the most obvious thing in the world. "On top of seeing you with Teddy that weekend, we later find out it was because he auditioned for the movie that's being made about your book."

"So?"

"So, I know how my sister works. She's always had this weird jealousy issue with you," he says. Bennett snorts. "Oh, shut up— it's true and you know it. She's always been jealous, so obviously when she saw that you had all these cool things happening in your life, she had to figure out a way to compete."

"But, of all things, she picked acting? What'd she think, that I'd miraculously get her a part in the movie or something?"

He shrugs. "I mean, that's why she practically forced your parents to invite us to your book signing. I'm sure she had some plan in her head that would get her on set to meet the actors. It was just too much luck that your assistant already had that planned out."

Bennett groans. "This is the most messed up situation. Jesus Christ."

Will's smile turns calculating. "Want to hear something even more messed up? Last night she passed out the second we got back to our hotel room, and I was already so pissed about Liz and my parents embarrassing us at dinner, I decided to snoop through Liz's phone."

"Oh, no . . ." Bennett says, bracing herself.

"I opened her Tumblr app when I got bored with reading her text messages, only to find that she has an entire fan blog dedicated to Teddy Sharpe. It's got, like, thirty thousand followers. Not even kidding."

"What?!"

"And that's not even the best part," Will says. "She made a post last night with the time and location of the restaurant we went to, promising Teddy would be there. That's why there was such a huge crowd out front when y'all got there."

Bennett's jaw goes slack. That had to have been the post those girls were referring to last night—it was all Liz. And the fact that she runs a Teddy Sharpe fan blog is so ironic Bennett can't wait to tell Teddy all about it.

Well, she *wants* to tell Teddy all about it. . . .

"I don't even know where to start with this blog thing. . . ." Bennett says to distract herself, and that's when she's struck with arguably the most brilliant idea she's ever had.

"Whoa—talk about a demeanor change there, B," Will says,

cautiously returning her grin. "You look like you just had a paradigm shift to end all paradigm shifts. . . ."

"Don't worry about it," Bennett says. This is going to be perfect. "We should get back. I have a few things I need to do before the set tour starts."

* * *

The set is between takes when Will and Bennett return.

Everything is in complete chaos per usual—PAs are running around making sure the cast and crew are happy; makeup artists are trying desperately to get in a last touch of powder; the actors are holding court in their director's chairs. . . .

Burt and the producers are having some kind of private discussion next to one of the filming monitors and the rest of the crew is in the process of fixing one of the backdrops. Bennett has to wade through a sea of crewmembers to go say hi to her family and to drop Will off with his. (To her delight, Bennett notes that Liz looks even worse than she does.) They're all standing with Emmy, looking a little overwhelmed with everything.

"I'll be right back—I need to talk to Burt for a sec," Bennett tells her.

She already has a general idea of how this conversation is going to go, hopefully, but she still feels a tiny ripple of dread as she heads across set toward Burt. Her gaze flicks over toward the actors out of reflex along the way, and her heart gives a panicked flutter when her eyes meet Teddy's. He immediately looks away.

Burt is huddled up with a group of producers, and Bennett just doesn't have the time to stand awkwardly and wait for a lull in the conversation.

"Excuse me, guys," she says, sliding up between the director and another producer. "Would y'all mind if I have a word with Burt for a second?"

"We still need to get that shot," Burt says after them as they head off in different directions. Then he turns to Bennett and folds his arms. "What's up, Bennett?"

"I need you to let my cousin Will over there be an extra in the raid scene we're filming later this afternoon," she says without preamble, and Burt looks at her like she's officially lost it. "An extra with *lines*."

"Are you kidding me, Bennett? You know we don't have time to set that up. There's too much paperwork that has to get done, and what lines are we going to give him? The script is set."

"It's not that much paperwork, and he won't even have to be credited. I'll figure out the lines while I'm touring my family around."

Burt frowns some more. "It's not that simple. . . ."

"I'll make sure the producers are on board with it, too. All you have to do is sign off."

"It's just not a feasible option today, Bennett."

"Come on, Burt," Bennett pleads. "I haven't asked you for anything during production, and I've done everything you've asked of me. It's just a few extra lines in the movie. That's it."

"Did he put you up to this?"

"*No*," she says. "He doesn't even know I'm asking you."

"Then why is this such a pressing issue if he doesn't even know you're asking?"

Bennett has to take a second to figure out exactly how she wants to word this. "Will's just super into acting. And he's sur-rounded by a family of assholes all the time. Giving him a couple of lines in a thirty-second scene will literally make him the happiest person on planet Earth today."

Bennett never pegged Burt as a softie, but she can see she's wearing him down.

"You know he has to stay and get all the paperwork done—photo release forms, liability waivers, the whole shebang," he says, pressing a finger to his mustache.

Optimism surges through Bennett. "I know. I'll make sure it gets done."

"And no promises that the extra scene will make the final cut."

"I know," she says. She already has a strategy in mind for that as well. "But you have to at least promise you'll consider it."

"Fine. Then consider it all done. But you gotta do something for me in return," he says, squaring off with her. Bennett already knows what's coming. She'd anticipated it, actually. "You have to give this PR thing with you and Teddy a shot. I mean really give it a go. I know you think it's a cheap—"

"Done," Bennett says.

"—scheme, but I—" Burt stops midsentence. "What?"

"I said, consider it done."

"Just like that?" he asks suspiciously.

She nods. "As long as you keep your word, Burt, I'll keep mine. But I get to do the PR thing on my own terms, with no interference from you."

He considers that for a moment, squinting at her like he's trying to see any cracks in her demeanor. Bennett keeps her cool, though. This is the segue piece in her plan—the most important component in setting everything into motion. And it's all hinging on Burt Bridges.

"Done," he says, holding out his hand.

CHAPTER TWENTY-SEVEN

Tanner lets Bennett borrow the baseball hat he'd worn to set. He told her he's doing her a favor. By then Bennett's too on edge to care about how bad her hair apparently looks, but she puts it on anyway.

Her plan is set into motion at precisely 10:02 a.m., when Burt comes over to introduce himself to Bennett's family. They don't actually get the set tour going until after ten fifteen, though, because Liz and her parents spend fifteen minutes gushing to Burt about what an amazing job he's doing (while subtly hinting at their family's "interest in acting"). Burt wants nothing to do with them after one conversation and finally sends them off on the tour so he doesn't have to deal with them anymore.

It takes an impressive amount of stealth and coordination to fill Emmy and Will in on the plan while they're touring around set. (Will almost blows their cover with his reaction to Bennett telling him she got him a spot in filming.) Thank goodness Bennett talked to the producers about Will before the tour started—her cheeks and face are so sore from all the fake smiling for pictures she's done so far, she probably wouldn't have been able to speak, let alone convince them to cast Will as an extra. They were surprisingly receptive to the idea, though.

Bennett and Will make sure to document every second of the tour, from beginning to end—proposing selfies around set; taking pictures with their families; making sure Liz looks as hungover as she feels in every photo. . . . They take so many pictures Will's phone dies halfway through. Just as planned.

Liz has one of those iPhone cases that charges your phone, and she's too hungover to care when Will asks if he can borrow it. She hands her phone over with an irritated shrug, and Will is practically bouncing when he gets back to Bennett's side.

"I started a group text with your family and my family so we can send each other all the pictures we've taken," Bennett says quietly. "Emmy's also in there—she's the six-four-six area code number."

It doesn't seem possible, but Will's smile actually gets bigger. It's taking up his entire face.

"I still can't believe you got me a spot in filming," he says, lowering his voice but keeping the giddy excitement in his tone. "This is going to be amazing—"

Bennett shushes him. "You're not supposed to know yet, remember? And we really have to sell this PR thing. . . . Knowing Burt, he'll probably change his mind and cut your scene just to spite me if we don't pull it off."

"No worries." Will shows her the back of Liz's phone case and presses a little silver button. Four white dots light up. His smile turns devious. "Fully charged. We got this."

Nodding, Bennett thinks back over her plan. The only things left to do are to break the news to the Will's parents about his role, then fill Olivia in on her job. . . .

And somehow convince Teddy to speak to her again.

* * *

"*WHAT?*" Liz screeches, her eyes darting between Bennett, Will, and Burt.

Everyone winces, and it takes a heroic display of self-control for Bennett not to laugh—she has to roll her lips back between her teeth and look away.

"Christ," Burt mutters. He turns to Will and his parents. "As I was saying, we'd love for Will to fill in for one of the extras this afternoon, but there's a lot of paperwork to get done. Will, are you over eighteen?"

"Er—no, sir."

Bennett panics. She'd completely forgotten Will needed a parental signature.

Burt nods. "You'll need a parent to cosign, then. Once Bennett gets everything green-lit with the producers and Emmy gets back with your paperwork, we can get you into hair and makeup."

"Emmy will be back in a few minutes," Bennett says. "And I already spoke with the producers about the script before the set tour."

"Don't you work fast, Bennett," Uncle Fletcher says. He doesn't look pleased. "Mr. Bridges, are there other openings for extras today? My daughter, Liz—"

"Sorry, but no. We only have room for one," Burt says; then he glances around the group. "But everyone is welcome to stay to watch filming this afternoon."

Uncle Fletcher and Aunt Susan gape.

Liz, on the other hand, sets her jaw and glares at the director's back as he walks away.

Bennett glances at her family to gauge their reactions. They'd been so enthusiastic about the set tour, but right now they just look uncomfortable. Bennett's parents are trying to keep up small talk while Tanner subtly congratulates Will.

"Bennett, I'm freaking out," Will says. He speaks softly, throwing glances in Liz's direction. Despite everything, he's still being considerate of his older sister—something that only Will McGeary would do.

"I'm freaking out for you," Bennett said. "You deserve it. Are your parents going to sign for you, though?"

Will grins. "They better. But I can forge my dad's signature better than he can."

"What's the scene he's in?" Tanner asks.

"It's the raid scene Katherine's involved in when she sneaks away from The Company to go on a rogue mission." Bennett feels her chest tighten as she answers. The scene that follows this one in the script is the reunion between Jack and Katherine—the same one from the first table-read. "Will's going to be one of the technicians in the warehouse that helps Katherine get out when she's detected."

Tanner high-fives him and says, "You're gonna kill it, man—"

There's another shriek from across set, except this time it's followed by Olivia running over and almost tackling Will into a hug. Emmy strolls up a minute later with a smirk on her face and paperwork in her hands, obviously already spreading the good news to the cast and crew. Olivia makes a huge deal out of congratulating Will in front of Liz and his parents. And it's so hilariously satisfying that Bennett kind of feels guilty.

"You're going to be spectacular, Will," Olivia says, megawatt smiling as she wraps Will into another bear hug. "This is just the start, too. Having a major production as the first thing on your acting résumé is huge. I'm putting you in touch with my agent after this."

Will looks like he's going to pass out. The rest of the McGeary clan looks like they're going to explode. Particularly Liz.

The only sour note of the day so far comes when Bennett's parents pull her aside and tell her they can't stay to watch Will film his scene. Tanner has to get back for a last-minute swing lesson before his big golf match later in the week, and her dad has a business meeting with Pontoon Paul back at the lake later that night.

"I wish y'all could stay," Bennett says, trying not to whine. "I still can't believe you guys came to the signing."

"So you were surprised?" her mom asks. "I was a little worried someone blew our cover."

"Totally surprised." Bennett grins.

"We had a blast, kiddo," her dad says as she walks them across the parking lot to their car. "Tell Burt thank you again for having us. And tell your friends we said bye, too."

Bennett hopes no one picks up on how much it hurts that Teddy isn't going to say bye to her family. "I'll let them know," she says.

They're about halfway across the set parking lot when Olivia calls out after them, "Hey, wait a sec, Caldwells! I didn't get to say bye!"

Because of course even a demanding major motion picture production can't keep Olivia Katsaros from being fucking awesome. She bear hugs everyone and stands with Bennett as her family drives away.

"Your brother's superhot, by the way," Olivia comments as she waves at the retreating car.

Bennett bursts out laughing. "Is that the real reason why you came over to say good-bye?"

"I may have given him my number last night when you weren't looking."

"Oh, God—thanks for that."

"You're welcome," she replies cheerfully.

"Hey, real quick, I have a favor to ask you," Bennett says, lowering her voice as they walk through the parking lot back to set. "So, I kind of had to cut a deal with Burt to get a spot for Will in filming today, but he made sure to tell me that there was a chance Will's scene would get cut in editing—" she explains, stopping when Olivia holds up her hand.

"Way ahead of you there, B. After witnessing the freak show that is his family last night, the boy must be protected at all costs. I'll make sure he's in all the right shots."

Bennett laughs at her use of "freak show," because, honestly, the phrase is about as accurate as it gets.

"Oh, for the love of God," Olivia mutters. "Speak of the devil."

Glancing up, Bennett follows Olivia's line of sight until it lands on Liz beelining toward them.

"Bennett? Can I talk to you for a sec?" she asks when she's still a good distance away.

Bennett sighs. "What's up, Liz?"

Liz is looking worse now than she was before the set tour— it probably has to do with her brother stealing back his spotlight. Real world lighting always shows Liz's true form.

Liz looks at Olivia. "Could you give us a second?"

Wrong thing to say to Olivia Katsaros.

"Actually, no. I can't," Olivia shoots back. "I'm gonna stand here and wait for you to get out whatever it is you think is more important than the conversation I was having with Bennett."

For one brief, beautiful second, Liz actually seems intimidated.

She looks to Bennett for some backup. Bennett looks back at her expectantly.

"Okay. Whatever," she says, getting her expression back to neutral. "So, you got my brother a spot in filming today?"

It's more of an accusation than a question.

"Yeah, I did," Bennett says. She almost starts to say why, but then remembers there isn't a damn thing in the world she needs to justify to Liz McGeary anymore. Especially when it comes to decisions about a movie that's based on her book.

"So, that means you can maybe convince Burt to open up another extra spot, right?" Liz tries again, and Olivia scoffs.

Bennett shakes her head. "Not really. It took some serious convincing to get Burt on board with a change like this. Especially since all castings had to be confirmed months ago during preproduction."

That last part is a total lie, but there's no way Liz knows that.

"Come on, Bennett," Liz whines. "This is, like, my dream! Please? After everything I've done for you—please do this for me?"

And the sad part is, Liz is being dead serious with that.

"Sorry, Liz. I can't," Bennett says, and it's almost scary how fast any trace of pleading on Liz's face vanishes.

"I can't believe how selfish you're being," she snaps, taking a step toward Bennett. Liz is a lot taller, and she makes a point to lean forward so it seems like she's looming over Bennett.

Surprisingly, it makes Bennett want to laugh.

"Yes. *I'm* the selfish one," she says.

Liz makes a face. "What is that supposed to mean?"

Bennett already has a response planned out about how selfish it is to be so unsupportive of her own brother's dream, but Olivia ends up beating her to the punch.

And she does so spectacularly.

"Jesus, it *means* that you're pretty much the definition of an asshole, Liz," Olivia snaps.

"Excuse me—?"

"So listen." Olivia gestures between herself and Bennett. "You're on our turf right now, sweetheart, and we don't have time for whiny, borderline psychotic bitches like you who get off on making people miserable. We have a multimillion-dollar movie franchise to get back to. One that most certainly doesn't include you. So, if you'll be so kind as to excuse us—which, don't hurt yourself, since any form of basic human decency seems to a stretch for you."

Pleased with herself, Olivia hooks her arm through Bennett's and pulls her forward, forcing a stunned-silent Liz to have to move out of their way.

"You are fucking awesome, Olivia," Bennett says, and she doesn't even care that she says it loud enough for Liz to hear.

Olivia shrugs. "I try."

Liz doesn't follow them, and Bennett smiles all the way back onto set, letting herself have a couple of moments before setting into motion the last leg of her plan. She and Olivia find Will and Emmy still rushing to get Will's paperwork done before he has to go into hair and makeup. Will is still using his sister's phone case and hands it and the phone to Bennett, telling her the passcode.

"You sure about this, Bennett?" Emmy asks.

Bennett nods.

"Sure about what?" Olivia chimes in.

"I'll let Will and Emmy tell you," Bennett says, squeezing Olivia's shoulder as she starts away from the group. "I've got one last thing I need to do."

* * *

Teddy is sitting in a director's chair to the left of the main set. Alone.

Which is probably the luckiest break Bennett's gotten all day. She had to take another minute inside her trailer to fully talk herself into what she's about to do.

When she swings open the trailer door to leave, the crew is already getting the set ready for filming that afternoon. Burt and the producers are posted up around Burt's favorite camera monitor, going over the itinerary. Will, Olivia, and a few of the other extras are swarmed with hair and makeup artists. The rest of the McGearys are awkwardly standing off to the side by themselves. . . .

Before they see her, Bennett skips down the trailer steps and ducks behind a door prop that a few crewmembers are carrying to the main set. She lifts her chin to Emmy as she passes by her and a huddle of personal assistants by the PA tables. Emmy wiggles her eyebrows and gives her a thumbs-up.

The knot in Bennett's stomach has worked itself into what feels like a serious medical issue. She's having a hard time catching her breath as she walks next to the guys carrying the door prop. When they veer off toward the main set, she finally breaks away and forces herself to head in Teddy's direction. She puts it off to the very last second, and by then she's pretty sure he knows she's coming, just refusing to acknowledge her.

"Hey—" She clears her throat when she stops in front of him. "Hey, Teddy?"

It takes a few painful seconds before he looks up from his phone. His face is neutral, but his body language says it all:

- 335 -

He's angled slightly away from her, arms crossed over his chest. It's clear the last thing he wants to be doing is talking to her.

"Hey," he says.

Bennett gathers most of her nerve and points to the empty chair next to him. "Do you mind if I sit?"

"Um." He glances at the chair, then back at her. "I mean, I guess not. . . ."

"Thanks," she says, ignoring how much his hesitation hurts. She sits next to him and he immediately starts fidgeting— alternating between looking at his phone and looking in the opposite direction of her. She waits for him to settle in (for her own sake, mostly), but Teddy reaches up and scrubs at the back of his head for a second, then stands suddenly.

"I'm gonna go—"

"Wait, Teddy," Bennett blurts out. His back is already to her and he barely twists around to look at her when she asks, "Can we talk?"

"Now?"

"Yeah."

"I'm supposed to be studying lines," he says.

Bennett knows he's been off-book for weeks now. "Please?"

He stands there for a moment, bouncing on the balls of his feet. Then he sighs and sits back down. "All right. What's up, Bennett?" he asks, and Bennett feels like she's going to throw up.

"I'm so sorry about this morning, Teddy," she rushes out, and she's pretty sure Teddy hadn't been expecting her to jump right into it. His eyebrows shoot up before his expression goes neutral again. "And I really want to talk to you about why I freaked out like that, but," she takes a deep breath, "but first I need to ask if you'll do me a favor."

Teddy snorts. "Yeah? What's the favor?"

"Well, for starters, I got Will an extra's role in filming today," she says, unsure of where else to begin and a little distracted by how he's inched all the way to the far side of his director's chair.

Teddy nods, still looking straight ahead. "I heard."

"Yeah," Bennett says. "And I kind of had to cut a deal with Burt in order to do it—and it involves you, so I wanted to talk to you about it before I did anything."

She watches Teddy's eyebrows knit together—then watches his expression harden with realization.

"You agreed to the PR scheme," he says.

"As a bartering chip," she says quickly. "The only way Burt would let me get Will in was if I agreed to it. On my terms, though. Not his."

Teddy's frowns deepens. "Your terms? So, I don't get a say in this?"

"Of course you do, if you want?" Bennett says, caught off guard. "I just assumed that—"

"You assumed, what? That I'd go along with whatever the hell this is and not worry about how it could possibly affect me or my career?"

"Whoa—hang on a sec," Bennett scrambles. "Of course you have a say in it! I just didn't expect you to agree to this at all, let alone want some kind of say in how to do it."

He snorts. "Yeah, well. I didn't expect you to ever be on board with a scheme like this, either, given that apparently it only takes a couple of tweets to set you off. But color me corrected, I guess."

Bennett sits back in her chair in silence, letting his words level her. She deserved it, she knows, but she honestly doesn't think she'll be able to recover from that one anytime soon.

"I'm sorry," Teddy mutters after a moment, still looking frustrated. "It's just—I'm still a little touchy from this morning. That wasn't cool."

"It's okay," Bennett says cautiously. "It was still warranted."

"Maybe a little," he admits, and Bennett can't tell if he's leaning more toward joking or being serious. "All right, so what're the terms of the favor?"

Bennett types in the passcode on the phone Will gave her and pulls up the home screen. She taps the messages icon, then the group text she'd started earlier, then picks out Emmy's number in the list of recipients. She sends her a quick text telling her where she and Teddy are sitting.

"Well," Bennett says, wading through some of the awkwardness still there between them. "I was talking with Emmy about the best way to go about this, and she and I thought it might be easiest to just get some candid pictures together. What do you think?"

Teddy stares at her for a moment instead of responding. Bennett feels herself starting to squirm under the intensity of his gaze. He gestures toward the baseball hat Tanner let her borrow and asks, "Did you wear that on purpose?"

"What? No—why would I do that?"

Teddy shrugs. "Never mind. Just—never mind. So you just want to get a few pictures, then. . . . Any other conditions I should know about?"

"Not really . . . other than Burt saying there isn't a guarantee any of Will's shots will make it through editing. We need to make this look as convincing as possible so he won't have an excuse for cutting anything."

"*Convincing*, candid pictures," Teddy repeats, and Bennett refuses to acknowledge any hidden meaning behind it. "That's definitely some shameless self-promotion right there. And you're seriously cool with this?"

"It's for Will," Bennett says. "And it's on our terms. I figured we'd only need a few pictures—Emmy said she could take them for us."

"Where is she?"

"She should be here somewhere." Bennett glances around. The set crew is in the middle of setting up the green screen for the raid scene; a lot of people are still rushing around, adding finishing touches at the last minute before filming. Bennett leans back in her chair and looks toward the set parking lot, right as she feels the phone vibrate in her lap.

A moment later, the phone in Bennett's hand vibrates with a picture of Bennett and Teddy from Emmy's vantage point— they're midconversation, and it actually appears sincere. The picture looks like it was taken from somewhere near the green screen being set up.

"Interesting plan," Teddy says as he leans closer to get a better look. Bennett's heart skips its way into her throat when she feels his shoulder brush hers. "So, she's going to creep around, take a few pictures of us, and then what?"

"We're going to post them on the Internet."

"Post them where?" he asks, incredulous. "My Twitter? *Your* Twitter?"

The phone vibrates again with three more pictures from Emmy. Bennett shows them to Teddy instead of answering his question. "Do you like any of these?"

"The second one," he admits.

It's a picture of Bennett smiling over at Teddy while he looks down at his hands. Bennett isn't even sure when that happened— but it's kind of adorable, and it kind of makes her heart hurt.

"Me too," she says. As she waits for more of them to come through, she looks over at Teddy and asks, "Why did you ask me if I'd worn this hat on purpose?"

"No reason," he skirts.

"Oh, come on," she says, saving more of the pictures Emmy sent.

"Nothing . . . I mean, it just reminded me of meeting you on the plane last summer." He smiles as he grips the back of his neck. "I kept trying to figure out why you looked so familiar, and at first I couldn't get a good look at you because you kept hiding behind the bill of your ball cap."

Bennett will never for the life of her understand why—out of all the amazing, wonderful, breathtaking things Teddy Sharpe has ever said to her—hearing about the baseball hat she doesn't even remember wearing on the plane last summer causes every single feeling she's ever felt toward Teddy to come pouring out of her with no way of stopping it, but here she is.

"*Goddammit,*" she mutters, turning away from him so he can't see the look on her face.

"What?" Teddy asks.

It takes her a second to look back at him, but when she finally does, she looks him square in the eye, gathers what's left of her nerve, and states for the entire planet to hear, "I am so fucking in love with you, I don't even know what to do with myself right now."

And leave it to Bennett Caldwell to drop the f-word while declaring the most important confession she's ever made.

Teddy freezes. Eyes wide, eyebrows raised, mouth slightly open.

"Wh-what did you just say?" he says, lips barely moving.

"To be honest, I'm not even sure," she admits, feeling the

aftershocks of a massive blush coming on. "It was definitely some crude variation of 'I'm in love with you,' though."

Repeating it only pumps more adrenaline into her veins. It's probably the truest thing she's ever said in her life, and it feels a lot more liberating than she expected (but still just as terrifying).

Teddy doesn't say anything else. His shocked expression is still there, but his gaze is unfocused. It looks like he's attempting to process everything but isn't quite making the jump. It's almost too much for Bennett. She glances back at the phone in her lap for something to do and sees another text message from Emmy. Her stomach gives a panicked jump as she reads it.

> Olivia just texted me and said Liz came looking for her phone case. Will told her you have it.

Bennett snaps into action. She opens up the pictures she saved from Emmy, making sure all the ones she liked are there before pushing the home button and swiping through the phone's apps. It takes her a moment to find the one she wants, and it takes her even longer to figure out how to work it.

"What're you doing now?" Teddy croaks.

"Posting pictures," she says, accidentally hitting another wrong button. That pulls up a page with more pictures from around set that Will posted before he gave Bennett the phone. She grins at all the notes they've already gotten.

"You're putting these on Tumblr?" Teddy asks.

Bennett looks up at his blanched expression. "Is that okay? Would you rather do something else? I won't post them if you don't think—"

"No, no. This is fine," Teddy says. "Tumblr is what you need if you really want this to explode."

Bennett nods, relieved Teddy is endorsing this while also trying to figure out how to create a post of her own in the app.

"Do you know how to actually work Tumblr?" She holds up the phone.

"Not really." Teddy leans over to get a better look at the screen. They both realize at the same time that there's a little pencil icon at the bottom center of the app. Bennett taps it and tries not to feel like a complete moron when it pulls up several different post-type options.

"Look at that. We're a couple of social media geniuses," Teddy comments dryly.

Six convincing candid pictures of Bennett and Teddy later (all with a caption involving #SHARDWELL), Bennett takes a deep breath as her finger hovers over the post button.

"You sure you're cool with this?" she asks. This is officially the point of no return.

"I'm cool with it if you're cool with it," Teddy says.

Bennett lets her eyes flick to his, holding them there as she mashes her finger down, unleashing the pictures of her and Teddy for all the Internet to see. It's almost anticlimactic, actually. . . . Just a tap of her thumb. Within seconds, though, notifications begin popping up.

"Whose account did you post those on?" Teddy asks.

Bennett smiles over at him. "Liz's Teddy Sharpe fan blog."

"Shut up," he says, like this is the best thing he's ever heard. "You've gotta be kidding."

"Nope," Bennett says, stuffing the phone back in her pocket just as her cousin closes in on them. "I'll tell you more about it in a sec, hang on."

Right on time, Liz comes to a stop in front of them.

"Bennett, I need my phone case back," she says, crossing her arms over her chest. "Will told me you have it."

"Hey, Liz," Teddy says. "I heard Will got a spot in the scene today. That's pretty cool."

"Yeah, supercool!" she sneers, dismissing him.

"Jesus, Liz, don't be such an asshole," Bennett says, and Liz seems a little surprised by the edge in her tone. Bennett doesn't care—she isn't okay with Liz talking to Teddy like that.

"Whatever, Bennett. I just need my phone case back so I can get the hell out of here."

"You're not staying to watch your brother?"

"Screw that. I'm too hungover for this shit," she says. "So? Where is it?"

Bennett reaches into her pocket and holds it up. "This?"

"*What else* would I be talking about? And why do you even have Will's phone anyway?"

Bennett's innocent expression turns into a smirk when she notices the phone's screen is illuminated with more incoming notifications. Likes, reblogs, private messages—there are already too many to count, and Bennett only sent the pictures out a few minutes ago.

"This isn't Will's phone," Bennett says, enjoying every second of the confused look that crosses Liz's face. "*You* have Will's phone."

"Jesus *Christ*, Bennett, I don't have time for this," Liz says as she reaches into the front pocket of her sweatshirt and pulls out an identical black iPhone to the one Bennett is holding. Minus the phone case. She mashes the home button a few times, then holds down the power button on the side. "What the—" she mutters.

"That's Will's phone that died this morning," Bennett explains. "*This* is your phone. Will switched them when he asked for your phone case to recharge."

Liz's eyes cut back to Bennett's.

"What," she says, her voice deceptively calm. "Why?"

Bennett stands up from her chair and takes a step toward her cousin, holding out her phone for her. "We needed to borrow your Tumblr blog for a little movie promotion."

Liz snatches her phone away and pushes the home button with her thumb. The home screen appears without her having to type in the passcode. Her eyes go wide. "Are you—are you serious? Why?"

"I needed to post some pictures," Bennett says. "And since you run a Teddy Sharpe fan blog, I thought they'd go nicely with that post you made with the time and location of our dinner last night."

"You run a fan blog about me, Liz? That's so sweet," Teddy says, barely able to contain himself. "Creepy as fuck . . . but kind of sweet, I guess . . ."

Liz ignores him. "What the hell, Bennett?! This is my phone; you had no right to do that."

"Oh, sure. I had no right to do that. Do you honestly want to get into all the stuff that you never had a right to do?"

"Oh my God—seriously? This is about payback from high school?"

"Actually, no," Bennett says, shaking her head. "This isn't even about you at all."

"Then who the hell is it about?"

Bennett turns around for a second to look at Teddy. He has a hand over his mouth, indiscreetly trying to cover up a massive grin. Their eyes meet and she returns his smile.

"At first this was completely about Will," Bennett replies, turning to face Liz again. "But then it became about me confirming to all thirty thousand of your fan-blog followers that I love Teddy Sharpe and that we're four thousand percent dating."

"God, you're such a freak, Bennett—"

"Fine with me," Bennett shoots back. "I've got family and friends and a bomb-ass career and I'm in love with a superhot, insanely talented actor." She looks her cousin dead in the eye and adds, "But that's no reason to be jealous, Liz. You've got thirty thousand fan-blog followers."

Liz slowly closes her mouth, setting it into a thin, straight line, and for a moment, Bennett feels a jarring twinge of guilt as she watches Liz struggle to mask the hurt writing itself across her face. Their relationship is boiling all the way down to this one confrontation, and that's when Bennett realizes it was never a relationship at all.

A fact that Liz solidifies when she looks at Bennett one last time and says, "Fuck you, Bennett. I don't regret a damn thing I ever did to you."

She throws one last glare at Teddy before turning and storming away.

Bennett stares after her for a few moments, trying to slow down her heart rate. She doesn't register how much her hands are shaking until she feels another hand close around hers. She turns around when Teddy gently tugs on her fingers.

"So," she stalls, dropping her gaze down to her shoes. "How ironic is it that Liz turned out to run a Teddy Sharpe fan blog?"

Teddy tugs on her fingers again. He's gotten up from his chair and is inching toward her.

"God, Teddy, I'm so sorry," she says. "Like, I don't have words. I freaked out this morning for the same reason that I freaked out in July—because every time I've got something good going on in my life, it always goes sideways when too many people start to find out. And it's awful to deal with. But it doesn't merit me being an asshole. . . ."

Teddy brings a hand up to her neck, tracing a thumb across her jaw.

Bennett leans into it, but she still can't bring herself to look up yet. "I just—I want you to know that for every text you sent in the fall I almost responded seven different ways. And I just, I'm really so in love with you, and—"

"Bennett."

"Yeah?"

"You're hiding behind that damn hat again."

Bennett can't help laughing and finally lifts her head.

Teddy grins down at her.

"And by the way," he says as he pulls her all the way to him, "that was the greatest thing I've ever witnessed in my life."

And then he's kissing her.

CHAPTER TWENTY-EIGHT

Will kills it as an extra.

Olivia decides the best way to ensure he's in all the right shots is to improvise—a lot. She throws unscripted lines at him left and right, constantly deviates from the blocking standards they spent an hour going over beforehand, and even creates an entire take where she pretends to break her ankle and Will has to help her hobble around. Will handles every situation like a pro, claiming he learned it all from acting classes, but everyone on set sees through it. He has raw talent. Even Burt Bridges makes a point to tell him so.

"Let me know when you get a booking agent, kid," the director says, and Will can barely form a coherent response when Burt hands him his business card.

The McGearys end up staying to watch—well, Uncle Fletcher and Aunt Susan do. Liz leaves to go sulk in the car. And to probably delete all the pictures off her Tumblr that Teddy and Bennett posted. Not that it matters. Bennett knows the damage was done within the first thirty seconds of posting. Like clockwork, Teddy gets calls from his manager and his agent asking if he wants the pictures taken down and how they should handle the tabloids.

Teddy says no, he wants the pictures to stay up.

He also tells them to confirm with the tabloids that he and Bennett are officially involved, but only if they ask first.

After he gets off the phone, he loops his arms around Bennett and says, "You good with that?"

She laughs, even though she's still breathless from their conversation earlier—a shy vulnerability that has her fully acknowledging that things are going to be okay between her and Teddy. She knows she put him through hell and back, and she wants to spend as much time as she can making it up to him, whether he likes it or not.

"Yeah, I'm good with that," she says, smiling and leaning into him. "I just—I told you I don't know what to do with myself right now."

He smirks. "Actually, I believe your exact words were 'I am so fucking in love with you, I don't even know what to do with myself right now.'"

She drops her gaze as another massive blush hits her hard (and it definitely doesn't help that she can't keep the dopey, lovesick grin off her face).

Teddy gently takes her face in his hands.

"If it makes you feel any better . . ." he says, brushing a thumb over her cheek. He presses a slow kiss to her lips, and Bennett is seriously worried her knees are about to give out. "I'm so in love with you, Mary Bennett Caldwell," he says, kissing her again, "I haven't known what to do with myself since July."

M. B. Caldwell (author)

M. B. Caldwell (born Mary Bennett Caldwell; May 20, 2000) is an American writer, screenwriter, and film producer. She is best known as the author of the *New York Times*–bestselling <u>young adult</u> series <u>Parachutes</u>.

Career

After secretly working on a rough draft for almost two years, Caldwell published her first novel, *Parachutes*, during her sophomore year of high school when she was only sixteen. She was put into contact with her literary agent through her English teacher. The film rights for the series were sold in 2017 and Caldwell was asked to help adapt the first screenplay. Filming wrapped in March 2019.

Personal Life

Caldwell was born in <u>Cornelius, North Carolina,</u> to Tom and Libby Caldwell. She has an older brother, Tanner. She graduated from <u>Davidson Day School</u> in May 2018. She is currently in a relationship with actor <u>Teddy Sharpe</u>, whom she met after he auditioned for the role of Jack in the film adaptation of *<u>Parachutes</u>*. Their relationship was highly publicized in the media after pictures of them together on set were leaked onto <u>Tumblr</u>, causing a wide range of Internet speculation that the two were involved.

EPILOGUE

These days there are a few things in life of which Teddy Sharpe is absolutely certain, and one of them is that his girlfriend is going to murder him if he doesn't hurry the hell up.

Well, *murder* is a stretch . . . but still.

"Rita! We were supposed to be downstairs ten minutes ago!" Teddy yells, rummaging through his duffel bag and flinging clothes across his hotel suite. "Do they really have to be solid black? All I've got are"—he grabs a fistful of socks toward the bottom and holds them up to the light—"gray Nike ones, and black ones with little purple polka dots!"

"THEY HAVE TO BE ALL BLACK, TEDDY," Rita yells back from suite's sitting area. "They'll throw off the whole ensemble if they aren't!"

Teddy pauses and glances down at himself. This could have all been avoided had he not been forced into wearing tight-ass dress pants that pull up at the ankle when he walks. His entire suit is too tight, actually. (You'd think custom-made would merit a little more comfort here.) And the fact that Rita just referred to it as *an ensemble* has Teddy putting on the purple polka dot socks anyway. He needs some normalcy.

He steps out of his room and Rita groans.

"How do you not have a pair of solid black socks with you, Ted? Jesus."

His manager is sporting a green cocktail dress and scary shoes that give her a few inches on him when she comes over to help straighten his jacket lapels.

"I didn't realize it was going to be this big of an issue," Teddy says, subtly shrugging her off. "Now come on, we gotta *go*."

The elevator ride down to the hotel lobby takes approximately twenty-seven years. Teddy spends it messing with his cuff links and listening to Rita explain the evening's itinerary again. He's only been to smaller, low-key movie premieres before, but the gist is pretty much the same: Red carpets. Fancy clothes. *Schmoozing.*

The elevator doors finally open and Teddy lets Rita walk out ahead of him. So far the concierge has been great about keeping paparazzi under control, but they can't do much about the crowd that's already gathered on the sidewalk outside the lobby's glass doors. It's the first thing Teddy sees when he steps off the elevator, and he banks hard left into a long hallway before camera flashes start going off.

"If you keep fidgeting with your jacket buttons they're going to pop off," Rita says, leading him toward one of the hotel's ballrooms. "And I didn't ask the tailor for extras."

Teddy fastens the top button and shoves his hands into his pockets.

The whole gang is already there when he walks into the ballroom—Olivia in a tiny white dress that looks like it's hard to breathe in and Will standing next to her in a blue suit, tugging at his pastel bow tie. They're surrounded by a horde of managers and publicists and handlers, and standing just off to the side of it all is Bennett Caldwell in a floor-length purple gown.

Teddy stops walking for a second.

She hasn't seen him yet, too engrossed in a conversation with Emmy to notice Teddy breathless and a little dazed in the entryway. Then Will yells, "Ted! You made it," and the focus of the room pivots. Greetings ring out; people beckon him forward; and when Bennett's eyes shift and land on him, Teddy's heart does one of those cheesy nervous stutter-step things that normally he's way too manly to acknowledge.

She looks stunning . . .

. . . and nervous.

"Ladies," Teddy says, strolling over with what he hopes is some composure. He stops next to Bennett, and it takes a heroic display of restraint not to reach for her. Teddy's been to enough industry events to know that it's too easy to smudge makeup or snag a cuff link on dress fabric—he's not about to let ill-timed PDA disrupt the perfection that is Bennett Caldwell before he has a chance to officially show her off.

"You clean up nice, Sharpe," Emmy says, locking her iPad and holding it to her chest.

"Back atcha, Em. Sorry to keep you guys waiting," Teddy says. He throws a wink at Bennett and tries not to smirk when her gaze flicks up from somewhere around his lapel region. Before he can shamelessly ask her if she digs the suit, though, Rita and one of Olivia's handlers call for them to gather around to go over the game plan for getting to the theater.

"We've got cars waiting behind the hotel at their loading dock," the handler says, turning to Olivia and Will. "We're in the first SUV—Will, as Olivia's date it's your job to keep paps from getting any up-skirt shots when she gets out, so make sure you step out first and block the doorframe until she's ready. And don't forget to button your jacket when you're on the carpet."

Handlers and jacket buttons. Jesus.

Rita steps in and says, "Teddy and Bennett, we're all in the car behind them, and Emmy and the rest of the crew are behind us. I can go over a few more logistics with you on the way over"—Teddy feels Bennett tense beside him—"and once we're through the red carpet, there's a waiting room for the cast and crew just inside the theater. We'll meet there before you go onstage with Burt to introduce the movie. Where's Otis?"

An older man wearing a hotel uniform steps forward.

Rita nods. "If you guys can follow Otis, he'll lead us all down to the loading dock."

As people start to file out, Teddy catches Bennett's hand to keep her from getting too far away. She angles back toward him, and he waits until the ballroom is almost cleared to step right up into her space, careful that only their fingers are touching.

He takes his time eyeing the purple fabric of her dress, from the one strap on her right shoulder all the way down to the hemline. This close, he can see all of the makeup she's had applied, can smell the amount of hairspray keeping her side braid styled. It's so different from how he normally sees her—he knows she prefers her jean shorts and baseball hats (most of the time, he does too)—but right now she looks every inch a red carpet smoke show, and it's making it really difficult for Teddy to remember the concept of personal space.

"*Jesus*, Caldwell," he murmurs, leaning in a little closer. "You care if I ruin your lipstick?"

Some of the tension disappears from her shoulders when she reaches up to slip her free hand into the hair at the nape of his neck. She shakes her head and pulls him in, but the angry sound of Rita's voice stops them less than an inch apart.

"No, no—no time for that right now!" she yells from the doorway of the ballroom. "We're late, remember? Save it for the carpet."

Bennett draws back, and Teddy catches another glimpse of all the nerves she's trying so hard to hide before she arranges her expression back to neutral.

Getting to their cars ends up being less of a production than Teddy was expecting. A few paparazzi figured out their plan and are camped out on top of the parking deck next door, but outside of that, everyone is able to slide into their designated SUV with minimal exposure. Once Teddy and Bennett are tucked safely into the backseat and hidden behind tinted windows, Rita hops into the front with the driver and the caravan pulls out into the New York City traffic.

"All right, guys," Rita says, turning around to face them. She pauses when she sees Teddy's arm propped up on the seat behind Bennett's head. "Ted, gimme a break here—you're gonna screw up your jacket's shoulder fit before photos if you keep your arm like that."

Teddy doesn't move.

Rita sighs. "Okay, anyway. This is your first event walking the red carpet as a couple. Paps will be all over you. It won't be like San Diego Comic-Con or any of the other press tour stuff you guys have done, and it'll only be worse at the LA premiere next week. Look at this as a practice round."

Teddy grins at the mention of Comic-Con. That was the weekend he finally got to introduce Bennett to his family, and they haven't really shut up about her since.

"I'll be right behind you in case things get overwhelming," Rita continues on. "I have no problem reminding paparazzi of their place, so just wave me over if you're getting uncomfortable. . . ."

Teddy sort of tunes her out after that, getting distracted when he glances over to check on Bennett again. She hasn't spoken since he met her down in the ballroom earlier. Sure, he'd anticipated this—eight months of dating has been long enough to learn Bennett's tells when she's anxious (among other things)—but now he's starting to worry that her nerves aren't just premiere-related.

"Rita," Teddy says as soon as his manager pauses from her couples PR lesson, "you mind giving us just a minute?"

Understanding appears on Rita's face and she nods; then she turns around and puts the radio on to give them some privacy.

"Caldwell," Teddy says, nudging her leg. "You good?"

Bennett gives him a warm, closed-lip smile, but she only holds his gaze for a second before dropping it again.

"Nice socks," she says.

It registers with Teddy that the polka dots he's wearing are almost the same color as her dress.

"You know, I could've at least been able to say I planned this had you told me what color your dress was ahead of time. That's why I had to go with an all-black suit in the first place. Now I'm gonna have to tell everyone on the red carpet that we're so in tune as a couple that we didn't even have to plan it."

Her nose twitches as she tries to hold back a grin, but it's still not the reaction he wants.

"Hey." He lowers his voice then. "You're still good with this, right?"

"What?"

"This"—Teddy gestures between them—"going public tonight."

"Of course I am." Bennett tilts her head to the side, eyebrows knitting together. "It's not like people don't already know anyway, right?"

That doesn't make him feel better.

"Yeah, but still . . ." Now Teddy's the one to look away, embarrassed for letting some residual insecurity from last February get the better of him. "I was the one who pushed for going to the premiere together. We're basically giving people written invitations into our relationship at this point. I don't want it to be uncomfortable for you—"

"Teddy."

Teddy peeks over.

Bennett sets a hand on his jaw to turn him all the way toward her. Then she gives him a slow, reassuring kiss that has him following after her mouth when she pulls back.

"I can't wait to walk down that carpet with you," she says, dragging her thumb across his bottom lip to wipe off her lipstick. "I can't wait to show everyone that we're together." She smirks as her voice dips low. "And *I can't wait* for this whole thing to be over so we can—"

"Heads up, we're a block from the theater," Rita announces from the front seat, and Teddy has never entertained the idea of firing his manager until right now.

Bennett leans away and takes a steadying breath in.

"I'm just . . . nervous in general," she says quietly, and Teddy gets it. He reaches for her hand.

"Your whole family's going to be there, and I'm going to be sitting right next to you," he says. "I think I'm actually more excited to see your family tonight than I am to see mine at the LA premiere next week."

"Oh? Even Liz?"

Teddy's eyes go wide. "Wait—the *whole* McGeary clan is coming?"

Bennett laughs, and Teddy's so happy to see a genuine smile on her face that he doesn't even call her out for scaring him half to death.

"She said she couldn't miss class," Bennett says dryly. "You know, with her shiny new PR and hospitality double major . . ."

Teddy shudders. The idea of that girl working in PR and hospitality. Yikes.

Their car slows to a stop in line outside a beautifully restored theater in between two skyscrapers. Up ahead, Teddy can already see a huge crowd and hundreds of cameras flashing. The line inches forward, and all too soon they're watching Olivia and Will step out of their SUV and into the spotlight.

Teddy and Bennett are up next. Teddy turns toward Bennett to gauge her reaction. Her eyes are trained through the side window, watching Olivia and Will begin their walk, but at least she doesn't look ready to jump ship yet.

Then their car door swings open.

Teddy steps out first, buttoning his jacket and thanking the event staff greeters. The screams he gets from the crowd are deafening, the camera flashes casting the entire scene in stark, lurid light. It's always intimidating at first to be the center of so much attention, and Teddy has a tiny moment of panic over what he's about to subject Bennett to. He turns back toward the car and leans into the doorframe, offering her a hand and his best smile.

"You ready for this?" he asks.

Bennett places her hand in his. "Just don't let me fall on my face."

"Don't worry," Teddy says, raising his voice over the roar of the crowd as she steps down onto the red carpet. "I've got my Buzz Lightyear briefs on for both of us."

The reaction from the crowd is overwhelming.

Photographers are yelling out their names and directions while the fans that showed up are screaming so loudly they're drowning everything else out. Teddy and Bennett move down the carpet slowly, laughing at the absurdity of what's happening and trying not to trip over each other. At one point Teddy almost gives himself a heart attack when he realizes he's standing on Bennett's dress, but by some miracle it's their only almost-mishap.

Bennett handles herself flawlessly for a first-timer—smiling and posing and letting Teddy hold her hand all the way through it. For someone so wary of the spotlight, she sure as hell looks good in it.

Up ahead, Will and Olivia are hamming it up for the photographers, striking outrageous poses and waving to the crowd. They're almost to the theater entrance, and even though Teddy hates the idea of leaving Bennett's side for even a second, he leans over and says "Wait here," before jogging ahead to grab Will and Olivia.

They line up that way—with Teddy next to Bennett and Bennett next to Olivia and Olivia next to Will, and the crowd goes absolutely wild. They pose for so many pictures that their handlers have to step in and subtly tell them to keep moving.

Finally, Teddy and Bennett reach the end of the red carpet, both a little flushed and pleasantly surprised by the whole ordeal. They're still in the photographers' range—and just because Teddy can't help himself, he wiggles his eyebrows at Bennett and says, "Wanna try to break Tumblr again?"

A smirk appears on her face.

She glances over at the photographers, then back up at him.

"Absolutely," she says, grabbing him by his jacket lapels and yanking him in for a kiss.

ACKNOWLEDGMENTS

There's really only one way to kick things off here, and it's by thanking my parents. They're the reason I was able to do this—in so many more ways than just one. Mom, you've encouraged me to keep writing since my fifth-grade literary masterpiece, *The Doggie Hotel*, and I can't tell you how much it means to me that I got my love for stories from the Oakley side of the family. Dad, this book is a direct result of our countless conversations about Strategic Coach and *investments*, but most important, it's a direct result of you telling me that if I'm going to do it, I better get going. I'll never be able to thank you guys enough—I just hope one day I can make my own kids feel as loved and supported as y'all have made Lindsay, Jay, and me feel.

Thank you to Jean Feiwel, Lauren Scobell, my editor Holly West, and the entire Swoon Reads/Macmillan team for everything you do. Holly and Lauren, that July afternoon phone call back in 2016 changed my life. Thank you both for believing in this story. And to Holly—thank you for your guidance and patience throughout this experience. *Love Scene, Take Two* has found a home on bookshelves because of you, and I couldn't be more grateful.

A Snorlax-size thank-you to Sam Pennington, for literally

e v e r y t h i n g. This acknowledgments section would be a novel in itself if I listed out all the things you've done for me, and I can honestly say that one of the best things to come from writing this story has been your friendship.

Thank you to all my Wattpad readers who have left countless votes and comments on my work, and thank you to the Swoon Reads community for being so welcoming. This story has always been for you, and it means the world to me that you all took the time to read it.

And finally, I have to give a major shout-out to my Internet pals Ashley, Ana, and Zoe. We've never actually met in person, but you've been riding with me in the HOV lane since the very beginning. And I absolutely love you for it.